AISURU

SHERELLE WINTERS

ON LANGUAGE AND HONORIFICS

THIS NOVEL IS PRIMARILY SET IN Hakodate, Hokkaidō, Japan. While it was written in English by my very American self, I strove to remain true to the culture of Japan.

While most day-to-day speech is easily translated to English, the people of Japan have quite a bit of ritualized speech that uses words that do not have simple English equivalents. Changing them to English would have required unwieldy or unnatural-sounding speech, so instead I retained their Japanese wording, with footnotes of explanation.

Japanese societal rules provide for an extensive set of guidelines on how people refer to one another, when one wishes to be polite. You generally refer to people by their family names, unless it is a very informal situation or the person is a close friend or a family member, or if you are speaking to someone inferior in station or position to you (such as, say, an underclassman).

Further, during polite speech, you add honorifics to a person's name to indicate your status/relationship with them, whether you are talking to them or about them. Leaving these out of my characters' dialog or their inner thoughts was never really an option to me: it is just too quintessentially Japanese.

Now, you could write a book on the various honorifics in the Japanese language (and, indeed, there are some on Amazon), but for our purposes, I'll highlight ones you'll encounter while reading *Aisuru*:

-san: the "all purpose" honorific, for use in almost any situation where one wishes to be polite; it's a generally safe go-to if you aren't sure which honorific to use

-kun: typically added to boys' names to indicate familiarity or endearment, or while addressing someone younger than oneself

-chan: another common honorific, primarily used to indicate endearment or familiarity with girls, or when referring to young boys and pets; it's also sometimes used among couples

-sensei: this title, which literally means "one who has come before," is used for teachers, doctors, and other professionals and can be used as a suffix or as a standalone title

For someone to drop an honorific altogether usually indicates an intimate relationship. This special privilege is usually reserved for lovers or spouses, younger family members, and the closest of friends, though it is also sometimes seen between members of sports teams and within a school class as a sign of their closeness. Conversely, one could drop an honorific as a sign of disrespect or to insult the person when talking to them directly.

In this story, mirroring real life, the characters introduce themselves in the ordering appropriate for their place of origin, meaning Japanese characters use last name followed by first name. And, just as you would call a pizza a pizza in a US-based novel, the foods herein are referred to by their Japanese names with footnotes to offer quick explanations for ones that may be less commonly known.

With all of that said, please join me as we head to Hakodate, where our story begins…

Sakura's Reality

Yachigashira-chō, Hakodate, Hokkaidō, Japan

Sakura Takeshi wasn't spending her birthday the way most eighteen-year-old girls do. She wasn't getting together with her school friends for karaoke. She wouldn't be going on a date with a boyfriend. There would be no cake, no drinking, and no wasting money on new things to celebrate. Of course, those girls would go on to be nineteen-year-old girls. She would not.

Sakura's plans constituted a more logical way to spend her final birthday. Well, maybe she would pick up a cake on her way home to share with Ito-san. Her favorite strawberry short-cake from the bakery down the road. Yeah, that would be good.

But, first, she had business to take care of, which is why she was now nestled in an overstuffed chair at the Seikat Legal Firm, sipping hot chocolate and waiting for her turn to see Hiko Aso, the gyōsei shoshi[1] who ran the small office.

---

[1] Translated as "administrative scrivener," this is a specialized legal profession unique to Japan. A gyōsei shoshi helps prepare various legal documents, including wills, inheritance claims, vehicle registrations, articles of incorporations, etc. They also regularly deal with immigration matters.

While she waited, Sakura studied the fish swimming in the massive aquarium that dominated one wall of the room, pretending she didn't see the looks of pity coming from the young receptionist. She hated those kinds of looks.

A buzzer sounded and the receptionist stood. "Takeshi-san, Aso-sensei will see you now. Right this way."

"Thank you." Sakura returned the woman's shallow bow before walking into the indicated office. As the door clicked closed behind her, Sakura moved forward to stand in front of his dark wood desk.

Aso-sensei was an older man, with a rather grandfatherly air and a bald spot forming on the top of his head. Much like his office had an old-fashioned feel, his clothes were a little dated, and he still preferred paper to computers. They'd first met three years ago, when he'd carried out the terms of Ito-san's will. He'd been sympathetic while also ensuring she understood everything thoroughly.

When it was time for Sakura to get her own affairs in order, he was the first one she'd thought of. When she'd first called on him, he'd warned her that he wasn't taking on new clients; he'd downsized his office the previous year as part of his plan to retire soon. Once she told him that she wouldn't live that long anyway, he'd shuffled some papers on his desk then declared that he had too much free time lately—one more client wouldn't hurt, and it wasn't like she was really a "new" client anyway.

"Good morning, Takeshi-san. Here is the formal will you dictated last time. I just need you to review it to be sure it was transcribed correctly and that everything is in place."

"Okay." She took the document from his outstretched hand and began reading it. The house and all her belongings would be sold. Two million yen[2] was bequeathed to her high school,

---

[2] Just under $20,000 US.

as promised when they'd accepted her into the school; five million to some local charities that were working to encourage the public to be more accepting of transplants and to be organ donors. It was too late for her, of course, but maybe someone else could be spared the same fate. Anything left after her final expenses and the other dispersals would go to the hospital that had kept her alive this long. From her calculations, it would end up being around twenty-five million.

"Yes, it looks correct. And this will make sure those people don't get a dime, right?" It was one of the main things that had prompted her to do a formal will, ensuring the so-called family who'd abandoned her wouldn't get so much as a speck of dust from her when she died.

"I promise. Though I doubt they will try to make too big an issue of it, as I'd make sure they knew how public their actions would be made." He replied with a firm nod.

"Good. Thank you."

"Now we just need to make it official. Did you bring your personal seal?"[3]

She nodded.

He called in his receptionist and one of his assistants to act as witnesses. "Please sign here at the bottom. Oh, and I need to confirm the seal with your proof of registration."

He opened the ceramic compact of red paste on his desk and pushed it toward her. After handing him the registration paper, she pulled her carved, jade stamper from its box and firmly pressed the stamp upon the page. The red lettering of the

---

[3] In Japan it is common to mark important documents with a personal registered seal, a jitsuin, in lieu of a signature. The format and contents of these seals is tightly regulated, with most being made by professionals and used for many years. When not needed, they are kept in a safe or other well hidden place along with the registration certificate verifying the person's identity.

kanji that formed her full name and the thin red border surrounding it stood in stark contrast to the bright whiteness of the paper.

Once the other two had signed, Aso-sensei applied his own seal to it then dismissed the pair with a thank-you. "All right, Takeshi-san, it's done. It will be fully registered by this afternoon."

"Thank you for your fast work."

"It's no problem. Truthfully, I wish you hadn't needed my services until I was far too old to be of use." Though his slight smile was tinged with sadness, it reflected no pity. Still, she hated making such a kind man look that way. With a deep breath, he slipped back into his professional mode. "When the time comes, I will be certain your wishes are carried out as you've stated here."

"I greatly appreciate it." Sakura stood and bowed deeply. "Good day and thank you again."

"Good day...oh, and Takeshi-san?"

"Yes?" Sakura paused at the door.

"I suppose it may be odd to say, but happy birthday."

She smiled at him and nodded in thanks before slipping out the door.

"Sensei, will I make it?" Sakura's voice trembled, belying her calm demeanor as she waited for Tenma-sensei's response. It had been almost eight years since her heart and lungs had been left permanently damaged by the quiet stabs of a knife. Her body had continued to grow as she matured, gradually increasing its demands on organs that were just as steadily straining to keep up. She wouldn't live to be an adult, she'd never marry, never have kids. All of that she had come to terms with, but there was one thing she wanted to do—no, had to do—first.

"I believe so, yes. Your illness is progressing as expected. As long as you continue to be careful, you should be able to graduate this spring."

"Good."

"Sakura-chan, you know as the end gets closer, it will get harder for you to live on your own. While I will do all I can to help you make it until then, you will probably have to check into the hospital for full-time care not long after." His heavy sigh weighed down the cold white room as he glanced again at the papers in his hand. She could almost see him willing the test results to change. "I'm sorry."

"It isn't your fault. You didn't do this to me."

"I know, but I'd hoped to at least be the one who could save you."

Sakura shook her head. "Tenma-sensei, it's because of you I've lived this long and that I even have a chance to fulfill my dream. Thank you."

She was well aware of the fact that he'd spent a lot of time finding treatments to help extend her life, including his personal time. He'd traveled to Europe and America, poring over the results of every study and experimental option he could find. It pained her to see how he took her pending death as a personal failure. She longed to find some words to comfort him, to let him know it was okay. Simple thanks seemed so inadequate, but it was all she had.

"No, it was nothing." He smiled another one of those small, sad smiles that made her heart ache to see. After a moment, he shook his head, as if trying to clear away the air. "How are things at school?"

"My studies are okay. We have exams coming up in a few weeks. Koga is still being his usual charming self, but I manage to avoid him most of the time. Oh, I have a new homeroom teacher. Mimomo-sensei…She's young and rather pretty, and she likes poetry. I bet you'd like her."

He laughed. It was a much better expression to see on him. "Oy, oy, are you trying to set me up on dates now too?"

"I heard the nurses saying you were thinking about doing an omiai?[4] A wife could be good for you." Sakura smiled. "Like you, she works too hard and is far too kind. One of my classmates was out sick the other week, and rather than give his assignments to a student to deliver, Mimomo-sensei brought them herself. Most teachers don't do things like that anymore. And on the first Friday of the month, she brings in a special treat for us at lunchtime, as if we're still little kids."

"She does sound nice." His smile faded. "Are you still keeping yourself distant from your classmates?"

"Of course. You know how I feel about it. I'm fine on my own." She smiled, making it as bright as she could. He didn't need to be burdened by her growing loneliness or hear how she cried herself to sleep when the fear got the better of her. He didn't need to know about the nightmares that blended scenes from the past and an imagined future that made it hard to sleep. He would just worry more than he already did. So, she lied with a smile, as always.

"Yes, yes, I know." He held up his hands in defeat. "I won't lecture today. I do worry, though, about you in that house by yourself. You aren't lifting anything too heavy or doing any strenuous cleaning, right?"

"I'm being careful, I promise."

"Good. Still, won't you consider hiring a housekeeper, someone to take care of cleaning and the like? It would be one

---

[4] A type of matchmaking meeting that could lead to marriage if the couple feels they are compatible.

less worry on my mind. Besides, don't you get lonely there by yourself?"

Sakura knew he mentioned his worries to guilt her into agreeing. They had one of these arguments every few months, him wanting her to be more involved with people in one way or another and her refusing. "I don't want a stranger living with me."

"You could hire a service, one that comes by once a week or even just once every two weeks. That wouldn't be so bad, right? They could do the cleaning and shopping for you. You must be careful of too much dust, you know."

"I'll think about it," she lied again, a smidge of guilt starting to gnaw at her.

"Sakura-chan…"

"I did have that emergency-alert system installed, so it isn't as if I can't call for help if I need it." Now it was her turn to sigh. "If it would make you feel better, I suppose I could start using the grocer's new delivery service."

"Good. Shall we call this round a draw then, eh?" They exchanged amused smiles.

After he'd given her the refills for her medicines, Sakura thanked him again. She was almost out the door when he called her back.

"I almost forgot…here." A small gift bag hung from his outstretched hands as he bowed slightly. Inside was a box wrapped in pretty pale-pink paper decorated with cherry blossoms. "Happy birthday."

"Tenma-sensei, you shouldn't have gone out of your way. I can't accept such a gift."[5]

---

[5] Gift giving in Japan is highly ritualistic. There are customs about how to hand someone a gift, how to accept it, what to say, and when you can open it. It is considered particularly impolite to accept most gifts without declining them first. The giver is also expected to belittle the gift they are giving, no matter what its true value may be.

"Oh, it's just a small token. Please, take it. I want you to have it."

"If you are sure…" Sakura carefully accepted the bag and returned the bow. "Thank you very much."

"It's nothing, really. Take care of yourself, and I'll see you in a few weeks."

"Yes, you too. See you later."

As Sakura made her way to the elevator, she paused in the windowed hallway. Hakodate City Hospital was close to the coast. From the fourth floor where Tenma-sensei's office was located, she could see the sunlit diamonds sparkling in the waves of Hakodate Bay.

At least she would be dying in a room with a great view.

"*Tadaima*."[6] Even after three years of no reply, Sakura called out the greeting automatically. Shaking her head at the pointless gesture, she carefully placed her shoes against the step in the entryway, slipped on her house slippers, and headed to the living room.

Like most of the house, the room was a blend of traditional and modern style. Rather than tatami[7] mats, the room had warm bamboo flooring with a rug in the center where the kotatsu[8] sat to keep her warm while she studied. It was also nice for reading or the occasional bit of TV watching. When the weather was nice, she'd eat her meals there to enjoy the view of

---

[6] A standard greeting called out upon returning home that is generally translated to "I'm home."

[7] A mat made of rice straw and covered with woven soft rush straw that is always twice as long as it is wide; they are used to cover the floors in traditional, Japanese-style rooms.

[8] A low wooden table with a heater built into the underside and usually covered with a heavy blanket or futon. People sit at the table with their legs under it and the cover over their laps, trapping the heat by their legs and enabling them to stay warmer.

the garden.

She stopped in front of the small, mahogany butsudan[9] nestled in the corner of the room, and pulled open the doors. Beside the memorial tablet bearing his name, Ito-san's face smiled back at her from a framed photograph.

"Ito-san, I'm back." Sakura slid open the shōji door[10] that led into the garden on the side of the house, letting in a cool breeze. The sweet scent of the recently bloomed cosmos rode along the breeze to perfume the room.

"Don't worry. I won't leave it open too long." She sat on her heels in front of the open door, holding the picture in her lap. After her parents had died, her father's best friend, Ito-san, had adopted her. It was he more than anyone who'd helped her cope with their deaths as well as her own. Now instead of warm hugs and a generous laugh, she came home to heavy silence, which she filled with empty greetings and one-sided conversations.

"The will is finalized. Those people won't get a dime of the money you saved for me. Oh, Tenma-sensei gave me a birthday present! He really is too sweet. Shall we open it?"

Setting the picture beside her, Sakura pulled the present into her lap. She used a letter opener to carefully split the tape on one end. Once she had pulled the corners up, she retrieved the small gold-and-white box nestled inside. The wrapping paper was folded with care and set aside before she removed the box's lid. Cushioned within pink-and-white tissue paper sat a large hair comb decorated with a pair of silk cherry blossoms, one white and one pink. Two streamers of matching ribbons ran from each flower.

---

[9] A personal shrine.

[10] A door consisting of a wood frame and a lattice of wood or bamboo that is covered in a translucent paper called washi.

"It's so pretty!" After running her fingers through her hair, she pulled a bit back and used the comb to secure it. "How does it look?"

Using the mirror from her school bag, she admired the way the bright flowers and ribbons contrasted her black hair.

"I bet this would go perfectly with my festival kimono." She tried not to think about the fact that she had no reason to wear it. It was still a lovely gift. "I'll wear it for him when I go back for my next visit, and I'll have to send him a thank-you note. Hmmm, I'll write it before I start dinner."

She lay back on the floor with her arms stretched out beside her as she stared at the large Kwanzan cherry tree in the corner of the garden. Its rich copper leaves waltzed in the irregular breezes. She could still remember Ito-san's excitement that first day as he showed her the sapling, a symbol of their becoming a family, which they planted together. Back then, they didn't know she was never going to get better, and she'd never imagined that their time together would be so short.

"Tenma-sensei asked me about school again. He didn't try to change my mind this time, though I know he doesn't agree with me. I mean, it's for the best, right? It's bad enough when people start pitying me. I don't need pity. I'm just dying. So are they. So is everyone. I just happen to know how long I have when most people don't." She rolled over onto her side so she could look at his picture.

"Besides, it would just make people sad. Making friends with people, getting them to like me when I'm just going to die in a few months. It would be cruel!" Tenma-sensei's question came back to mind. "No, I'm not lonely! I'm not! I don't need anyone anymore. I'm fine on my own."

Even to her own ears, her declaration was tinted in shades of desperate denial. A heavy sigh escaped her lungs as she reached for the picture and hugged it against her chest, willing her tears back. "Hey, Ito-san, do they have cherry trees where you are now? When I join you this spring, can we lie under them and watch the blossoms fall like we used to? You could tell me those stories again, the ones about that boy you met once, long ago."

Kazuki's Reality

Throklana, First Kingdom of Jalathumesa

"My Prince! My Prince! Prince Kazukiarama!" Reito's call was almost as sharp as the clicking of his heels as he stalked down the hall. Some people swore he put nails into the bottoms of his boots to make them so loud. "My Prince, hurry please. There is much to be done."

As Reito walked, he scribbled something in the faded leather-bound book he was perpetually writing in. As the king's attendant, the red-furred kitsune[11] was meticulous about keeping records of the king's schedule, reminders to be given, and anything else he felt would be of use. While Reito temporarily served the same role for him now, Kazuki suspected the notes being scribbled were for when his father returned, a report of his sons' performance (or lack thereof) while he was away.

It had been four months since King Toramaru had announced that he was going on a pilgrimage alone. No one knew where he'd gone or why. Even Reito, who had served as the

---

[11] A supernatural creature with characteristics similar to a fox, often believed to be one that has lived fifty to one hundred years, at least.

king's right-hand man for every one of the 950 years of his rule, had been left behind, despite it being well known that they were close friends as well as master and servant. If being kept in the dark like the others bothered him, he wasn't letting on. From the way Reito had calmly continued his general duties, Kazuki suspected he knew exactly where the king was if not why. But no amount of begging, or torture at the hands of an enemy, would ever make Reito betray the king's confidence.

With a heavy sigh, Kazuki moved out from behind the pillar where he'd hidden when he first heard those boots clicking. "Yes, yes, I'm coming. Must you call my full name? Kazuki is sufficient."

Without breaking stride, Reito turned and led the way back toward the throne room. Though the motion caused Reito's bright auburn tail to whirl around him, it quickly settled back into place behind him as if it dared not act unruly or disorderly.

"Now then, Prince Kazukiarama, there are citizens' concerns to be addressed. You have the weekly meeting with the advisory council, and some correspondence to respond to." Reito glanced back down at his book. "Oh, and Princess Aya has come to visit, so you must properly greet her later."

Kazuki mentally cursed Yuji for leaving him to deal with this mess. Why his brother loved this stuff was beyond him. If something didn't change soon, Kazuki might be stuck doing it for a millennium. The thought made him shudder.

"Reito, has there been any word from Yuji?"

"No. Nor have we found any sign of where he might be staying at the moment."

"I see." Why had Yuji left the castle so suddenly? The last thing he'd said to Kazuki was that he'd never forgive him, but for what? Try as he might, Kazuki could not think of any wrong he'd done against his brother.

Kazuki paused while Reito opened the door to the throne room then continued inside down the rich blue carpet, which acted as a path to the front of the room and to the royal receiving area, where three thrones sat. Normally, their father would be sitting in the large, dark wood and velvet throne in the middle. Yuji would be sitting to his right, watching as his father handled matters of state. As Yuji approached full adulthood, the two had started having even more discussions, with the king soliciting his son's opinion in some matters as a way of evaluating him. Some days they would be together from sunup to sundown.

A lesser man might have been jealous of the time and attention their father gave his younger son, but Kazuki didn't mind. It was all in preparation for Yuji's ascension to the throne, and it gave Kazuki more free time to pursue his own interests. The only thing he missed was the time with his brother, but he knew that they were reaching the age when they couldn't spend all their time playing and having fun. Once Yuji ascended the throne, he'd practically need an appointment to even see him. He used to worry about losing that close relationship, but now it seemed he, somehow, already had.

Without the low hum of conversation and their father's imposing presence, the empty throne room seemed especially large. The sound of their footsteps bouncing off the walls only made it worse. Kazuki walked over to his own seat, to his father's left.

"My Prince."

Reito stood beside the large center throne. Of course. Kazuki was acting king now, so he must sit so that he was directly facing whomever he might be giving audience to. He hesitated a moment before settling into the throne. Even after two weeks of temporary rule, he still felt like he was a young child again, feeling so small and unworthy of sitting there. It wasn't where he belonged.

"Now then, first the concerns from the citizens," Reito said as he placed a lap table across Kazuki's thighs then dropped a stack of files on top of it.

"What? This many? But I did nearly as many yesterday." All citizens of Throklana were free to bring questions, problems, etc., to the king's attention. These concerns were received by special liaisons, who sorted through them and did any research that might be useful, adding it to the request, which was then passed to the king. If a concern seemed especially dire or important, they could escalate it directly to the king through Reito. On the whole, the system worked well, with most concerns being presented to the king within a day or two. Which meant that most of the ones in the foot-tall stack had been filed just yesterday.

"It was two days ago. With the king away, the citizens are growing more anxious. Unfortunately, rumors of Prince Yujinasanarama's departure are starting to leak outside the castle as well. Most are minor things. It is only ninety minutes until the advisory council arrives. These must be handled before then."

"You want me to get through all of these that quickly?"

"Had you arrived earlier of your own volition, you would have had more time. The pile would also be smaller if you did them daily as your father does."

"Fine, fine, where's my pen?"

After handing him the quill and ink, Reito reclaimed the top third of the files, which had been turned perpendicular to the rest. "These are predominantly basic questions of law or the like that do not need a personal answer. I shall handle them."

"Thank you, Reito." For all the droll lectures Reito had

treated him to in the last few weeks, Kazuki realized that he never left him hanging in the wind. It was probably more for the people's sake and his loyalty to the king that Reito supported him, but still, Kazuki knew that without him, the kingdom might well be in ruins by now.

Reito nodded then carried the files to his desk to the right of the throne area, setting to work without hesitation. Letting another sigh escape, Kazuki picked up the first folder from the stack and flipped it open.

"To our beloved king…"

King…I am no king, nor do I wish to be. Hurry home, Father.

Kazuki was signing the last of his responses when the throne-room doors opened. His attendant, Karasu, ducked inside and hurried the doors closed again. Karasu had been with them since the day Kazuki found the young tengu[12] badly wounded and starving in the streets. He was a dear friend to his brother and him, and they both doted on him like they would a baby brother.

"Master Kazuki! Lord Reito! The advisers are gathering."

"Finished just in time then." He handed the stack of files back to Reito as Karasu sprinted across the room to throw his arms around him. Kazuki stroked his hair with a smile and returned his hug. "How did it go?"

Karasu grinned up at him. "Not too bad. Today I got to try a wooden sword! Master said I showed good promise."

To keep the boy occupied and to try to make up for Yuji's

---

[12] A legendary type of being in Japanese folk lore, thought to take the form of a bird of prey, particularly a crow.

absence, Kazuki had named Karasu as his attendant. Though he was too young yet to assume his full duties, it allowed him the freedom to stay with Kazuki most of the time while he was temporary king. The advisers had grumbled a bit at first, as Karasu had no formal education, but had relented on the agreement that Karasu begin training immediately. As such, each morning was spent on various lessons, including the fighting skills necessary for one expected to protect his master.

Reito coughed under his breath in warning before making his way down the blue carpet road to admit the advisers.

"I guess it's time." Kazuki straightened himself in his chair while Karasu darted over to Reito's table to watch and learn from Reito.

Led by Matsushita, the mujina[13] who served as head adviser, the eight council members filed into the room and stood in a semicircle in front of the throne. The two recorders strode to the two tables positioned opposite Reito's. The tables were set at an angle from one another, with low, thin pieces of wood framing the front and sides so that neither recorder could see the others' notes. This ensured both would take full, accurate dictation of all that was said and done in the meeting, as the notes would be compared later and discrepancies had to be explained by both.

The council was infamous for their long-windedness. After one council meeting had droned on for over eight hours, Kazuki's father had decreed that all council meetings would be held with the council standing, to encourage them to keep it to a minimum. Thus far, it had worked quite well, encouraging the council to not only keep their reports to the point, but also to discuss the issues thoroughly amongst themselves to avoid hashing out their thoughts before the king.

---

[13] A yokai that shares characteristics with a badger.

Still, Kazuki wouldn't mind if they were even shorter. An hour was too long to listen to their babbling.

The council members knelt down, their left hands on their chests as they said in unison, "My Prince."

Once they were on their feet again, Matsushita took two steps forward. With his spectacles set on his snout just in front of his eyes, Matsushita looked every bit his meticulous self. He was the sort of person who answered a simple question, like whether it was raining, with a long answer on all the conditions of the atmosphere that contributed to the current weather before actually giving the desired answer. He was a chief reason for his father's standing rule.

The thick chunk of paper flapping around in his gesturing hand made Kazuki groan inwardly. Definitely not going to be a short one.

"My Prince. Fruit production appears to be going well, due to a mild cold season and a good amount of rain during the growing season. We have received reports from 80% of the fruit producers that indicate we will have an above-average crop. Though we have only received reports from 43% of the vegetable and herb growers, they have been reporting similar results. Thus plant-based foods should be in good supply this year." As he droned on in that thin voice, he would glance at the papers in his hand to consult whatever notes he'd made. "There are some concerns regarding meat foods, however. An unidentified malady has appeared in the kagorin bird hatcheries. It seems to have no lasting effects on the birds themselves, but according to the reports, infected parents are producing eggs with thin shells and stillborn chicks. If the cause of this disease is not found soon, we may face an egg shortage as well as a shortage of new birds."

He stopped and looked up over his spectacles. Kazuki hesitated, knowing without it being said that his response would be evaluated by the council after the meeting.

"What progress are our researchers making?"

"They are still gathering reports from all the farms in which it has appeared to try to trace all movements of involved parties and animals. Meanwhile, they have studied samples from the infected birds and the ruined eggs, but thus far have not been able to determine much about its nature except that it does seem to be isolated to domestic kagorin at this time."

"I see. Ensure the researchers have quick access to any resources they need for their studies. If necessary, I will authorize the capture of a limited and controlled number of wild kagorin birds and their eggs to compare to our domestic flocks, but they must submit a formal request specifying the number of birds that will be affected beforehand. We must keep the conservation of wild populations in mind and I fear excessive harvesting could cause contamination of the wild flocks, which would be disastrous. Send out advisory notices to all hatcheries summarizing what we know and urging them to report any appearances of the disease in their flocks. Look into what we can do to aid anyone who might suffer catastrophic losses, in the form of financial compensation and helping them in recovery."

Kazuki waited to see how the council would respond. Had he adequately addressed those who would be affected? Were his commands an appropriate balance of leadership and compassion? He was relieved when Matsushita nodded.

"Yes, My Prince." He flipped to the next page. "Mining of precious stones remains steady overall. However..."

Nearly two hours later, Kazuki was ready for the meeting to be done! In addition to addressing the kagorin situation, Kazuki had listened to the reports on every other meat animal, major crop, and raw material of importance. He'd also given his approval for the expansion of a small town in the western part of the kingdom, based on the earlier reports already heard by his father. Requests were made to expand the lakmanine mining operations, but he'd asked for further studies on the potential impacts it would have first. Surely they had covered everything by now?

"Any other matters to attend to?" Kazuki tried to keep a hopeful lilt from staining his voice as Matsushita flipped his notes closed.

"Yes, My Prince, there is the issue of Prince Yuji. People are beginning to express concerns over not seeing him in the castle or about in the town. We considered letting it be known that he was traveling, perhaps with the king, but then today no less than three reports came in saying that he had been seen near the outskirts of town."

"I see. No one would believe the story if he is seen again, and it would only make them wonder more if a lie is told. And Yuji has made no attempt to contact me at all, so I can't be sure when he'll return."

Matsushita gave Karasu a pointed glance. Kazuki was well aware that some in the council believed the boy knew where Yuji was hiding.

"He has not attempted to contact anyone at all," Kazuki continued with a firm tone. "For now, continue sending out the messengers with the request that he at least come talk. If he doesn't want to come to the castle, we can meet somewhere else. As for the people...you said he was seen near the outskirts of town. Near the mining area?"

"Yes, actually."

"Good, then if anyone questions, he is inspecting the mines himself to consider the option of expansion. Yuji has always been a hands-on leader, so people will believe that, and it should help keep them calm a while longer."

"Very well, My Prince."

Finally free from the advisers, Kazuki made his way back to the living quarters of the castle, Karasu close at his heels. Before they left the meeting place, Reito had quietly patted his shoulder. Kazuki took it to mean that Reito had approved of his handling of the meeting. It was a small consolation at least.

"Master Kazuki?" He could detect the worry in Karasu's voice. "Master Yuji will come home, right?"

"I hope so. If only he would contact me. I'm certain whatever is wrong we could fix it if he would just talk to me."

"I wish there was something I could do."

Kazuki smiled at him and ruffled his thick black hair. "No worries. I'd much rather you not get put in the middle of whatever argument this is. Just keep praying for us and be ready to welcome him home when he does return. This will all surely blow over soon enough."

"Okay."

"Meanwhile, I think I'll rest a bit before dinner. Those meetings are exhausting."

"No kidding! I thought they'd never finish the way they kept going on and on." Karasu held up his hands and mimicked talking heads while rolling his eyes.

"Just imagine, it used to be even worse!" They were still laughing as they reached Kazuki's chambers. "I'll see you in a few hours for dinner, all right?"

"Have a good rest, Master Kazuki!" Karasu darted off, probably eager to go practice the maneuvers he'd learned earlier in the day.

As the heavy door closed behind him, Kazuki began unclasping his jacket. He walked through the sitting area, pausing to snag a ringa fruit from the bowl on the table to snack on. Continuing to his bedroom, he froze as he spotted the woman sitting on his bed. *Dafnikar, forgot she was here.*

"My Prince." She stood, her long red hair flowing down to nearly her knees. Her pale skin was as smooth as a kagorin eggshell, with the same luminescent quality. The red stripes that lined her cheeks and neck were striking without being too flashy. No one would find fault with the curves of her body. The well-modulated tone of her voice spoke of her high breeding and class. She was beautiful, a desirable woman by most any yokai's standards, and she was probably the last person he wanted to see.

"Aya, what are you doing here?" Kazuki didn't bother hiding his annoyance.

"Oh, Kazuki, don't be that way." She walked over and kissed his cheek. "I'm your future mate after all."

"That hasn't been decided yet. Either way, it doesn't mean you can just walk into my bedroom whenever you wish."

"But I never get to see you! You haven't come to visit in months, and when I come to see you, you're always 'too busy' to even say hi." She pouted in a way that seemed designed to be cute.

He brushed past her to drop his sash on his dressing table. "I am busy. You know my father is away. There is a lot to be done in his stead. Now go back to your room, please. I'm tired and want to rest a bit."

He finished taking off his jacket and dumped it beside the sash. He moved to the edge of the bed and sat to remove his soft leather boots. Instead of the door closing as he anticipated, a sniffle filled the room behind him. *Dafnikar!*

"Kazuki, do you hate me that much? Am I such a burden to you?"

With a heavy sigh, he stood and walked over, laying his hands on her shoulders. "I don't hate you, Aya. You know that. We've been friends since childhood. I just don't love you that way. To me you have always been like a sister, not someone I could view as a lover. As such, I want to see you truly happy with a man who will love you and treat you the way you deserve. That man just isn't me."

"But I love you!" She leaned her head into his chest as she cried. His arms went around her naturally, and he rubbed her back with slow strokes, as his mom had always done for him when he'd been upset or frightened. As her tears dampened the front of his shirt, he wished more than ever that Yuji would hurry home. It should be him here comforting Aya, him here so she could see that it had always been Yuji, not Kazuki, she was meant for.

Once her sobs quieted, he set her gently away from him and handed her his handkerchief. "I am sorry, Aya."

"I know." She wiped her face, but it did little to help as fresh streams continued escaping.

"Please, return to your room for now. I would hate it if people started smearing your reputation because you're in my chambers like this. I promise I will join you for dinner later, after I've rested a bit, okay?"

"Yes, you're right. Father will yell at me. I'm sorry." She nodded toward him then walked back to the door, still wiping her face to try to remove the evidence of her crying. She paused just inside the frame and turned back. "You promise?"

"Promise." He held up his hand with his first two fingers pointing up, pressed together. She smiled at the gesture, a hold over from their time as kids. It was how the three of them had always signaled a binding promise between them.

Moments later the door to his chambers closed behind her. Relieved, he quickly locked it then returned to his bedroom and finished changing into his sleeping pants. He lay down, but found himself tossing and turning. He was still tired, but now it seemed the sleep he wanted was in an elusive mood. A cacophony of thoughts demanded attention, from the kagorin bird issue to Aya to Yuji. He longed to have his brother home, he longed to be free to while away the day in his studies, having fun as he used to.

Frustrated, he rolled onto his back and shifted his hands behind his head while he stared at the ceiling. It was covered in a mural of his own design, featuring his favorite scenery and snippets of favorite memories. Many featured Yuji, of course, with a few of Karasu that he added after the bird had joined their family. One or two scenes even included Aya, though from long ago, when they were Karasu's age.

His eye was drawn to a small scene where a younger version of himself stood beside a young boy, a human boy. Their arms were around each other's shoulders with big smiles on their faces as they stood in front of a pale-yellow house.

"Hiro." He smiled to himself as the liquid warmth of nostalgia flowed over him. How long had it been since that visit to the human realm, the realm where he'd met his friend and promised to return? Many years, to be sure.

"I wonder how you are doing, my dear old friend. I suppose by now you must be done with school, out working in the world somewhere. Did you ever ask that girl to go out with you, eh? Do you still remember me even? Once Yuji agrees to talk and comes home, I'll come see you again and beg forgiveness at my taking so long, I promise."

CHANGING DAY

CHATTERING STUDENTS FILLED the halls of Saigonohi High School after the final bell, eager to escape campus before the heavy gray clouds above carried out their implicit threat. In each classroom, pairs of students assigned clean-up duties[14] for the day worked quickly to get their chores done.

From the second floor in class 3-A,[15] Sakura watched the boy assigned to work with her greet his friends by the school gate. He pointed back toward the school, sending the group into a laughing fit as they headed down the street. Had he told them that she'd bought his lie about needing to go medicate his cat? As if she were that stupid. She knew he was lying before he even finished spinning the tale.

Of course, she wasn't supposed to be there either, but apparently no one had told Mimomo-sensei not to assign her duties. It happened sometimes, usually with new or substitute

---

[14] In Japanese schools, students are expected to help keep the school and classrooms clean, with pairs of students often assigned small, daily morning and afternoon work, such as cleaning, preparing the board for the next day, and completing a class log for the day that documents absences and events.

[15] The classroom number indicates the students' year. Japanese high schools have three grades rather than four, so third-year students are equivalent to American seniors.

teachers. She could complain and refuse to do it, but in an odd way, she liked it. It helped her feel more normal, if only for a little while.

Besides, her assigned partners always found reasons to skip out. A doctor's appointment, a dying relative, a pet needing care, some young sibling they had to pick up. Same old stories. They could at least try to be more creative. Though why they bothered, she didn't know. It wasn't as if they apologized or showed any shame if they were caught in the lie. Like the boy whose supposedly dead grandmother attended the school's athletic festival a week later looking quite spry and healthy.

Sakura would nod, straight-faced, and let them excuse themselves. But she stayed and did what she could. Ito-san would be disappointed in her if she just did nothing and left the class suffering at the work going undone. At least with her "partner" gone, she could work alone. It was easier than working with someone else; after all, it is significantly easier to snub someone who isn't there.

It was exhausting pretending she didn't hear their pathetic attempts at engaging in social-obligation chit-chat with her. Though after three years together, most of her classmates knew her as an ice queen and didn't bother talking to her at all.

She washed the chalkboard with a damp cloth, straightened the desks, and then finished writing the entries into the class log. The chalk erasers she left on the windowsill and the sweeping would have to be done by someone else. She was not going to risk a coughing fit from the flying dust. With the room as clean as she could manage, she carried the trash to the outside incinerator. Steel-gray clouds hung low in sky and the smell of pending rain saturated the air.

Few students loitered in the halls as she made her way to the teacher's lounge to turn in the log book. When she reached for the door, it suddenly slid open. The vice principal stormed out, forcing her to take a few steps back to avoid getting bowled over. *Damn.* She'd almost made it a whole week without seeing Koga.

He smiled down at her, an expression as bogus as the cheap toupee he used to cover his balding head. "Good afternoon, Takeshi-san. I've addressed the situation regarding your being assigned duties. It won't happen again."

"Thank you, Koga-sensei. Your efforts are appreciated, as always." Sakura's response was as insincere as his concern, and they both knew it. He'd been the first, the last, and the loudest to try to deny her entrance into Saigonohi, arguing that they shouldn't waste school resources educating someone who had no future. It was only the disclosure of her considerable financial assets with subtle hints at a future bequest that had won her admittance.

"If you'll excuse me, sir, I'll turn this in so I can go home."

"Of course. If you've missed the tram, with the rain, you should take a cab. Use the phone inside to call for one."

She waited until he was well down the hall before entering the room. Mimomo-sensei, normally cheerful and positive to excess, was hunched at a desk. Tears streamed down her face despite her best efforts. Two other teachers in the room were doing a pathetic job of pretending they hadn't watched her get chewed out by Koga. It was the young woman's first year at the school, and it would be like Koga to "forget" to tell her about Sakura's situation. In fact, she was certain he had done it on purpose. How else had he already known that she'd been assigned clean-up duty? He'd probably been keeping an eye on their room, checking the board daily until it happened.

As Sakura approached, the young woman jerked to her feet and bowed deeply.

"I…I'm so sorry, Takeshi-san. I had no idea. Is there anything…" Her brown eyes settled on Sakura, her pretty face heavy with sorrow.

Sakura forced down her own feelings and slid the book onto the desk. "Here is the log. I didn't clean the erasers or sweep."

Turning on her heel, she walked out. There was little value in trying to ease the woman's discomfort now. Perhaps her having to endure one of Koga's infamous tirades might put an end to her constant attempts at reaching out to Sakura. Despite her liking toward the teacher, it would be better for them both if Mimomo-sensei just followed the example of other teachers and ignored her presence beyond grading her work. More than likely, the other two in the room were advising her to do just that. Because of their "hands-off" policy, the teachers tended to give her a ridiculous amount of leeway. If she'd been inclined, she could act like a world-class brat and make their teaching lives hell. Fortunately for them, she was a "good girl," and all she wanted was to get through school with little incident.

After exchanging her school slippers for her street shoes, Sakura headed outside. A heavy sheet of cold rain bordered the entry overhang. She debated calling a cab after all, but the idea of doing something Koga suggested grated on her nerves. Nor was she in the mood to wait around another hour. She had a well-made umbrella to shield her from most of the rain. Combined with the thick black scarf wrapped around her neck and her matching, long, waterproof coat, she should be able to stay warm and dry enough.

In good weather, she enjoyed the half-mile walk home with Mount Hakodate dominating the view along the way. Though she couldn't see the bay, she usually could catch its sweet salty smell on the breezes that normally accompanied her. Today there was nothing but the wet smell of rain riding on a chilly wind.

She pulled her coat tighter as she turned into a small park of trees. The barren branches of the apricot and plum trees lent a sinister air to the day's monotone scene. The delicate blossoms of a few late-blooming cherry trees plastered to their branches, desperately holding on, when in nicer weather they would drift around like white-and-pink snow.

Just past the park, a large house with flower gardens in the front graced the end of the block. Its green-thumbed owner kept it in full color year round, much to Sakura's envy, though cloaked in the dull gray shroud of rain, even the cheery autumnal orange and yellow flowers looked morose and dull.

Some students from her school ran by her as she passed the corner store. A girl with blond pigtails looked back, probably questioning her sanity. If she were healthy, she would be running to get out of the rain too, but that would be even more dangerous than deciding to walk in the rain because of that pissant Koga. She should just duck into the store, or the café beside it, and wait out the rain, but there were only two more blocks to go.

Kazuki,

I wish to talk. Please, meet me by mother's grave tonight after dinner.

I miss you, big brother.

Yuji

Kazuki read the note one last time. A servant had handed

it to him just after lunch. Having to wait so many hours had nearly driven him crazy. Yuji was finally ready to work things out! His brother was a gentle soul, kind and generous, selfless to a fault. Kazuki knew he must have done something truly despicable to his brother, but what? No matter what his grievances were, Kazuki resolved to carefully hear them out and properly apologize.

"Master Kazuki?" Karasu sat on his bed beside him, staring at the wrinkled paper in Kazuki's hand. "Do you think you'll be able to mend things?"

"I hope so. I will give it my best, to be sure. This foolishness has gone on long enough! It's time for Yuji to return home where he belongs."

"You know, I've been thinking. Maybe he misunderstood about Princess Aya somehow?"

Most knew Yuji was in love with her, and as such, Kazuki had already sworn he would never accept her for his mate. But maybe Yuji had started to wonder. The advisers had been adamant that the formal refusal not happen until the king returned, so it could come from him rather than Kazuki. Otherwise, it might be seen as a disgrace for Aya. But had Yuji thought he'd been stalling somehow or that he had changed his mind?

"Maybe you're right. He doesn't always think clearly when it comes to her; she is perfection in his eyes. If Aya repeated her claims of loving me to him, combined with her repeated insistence that I visit with her, he might think I would have no choice but to fall in love with her. It may not be that he is angry, but heart broken and thinking I've betrayed him. This just won't do, not at all. I must set him right. I'd die before I'd take his love from him! And adviser demands or not, as soon as I get back, we are sending the formal rejection of the mating proposal so there is no more question."

"Good idea! Then Master Yuji can propose instead. I'm sure once Princess Aya sees how much he loves her, she'll accept."

"Exactly." Kazuki glanced out the window. The orange and red glow of the setting sun had disappeared. The first stars had already appeared to dot the darkened sky. "Well, it's about time. I'll be back soon."

"Can't I come with you?" The boy pleaded as he gripped Kazuki's sleeve.

"Not this time, old friend. I wouldn't want you to get pulled between us, and I suspect we'll say some harsh words before we can make amends. Don't worry, we'll be home soon, both of us."

Kazuki ruffled the boy's hair affectionately then stood and retrieved the lakmanine stone from his dresser. He glanced at the sword that hung on the wall, cradled in its ornately carved, wooden frame. When leaving the castle, he would be expected to take it with him, but even as he considered it he laughed to himself. This was Yuji. Weapons were not needed tonight.

He gave Karasu one last reassuring smile before picturing the flower-filled area where his mother had been entombed.

"Stone of water, stone of air, take me hence to the place I desire." His vision filled with rays of white-and-blue light that blinded him to the world around him. A strong whoosh of air flowed over him as he felt the ground disappear beneath him. Moments later, it returned again and the lights faded.

Like silhouetted sentries, the trees surrounding the glad seemed to guard the square tomb housing his mother's ashes. A pair of torches burned at the entrance, but in such darkness, their faint light was more unnerving than uplifting, the sliver of moon above barely brightening the area.

"Yuji?" When no reply came, Kazuki walked forward to

stand between the torches and bow. "Mother, I hope you will smile down on your foolish children so that we can resolve things tonight. We'll bring a proper gift to apologize for making you worry as soon as we do. You have my word."

A noise emerged from the edge of the forest a few meters behind him. There, a pale figure stood, made only paler by the loose-fitting white outfit he wore and the long white hair flowing down his back.

"Ah, Yuji, there you are! I'm so glad you called for us to meet."

Kazuki stepped into the darkness toward his brother. Yuji remained where he was, letting Kazuki make the first move. The wind shifted, carrying his brother's scent to his nose. How long had it been since he'd smelled that familiar fragrance? *But was it familiar?*

It was his brother's scent, to be sure, but it seemed a little off. He hesitated a moment, then continued forward. After weeks away from the castle and his nightly scented baths, of course Yuji would smell a little different.

"My brother, please! Tell me what has led to this, to you leaving us and your anger with me." It was all he'd intended to say at first, but his pain at their separation overwhelmed him and he was unable to stop himself. "Whatever I have done, I will make amends! If it is about Aya, I'll send the rejection this very night and beg forgiveness for making you worry. Just please tell me what I can say or do to heal this rift."

Yuji stood there, only meters from him, but said nothing. No smile, no shrug, not even a scoff to acknowledge Kazuki's passionate plea. He just continued to stare at him. At least, Kazuki presumed he was staring, as he could only just make out his eyes in the low light.

The silence stretched on until it became too much to bear.

"Yuji? Please, say something, anything."

Finally, Yuji shrugged then pointed behind him. At the same time, he heard a rock shifting near the grave. Had Karasu followed him? He turned toward the sound, but saw nothing moving in the dim lights.

A second later, he felt movement beside him. Instinctively he dodged to the side as a sword sliced the air. Before he could fully react, Yuji's claws had ripped into his shoulder as he whirled back around to face his attacker, his brother.

"Yuji?" As if he were standing outside his own body, Kazuki watched as Yuji brought his sword back up, intent on running him through with it. His body reacted on its own, blocking the blow with his wrist and knocking the sword away. He shoved Yuji back, but his brother growled and came at him with claws and teeth bared.

They wrestled there on the ground in front of their mother's grave, Kazuki trying to defend himself even as his sluggish mind refused to accept that his brother seemed intent on killing him.

"Yuji, please, stop this!"

Yuji managed to pin him down with one hand as he raised the other above them. Where had that knife come from? Had he hidden it in his sleeve?

"Die." The first word his brother said was not the one he'd ever thought it'd be.

From the corner of his eye, he spotted something sparkling near his hand. The lakmanine stone. Wrapping his fingers around it, he quickly said the chant in his mind while mentally picturing his room in the castle. Just as the lights enveloped him, he thought he heard a voice call to him. *Kazuki, this way.*

The rain had slowed to a light mist by the time Sakura reached the white picket fence enclosing her yard. In some ways, it was worse than the heavier rain, as it was more easily pushed by the wind, enabling it to get past her umbrella and coat that much faster. She would be glad to get out of it and into dry clothes. A warm bath before dinner wouldn't be a bad idea either.

In the approaching dusk, her gardens were a mix of shadowed, darkened shapes. The pale stone paths seemed to glow in the waning light as she opened the gate and walked in. Having stepped in a mud puddle on the way, she'd decided to enter through the side door so she could leave her shoes outside rather than track the dirt and mud into the foyer.

As she passed the cherry tree, she paused and laid her hand against it. Despite the chill in the air, its trunk felt warm, almost as if it were pulsing with life. She hoped whoever bought her house took good care of it. Perhaps she would leave them a letter, explaining its meaning to the new owners and telling them the joys of waking up to find it awash in a seemingly endless supply of purplish-pink blossoms in the spring. The blossoms sometimes got in the house as they drifted around, but it wasn't too much of a bother. She hoped to see it bloom one last time, at least. A final memory of it to take with her to the afterlife.

"Maybe you'll bloom early for me this year."

She stroked the trunk then turned to head inside. She'd been out in this weather long enough. Halfway down the path to the side porch, something, a sound perhaps, made her look back toward the tree. In the spot she'd stood moments before lay a large, unmoving mound.

Helpful Insanity

"HELLO?" SAKURA CALLED out uncertainly. It didn't look like a branch broken by the wind. Was it a large dog? A person? How had it even gotten under the tree without her seeing it cross the yard?

When the mound remained motionless, she crept forward. As she neared, she realized it was a person, crumpled up as if in pain. Her usual caution forgotten, she dropped her umbrella and darted to his side.

"Hello, are you okay?" He groaned in response as she shook his shoulder. A warm wetness coated the tips of her fingers as she pulled away her hand. In the low light, something darkened her hand. Blood? Multiple tears littered his shirt, the pale skin underneath marred with wounds.

"Wait here. I'll call for help."

She stood to run into the house, but he grabbed her ankle. The hand gripping her had the usual five digits, but each slim finger was tipped with extraordinarily long, pointed fingernails. They were almost claw-like. He was looking up at her, his long, white hair plastered against his face by the rain. His ears were large and came to a point near the top. Such deformities would have made him an easy target for some of the local thugs that roamed the nearby shopping district at night. It was early for them to be out, but if he'd stumbled into one of their hangouts, no one would notice them attacking.

"Hiro, is that you?" The weak voice sounded unsure and confused. Before she could respond, his grip slackened and he fell unconscious again. *To use Ito-san's given name like that...was this man a close friend of his?*

A sharp gust of wind blasted her. She couldn't just leave him there, but she was getting colder and wetter with every passing second. She tossed her umbrella on the porch before hurrying inside. It would be easy to call emergency services, wiping her hands of him. Her sensible side said to do just that, but her instincts were telling her that someone so unusual look-ing would not be well served by local authorities. If he was a friend of Ito-san's, she was obligated to do something to help him. Besides, she was curious to know who he was. She could only think of one person, other than her dead father, that Ito-san had called a close friend. *But those had just been fairy tales to calm a frightened child, right?*

Decision made, she turned the kerosene heater to high and set some blankets, towels, and the first-aid kit on the floor be-fore heading back outside. He was still unconscious. She turned him on his back while keeping her arms threaded under his.

"Here we go." Her shoes slid in the wet mud, sending her to the ground butt first. Cold water soaked through the skirt of her school uniform. Gritting her teeth, she got back up and re-sumed her previous stance. She shifted her feet slightly to find better purchase then tugged. Five centimeters down, only 411 more to go before they would reach the porch.

Tug by tug, she somehow managed to drag the heavier man along, aided by the slippery mud while questioning her sanity.

If this wasn't overexerting herself, what was? At times, his feet shifted a bit as if he subconsciously tried to help, but his eyes remained shut. How she got him up the two steps to the porch without falling again, she didn't know.

Once his feet cleared the doorway, she let herself fall backwards with the man lying half on top of her as she tried to catch her breath. The burning in her arms, legs, and back were background noise to the tortured screams of her lungs. Every ragged breath was pure agony. The pounding of her heart filled her ears in protest. If she lay there, would the vise grip tightening in her chest make her heart stop beating altogether? Tempt death by lying there and waiting, or try to finish helping the man she may have just killed herself for?

With a grunt, she dragged herself to the school bag she'd left against the wall. She grabbed two containers from the front pouch and set them beside her. *Control the breathing first, then the heart.* With practiced, if shaky movements, she positioned her inhaler and breathed in as she pressed the top. With the dose delivered, she held her breath and counted to ten.

The inhaler fell to her lap as she grabbed the spray bottle. A moment later, the needed dose of nitroglycerin was under her tongue. She closed her mouth and started the timer on her watch. When she'd first started using it, she'd learned not to watch the time count down. It only made the five minutes of stillness seem even longer.

Finally, her heart dropped out of warp speed and the usual sharp pains began stabbing her head.

"Okay, we've got maybe ten minutes."

With slow, uneven steps, she made her way back across the room to slide the paper door shut. There was no time to be shy. She pulled at the man's wet clothes, but with him lying so still she couldn't get them off. The sleeves of the white shirt and the legs of the matching pants were puffy like parachutes. Even wet, the fabric felt like silk. But she couldn't find any buttons or clasps that might help her remove them. Whispering a promise to replace them later, she used the scissors from her first-aid kit to cut them off. She left the sand-colored loincloth covering his groin untouched. Averting her gaze from that spot, she managed to tug the ankle-high, tan-and-white moccasins from his feet.

She used the towels to dry his skin with quick, rough strokes. His long body was lean but well muscled. From the expensive nature of his garments and the gold chain and pendant around his neck, she guessed he was well off. And yet, his ears and fingernails were so odd, why didn't he pay to have them fixed so he would look normal?

The man moaned and shifted a bit, then went still again. As she wrapped a towel around his long hair, she noticed his mouth had come open. *Are those fangs?* With one finger, she gently pulled back his lip, revealing that his eyeteeth were indeed long and sharp. The rest of his teeth were more regularly sized, but also pointed. *What sort of genetic mutation could cause this?*

It was something to find out later, though. For now, she turned her attention to his wounds. Most were sets of marks with ragged edges, grouped in threes and fours. They reminded her of claw marks like she'd seen in books on big cats. Glancing back at his hand, she realized that he, likely, could make such wounds. Which meant someone else was like him—someone who had attacked him? The thought made her uneasy. She could feel her mind growing fuzzier. She quickly dabbed the wounds with antiseptic and taped bandages on them.

One of the wounds was noticeably different from the rest. On his side, a long, straight, clean line was bleeding more than the others. She froze at the sight. That kind of wound she knew: the wound left by a sharp blade. A shudder ran through her as she forced the image of a blood-soaked knife aside. She taped the largest bandage she had on the wound, adding extra gauze to soak up the blood, then threw the blanket over him to keep him warm.

"I hope this will be enough." Her voice sounded thick and muffled to her own ears. Quickly, she pulled off her wet clothes, throwing them on top of his in the nearby pile. As she dried herself, her arms grew heavier with every second. After dropping the towel twice while drying her hair, she left it on the floor and tried to stand. Her body refused to obey. Time was up.

The effort it had taken to bring him into the house and the powerful medicines she'd taken to stay alive were demanding their due. She'd never make it upstairs to her own bed. Unwilling to risk catching a cold by sleeping in the open air, she crawled under the only blanket available, turning her back to the stranger. Before the darkness claimed her, she prayed to the gods that she wouldn't come to regret her impulsive rescue.

When Kazuki awoke, he had a vague sense that something was not right. Blinking away his lethargic state, he looked up to see a plain white thing that he supposed would pass for a ceiling; the walls of the room just as plain. Functional enough, he supposed, but he was clearly not in any room in the castle.

His head felt heavy. When he reached up to touch it, he found a rough cloth covering it. Pulling it away, he held the dark-blue thing in his hand, studying it curiously. It looked much like a drying cloth, though of rather low quality. With a mental shrug, he dropped it beside him then pushed himself into a sitting position.

A sharp pain speared through his side. Glaring at the spot, he noticed his wounds were covered with clean cotton squares. The scent of bitter medicines burned through his nose, as did the overwhelming scent of humans. Was he in the human world? But how?

He remembered grabbing the stone to escape Yuji's silent onslaught. Just as the gem had activated, he'd heard a voice calling him. He was certain it had been Hiro's voice, but he couldn't remember exactly what it had said. Perhaps the gem had erred and read his flash of recognition as his desired destination.

Inhaling deeply, he realized that the most prominent human scent wasn't Hiro's. It was distinctly feminine and came from beside him. Looking down, he found a woman curled into a fetal position, sleeping. A trail of dirt led from a spot a few feet behind them through a door. Someone must have dragged him inside, but who?

This girl looked too small and weak to have been able to move him an inch, but the only scent he could detect was hers, and his sensitive ears couldn't pick up any movement anywhere else in the house. As far as he could determine, they were alone.

Long, jet-black hair framed her ghostly white face. His sitting up had loosened the blanket, revealing her to be in the same state of near nakedness as he was, except for the thin white top covering her torso. She was far too thin for his taste, but decent looking enough for a human he supposed. Was she perhaps a concubine left for his use by whoever owned this estate? Probably not. He was pretty sure humans didn't do such things anymore.

The girl's breathing took on a ragged, harassed quality. Her eyes pinched tightly together as she moaned and thrashed about. As a whimper escaped her lips, he shook her shoulder to wake her from the nightmare. She bolted up, her eyes wide open in fear, her breathing coming in short, rapid spurts as tiny tremors racked her body. He rubbed her back in small circles to offer her comfort until she could regain her composure.

"Are you okay?" He kept his voice low, not wanting to frighten her any more.

"Yes. It was just an old memory." After a few deep breaths, she turned to look at him. There seemed to be no fear in her gray eyes, only mild curiosity.

"I see. Well, it would seem I am in your debt. You aided me when I was in need. *Arigato gozaimasu.*"[16]

"It was nothing. How are your wounds?" Her arms trembled as she reached to check his bandages. Again he didn't get the impression that she was afraid, at least not of him. Perhaps the shivering was a remnant of the nightmare or the slight chill in the air.

He already knew none of his wounds were serious. They would be fully healed in a few days, at most. For now, he kept that knowledge to himself and sat quietly while the girl finished her inspection. When she was done, she shifted her legs under her and tried to stand. He caught her as she fell, ignoring a fresh spurt of pain from his side as he gently eased her back to the floor.

"Are you sure you're okay?"

"Yes, I'm sorry. I'm just a little tired. I'm sure you must be hungry. I'll make dinner in a few minutes. It shouldn't take long."

"Truthfully I am, but please rest as long as you need. It would be hard for you to make anything if you hurt yourself

---

[16] "Arigato" is the general Japanese word for "thank you." In adding the "gozaimasu," however, Kazuki is giving the phrase a more formal and respectful tone. Similar to the difference between "Thanks" and "Thank you very much."

from falling."

He almost missed the brief smile that lifted the corners of her mouth. With a sigh heavy with resignation, she crawled around him to sit against the wall, pulling some of the blanket with her to cover herself.

Unbothered by his own lack of clothing, he skipped the blanket and moved beside her to give himself a better view of the room.

It was only six tatami[17] in size, smaller than some of the castle's closets, but he didn't feel as claustrophobic as he would have expected. Dark shelves lined the wall opposite where they sat, with various odds and ends filling the little square alcoves. To his delight, a large black box took up the center section of the wall. A television! Though he had heard much about them, he'd never had the chance to watch one. He'd long wondered why humans found them so enjoyable. In the corner near the sliding doors, sat a small wooden rectangular cabinet of some kind, positioned on a matching stand. The wood was dark and had rich red tones in it. The handles on its doors were a dark metal he didn't recognize. It was a rather pretty box.

Though the knick-knacks had changed and the television was new, the smell of the house was familiar. This was definitely Hiro's house, or at least had been when they'd last met. Every place had its own unique core scent; only the nuances changed with time. Had Hiro moved? From his studies of humans, he'd learned that they changed residences quite often, and it had been many years since they'd seen each other.

"Um, I'm Sakura. Takeshi Sakura." The girl's quiet voice had a slightly husky quality.

Kazuki debated how to answer. What he should tell her?

---

[17] A unit measuring about 6' x 12'.

The human world was not the place it once was; travel advisories had been issued long ago to his people and were renewed every decade. Revealing one's true nature to the wrong person might result in a violent response or, worse, capture and scientific study. It was safer to reveal oneself only to those who already had long ties to his world and could be trusted. Otherwise, it was recommended to use a glam spell to appear human throughout one's travels.

Still, this girl had already seen him in his true form and sat beside him with no hints of ill intent. Wrapped in the comforting scent of the house, he decided to take a chance.

"Kazukiarama Yygralenu Throklamanasa. Please, call me Kazuki. Seeing as we are being rather informal at the moment, may I call you Sakura?"

"If you wish. You have an unusual name."

"Yes, I suppose it is, to a human."

She stared at him a long minute before replying. "You say that as if you yourself are not human."

"I'm not. I am what your people call a *yokai*. Crown prince to the throne of Throklana, first kingdom of Jalathumesa." Other than her eyes opening a little wider, her expression barely changed.

"I see. So Ja…ja…la…"

"Jalathumesa. I believe you call it *Oni no Sekai*[18] in your tongue."

"Oh. Um, so, where is it, Oni no Sekai?"

"I guess the best description is that it's in another plane of existence. It is not a place you could walk to or reach by normal means, but our worlds are connected through various portals."

"Wait, so there is a portal to your world in my yard?"

"Ah, no, though there is one in this area, I believe. I arrived

---

[18] Roughly translated to "The Demon World."

via a transportation gem. It allows us to travel to any place that we've been to at least once before, no matter which world it is in."

"I see." She nodded as she turned away from him. Did she doubt what he was saying? From what his father had told him, many humans had so lost their belief in those with supernatural natures that they could deny even what they saw with their own eyes.

"I think I'm okay now." She made another attempt at standing, this time staying on her feet. She looked at him, but he couldn't decipher the look's meaning. "I'll go make dinner, though I should apologize in advance. Nothing I can make is likely to be like the royal foods you would be used to."

"Oh, anything will be fine. I quite enjoy human foods." His stomach growled. He'd gained two kilograms when he'd last visited from eating so much.

The girl hesitated a moment, then left him the blanket, quickly wrapping herself in one of the towels lying on the floor. Before leaving the room, she picked up a pile of wet clothes and a pair of muddied white shoes from nearby. He focused his senses to keep track of her. Her bare feet padded through the house, first to the front area then back down the hall. Moments later, the house filled with a mechanical humming and he could hear water running. The gentle vibration of a machine reached him through the floor.

From there she went into the room opposite from where he sat. Small wooden doors opened and closed, followed by a larger door that sounded as if it had a seal of some kind. Guessing it was a refrigerator, he surmised she was now in the kitchen. His stomach growled in anticipation. He'd eaten his morning meal as usual, but he couldn't remember eating anything else since. He'd been so excited to make up with Yuji that he'd decided to hold off on dinner in hopes that they could eat together.

Pushing aside thoughts of Yuji's betrayal, he contemplated what he should do now. If he returned home, there was every possibility Yuji would come after him again, forcing him to defend himself. Would he have to hurt his brother, or worse? An image of Yuji lying in his arms flashed through his mind. No, no, he couldn't bear the thought. He couldn't hurt his baby brother. There had to be some explanation, some way to stop all this. But if he went home and somehow captured Yuji to force him to talk, the advisers might force his hand. If they learned of Yuji's attack, it might be ruled treason, and his brother would be executed.

I'll stay here. I wanted to come visit soon anyway, and at least if I'm here, things might settle down. Maybe Yuji is sick or something. Once Father returns, he can make sense of this. Until then, perhaps that girl will be generous enough to let me stay the night. Then I can go find Hiro tomorrow. If she lives in his old house, she might even know where he is.

Satisfied with his plan, he rested his eyes while he awaited his meal.

RISKING CONNECTION

AFTER LEAVING THE LIVING room, Sakura had taken their wet things to the laundry room to wash. She wasn't entirely sure how to clean his torn garments, though as she held up his pants she realized they looked more like rags than expensive clothes. She'd practically cut them in half and then some to get them off. There was no saving them. She put her uniform and wet under things in the washer then headed into the kitchen to throw his ruined garments away.

As she stuffed them into the trash, a deep blue gemstone dropped to the floor. The rich color reminded her of a sapphire she'd seen in a book of famous gems. Holding it up to the light, she could see it was very clear despite its dark color. The multitude of facets on it made it sparkle. It was one of the prettiest stones she'd ever seen. He would surely want this back. She quickly checked the clothes for any other items that might be hidden in them. Once she was certain nothing else remained, she put the remnants in the trash can and set the stone on the counter.

Sakura realized she was remarkably calm, all things considered. She was standing in the kitchen, wrapped in a towel, putting on water to boil so she could prepare dinner for a yokai.

She'd already started to suspect who and what he was from his first words to her, but she pinched herself to make sure she was actually awake. This Kazuki had to be him, Ito-san's friend. When she was still recovering from her wounds, Ito-san would tell her many stories, including some about a yokai he'd met as a child. They spent several weeks together having fun adventures before his friend had returned home, promising to visit again one day. At the time, she thought he'd made them up to keep her from dwelling on what had happened. Yet now, she remembered how he always ended the stories by saying how much he looked forward to introducing his friend to his new daughter with the nostalgic look of someone recalling fond memories.

Of course, in none of those stories had Ito-san mentioned that his friend was also a prince, much less such a beautiful creature. Looking down at her white camisole and flower-patterned panties, she felt her cheeks warm. Had she really sat side by side with a prince like this while having a conversation? At least she'd had the sense to pull the blanket over her, and he'd been a gentleman enough to not mention it. Given the odd circumstances and the fact that he'd been even less dressed than her, she suspected he wouldn't consider it too much of a mark against her character.

Not that she planned to go back looking the same. She dropped the vacuum-sealed curry mix in the water and started the rice cooker then went upstairs to her room to change. She debated dressing nicer than she normally would for an evening at home, but she was still tired and it was already getting late. Prince or no, he'd just have to settle for seeing her in her well-worn pink sweats.

Once she was more decent looking, she crossed the hall to Ito-san's room. It was mostly empty now, other than for a few stacked boxes. All the furniture was gone and most of his clothes had been given away to charities, but one of the boxes held some clothes she'd overlooked at the time and then never got around to dealing with. There were a few pairs of pants in it, but as she pulled them out, she realized they were all too short to fit her guest. Kazuki seemed to be much taller than her own 165 centimeters, maybe closer to 195, whereas Ito-san had been 175 centimeters at best. If any had been looser fitting, they might have worked, but they were all tighter cut slacks that he'd worn to work. At least she found an oversized tee-shirt that he could wear as a top.

"Wait, wasn't there…?" Sakura moved to another box, one containing pictures and personal mementos. Shifting aside the mix of framed and loose prints, she spotted the silver frame she was seeking and pulled it out. She'd discovered the picture hidden inside Ito-san's dresser when she'd packed up his things. A young Ito-san stood smiling as he stood beside a taller boy. Their arms were on each other's shoulders, huge smiles on their faces as they stood in front of her house, though the house was painted yellow then. The boy had white hair that went past his shoulders and purple eyes, just like Kazuki. Though unlike Kazuki, the boy in the picture looked decidedly human, other than for his hair and impossibly colored eyes.

"This has to be him. Kazuki really was Ito-san's friend." She stood, carrying the picture and the shirt as she made her way downstairs. How could she tell him? After all this time, he'd come back, but it was too late. Putting off the moment a few minutes, she stopped in the kitchen to check the curry. *You can't very well tell him while we're eating. Just get it over with already.*

With a deep breath, she forced herself to go to the living room. He'd wrapped the dry towel she'd left behind around his waist, apparently realizing that it probably wouldn't work well to sit around in a loincloth long.

"I had to cut your clothes off earlier, so they aren't wearable anymore. For now, I found this shirt that might fit you. I couldn't find any pants, though. I'm sorry. Tomorrow I'll go to the store and get you some new things to replace the ones I destroyed." She pulled out the kotatsu and set it up in the middle of the room while she talked. Anything to delay the inevitable.

"Thank you, I suppose it is a bit chilly to sit around like this too long." He pulled the shirt over his head. It was a little tight, but it was long enough to go down to his hips.

"Oh, and this fell out of your pants." She pulled the gem out of her own pocket and returned it.

"Ah, thank you. I was afraid I had lost it. This is the transportation gem I mentioned. They are wonderful tools, but rare because lakmanine stone is difficult to find and it is the only mineral we've found that can be enchanted for transportation, something to do with harmonics and the like."

"I've never seen anything like it. It is so beautiful. I hope it isn't damaged?"

He turned it around in his hands as he examined it. "It doesn't look like it. They are quite strong, harder even than your diamonds. Smaller chips are sometimes used in fine tools for carving, and when they were more common, they were used to make small knives. We have one on display now in our historical museum."

"Amazing. I'm glad it's okay."

"As am I."

Sakura gave herself a mental kick to stop herself from stalling anymore. With grim determination, she sat on her heels in front of him. "Um, you said earlier that it can take you to any place you've been to before, right?"

"That's right." He smiled at her as if he'd anticipated the question.

"So then you've been here before, to this house I mean?"

"I visited your world with my father, some twenty-five of your years ago. While we were here, I met a wonderful friend who lived in this house, a man named Hiro Ito. Perhaps, you know him?"

She nodded and held out the picture. "Is this you?"

"Yes, it is! I knew I was in the right house, but I thought perhaps he moved since I couldn't smell his scent very strongly at all. Where does he live now? There is so much we have to talk about." He was practically radiating happiness as he leaned toward her, so eager to hear her answer.

"Um, I…I'm sorry. Ito-san…he died…three years ago."

He went still. "Died?"

"Yes, he was killed in a car accident." She could still remember that night as she'd sat waiting for him to come home from work. Long after their dinner had grown cold, he still hadn't arrived. It was late at night when the cops knocked on the door. They'd taken her to the hospital to see him, but Ito-san had been killed instantly. She hadn't cried after her parents died, but standing beside her guardian's bruised body, his face covered with a white cloth, she'd gone on and on until her tears had run dry and her head ached.

Kazuki's anguished voice ripped through her. "Hiro…I'm sorry. I'm so sorry, my friend." His head dropped, tears running freely down his cheeks. Ito-san hadn't any family besides her, and he'd only had a few friends, so the funeral had been a small affair. Watching Kazuki crying, she wished she'd been able to reach him back then, to tell him sooner. He might have understood her own pain at the time, this man who was crying so earnestly.

Before she realized what she was doing, she shifted closer to him and wrapped her arms around his head, holding him close until he calmed while fighting back her own tears. When she was certain he was done, she retrieved a box of tissues for him so he could dry his wet face. When he blew his nose, it was quiet and understated, the sort of gesture that seemed fitting for a royal person, even one who'd just been crying like a child.

"Forgive me, Sakura. I imagine this display must look rather frightful. I just never imagined he would be gone already. Of course, I knew he would pass long before me because of the differences in our lifespans, but still." He straightened himself more fully, clearly trying to recompose himself.

She walked over to the butsudan and opened the doors to show him Ito-san's memorial. "I visit with him here. I figured his spirit would much rather stay here than some lonely cemetery. I'll leave you to talk to him, if you like, while I finish dinner."

"Thank you." He walked over to the shrine and sat on his heels. After clapping his hands together in front of his face, he bowed. She pulled the living room screen closed to give him privacy as she quietly made her way to the kitchen.

Three tablets stood inside Sakura's shrine. Two had the same family name, Takeshi. *Wasn't that Sakura's family name as well?* Were they her grandparents perhaps? The third tablet bore Hiro's name.

"Hello, old friend." Kazuki smiled at the picture of Hiro nestled in the shrine. Even if there had been other photographs in the cabinet, he'd have known which one was Hiro. Though obviously older than the boy he'd once played with, Hiro stood under a large cherry tree wearing that easy-going smile Kazuki remembered so well. His body was a bit taller, but still lanky with a slightly awkward air about it. Those thin-framed black glasses perched at the end of his nose didn't look very different from the ones he'd worn when he was ten.

"It has been so many years since we last met. Alas, far too many. How I wish I'd returned sooner, that we could have had one more chance to talk. I hope you did not think I forgot you? Not ever, I promise. I foolishly thought I had more time. Never did I imagine you would leave the world at such a young age." He paused, regret settling over him. "I wonder, was it your voice I heard when I fled Yuji? Did you guide me here for some reason? This girl, Sakura, is she your daughter perhaps? Your family names are different and you look nothing alike, yet I could feel her sorrow when she told me of your passing."

His ears twitched. Sakura was returning.

"We shall talk more later, my friend." He bowed one more time before closing the cabinet and walking across the room to open the door for her. They reached it at the same time. She paused, seemingly surprised by his actions, but he was glad he'd done it. The large tray in her hand would have made it hard to open.

Sakura thanked him as he stepped aside to let her pass, his stomach growling at the delicious smells coming from the dishes on the tray. She carried the meal to the kotatsu and set the tray on the floor beside it. It took him a moment to remember how to position his legs under the table, but he managed to do it without knocking things around.

He waited patiently while she transferred the dishes to the table. His mouth watered as she set a large bowl in front of him and a large spoon. A thick broth with chunks of onion, carrots, and potatoes covered a healthy serving of rice. Curry! He wasn't sure what kind of meat it was, but he was sure it would be good. A bowl of miso soup joined the larger bowl. After setting the teapot in the center with sugar cubes and milk, she joined him at the table then poured them some tea.

"I hope venison curry is okay." She gestured at the bowl. "I'm sorry I couldn't make something more grand."

"Please don't worry yourself about it. It's been a long time since I've gotten to enjoy the foods of your world." He took a bite. The sauce was thick with just a hint of spiciness and the sweet tartness of apples. "This is quite delicious!"

"Oh, it's just a packaged one; I didn't do anything special really." A blush stained her cheeks.

They ate in companionable silence for a while, his stomach demanding he focus on filling it versus engaging in conversation. Once the edge had worn off, he asked her if she was Hiro's daughter.

"In a way. He adopted me eight years ago, after my parents died."

"I see." That explained the other two tablets. "I'm sorry for your losses."

"Thank you." She gave him a brief, polite smile. How many times had she heard those words before?

"So now you live alone here?"

"Yes, Hiro left me the house in his will. He wanted me to have a safe place to live for the rest of my life, without having to worry about the financial aspects."

"That is so like him. He always had a kind heart."

"Um, he really treasured you, as a friend." Her smile was genuine, almost shy. With the solemn look she'd worn most of the night, she'd been decent enough looking, but smiling like that, she looked cute. "He told me stories about you all the time, though honestly, I didn't believe them until tonight."

Relief filled him. He'd worried if perhaps Hiro had been angry about his unintentional silence. He should have known better. Hiro wasn't like that. *Yuji wasn't either, once.* Mentally he shook his head. There had to be an explanation; there just had to be. For now he pushed the thoughts aside, focusing on the girl in front of him and his lost friend. "As did I. I often catch myself looking at our picture, a copy of the one you have, remembering those days. Come to think of it, Hiro was much like you. Seeing me like this, in my true form, he wasn't at all afraid."

"Why would anyone be afraid of you? I mean, I suppose people often associate yokai with monsters, but you don't look scary at all. If anything, you look more like one of those pretty heroes you often see in shojo manga series."

"Really? Well, it's true, like humans we yokai come in many different shapes and sizes. Some do very much resemble the monsters of nightmares, and often have the personalities to match. Others have animal forms, and so their regular forms have features in common with those true forms. Many are more like me, though, with only minor differences between us and humans appearance wise. Of course, members of the royal families have always been known for our extraordinary beauty." He finished the statement in as casual a tone as he could muster, curious to see how she'd take it. Sakura blinked a moment.

"So I see." Her eyes crinkled at the corners in amusement as she gathered up the dinner dishes. "I'll be right back."

As he waited, he thought about his situation. With Hiro gone, he had nowhere to go. Of course, he'd already considered just using a glam spell and hanging out awhile on his own, but he'd looked forward to visiting with Hiro. It was so much more fun to stay with someone you knew than to live in some hotel by yourself. Soft, padded steps came from the hall. Well, he now knew one more person in the area, that he had a connection with too, but would she welcome an unexpected house guest for a week or two?

When Sakura returned to the living room, she brought two bowls of ice cream with her. It seemed like a good treat to offer her guest after having made him cry earlier.

He smiled as she set the bowl in front of her. "I love ice cream!"

"Me too. Even though it's technically too cold for it, I still like to make some every few weeks to have on hand. This one is black cherry, which is my favorite."

Kazuki scooped up the first pink spoonful and popped it into his mouth. His eyes closed as he moaned under his breath. "Mmm, so good! I think it may be mine too."

It was fun seeing someone else appreciate food she made. As they ate, she kept thinking about how he had arrived. She was so caught up in realizing Hiro's friend had returned that she'd almost forgotten he'd been wounded.

"Kazuki-san…"

"Please, just Kazuki is fine." Another smile. As if he wasn't handsome enough, when he smiled so freely even she couldn't help but take notice. She wondered if he had a wife back home or a girlfriend at least. But that wasn't what she needed to ask him about now.

"Oh, okay. Um, Kazuki, why did you come here? I mean, I don't imagine it was to see Ito-san, when you had so many wounds on you. And from the way they looked, I'm guessing they were from another yokai?"

His smile dropped as he put down his spoon. He almost looked like he wanted to cry again.

"No, much as I wish that had been why I came, it was truly an accident." The confidence had fled his voice, leaving it soft and humble. "I was trying to return to the castle, but at the last minute I heard something, a voice maybe, and I ended up here. Please, don't misunderstand. I would have truly been happy to see Hiro again and, in fact, had planned to come in another few weeks. It just wasn't my intention to come this evening."

Knowing Ito-san, he wouldn't have minded at all that the visit had been unintentional, so it didn't bother her either, but that didn't explain the injuries. The way Kazuki was watching her, his eyes sharp and assessing, he was no doubt trying to decide if he should tell her the rest of the story. She was curious to know more but also hoped he didn't say any more, that he would just leave it at that. He could head home and get back to his princely life, maybe remembering her now and then—there must be no promises to return.

Sakura was so lost in her own thoughts, she almost missed Kazuki's brief nod before he rested his elbows on the kotatsu top with his fingertips touching the front of his face. "My kingdom, Throklana, is ruled by a hereditary monarchy. Each king rules for up to one thousand years before he must abnegate the throne. The crown is then passed down to the departing king's oldest child. However, the second child can become king if the crown prince declines the throne, if he dies before having a child of his own, or if the citizenry find him unfit to rule."

"Wait, did you say one thousand!? Then how old are you?"

Her reaction drew a brief smile from him. "I turn 370 this year. Time in our worlds pass differently, though, so it is not as long as it may sound."

"Okay, I think I follow. Are you your father's eldest son?"

"Yes. My father has now been king for 950 years, so the end of his rule is approaching."

"So then you'll be king in fifty years?"

"I have a younger brother, Yuji. I've loved him from the moment he was born and I swore to protect him like a proper big brother. He is my best friend, second to none. There is nothing I would not do for him." He paused, rubbing his chin with the tips of his fingers. "In truth, I have no desire to be king. I'd much prefer to continue my studies and aid our people some other way. Yuji loves it, though. He thrives on the mental challenges of politicking and has the right nature to be a good ruler. As such, I swore many decades ago that I would decline the throne when the time came, which means he is really the crown prince, though it is not official yet."

"Oh." It sounded like a good system to her. Why force someone to be king if he didn't want to be? So why did she have a bad feeling about where this conversation was going?

"A few weeks ago, Yuji turned against me, storming out of the castle. He hasn't been home since."

"But why?"

"I wish I knew. He hasn't spoken to me, and even when he left, it was so sudden. The night before nothing had been different that I can recall, but in the morning he yelled that we were no longer brothers and left."

He told her of the note he'd received and of Yuji's attempt on his life at their mother's gravesite. Sakura felt her breath catch as he told of his escape. Taking a sip of her tea, she sought refuge in its warmth. Again, she found herself wanting to hold him and comfort him.

The circumstances were different, of course, but she certainly knew how much it hurt to have someone you love turn on you, to want you dead. She shuddered at the thought of that knife, descending with lethal malice. Ruthlessly, she shoved her thoughts back into their prison and concentrated on refilling their teacups.

"You said earlier the citizens could also reject a ruler if he was unfit. Would your brother still be able to take the throne if he killed you?"

He shook his head. "No, it would not be allowed. He would be imprisoned, possibly even executed. As we are our father's only children, he would either have to find a second mate and have a child with her within fifty years or the throne would go up for grabs to whoever may be found worthy. If the people learn about this ongoing feud, and Yuji's attack on me tonight, they may turn against him anyway and he would lose everything. He knows this, so why he would take such risks, I do not understand."

"What about your father? Can't he do anything?"

"Alas, he left on a trip some months ago. We have told our people that he is visiting other kingdoms, but in truth, I know not where he is. No one seems to. Even Reito, my father's attendant, was left behind and claims to know nothing."

"You don't believe him?"

"Reito is as dependable and trustworthy as they come, but I also know he would never betray my father's confidence. If he was sworn to secrecy, he would lie to the gods themselves. It seems almost impossible that my father would just leave and not tell Reito where he is going. But even if he does know, I'm not sure he can communicate with my father. If he could, I think Father would have come home by now to sort it all out. I'm sure once he does return, he can talk some sense into Yuji."

Sakura regarded the forlorn-looking yokai sitting across from her, taken aback by the whole messy situation but not least by his presence. She spoke carefully, "So, what will you do now?"

Kazuki looked up at her with a hopeful expression. "Actually, I wondered if perhaps you might let me stay with you here, for a little while. Yuji would not think to look for me here, so we would be safely separated until Father returns. Of course, I'll gladly pay for the room and board, just name your price."

Sakura couldn't help laughing. "Somehow I doubt there is an exchange rate for the money of your world and mine."

"True. My people do not consider the same metals precious that yours do. Most business conducted between our worlds is in trade of materials and the like, rather than money, but I don't know how useful any such materials would be for you, and I presume you are not a trader who could sell them readily. Hmm, then might I offer to pay with myself?"

Her eyes opened wide as she stared at him. She could feel her eyebrows arching high. Surely he wasn't offering that?

He quickly shook his head and waved his hands in front of him in denial. "I didn't mean it that way, forgive me. I meant it as an offer of my services around the house. What do you call them?…chores, yes, chores. I admit I have not done much in the way of housework, but I'm strong and a quick study. No task would be too menial. I would be glad to help you however I can."

She sighed in relief, and perhaps a bit of disappointment. Having a man who looked as good as he did wanting her would be thrilling. Of course, if she tried more than a momentary fantasy she would likely be dead. Talk about unsexy. Pushing aside her unruly thoughts, she realized she needed to give him an answer. The longer he stayed, the more they would *bond*, the more likely he would remember her later. He'd already lost his friend and possibly his brother. Pushing him away would be kinder, for both of them.

"I don't mind, I guess, but your appearance would likely

draw unwanted attention from others." *Did I really just say that out loud?*

"Oh, that won't be a problem." In an instance, his ears shortened to a more normal-looking height retaining just the barest hint of a point. His claws retracted and changed to ordinary human fingernails. The fangs that occasionally flashed as he talked vanished. Before her eyes, he'd changed from a yokai to a regular, albeit handsome, guy in his early twenties. That would certainly get the neighbors gossiping, not that she cared what they thought.

"Wow, how did you do that?"

"It's a glam spell. We use it when we travel to foreign lands and need to be in disguise. If my normal appearance doesn't bother you, though, I'd rather not use it when I don't need to."

"No, it doesn't bother me at all."

"Wonderful!" He resumed his regular appearance. "Well then, if I might impose on you a bit, I'm still a bit dirty from the day's events. A bath would be heavenly about now."

"Of course, this way." He followed her upstairs. She gave him a quick course in operating the shower, and the tub, should he want to soak. After admonishing him to keep his bandages dry, she went back downstairs. It was getting late, and she still had homework to do. Half an hour later, a cleaner, happier Kazuki rejoined her.

"That's much better, thank you." He glanced around at the textbooks and papers she had spread out. "So many books. What are you doing?"

"Studying. I have school tomorrow."

"Of course, as I recall, your schools run six days a week, yes?"

"Yes. Tomorrow is Saturday, though, so it's just a half day."

Seemingly content to leave her to her studies, he lay down

on the floor nearby. It took her a moment to realize he was reading her history book. Catching her surprised look, he gave her a chagrined smile. "Forgive me, I began reading it without even thinking. I have a great fondness for books, especially ones on history."

"It's okay. I've already finished with that one tonight. I'll need it back in the morning, though." She looked back down at the math problem she'd been working on before his actions fully sank in along with another realization. All this time, they'd been conversing in Japanese. "Do all yokai speak and read Japanese?"

"No, mostly scholars and those who have dealings here. Of course, it is also expected that members of the royal family learn multiple languages to help with foreign relations. Thus I can speak Japanese, Cantonese, Dragon, and smatterings of English, Spanish, Okami, and Raptor."

"Dragon?"

"It is a fairly easy language to learn, really. Not nearly as difficult as Japanese or Cantonese. Humans seem to have a penchant for creating complicated languages. Of course, reading other languages is a far different matter and much harder to do. Thus far I can only read English and Japanese with any ease. I imagine it will be a wonderfully different experience reading an actual book from your world versus our study guides."

She couldn't decide if she was amused or amazed at his linguistic abilities. It was tempting to ask him what Dragon sounded like, but she really needed to finish her assignments. Perhaps later she'd see if he would demonstrate. For now, she just pointed to a larger book near his leg. "If you have trouble with any words, that's my dictionary."

"Ah, that will be most helpful. Thank you."

Audacious Request

HOW LONG HAD IT BEEN since Kazuki had been able to just spend some time reading? Since his two hundredth birthday, most of his time was taken up by a schedule of political meetings, responding to correspondence, attending balls. Even dinners were rarely quiet, as there were often visitors from other countries to be entertained. But tonight there was no pressure and no desperately trying to feign interest in the droning chatter around him.

He had just finished the first chapter of Sakura's history book when she closed her notebook and began putting her things away. "All done for tonight?"

"Yes. How did you like that book?"

"It was interesting to learn more about what you call the Western world. I have not had the chance yet to visit these places, though I have learned some from my studies of the English language. Such a richly diverse set of cultures! Though I must admit, the writing is a bit dry for my taste."

She chuckled as he handed it back. "Yes, sometimes I wonder if textbook writers actually like history that much. They always write it in such a boring fashion. You might find the ones in my library more interesting."

"You have a library? Here? Where?"

"Yeah, I love books. I'm a bit tired, though. If it's okay, I'll show you in the morning along with the rest of the house."

"I look forward to it!" A yawn escaped him as Sakura opened the sliding door of the closet and reached inside for a large, folded, white object.

"Let me, please." He darted forward to help her with it. No sense waiting until tomorrow to be useful, after all.

"Thank you. I hope you don't mind sleeping on the futon[19] in here tonight."

"Oh, so this is a futon! I have read about them, but I had not seen one. Where does it go?"

"Here on the floor. We just need to put the kotatsu away to make more room."

He obediently put the futon down where she indicated. It seemed to have a plush padded bottom and a blanket. They were thick enough, he supposed, but it didn't seem very comfortable to him.

"I do not mean to seem ungrateful, but you wish me to sleep on a floor?"

"Um, well, it is technically on the floor, so I guess so. Tomorrow we can clean up Ito-san's room, if you like, and move it there."

"I see." He did recall that futons were a traditional form of bedding in Japan. He supposed he couldn't complain if it was the best she had to offer. "And you sleep on one of these as well?"

"No, I have a bed, upstairs in my room."

---

[19] Japanese futons are bedding sets consisting of a padded mattress and a quilt that are pliable enough to be folded up and stored out of sight when not in use. American-style futons were inspired by the Japanese futons, but are usually dual-purpose mattresses, larger, thicker, and less pliable than the originals, that act as both sofa and bed thanks to the folding frames they rest on.

Kazuki glanced down at the futon again, then back at Sakura. So there was at least one bed in the house, presumably a proper one with at least a mattress, raised off the ground. Granted, he had roughed it before, having gone camping many times with Yuji and Karasu, but seeing her troubled expression, he found himself feeling a bit mischievous. "Well, if that is the only bed, then it would only be fitting for a person of my station to sleep there. Surely you would not expect royalty to sleep on the floor like a commoner? Of course, as you are a lady, I could not in good conscious demand you sleep on the floor in my stead, so the most sensible solution seems to be that we share this bed of yours. I trust it is big enough?"

He braced himself for an outraged response. Thus far, she'd been very calm and composed, almost oddly so for a girl her age. Seeing her in a bit of spirit would be fun. But she didn't yell or even ask if he was crazy. Instead, she stared at him a moment, her eyes perhaps open a little wider than before. He struggled to keep a straight face, not wanting to let on that he was teasing just yet.

A flash of emotion crossed her face, but it was too fleeting for him to decipher it. When her cheeks turned pink, he realized his request may have come across as a solicitation. That was the furthest thing from his mind, but before he could correct that idea she nodded. It was such a slight movement, he almost missed it.

"Okay, I suppose you're right." Her voice was soft as she shyly tucked her hair behind her ear. It took him a moment to process what she'd said. She'd agreed? He could almost hear his mother yelling from the afterlife at his outrageousness.

Feeling a little guilty, he said, "Good. I mean, thank you. Please be assured, I shall be a complete gentleman. I would never be so untoward as to abuse your kindness."

She nodded then crossed the room to turn off the heater and the kotatsu. Taking her hint, he returned the futon to the closet. Once they were done, Sakura went into the hall to lock the front door and turn off the small light that illuminated the entryway. He followed as she went upstairs. The bathroom she'd shown him to earlier was across from where the stairs emerged. Doors stood on either side of the landing.

"This is my room." She continued through the door on the left and he followed, guessing that the other door had led to Hiro's room. After grabbing some clothes from her dresser, Sakura started back out of the room. "I'm going to take a bath. Please make yourself comfortable."

He stayed there, standing in the middle of the room, until he heard the bath water start. He still wasn't sure why he'd made such a ridiculous demand of her. Maybe it was her waif-like appearance that made him want to stay close by, in case she had another nightmare.

Though the rest of the house had been stark, Sakura's room had a few personal touches. The dressing table by the door was almost oddly neat. Every other woman he knew had such tables crammed with make-up and accessories, but Sakura's held little. There was a photo, a hair brush, a small bottle of perfume, and a pretty hair bow. The flowers of her namesake decorated the piece, with long colorful ribbons. No doubt it went well with her hair, but he found it hard to picture Sakura wearing such a frilly piece.

The photo featured a younger version of Sakura with Hiro standing behind her, his hands on her shoulders. It was hard to reconcile the smiling, relatively healthy-looking girl with the thin, pale girl he'd met tonight. Had Hiro's death been even harder on her than he'd thought? *Don't worry, Hiro. You know I would never misuse your daughter.*

He moved to the bed nestled in the corner. It seemed big enough for two, though it was much smaller than his own bed, which could have easily slept five with room to spare. Giving it a little bounce, he decided the bed would be comfortable enough. It wasn't the sumptuous bedding and plush pillows he was used to, but the dark-purple bedspread looked warm.

On her bedside table sat a glass of water, a small round case, and a novel. To his amusement, it was about a yokai, only this one was a young girl that ate books to live. The idea both horrified and fascinated him. Maybe she'd let him borrow it when she was done reading it.

Near the book sat a simple black leather watch and a gold locket decorated with an etched flower. Curious, he picked up the locket. A cropped version of the picture of Ito from the shrine was tucked into one side while the other side contained a picture of a woman with shoulder-length black hair. She resembled Sakura. Though the woman smiled in the picture, her gray eyes seemed tired and sad. He clicked it closed and put it back on the table.

He looked around the room again, but there were no other pictures. A few books lay on the desk near the window, but none looked like a photo album. Perhaps she just didn't like photographs much? With a shrug, he settled back on the bed to wait.

As hot water sluiced over her, Sakura wrapped her arms around her chest. What on earth was wrong with her? Why was Kazuki now a guest in her house, much less waiting in her bedroom to go to sleep? Her bedroom! She'd intended to just apologize and decline when he'd asked to stay, but then *yes* had come out before she knew it. Was it some strange sense of obligation to help the friend Ito-san had talked so fondly about?

She knew it must have taken an incredible amount of trust to tell her what he truly was and to share his story with her. It would have been easy for her to call the police or some lab to come study him. Was it because of her connection to Ito-san, or did he have some special magic that let him know she meant him no harm?

Magic…was it magic that made her say yes? Had he beguiled her into accepting not only him living with her but also sleeping in her bed tonight? Even as the thought crossed her mind, she shook her head. He seemed like an honest and sensitive person, not the sort who would resort to such trickery.

She meant what she'd said earlier, about not fearing him. Even before he'd promised he had no ill intent, she hadn't worried that he would attack her in her sleep or something. From the look on his face, he might have been more shocked that she'd agreed to his silly demand than she had. It wasn't as if he'd even really meant it. She could tell. She could have just said no and he would have agreed to sleeping on the futon. Heck, she could go in there right now and say she had changed her mind, and she knew he would be okay with it.

So why don't you?

Her cheeks grew warm as she hugged herself tighter. Earlier, he'd pulled her from her nightmare, but it had actually been the second time she'd woken up. Perhaps an hour before, she'd drifted awake. During their sleep, she'd turned around so that she'd be facing him, her hands lightly touching his arm. They'd been close enough for her to feel the heat from his body, a deliciously warm sensation. Maybe she'd said yes just so she could feel it again, the warmth of another person close to her.

She grabbed her loofah, poured on a dollop of her jasmine-scented body wash, and scrubbed herself clean. It would be rude to dawdle too long while he was waiting for her. A soaking bath would have to wait until another night. Once she'd finished rinsing off, she turned off the shower, dried herself, and threw on her long nightgown. The fabric was thick, so her body wouldn't show through, and it came down just past her knees. It should be modest enough for mixed company. After quickly taking her medicines and brushing her teeth, she went back to the bedroom.

Kazuki sat on the edge of her bed, reading the novel that had been on her nightstand. As she walked in, he looked up with a chagrined expression. She smiled. His love of reading was too cute for her to be mad that he'd gone through her things.

"That's the sixth book in the series. I have the first five in the library, if you want to start from the beginning."

"Oh, that's why it seemed a bit confusing. The writing is quite good, though, so yes, I'd love to, thank you."

"No problem." She pulled her hair into a loose ponytail as she walked over to the bed. "Do you mind sleeping near the wall? I sometimes have to get up quickly during the night."

"Certainly." He slipped under the covers and slid over as requested, lying on his back. Once he was settled, she clicked off the light and joined him. If she lay on her back too, their arms would probably touch. It was tempting, but she lay on her side instead, turning her back to him.

"Good night."

"Good night…and thank you, Sakura."

A soft beeping pulled Kazuki from his sleep. Seconds later Sakura shifted beside him, her arm reaching out to hit a button on the watch on her table, stopping the sound. Her arm burrowed back under the covers. She didn't seem to notice that he had shifted during the night or that her back was now pressed against him and his arm was around her waist. Though she was thin, she was still soft with gently curving hips.

He should really move himself before she misunderstood and thought he was trying to molest her. Lifting his arm, he started to scoot back when he noticed her looking at him. Once he'd moved away a little, she sat up and yawned.

"Good morning." She didn't sound angry.

"Good morning, I'm sorry about…"

"It's okay. You were asleep. It happens." She yawned again and stood. "Be right back."

She returned a few minutes later, her nightgown replaced with a white blouse and a mid-calf-length, dark-blue skirt. The items looked similar to some of the wet things from last night. Her hair was now freed from its ponytail and brushed straight.

"I'll show you the rest of the house right quick then make breakfast."

"Great!"

As he'd already suspected, the room directly across from Sakura's was Hiro's bedroom. It was bare except for some boxes and an upright piano covered with a black cloth.

"Oh, I didn't realize Hiro played piano. It's a lovely instrument."

Sakura made a sort of hum sound, but didn't comment. Instead she led him back out of the room, closing the door behind them. "That's really all that's up here other than that closet there and the attic access. There isn't anything in there, though, so let's go downstairs."

The laundry room she'd used last night turned out to be tucked under the stairs, maximizing the home's space nicely. Near the base of the steps was the one door he didn't know, and to his delight it was the door to heaven. The shelves in Sakura's library bowed under the weight of all the books crammed in their spaces. She had a wide range of reading tastes, if what he gathered during his quick glance over the selection was any indication.

Through the window, he could see a garden on the side of the house. A vibrant mix of colorful plants and grasses painted a lovely scene around the large cherry tree on one end. Near the base of the tree, one batch of flowers was crushed and a set of marks marred the sand-filled path that wound its way from the gate to the back door. Sakura had dragged him that far? His mind reeled. He owed her so much!

In the spacious kitchen, light-colored wooden cabinets lined the upper half of the room. A matching set lined the bottom half along with a stainless-steel stove. A small stainless-steel fridge was tucked at the end of the cabinets in the corner of the room. In the center sat an island, topped with wood rather than the dark counter that topped the other cabinets. The room also had a small table with four chairs.

"Please, sit there and I'll make breakfast." Once the food was started, she ducked out of the room, returning moments later with a long rectangular box that was divided into seven colored compartments, one for each day of the week. Through the semi-translucent lids, he could see that the compartments were further split into four segments. Most were empty except the ones marked for Saturday. Inside those he could see various pills. As he wondered what they were for, Sakura set a cup down in front of him. Steam rose off the creamy brown liquid.

"This is coffee. I wasn't sure how you'd prefer it, so I made it the way I usually drink it. I can make it a different way if you don't like it. Blow on it a little to cool it before you sip it."

It was slightly bitter but the overall taste was sweet and

milky, with a pleasant undertone he couldn't identify. As the liquid flowed down his throat, it made his body feel warm all over.

"I like it."

"Thank you." Sakura walked back over to the counter and picked up the box of pills. She removed the pills from the first compartment and swallowed them with a glass of water. He was confused. That seemed like a lot of medicine to take at one time. They had a bitter smell, one he'd smelled on Sakura twice last night. Had she taken pills then too? He stayed quiet while she finished their meal.

"Breakfast is served." She set a bowl of miso soup and another of steamed rice at each of their seats, followed by two more dishes. "The fish is steamed mackerel and this is tamago-yaki.[20] It's made from sweetened eggs."

It all smelled wonderful, but he still was curious. "Sakura, those pills you took…?"

"They are medicines." She frowned. "Do you not have those in your world?"

"Yes, of course, we have many made from herbs and the like. But usually medicines are only taken by those who are very sick?" He deliberately framed it as a question, but she simply nodded and started eating. Taking the hint, he let it drop, for now. She seemed healthy to him, other than for her pale coloring, but whatever her reason for taking so many pills, it shouldn't matter to him.

He realized last night as he lay beside her that he needed to be cautious in his dealings with her. After all, she was a human, so she would not be long in the world. It was one thing his father had warned him about repeatedly once Kazuki had started

---

[20] A type of omelet made by rolling together several layers of egg using a rectangular pan; the eggs are flavored with rice vinegar and sugar or soy sauce.

studying human cultures. *Remember, Kazuki, their lives are very brief compared to ours. In the time it took you to grow to an adult, two generations of humans were born and died. I will not say not to befriend them; I just want you to keep the inevitable in mind.*

Taking a bite of his eggs, he shifted the conversation back to more neutral territory.

"This is quite delicious."

"Really? It isn't much, but I'm glad you like it. What do you usually have for breakfast, at home I mean?"

"We usually have a large table set out with a variety of things to choose from: fresh fruit, pastries, and sliced meats, along with boiled or scrambled kagorin eggs."

"Kagorin?"

"It's a large bird with a fierce-looking hooked beak and sharp claws on its feet, but it is very docile. Some households keep one or two females for gathering eggs. They have pretty blue and green feathers, which are used for decorations, and soft black down used to stuff pillows. They were one of my mother's favorite birds, so we have a large flock at the palace."

"They sound kind of like an ostrich, but with prettier colors."

He recalled the large black-and-white bird from his zoology books. "Now that you mention it, yes, I suppose they are similar."

They finished the rest of the meal in silence. He'd expected her to ask more about his world, but she seemed lost in her own thoughts. After putting away the dishes, they went back to the living room. A dark-blue blazer that matched her skirt hung near the room's entry. That's when it clicked what the outfit was.

"That's your school uniform!"

"Yes, I have class this morning."

"Oh, I was hoping you could show me some of the city today. Perhaps I could visit your school instead?"

"Um…" She glanced downward, reminding him that all he had to wear was Hiro's old shirt.

"I guess I can't really go anywhere like this." While the glam spell could change his physical appearance, it couldn't make him new clothes. He certainly wasn't about to walk around in public with just his loincloth and this plain shirt.

"Not unless you want to be arrested. Even if you did have clothing, the school has strict rules about visitors. Unless campus is open for an event, people can't just drop by."

"I see." He had always wanted to see a human school. His father had sent both him and Yuji to a regular school, wanting them to be connected with their people rather than being kept separate all the time. Were their schools similar or vastly different?

"It's a half day today, so I'll be home around lunchtime. I'll pick you up some pants and stuff on the way, so you'll have something to wear out. Then we can go shopping to get you something better to wear."

"Thank you."

"Here, this is the remote for the TV. Push this button to turn it on and off. These two control the channels, and these two change the volume, okay?"

"Okay." He might miss out on seeing her school, but he at least would get to watch some TV while she was away. Sakura put on the blazer and picked up her book bag.

"If you get hungry, there is some fruit in the fridge and some more rice in the cooker. Just help yourself. I left a pot of tea as well. If it gets cold, just hit the button marked 'warm' on the pot and wait for the light to turn back off."

He nodded. "Got it."

She nodded in return, turned, and left the room. Seconds later, looking somewhat nervous, she came back. "Next week. If you're still here then, my school has a Visitation Day for parents and guardians. Campus will be open for tours and stuff. You could pretend to be my guardian and see it then, if you want."

"Really!? Thank you. I look forward to it!" He was so happy he nearly ran across the room to hug her. A real human school!

"I'll be back soon." This time she smiled before turning to leave again.

He looked around the living room. What to do first? With his lack of proper attire, exploring the city was out. Besides, it would be more fun with someone along who could teach him about the wondrous things he was certain awaited.

Despite the circumstances, he was elated. Finally he was here in the human world and could truly study it at his leisure as he'd longed to do for so many years! Since his visit where he'd met Hiro all those years ago, he hadn't been able to come back. At first because he was "too young" and then because his father had insisted he wait until it was formally announced that Yuji would be the new king.

An announcement that was due to take place in the twelfth cycle of the year on their father's 1500th birthday, presuming Yuji wasn't ruining everything with his misbehavior of late. *After all this time, would you really just throw it all away, little brother? The kingdom, Aya, Karasu...me?*

Kazuki pushed the thoughts aside. For now, he could start what he'd been planning for months. His extensive study of humans! As if it were calling his name, he made his way back to

Sakura's library, snatching up the first volume of the novel series she was reading and a thick book on "Western" history that she'd pointed out earlier.

Back in the living room, he set the books down.

"Good morning, Hiro! What do you think, reading or seeing what this TV thing is all about?" He directed his question at the closed butsudan. "Yeah, I think so too."

With a beep, the television screen lit up and majestic music filled the room. A show was just starting that seemed to be a cooking competition of some kind, with an extravagant stage, a colorful host, and fun commentary from the people judging the results. He was so engrossed in the show, he ended up not reading at all until it was done.

The next show had a set of guests talking about such a random assortment of topics, it was hard to follow. Deciding it was best watched with an interpreter, he turned the TV off and glanced at the two books beside him.

"Wait a few more moments, then I shall decide which of you to enjoy first. Till then…"

He walked over to the butsudan and pulled open the doors. Fresh flowers from the garden were now inside, along with a cup of green tea and a bowl of rice that Sakura had put in for her morning offer.

"Good morning again." He bowed before sitting on his knees in front of the cabinet. "Thank you for trusting me enough to lead me here. At first, I wasn't sure it was you whose voice I heard in that moment, but now, I am certain. You wanted me to come here to meet her, yes? She is a very sweet girl. Kind, like you, though perhaps a little more reserved than you were when we met."

He'd come to the human world with his father and Reito for a business trip. Bored with the chattering of the adults at their host home, Kazuki had slipped off on his own. At a park nearby, he ran into a dark-haired boy tossing a ball alone. Hiro had run over, introduced himself, and asked if he wanted to play catch with a big grin. By the time Kazuki's father had come to fetch him, they had become the best of friends as only kids can do. Where Sakura was more closed in her revelations, Hiro had happily shared anything and everything about himself.

"It still seems strange, to think of you gone. This house, it feels so empty now. It is as if she is only existing rather than living here. To endure here alone, I know she must be strong, but the air has a heaviness to it, a sorrow too deep to miss. I think perhaps you are worried about her in such a lonely atmosphere. And the pills, that box made to hold so many pills…Why does she need them, and why does her scent—tainted with that darkness—remind me of my mother's?"

New Day

AS SOON AS SHE SAW THE first student wearing her school's uniform on the street, Sakura donned her protective mask—the cold, stuck-up persona they had come to expect of her. It wouldn't do for them to know she often hummed to herself while walking, or see her stopping to admire flowers. Once there was a chance any of her classmates might see, it was eyes straight ahead, an almost stiff march, and a dash of dismissiveness added to any glance she gave them.

Wordlessly, she switched out her shoes and headed to her classroom. All around her, early morning chattering filled the silence she left in her wake, the joyful noise of friends greeting each other as if they hadn't just been together yesterday.

With a steadying breath, she pulled open the classroom door and stepped on stage. As much as rudeness grated on her, she didn't call out the standard "good morning," just marched in with that practiced air of self-importance and headed to her desk. After three years, her classmates ignored her as much as she ignored them.

Surreptitiously looking around while she took her materials out of her messenger bag, she couldn't help but notice that she was the only one, this late in her school career, who still sat alone. For the first time in a long time, she felt a pang of envy toward them.

It's better this way…Quit feeling sorry for yourself…

With a soft sigh no one would hear, she picked up her bag to hook it to the side of her desk then paused. Across the room, a girl with long blond hair tied up in pigtails was looking at her. When their gazes met, the girl turned her attention to her desk, her cheeks pink. Of all their classmates, she was the only other one who was alone, though Sakura doubted that was usually the case. Indeed, moments later, another girl joined her.

Sakura put the staring girl out of her mind and began reviewing her notes for her first class. If nothing else, keeping her classmates at bay left her plenty of time to study. Not content to just graduate, she wanted to go out on a high note. It was a pointless achievement, all things considered, but she was rather proud of having one of the top class rankings and one of the highest practice exam scores among the third-year students. *At least when I do die, I can face Mom with my head high.*

Most days, she had no trouble tuning out her worries to study, but today her mind seemed determined to focus on anything but. Giving up, she stared out the window, her chin resting on her hand as she twirled her pencil in the other.

After so many years alone, her solitude was like a blanket loved for its familiarity while hated for always being too short. Yet that man's presence last night hadn't disturbed her. She hadn't been annoyed at his reading beside her, and she'd had no trouble falling asleep with him lying so close beside her. Waking up with his arms around her had given her a sense of safety and security she hadn't felt in a long time or even realized she'd been missing. She'd even pretended to be asleep a little longer to revel in that warmth, only "waking up" when he began moving.

"Takeshi-chan?" The blond girl was standing by her desk. Her child-like voice fit the somewhat immature pigtails she sported. Sakura tried to recall her name, but drew a blank.

"Yes?" Sakura carefully schooled any curiosity from her voice, aiming to sound just slightly annoyed.

"Um, Kagura-sensei is going on maternity leave after today. The baby is due soon, you know? So we're collecting money from everyone to give her a gift from the whole class." The girl kept shifting her hands and feet as she talked.

The others in the class didn't even attempt to hide their staring, as if waiting to see how she would coldly dismiss the girl. It would be an in-character response and Sakura briefly considered it. The girl stood there, still looking nervous but almost excited too as she stared directly at Sakura. Being bitchy just to feed her act didn't seem worth the effort, or the eventual guilt. It wasn't as if this girl in particular had done anything to her, and Kagura-sensei had always come across as genuine in her kindness toward Sakura.

Since she could afford it anyway, she handed the girl two one hundred yen bills.[21] "Will that be enough to cover my share?"

"Oh, yes, arigato godaimas." The girl smiled, that same carefree, wide-mouthed grin she'd given her friend earlier, then bowed several times before scurrying off back to her desk.

"Rich people love showing off, eh?" The stage-whispered remark came from a girl two seats behind. Figures they would find something to be annoyed about no matter how she'd responded. Turning her attention back to her notes, Sakura thought she spotted the blond girl watching her again, but when she glanced up, the girl was chattering away with her friend.

As the day wore on, Sakura's thoughts kept returning to

---

[21] Approximately $20 US.

Kazuki. How would he spend his first day alone in the house? Was he reading one of the books from her library, watching the TV, or maybe just lazing the day away? He could just decide to leave, but she didn't think he'd be so rude as to disappear without saying goodbye, and he'd seemed earnest in his desire to stay. Still, her plebeian home must be so boring to someone used to spending his days in a castle—he couldn't really want to stay long, right?

The vibrating at her wrist surprised her. It was the first time in years she'd needed her watch to remind her to take her medicine. Her medicine regimen required her to take several doses during the regular school day. To avoid anyone spotting her pills, she kept the doses in a cute character bag tucked in her skirt pocket. The larger pillbox was carefully stored in the middle of her bag, where it wouldn't be visible if she had to get anything from inside. Only the nitro spray and inhaler were kept in the bag's front pocket where she could reach them in an emergency, but even those were covered by a handkerchief.

Usually, she took her doses between classes as much as she could, but she'd missed her chance at break. She raised her hand to request permission to go to the restroom. Kagura-sensei, the very pregnant history teacher, let her go with an understanding smile. It was at least easier to take the dose, as the bathroom was completely empty, unlike during breaks when she would have to take it while sitting in the toilet area with a small cup of water she'd slipped in with her.

After school let out, Sakura headed home, pausing at the corner store to buy a small onigiri[22] to eat so she could take her

---

[22] A rice ball made with sticky rice that is lightly salted and formed into a shape, usually a triangle or an oval. They can be served plain or wrapped in seaweed and/or filled with various ingredients, such as ume (pickled plum), salted salmon, bonito flakes, or salty cod roe.

lunchtime dose. Kazuki hadn't pressed further with his curiosity about her pills, but he seemed bothered by them. It would be less troublesome to avoid taking any more in front of him. Just as she did at school, she could take them in the bathroom or, like today, on the way home.

While she was there, she picked up a pair of sweats for him to wear on their outing. They weren't very nice, but at least they were clean and not completely hideous. It would do until they could go shopping anyway. When she reached the house, she found him eager to go out.

"Here are some clothes for you to wear."

"I see. Thank you." He turned them over in his hands a moment, then shrugged and went into the bathroom to change. Sakura quickly switched out her school uniform for a pair of black jeans and a long-sleeved white blouse. Shivering from the chills the beta blocker often caused, she layered on a sweater and grabbed her coat before they headed outside.

"I'm sorry, I couldn't find you a coat," Sakura said, pausing in front of the door to turn the key in the lock.

"It's fine. It's cool but not unpleasant. I can handle it." As they continued down the paved walkway to the sidewalk, Kazuki asked, "Where shall we go?"

"The Kanemori Warehouse, down by the bay."

"Kanemori?"

"It was originally a set of commercial warehouses, the first in Hakodate actually. Now the buildings house shops and a few small restaurants, but they tried to retain some of the original feel of the place." From his apparent love of history, she thought he might enjoy the place. The way he smiled seemed to confirm it.

"That sounds like a wonderful place to see. Let's hurry!" A moment later, Kazuki jumped to the side, almost hiding behind her. "What on earth was that?"

"What was what?"

"That thing that just flew past us." He pointed down the road as the last *whir* of a car faded.

"The car?"

"That was a car?" His eyes were open in shock. "I remember seeing a few when I was here last, but they were not so fast or quite so loud." When another car passed a minute later, he flinched a little but held his ground. "I don't suppose we will get to ride in one of those?"

"Sort of. We're taking a bus, which is like a big car but it holds more people." She paused, tilting her head to the side as a snippet of their conversation from the night before came to mind. "You said before that you couldn't 'smell' Ito-san in the house much anymore, so I guess your senses are sharper than ours?"

"Yes, most yokai possess a more sensitive sense of smell and better long-range hearing than humans."

She'd never really thought of her world as loud, but trying to imagine it with his kind of hearing, she realized it must be like standing right in front of an orchestra pit. "Do the city sounds hurt you?"

"If I listened fully, it would hurt some and likely make my head ache. Fortunately, I can adjust my senses down to nearly human levels."

"Oh."

They continued on, walking in silence for a few minutes. It was strange to think about, how her world might sound and smell from Kazuki's perspective. She took a deep breath, trying to take in all the scents that she often overlooked. The light hint of woodiness from the trees that lined the street. A few teases from the fall flower gardens in the neighborhood. Briny fish from the seafood market a block away. The ashy scent of the passing cars. And under it all, the light hint of saltiness from the ocean breezes, evident even this far away, along with the clean, crisp air coming down from the mountain.

"What about your eyesight? Is it also better?"

"Not as much, at least not for me. I can see a bit better in the daylight than you might be able to, but at night it's about the same." Kazuki shrugged. "Some other yokai, though, have incredible sight, especially those who are what you might consider animal-based. For example, tengu can see for great distances." He glanced at the road as another car went by. "Might I ask, will this bus move as fast as those cars?"

"Only for a few minutes, at most. They stop frequently, so they never really pick up much speed unless they go on the highways."

"I see. It is a bit unnerving to have them pass you at first, but I should like to try one. With a transport gem you move to your destination in a near instant, so you don't feel it much, and our carriages move much slower than these cars."

She glanced at him, surprised. They clearly had magic in his world, so they must be advanced. Why did they not have some sort of high-speed transportation other than those rare gems? "So you don't have cars or trains or anything like that in your world at all?"

"Not in Throklana, no, though we could have such things if we chose. We have enough dealings in the human realm that importing is a simple matter, and it's something a few other kingdoms have chosen to do. In our kingdom, though, both my father and his father before him felt the potential negative impacts would outweigh the benefits, so only very select technology has been allowed."

"So those carriages are drawn by horses then?" She asked

as they stopped at the corner for the red light.

"A variation of them, yes. Larger breeds of horses from this world were imported some several thousand years ago and then selectively bred with a similar creature, a *grenoin*, in our world. Our smallest breeds now are as large as the ones you call 'draft' horses, while the larger ones are as tall as me at the shoulder."

"Wow! That's a huge horse! It would be kind of cool to see, though a bit scary too."

"There is no need to fear them, despite their size. Our breeders were careful to also breed for a gentle nature, and high intelligence too."

"That's good." She wanted to ask him more, but the signal changed and they continued across the street where their destination awaited. Other passengers stood near the pole that marked the stop. "This is where we'll wait for the bus. It shouldn't be too long."

The thing Sakura called a bus pulled up in front of them. The hulking metal beast dwarfed the speeding cars, though it was relatively quiet for its size. He followed as Sakura got in line to the door. Once inside, he mimicked her motion of pulling a piece of paper from the machine then followed her to the back where she sat on the bench seat. Only a few other people accompanied them on this particular bus.

"What's this paper for?"

"It's your ticket so we can pay when we get off, so make sure to keep hold of it."

"Okay." The bus lurched forward as it pulled away from the curb, and Kazuki grabbed the seat to hold himself in place. If his claws had been out, they'd have easily ripped through the shiny leather covering them.

"Are you okay?" Sakura was watching him.

"Yes, of course." He forced himself to relax his grip as the movement smoothed. He'd already let the car thing startle him. At this rate, his companion might think he was some sort of coward. "I was a bit unprepared for that take-off. It is rather sudden, yes?"

Sakura nodded briefly in response. "I'm sorry. I should have warned you about that."

"It's okay." Oddly, his stomach lurched a bit as the bus continued trudging along. Not wanting her to get suspicious, he turned to look out the window beside him. The people on the sidewalk, the trees, the buildings, all were still visible, yet their lines blurred as they moved along. Beside them, the cars on the road were now almost sharp and easy to see.

Looking out the window seemed to relax his stomach, so he gave in to his curiosity to see the view from another angle. With his knees on the seat, he turned to look out the back window. A small hand tugged on his shirt.

"Kazuki, you're not allowed to do that," Sakura whispered.

"Oh?" He turned around and plopped back down beside her. To his embarrassment, he realized some of the other passengers were staring at him. He presumed the issue was with his feet being on the seat; humans could be very particular about such things. Though he knew he'd gotten his moccasins spotless while Sakura was in school, to them shoes were "dirty." *When in another's world, you must strive to honor their customs.* It was a rule of traveling his father had drilled into them. Remembering his lessons from his previous visit, he gave several small bows in apology.

"I'm sorry." Sakura gave him a reassuring smile as the other passengers turned their attention back to their own affairs. He gestured at the window beside her. "What about that one? Can

I go look out it?"

"No, you must stay seated. It isn't safe to move around while the bus is moving."

"Oh. Okay." He resigned himself to enjoy the single view out his window, in a way relieved. As before, turning to look at Sakura or even the other passengers had made his stomach flop all over the place.

When the bus stopped to pick up more people, he quickly moved to Sakura's other side. "There, the bus wasn't moving then, so it was okay, right?"

"Yes, I suppose it's fine then." She shook her head slightly, an amused expression on her face.

At each stop, Kazuki moved from one side to the other so he could try to see as much as possible. The buildings had so many different designs, he wished they could walk some of the streets just so he could study them up close.

At one point, while the bus stopped at a traffic light, he noticed a strange vehicle beside the bus. Unlike the cars, the trucks, and the bus itself, this odd thing only had two wheels and no enclosure, but was incredibly loud.

"Sakura, what is that?"

She leaned over him to see. Her light perfume tickled his nose.

"That's a motorcycle. They can be crazy fast, and because they're small, they're easy to maneuver."

"It looks like it would fall over all the time?"

"The rider has to use his body to keep it balanced. When he's stopped, he uses his legs, see?"

He looked again and realized the rider had one foot on the ground. Once the light turned green, the man picked up his foot and rested it on the bike, taking off into the distance. "You have so many kinds of vehicles here. It's amazing! I wouldn't mind trying one of those too."

"You have to have a special license to drive one and someone who could teach you. It isn't something I can really do."

"Too bad." He supposed it would take a lot of strength to keep those bike things upright, which Sakura did not appear to have much of. Perhaps they could find him a teacher later, but for now, he was content to let it drop.

A few minutes later, Kazuki realized the buildings were spaced out further and that he was seeing something between them. He squinted a bit, trying to make it out. It looked like…water?

"Sakura, Sakura, there. That water. What is that?"

"That's Hakodate Bay. We're almost at our stop."

"We'll be near that water? Can we go see it, please?"

She laughed. "Yes, Kanemori is on the dock, so you'll be able to see it pretty well."

"Yes!" He could barely keep still. It looked massive, far bigger than any lake he'd seen. Sakura said it was a bay, which he recalled was something that emptied into the ocean. Jalathumesa had oceans, three in fact, but he'd only been to one. It had been incredible to behold an endless expanse of water.

"Kazuki, we're getting off here." Sakura stood and led the way to the front of the bus where she put her ticket into a machine and waved a card with her picture on it over a box. Something beeped. Kazuki fed the machine his own ticket, but wasn't sure what to do next. Sakura dropped some coins in the box, which triggered another beep. "This way."

It was a few blocks to the Kanemori place she had mentioned. Near Sakura's house, the mountain's smell was more dominant, but here, it was all water and seafood. A sharp, but not unpleasant scent. The sound of waves lapping against the shore structures was kind of relaxing.

"That's Kanemori." She pointed to a set of long, red-brick warehouses ahead, arranged in three pairs of buildings. One pair, which a sign identified as "Bay," had a waterway running between them with green vines climbing along the sides of each building up to the roof. As he looked around at the water, he saw objects floating atop it.

"Are those boats?" The few he saw seemed rather small to be boats, though perhaps they were just rowboats.

"Yes. We can't ride one, but we can look at them, if you want."

"Yes, please—the water first."

With a smile, she went down a walkway to the port area on the other side of the buildings. Smaller boats with multiple long sails drifted up and down in the waves, the thin lines tying them to the dock seeming to be all that kept them from answering the bay's inviting call.

"Amazing. They are much smaller than our royal ship, yet appear to have more complex designs. Are they fast, like cars?"

"The ones with motors are pretty fast, while the ones with sails tend to move slower unless the wind is strong. These are mostly personal boats, though. Sometimes a cruise ship comes through—those are much larger—but I don't see one nearby right now—they have to go slow this close to land, to avoid hitting anything."

"Oh, do so many people have their own boats?"

"I don't know if it is a lot of people, compared to the whole population, but I guess around here quite a few people have them. It is a port town after all."

"I'm rather glad I ended up here. There is so much to learn that is not found in my books at home. While you were at school, I was reading one of your history books. It talked of the early history of Japan and of the samurai warriors. I so wish I could have met one. My father used to tell me tales of them, but alas, when I first visited here, I learned they were long gone." He still remembered Hiro falling over with laughter when Kazuki had requested an introduction.

"Yes, but some people still trace their histories back to samurai lines, and many of their ideals live on." She turned to look at him. "So, what would you like to do next: eat or shop?"

As the scents of pastries, meats, and seafood filled his nose, his stomach growled its preference out loud. He blushed as Sakura laughed. "Food, please."

She led him to one pair of buildings. He expected to see just one or two places to eat, but there were dozens, serving different foods of wide-ranging varieties. How on earth did anyone pick just one from so many choices?

"How about we eat there?" She pointed to a café, its glass shelves lined with a tempting array of sweet and savory items.

"Those all look delicious. I think that will do nicely." As they browsed the displays, they admired the beautifully decorated, bite-sized soufflés, pastries, and other treats.

"There are so many to choose from. I am not sure what to get. Why don't you decide for both of us?"

"Okay." Sakura ordered two of the cheese soufflé-cakes, a pair of the chocolate cakes for dessert, and two cups of tea. The moist cakes were marvelous; their rich flavors danced on his tongue. And the chocolate, oh the chocolate. He'd forgotten how good it was! He made a mental note to take a lot home with him when he left so he could have it more often.

After lunch, Sakura left him alone briefly to go the bathroom. When she returned, the bitter tinge of the pills she'd taken that morning was once again around her. Had she taken more while there?

"Are you okay?" he asked, torn between curiosity and not

wanting to pry. He was just a visitor after all.

"Yes, I'm fine." She said it kindly enough, but the pinched expression on her face didn't encourage further prodding. Still, he found himself watching her more closely as they browsed the various clothing stores, looking for signs of what her mysterious illness was that required so many pills.

Kazuki left most of the shopping selections to her, other than commenting on choices she held up. She would know best what was appropriate for him to wear in her world after all.

After she'd gathered together several shirts and pairs of pants, she gave him an odd little glance then held up another garment.

"So what do you think about this shirt?"

It was the most hideously colored thing he could have imagined, an orange so outrageously bright that it physically hurt to look at. And what was that on the front? He supposed it could pass for a face, but only barely with that grotesquely inflated tongue sticking out of it.

"No way." It slipped out before he could stop himself. "I'm sorry. That was rude. I meant to say, that isn't quite to my taste."

Sakura laughed and put the shirt back in the pile. "I didn't think it was. I just wanted to be sure you weren't agreeing with everything to be nice."

He chuckled and shook his head. "I promise, I am not. I truly have found no fault in your taste…well, other than for that monstrosity. That color is unreal."

"It is awful, isn't it?" she said with a smile before leading him back to the dressing rooms. "Here, why don't you try these on? If they fit okay, then whichever you like best you can wear out, if you like."

"Oh, thank goodness." He darted into the curtained area.

Though he was grateful to Sakura for bringing him the clothes that had let him leave the house, he was even more grateful to be out of that drab outfit. *Though at least the sweats weren't supernatural orange.* He chuckled to himself as he put on his favorite of her selections, a dark blue button-up shirt and a pair of dark blue pants she'd called "jeans", and headed out.

The new clothes were a definite improvement and made him feel more like himself. As they left the store, he noticed several women giving him appreciative glances when before he'd gone almost unnoticed.

Seemingly unaware of the stares now aimed at them, Sakura paused in front of a different store. "I suppose we should also get you a suit, for visiting the school."

"All right, but I am curious. On the bus you showed a card to pay for your fare, but then gave him coins for mine?"

"Yes, I have a bus pass, so I don't have to pay for each ride. But since you don't, we had to pay cash."

"That makes sense. But here, as we've shopped, you handed people another card?"

"Yes, it lets them take the money straight from my bank account rather than my having to carry a lot of cash around."

"Ah, that sounds quite convenient. I never thought to ask the cost of any of these items. I wonder if perhaps I am imposing too greatly on you." He was unused to caring about the cost of items, but his family had plenty of money, while Sakura's situation might be different. After all, she was so very thin. The idea that he might be using up a large part of her precious funds just to clothe him was distressing.

"No, not at all. I have quite a bit of money sitting around that I never use." Her wry smile assuaged the guilt gnawing at him. "Hmmm, I guess some people would even say I'm rich. My classmates seem to think so. I suppose from their point of view I am. It isn't as if I earned any of it. It was left to me by my parents and Ito-san."

For a moment her smile fell, and the sorrowful expression she'd let slip before at times reappeared. She shook her head then smiled at him again, a fake cheerful smile. "Anyway, it's kind of fun to finally have someone to spend some of it on for a change."

Maybe it was as she said. He certainly had far more fun spoiling Karasu or buying gifts for others than he did when shopping for himself. "Yes, I think I know what you mean."

Deciding her build must just be her natural size, he watched her flick through the racks of suits. Finally she pulled out a dark-gray suit and held it toward him.

"I think this might work."

"That does look nice." It was soft and felt as if it were made from a high-end fabric. The color was pleasing too, so he carried it to the dressing room to try on, along with a white shirt and a pale-violet tie.

Glancing at himself in the mirror, he thought she'd made a fine choice. He walked back out to show her and to see it in the larger mirrors.

Sakura reached up to fix the necktie he'd found too complicated to do. With her so close, the light perfume she wore filled his nose. He'd noticed it before, but only now did he pay attention to it—of course it would be cherry blossoms. For a brief moment, he felt a tinge of awareness of her as a woman. *Hiro's daughter...off limits!*

Finally she stepped back. "What do you think?"

"I like it." He preened a bit in front of the mirror, hoping to steal another smile from her. "You have a good eye."

"Thank you."

Before leaving the store, the sales clerk took Kazuki's measurements so the suit could be tailored to him before being delivered to Sakura's house. At that point, Kazuki figured they had to be done, but Sakura led him around to the shoe store for a pair of comfortable sneakers, for everyday use, and polished black dress shoes to go with the suit. Then they had to get a few "accessories" as Sakura called them, which included a wallet, a watch, cufflinks, and the like.

As they started to leave, they passed a women's clothing store. Kazuki grabbed her hand and tugged her inside.

"Sakura, we've only shopped for me all day. You should treat yourself as well. This dress here. I think it would be quite flattering on you."

It was a white dress with a sleeveless design and a knee-length skirt covered by a slightly longer, sheer skirt. The bodice had a few silver beads for decoration. It was pretty, but with the sort of basic design that she seemed to favor, at least from the clothing he'd seen so far.

"I don't need anything, really." Granted, it was her money being spent, but he'd never gone shopping with a woman who hadn't wanted to buy tons of stuff for herself. Yet even as a dark look crossed her face, she reached out and fingered the fabric of the dress.

"Please, it wouldn't be fair if you went home with nothing."

"It is cute, I suppose." Her heavy sigh filled the space between them. "The hair bow would go with it…"

Deciding she must mean the one he'd seen in her room, he nodded enthusiastically, hoping it would be enough to make her lose that forlorn look. "Yes, it would, very well indeed!"

When she lifted one from the rack, he almost cheered aloud. A few minutes later, she'd tried it on and purchased it, though she had looked more grimly determined than happy. It was something, he supposed.

"It's getting late. We should head back," Sakura said. Outside, the sun had already set. He realized at some point her breathing had become labored. It wasn't enough that most people might have noticed, but his sensitive ears could tell the difference, so he'd insisted on carrying all of the shopping bags. It was a little awkward, as he held most of them on his uninjured side, but he was concerned it would only strain her more to carry any.

On the way home, they stopped at a convenience store where Sakura picked up some bento boxes for dinner. Though it was "cheap" food, it meant she wouldn't expend any energy cooking. After eating, she stood from the kotatsu.

"I should go clean out Hiro's room for you. I'm sure you'd rather sleep there."

Reaching out for her hand, he gave her a gentle tug so that she plopped back down beside him. "It is fine. I do not mind the current setup at all. Please, sit. It's too late at night, and doing such physical stuff right after eating will make your stomach cramp." Though she was clearly exhausted, he figured it was wiser not to point that out.

As they lay in bed later that night, Kazuki listened to her slow, even breaths as she slept beside him. While they'd done a lot, her level of tiredness seemed abnormal. He again wondered what was wrong with her health. Throughout the day, she'd made more trips to the restroom, all for show. Every time she'd come back smelling of the pills. Despite his earlier self-assurances that she was naturally thin, he knew it had to be more than that. But what? And why did it bother him that she was so determined to keep it from him?

Sitting quietly with a woman, encouraging her to lean

against him, sharing her bed. These were not things he ever imagined he would enjoy doing. He'd had his share of concubines in the castle, but he'd never slept with them. They were not even allowed in his personal chambers; liaisons always occurred in their rooms or in other rooms in the castle made just for such a purpose. When they'd finished their sexual activities, he'd always returned to his own room to sleep.

Yet here he was, lying beside Sakura. She had pretty features, especially those gray eyes with their long lashes, and was attractive enough that he wouldn't object to having sex with her. But, it wasn't at the forefront of his mind. He liked talking to her; he'd even had fun shopping for hours with her.

At first she'd been a bit stiff and quiet, but after a while she'd become more animated and alive, allowing herself to smile and laugh with him. A few times he'd noticed her staring off into space, with that haunted expression that left him with the strangest urge to pull her close and offer her comfort, though against what, he didn't know.

From little things she'd said and more that she had not, he suspected she had no family left at all, nor any friends. When he'd asked about school, she'd told him a lot about her studies and mentioned some of her teachers, but never any other students. Her house was oddly absent of mementos of her life other than the photo in the shrine, the one in her room, and the locket.

He wanted to ask her about it, but he was torn between wanting to keep an appropriate distance from his human host and his growing desire to know more about her. Feeling Sakura shiver beside him, he adjusted the blanket to cover her shoulder. *Appropriate distance my ass.*

Part of him wanted to flee and forget he'd ever met her, but he knew it was too late for that. He owed it to Hiro to discover the truth, even though it meant being close to another human who would die long before him. This time, though, he would make sure he did come back to see her often; he wouldn't leave it for decades, only to get back too late.

Dangerous Surprise

As they ate breakfast, Kazuki wondered what wonderful places they might see today. Sakura was wearing a pair of black jeans and a long-sleeved, pale-blue blouse. No uniform meant she didn't have school, so they should have all day to go sightseeing! Maybe they would go to the mountain or to some of the famous places he'd studied, like Tokyo Tower.

"Um, Kazuki?" Sakura set her chopsticks on the edge of her empty plate. "Did you mean what you said before, about helping around the house as a way of paying for staying here?"

"Yes, of course. It would be inexcusable for a gentleman to go back on his word." He held his hand up to his chest as he spoke.

"Good. There is some cleaning that needs to be done today, and I'd also like to fix the damage to my garden." She cleared away the breakfast dishes and handed him an apron. "You'll need to wear this while you clean."

"Oh, okay." He gave the frock a dubious look, but slipped it over his head. It was white with lace along the edges and went down to his knees. Sakura tied the ribbons for him, making a large bow in the back.

"Perfect." He could swear a hint of a smile teased the corners of her lips. "Do you know how to dust?"

"I think so, yes."

"Okay, here you go." She handed him a stick with a bunch of feathers tied to the end, a soft cloth, and some cleaning spray. "Please dust all of the shelves in the living room, the library, and the cabinets here in the kitchen. I'll start the laundry and clean the upstairs bathroom. Call me if you need me."

"Yes, ma'am!" He saluted with a grin. As she walked out, he got to work running the feather duster over the fronts of the cabinet doors and drawers. Trying to mimic what he'd seen watching the servants clean the castle, he made sure not to go too fast. As he dusted the counter tops, he moved each item aside to dust under and behind it.

Once he was done with the duster, he presumed she wanted him to wipe some things down with the cloth. The servants used buckets of soapy water to clean some of the floors, but he wasn't sure about this spray bottle. He pushed the trigger, barely avoiding hitting himself in the face with the cleaning solution.

"Woops! Well now I know which way to aim it, but what do I use it on?" He skimmed the label on the back of the bottle. "Oh, any surface, and I just spray it on the cloth. That's easy enough."

A few minutes later, he wiped his brow with the back of his hand as he surveyed the kitchen. It seemed to gleam a bit. "Not bad! Next!"

He headed into the living room and cleaned the shelves and the TV.

"Good morning, Hiro!" He bowed in front of the butsudan before he polished its outside surfaces, working slowly so as not to disturb the contents. "I bet you're laughing over there at this sight, eh? The advisers would have a fit if they saw me now.

There you go, all clean."

As he moved into the library, he thought about home. He should send word to let everyone know he was okay. There were enough missing rulers in Throklana as it was. The people certainly didn't need to think he was out of touch as well. With the transportation gem, he could send a letter back to indicate where he was. He wouldn't tell them about Yuji's attack, though; the potential fallout could be too disastrous.

He heard Sakura moving around upstairs. *I'll just say I'm visiting the daughter of a late friend to be sure she's okay and will be home in a few weeks. Not quite the truth, but close enough. Reito can take charge while I'm away.* As he dusted the shelves of books, he decided maybe he wouldn't say exactly where he was, so they couldn't try to force him to go home. Still, he needed to make sure they could contact him in an emergency. If he sent a leaf from Sakura's cherry tree with the letter, they could use it to reach him through the tree. That should be enough to keep the advisers from going nuts and keep Karasu from worrying about him.

Sakura was coming down the stairs just as he exited the library. As soon as she saw him, she seemed to choke back a laugh.

"All done?" Her voice sounded normal enough. Maybe he'd just imagined it.

"Yep, what's next?"

"Hmm. Inside, the last thing to do is to polish the floors." She put away the duster and sprayer and handed him another clean cloth, folded up into a long thick rectangle. "Just run over all the floors with this. Make sure to switch to a clean bit regularly. The laundry should be done now, so I'll be upstairs hanging it to dry."

"No problem." He went back to the kitchen to start, moving to the corner furthest from the door. "If I remember right…"

He knelt down with the cloth on the floor under his hands and began pushing it forward. It was slow going at first, until he was sure of his balance and step. The living room went faster, but it was more fun in the hall with the longer length and a single small table and the stairs as the only obstacles. The library, with all its shelves as well as a desk and chair, reduced him to doing short sprints.

Once he was done, he found Sakura sitting outside on the porch step drinking a cold beverage. When he joined her, she handed him a glass. "For you."

The liquid inside had a translucent look, but it wasn't clear like water. It was tart, yet sweet at the same time. Until he'd taken that first sip, he hadn't noticed he was thirsty. He drank some more before asking what it was.

"Lemonade. Basically water with lemon juice, sweetened with sugar to cut the tartness."

"It's good. Thank you."

"No, thank you. It's been a while since the house has been so clean. I appreciate it."

"You know, at home, dozens of servants clean the castle each day. I never really thought about the amount of work it must take. I must remember to show them my appreciation more often and tell them thank you."

"I'm sure they will like that."

Setting his empty glass beside him, he stood and turned to face her with a smile. "So, what next, my lady?"

"I guess first you can take off that silly apron." There was no question she was amused now.

"Silly?"

"Yes, you don't have to wear one to clean. I just thought it would be fun to see you in it."

"So you deliberately set out to make sport of me?" He

growled in mock outrage and held up his hands as if he were going to attack her. She broke out laughing, falling back on the deck as she rolled onto her side. Watching her laugh so freely, he had his first real jolt of physical awareness of her. When she was so relaxed and happy, he could spend hours watching her.

After her laughter calmed, she sat up and cupped her hands in front of her face. "I'm sorry. I shouldn't tease you."

He untied the bow and pulled the apron over his head before lightly tapping the top of her hair with his fingers. "I wondered why you seemed so amused all day."

"It was silly looking, but kind of cute too." She paused, gathering the apron in her lap. "I know! When we're done with the chores, there is a place nearby that sells really good ice cream. We can go there for a treat."

"I guess that would be an acceptable punishment." He grinned at her. "So, what's left?"

"We just need to fix up the garden a bit." Sakura stood and walked through the garden, pointing out the areas that needed attention. "The sand here needs to be raked smooth again. I already checked the flowers by the tree, and I think they will recover. We'll just give them some plant food and trim off the damaged bits. I also have a few pansies to plant in this patch here."

Kazuki followed her down a small path leading to a shed tucked just behind the house. Inside she grabbed a long rake, a pair of odd-looking scissors, and a tray of colorful flowers. The little faces on them made him laugh. "Can you bring that bag of soil and that mulch? We'll also need that bottle of plant food."

"Sure."

He tossed the bag of mulch on top of the soil and lifted both easily. Once they were settled securely on his shoulder, he was able to pick up the bottle. As he was coming around the corner,

Sakura cried out. He dropped the bags and dashed around the house.

"Return Master Kazuki, you ugly witch, or you will face my wrath!" Karasu stood in the garden, his wooden sword aimed at Sakura, who lay on the ground in front of him as if she'd been pushed.

"Karasu!" Kazuki called out sharply. "What are you doing to Sakura?"

"Master Kazuki!" The boy ran over to him and threw his arms around him. "I've been so worried! Don't worry, I'll free you from this human."

Kazuki bopped him on the head. "Calm down. Do you really think a human could put a binding spell on me, eh?"

He walked over to help Sakura up. When he reached her, she glanced up at him but something was wrong. Her breathing was coming in ragged, gasping spurts.

"Sakura? Sakura? What's wrong?" He knelt down, putting his hand on her cheek. It seemed like she was struggling to speak. "Karasu, what did you do to her?"

"Nothing, I swear! I didn't even hit her. When I jumped out she fell over herself." He joined them, looking down at her with disdain. "Come on, get up! I didn't hurt you."

Sakura grabbed Kazuki's arm in a shaky grip. He leaned over, adjusting his hearing up to catch her staggered whispers. "Inhaler…school bag…need…inhaler."

"In your bag? I'll get it."

Fear drove his feet as he rushed inside to find her bag. He dumped the contents out in his rush. Amongst the books and papers was a strange-looking thing. Was that the inhaler? Uncertain, he took it along with the spray bottle that had landed beside it and ran back outside.

"Here, is this it?" He thrust the first one into her hands, but they were now shaking so much she dropped it. Wrapping his hand around hers to help steady them, he placed it back in her palms. She lifted it toward her mouth, wrapping her lips around the small bit that jutted out from the cylinder. Realizing she was trying to push down on the top, he adjusted his hands so he could aid her. When her finger flexed, he pressed with her. Hissing emitted from the cylinder as she inhaled deeply.

Sakura let one hand fall and limply moved it toward the bottle he'd set in her lap.

"Now this one? Okay." Letting the subtle movements of her muscles guide him, he helped her raise it to her mouth and sprayed a dose under her tongue. The tension eased from her body. After a few moments, she took another breath from the inhaler and relaxed, falling against his chest.

"Sakura?"

"I'll...be...okay..." Her voice was still weak, but her breathing was returning to normal. Trusting that the things she used would make it better, he gathered her into his arms.

"Karasu, Sakura needs to rest. We can talk once I've put her to bed."

Certain Sakura was sleeping naturally, Kazuki slipped back downstairs. He kept his senses on high alert so he could monitor her breathing, just in case. Sakura's health was worse than he'd suspected. Bad nerves, perhaps? There were those in the kingdom for whom a bad fright caused panic attacks, which were not dissimilar from what Sakura seemed to experience. He wasn't sure how the oral treatments helped, but Sakura could explain once she was feeling better. This time he would not let the matter drop if she tried to ignore his questions.

Meanwhile, it looked like he wouldn't have to send that letter home after all. But how had Karasu found him here of all places? The boy was sitting outside on the porch, leaning back on his hands while he stared at Sakura's tree. Knowing his dislike of small spaces and of humans, Kazuki wasn't surprised he hadn't come inside.

Karasu turned as he approached, grinning up at him. "Master Kazuki!"

Kazuki did not return the smile. Instead he stopped in front of him, arms crossed. While Karasu couldn't know about Sakura's condition, it didn't excuse his behavior. "Karasu. You know better than to just attack people, especially those weaker than you. And a gentleman would never raise a sword to a lady without cause. Explain yourself."

"I…" His grin fell away and his head drooped. "I thought she had captured you. It was stupid, I know, but I've been so scared. I thought Master Yuji had…you didn't come back for so long…I…"

Fat tears rolled down Karasu's cheeks. His anger forgotten, Kazuki crouched down and pulled the boy into his arms. "It's all right. I did not mean to worry you so."

Kazuki held him until his sobs subsided. Sometimes he forgot that Karasu was still a child. With Yuji already gone, it was to be expected that Kazuki's failure to return might cause him to get upset and act rashly.

"I should have sent word to you yesterday. I did not mean to let two days go by without letting you know anything."

"Master Kazuki, it's been almost two weeks since you left to meet Master Yuji!"

"Two weeks? *Dafnikar*, I forgot time passes faster in our world than here. I truly am sorry."

Karasu wiped his cheeks dry with the sleeve of his shirt. "At first, when you didn't come back, I thought maybe you were still talking. But then it grew later and later. I went outside to wait for you there. Hours later, I spotted Reito returning with a nasty wound."

"Reito? What happened?"

"He came to your room not long after you left. When he learned you had already left, he followed you there. He said Master Yuji attacked you. At first he thought you were fighting things out, but then he realized Master Yuji was seriously trying to hurt you, so he came out of hiding and attacked him just as you disappeared."

"I see." So maybe it was Reito who had called his name, not Hiro like he believed. The voice, though, really had sounded more like Hiro's. "And Yuji?"

"They fought. Then Master Yuji fled into the forest."

The ruse was over before it even began. The advisers wouldn't sit idly by knowing Yuji had made an attempt to kill him. Kazuki covered his face with his hands. "Have they caught him yet? Will they execute him?"

"No. The advisers don't know about any of it."

Kazuki jerked his head up and stared at Karasu. "What do you mean they don't know? Have they not wondered where I was?"

"After Reito returned to the castle, we snuck back inside and I helped him treat his wounds. In the morning, he assumed your form long enough to announce that you needed to visit the human world to address some issues with operations here and that you'd return in a few months. Oh, and that I would be going with you while Reito would handle any day-to-day matters."

"Wait, Reito lied? Reito!?"

"I know! I figured he'd tell the advisers immediately." Karasu looked down at his hands, holding them in front of him as if evaluating their strength. "When I asked him about it, he said that 'as attendants, we must use our minds, our bodies, anything, and everything to protect our masters.' If the advisers knew the truth, the kingdom would be in turmoil, you'd be hidden away for your own safety until Yuji was found, and the king would have to face the possibility of one his sons having tried to…having tried to kill the other."

Somehow Reito had hit on the perfect excuse for Kazuki being gone several months—the time difference meant that even if he stayed just a few days, a long time would pass in his own world. "Wait, but how did he know to reference the human world? And for that matter, how did you find me?"

"Before you disappeared, he heard you say 'Hiro.' He remembered he was that human friend you told me about. He was able to find a portal not too far from here that I used to come search for you."

"I see. It's good Reito remembered that." Kazuki heard Sakura moving upstairs. "It looks like she's awake. Come, I'll introduce you, and you can apologize for your ill treatment of her."

"Yes, Master Kazuki."

Angry Boy

THE PAIN THREATENING TO SPLIT her head apart made Sakura wish she'd stayed asleep longer. The nitro headache hurt more than it ever had before. She knew she'd had a breathing attack and had vague memories of Kazuki helping her with her medicines, but why had she had one at all?

One hand on her head, she tried to sit up so she could get some painkillers. The room began to lurch and spin. She lowered herself back down, lying on her back and closing her eyes until the dizziness subsided.

"Sakura?" Kazuki's voice was so low she almost missed it. She opened her eyes slowly and watched as he walked across the room and sat gingerly on the edge of her bed. "Are you okay?"

"I…" She started to say she was fine, but something in his eyes told her that he'd know she was lying and that he wouldn't appreciate it. "My head hurts, and I need some medicine. In the drawer over there, there should be a green-and-white box with pills in it."

"Okay." Kazuki retrieved the box and handed it to her. Her hands still shook slightly, but she managed to push two aspirin through the blister pack and swallow them, followed by some gulps of water from the cup by her bed.

"Thank you."

"Is there anything else I can do for you?" Worry wrinkled his forehead and darkened his eyes.

"No, I'll be okay in a while. I just need to sleep a bit more and the pain will go away."

"What about earlier? It was as if you couldn't breathe."

"I have a medical condition that causes me to have attacks like that if I overexert myself, and sometimes if I have a sudden scare or shock." *Major understatement? Check.*

"Then, those pills you take…are to help with that condition?"

"Yes, they keep it under control most of the time. The inhaler and the spray help if I have an attack, though." She covered his hand with her own. "Kazuki…thank you for helping me. I…I'm glad you were there."

And thank you for saving my life. If he hadn't been there, she never would have reached her bag in time. How many times had she gone out in the garden just like that, her medicines far away in the house? She needed to be more careful about keeping them on her at all times.

"But, of course, in a way it was my fault you were startled." She spotted movement by the door. A young boy leaned on the frame. "Sakura, this is Karasu. He is like a little brother to me, and he also serves as my attendant. Karasu, come meet Sakura."

Now she remembered. She'd heard a noise and walked toward the gate to investigate. Then the boy had jumped out with a sword in his hand. She'd stepped back, tripping on the garden hose, then her breathing had cut off. Sure, the kid had surprised her, but it was the first time she'd had an attack from such a small scare. Tenma-sensei would need to be notified, and she'd have to come up with a story to explain the bigger attack and the smaller one while leaving out any mention of Kazuki.

Karasu sauntered from the doorway to stand beside Kazuki. He looked to be maybe ten years old with a darker complexion than Kazuki, more like milk tea than cream. His short, spiky black hair looked fun to ruffle. If it weren't for the way he glared at her, he would be cute.

"Hello. I'm Karasu. Nice to meet you." His grimace belied his words.

"I'm Takeshi Sakura. I'm happy to meet you, Karasu-kun. I hope my collapsing like that didn't frighten you."

He shook his head and seemed to whisper something under his breath, but she couldn't catch the words and, from his lack of reaction, Kazuki, she presumed, hadn't noticed.

"Karasu?" Kazuki glanced back at the boy and made a forward motion with his hand. As soon as Kazuki turned around, the boy went from death-glare mode to brilliant, sweet smiles.

"Oh, yes, I'm terribly sorry for threatening you, Lady Sakura." Kazuki gave him an approving nod and turned back to her. As soon as he did, Karasu's sweet smile disappeared and the glare returned.

"Forgive him, please. He was worried for my safety because of my long absence from home."

"Of course, don't worry about it. It was an accident. You had no way of knowing." Karasu answered her smile with another dirty look, until Kazuki looked back at him. She had to hand it to the kid, he could flip his facial expressions with amazing speed.

"Master Kazuki, since Lady Sakura is okay now, shall we head home?" Home? Was Kazuki leaving already?

"No, no, I plan to stay here for a while yet. I am enjoying it here, and I cannot miss the trip to her school that Sakura has promised me."

Relief flooded through her, even as she made sure not to let it show.

Karasu's smile faltered. "But, what about the kingdom?"

"It will be fine with Reito taking care of things. We'll send word back to him in just a bit, though, so he'll know you found me and to make it easier for him to contact us. Meanwhile, it will be just as I talked about not too long ago, a wonderful trip to the human world!"

Sakura yawned as her drowsiness kicked in again. She'd figure out the boy's problem with her later. For now, she needed sleep.

Kazuki adjusted the blanket around her. "Get some rest. Karasu and I shall finish the garden work as you instructed earlier. If you need me, just say my name. I'll hear you. I promise."

"Okay." She rolled onto her side and tucked her hands under the pillow. "I'm sorry about the ice cream. We'll get it another day, I promise."

Karasu followed as Kazuki returned to the living room. He walked over to a bag on the floor and stuffed the books, pencils, and other junk lying around it inside, except for one notebook and a pen. "First, we better send word to Reito that you made it okay and that I'm well."

He sat outside on the deck and began writing on the paper. Karasu followed, sitting beside him.

"Master Kazuki, I don't understand. I thought you'd be with your friend Hiro, but you're staying here with that weak girl."

"Yes, I think that's why the transport gem brought me here. But I returned too late." He pointed back toward the cabinet in the living room. "Hiro died a few years ago."

"I'm sorry." Karasu shifted so he could see inside the

shrine. The smiling man in the picture was not quite what he'd envisioned when he'd imagined Kazuki's human friend. He looked nice enough, but weak and wimpy like the girl upstairs.

"So she's his kid?"

"Yes, he adopted her when she lost her own parents. Despite having no obligation to me, she took great risk to herself in helping me when I was wounded, then so generously allowed me to take refuge here."

"I can understand not going home yet, but with Hiro gone, why stay here? We could travel around and see places." Kazuki had always talked about doing a grand tour of the human's world, so maybe that was the best tactic to get him to leave.

"Karasu, really, I owe Sakura for her help. It would be rude not to repay her kindness in some way, and how could I face the thought of Hiro if I turned my back on his daughter when she is ill? So I shall do what I can, even if it is just cleaning the house and fixing the mess I made in the garden here."

"Are you…in love with her?" Karasu wasn't sure he wanted to know, but the question had popped out before he could stop it. Kazuki laughed but it didn't relieve the strange anxiety that was strangling Karasu's heart.

"Of course not. Don't be silly—we only just met! Besides, I would never fall in love with a human. She is Hiro's daughter and we are becoming friends, I'd like to think, but she is still a human."

Exhaling the breath he'd forgotten he'd held, Karasu forced himself to relax. Of course Kazuki wouldn't fall in love with such a short-lived species. It would be the height of foolishness for any yokai. And Kazuki was an honorable man, so it made sense he felt obligated to return the girl's favor. Still, it bugged him. She bugged him. A lot.

While Kazuki continued writing his letter, Karasu figured

he might as well find a roosting place. If they were staying, he was not about to sleep in that cramped little house. He walked over to the large cherry tree in the corner. It was a lovely tree with strong thick branches. A warm feeling flooded through him when he put his hand against the trunk.

Images flashed through his mind of the tree when it was bigger than a sapling, but shorter than it was now and with far fewer branches. Younger versions of Hiro and that girl watched as the tree was set in the ground in the garden. Her small hands helping as they patted soil around it. The man reading her stories. The two resting, separately and together, against its trunk, talking to it. The girl, curled up into a ball, crying in the shelter of its roots while holding a picture of the man—the picture that now sat in the shrine.

Happiness, love, and sorrow. A blend of emotions, but it was the affection the tree held for his human caretakers that came out the most.

"You're well loved. Do you mind if I make my home in your branches for a while?" Of course, he could have just done so anyway, but he preferred to ask permission to show his respect. It also made for a more comfortable sleeping spot. The tree responded with a feeling of welcome. "Thank you. I'll return this evening then."

"There, done," Kazuki called out from the porch. "Karasu, could you bring me a few of that tree's fallen leaves? We'll use those to give Reito a channel for communicating with us, if needed."

He gathered a handful of the leaves from the ground then touched the tree's trunk again. "Is it okay if we borrow some of your magic to talk with our friends back home? It's a mild spell and will bring you no harm."

This time the tree sent him a feeling of acceptance. "Thank

you again."

Karasu carried the leaves back to Kazuki, who tied them in a small bundle with the letter. Once it was ready, Kazuki carried it over to the base of the tree and set it down by its roots. Karasu kept watch for any passersby while Kazuki pulled the transportation gem from his pocket.

"Stone of water, stone of air, through distance, space, and time, this letter to Reito's hand must fly." As he spoke, he held the gem against the letter. It disappeared in a blue flash of light.

"Now then, let's attend to Sakura's garden." Kazuki smiled and patted Karasu on the shoulder.

"Okay." He would help, but only for Kazuki's sake and for the sake of the tree. If it happened to make that girl happy too, it couldn't be helped.

Painful Past

KAZUKI GLANCED AT THE CLOCK on the wall. Five minutes had passed since he'd last looked. He resumed pacing the length of the living room. Sakura told him that weekdays were regular school days, so she would be home at four rather than close to noon like on Saturday. Yet now it was after five and she still wasn't back.

They hadn't had a chance to talk since she'd had that attack, as she'd called it. He'd intended to question her thoroughly about her condition, but she'd slept long into the afternoon. When she woke up, she seemed so tired he encouraged her to just rest. So she'd ordered them pizza for dinner—a most delicious and efficient food—and they'd watched a movie before calling it a night.

"Master Kazuki?" Karasu sat in the doorway, watching him, as he had the last hour or so.

"By the gods, where is she?"

"Maybe she decided to hang out with her friends or something."

"She doesn't have any." Five more minutes had passed.

"School was out long ago. What if she had another of those attacks? Five-thirty, if she isn't home by then, we are going to look for her."

Three minutes later, the front door opened. "Tadaima!"

He ran into the hall and pulled her into his arms before she could even change her shoes. "Sakura! Thank the heavens."

"Kazuki?" Wrapped in his arms and pressed against him, her muffled voice sounded confused.

"You are so late. I was worried, so very worried."

"I…" Her arms came around him and she patted his back. "I'm sorry. I should have let you know I would be late."

"Yes, you should have. Master Kazuki has more important things to do than waste time worrying about you." Karasu's caustic remark from the door brought Kazuki back to his senses. Embarrassed, he set Sakura away from him. Her cheeks were tinged pink.

"Sorry, I just thought…after yesterday, I was afraid you had collapsed again."

"No, I'm fine. I had a doctor's appointment, that's all." After changing her shoes, she went into the living room and set her bag down. "I'll show you how to use the phone later. Then I can call if I'll be late again, okay?"

"Yes, that would be good." He kept staring at her, looking for any sign that her condition was worse, all of his senses indicating she was the same as she had been when she left that morning. "Um, I'll bring you some tea."

He fled to the kitchen, busying himself by brewing tea and cutting up fruit for a snack. Sakura had lived on her own for several years and he'd only been there a few days. It was easy to believe it slipped her mind that she had an appointment after school. But, still, she didn't seem the sort of person who would forget to mention something like that. Maybe she really had collapsed and was hiding it, like she tried to hide how many pills she took each day.

I'm going to drive myself crazy. It was the fear, the fear of not knowing the full story that was fueling his suspicions. This time, they would talk and he would get the truth.

Tray in hand, he started back to the living room. Just before he reached the door, he heard Karasu's voice. "You really are a rude and self-absorbed human. You probably worried Master Kazuki on purpose just to get him to pay attention to you."

Kazuki moved more quickly. Karasu stood in front of Sakura with his hands on his hips as he abused her. "Karasu, what are you saying?"

"Master Kazuki!" The boy jumped back from her, guilt flooding his face. "I..."

"That was uncalled for. Why would you say such things to Sakura?" He set the tray down on the kotatsu before facing the boy. "Apologize at once."

Looking toward the wall, Karasu mumbled an insincere apology. "Karasu!"

"It's all right, Kazuki. It was rude of me to worry you like that." Sakura's voice held no anger, rather she sounded ashamed as she looked down at the tabletop. "While he spoke roughly, I'm sure Karasu-kun was just annoyed that I put you out."

Kazuki suspected there was more than that. He'd never seen the boy act that way toward anyone, not even the advisers, who regularly "put him out" so to speak. But, for now, there was a bigger issue to deal with, and he couldn't let this distraction throw him off course.

"Fine. If you are willing to forgive him, I'll say no more for now." He joined her at the kotatsu. "But I do wish to speak to you about those attacks of yours."

"What more do you want to know? I explained it yesterday."

"You told me that you have these breathing attacks, but not why. That is why I worried so, because I do not truly understand what is wrong."

"Like I said, they only happen if I push my body too much. Yesterday, I only had one because I hadn't fully recovered from the last one yet. I rarely have them."

Kazuki could tell she was avoiding giving him any real details. He knew he should just drop it. It wasn't any of his business anyway. Except it was, because she was his friend and Hiro's daughter. If he knew what was wrong, perhaps he could help her somehow.

He leaned on the table and watched her. She returned his gaze, steadily at first but as the minutes ticked on, she started glancing away. For once, his royal training was coming into use. His father had taught them the art of waiting out the other side of a negotiation quite well—he could sit like this for hours if necessary.

Karasu jumped up from the doorway. "You two are driving me nuts! Let me know when dinner is ready."

He darted into the dusk-shadowed garden and looked around before morphing into his crow form. With a furious flapping of his wings, he was gone.

Wide-eyed, Sakura stared at the garden. "He..."

"Hmmm?"

"Karasu-kun?"

"Oh, yes, he is a tengu. He can change at will into his namesake."

"I see." Sakura stared out the door a moment longer before turning her gaze back to him. "Can you also transform like that?"

"No, I do not possess shape-shifting magic."

"I see."

They lapsed back into their silent war, the stilted conversation having done little to ease the tension. The minutes ticked by. She poured them another cup of tea, but still he watched and waited. A breeze picked up outside, bringing a chill into the room. Sakura stood and walked over to the door, no doubt intending to close it.

A pale-pink flower drifted in on the breeze, floating around in front of her before it landed in the shrine beside Hiro's picture. After sliding the screen closed, she picked up the blossom, cradling it in her hands. She returned to the table and sat down and held it out for him to see.

"It's a winter cherry blossom." Her voice was soft, like it was when she talked about Hiro. "I don't know of any winter cherry trees in this area."

She looked over his shoulder at the shrine then back down to the flower in her hand. Her eyes closed as she held it against her chest as if she were saying a prayer. When she opened them again, she squared her shoulders and took a deep breath. "You remember, I told you my parents died."

"Yes." He relaxed his gaze. It wasn't what he expected her to start with, but if she was ready to talk, he would let her tell things in whatever order she wanted.

"My mother was a good woman. Very gentle and sweet natured. She worked at a daycare. Even when she was angry, she never yelled or said a harsh word. My father loved her very much. They were high-school sweethearts. When things were good, he was kind and loving, but things weren't always good."

"He was abusive?"

"No, not really. He never hit her or threw things or anything like that. But, he had a disease called integration disorder[23]. It's a mental illness that makes it hard for someone to tell the difference between what's real and what's not. It can cause them to have delusions and to sincerely believe that someone is hunting them."

"I did not know such diseases existed. It is a scary thought, an illness that could make one lose their mental soundness."

"Father took medications, which helped, but sometimes he would stop taking them because he didn't like them. A psychiatrist told me that the medicines had become part of his paranoia, that he thought they were part of the plots against him. When he was off the medicines, he would talk about 'bad men' in black suits who were looking for him. I remember my mom would cry and they would argue; then he would go back to normal. I think he would start taking his medicines again when she got upset. He really did love her."

She paused and took a sip of tea. He could see a tremor run through her.

"When I was ten, we lived in a little single-story house in Hitomi-chō, across town from here. The elementary school I attended was beside my mom's daycare, so I always got to walk home with her. We would have an afternoon snack and talk—mostly I'd babble silly things about my school day. Mom would make dinner while I did my homework.

"Then one night, Father came home from work early. I hadn't even finished getting my books out when I heard the front door open. He didn't say anything when he came in, didn't call out tadaima or anything, but I knew it was him, and so I was happy. Whenever he got off work early, he'd always help me with my homework and it was fun."

---

[23] The term used in Japan for what is commonly referred to in the US as schizophrenia.

Another drink of the tea, as if it were a magic potion giving her the strength to go on.

When her father rushed into the dining room, his hair was disheveled, his suit rumpled as if he'd slept in it. He came straight to Sakura, picking her up and hugging her tight. Despite the strange way his hands were twitching, she didn't mind it, as his familiar scent enveloped her along with the warmth of his embrace.

"Welcome home, Papa!" She smiled at him as he pulled back a little, but he didn't return her grin. Instead, he stared at her, a strange look on his face. "Papa?"

"Sakura, my sweet little girl. Don't you worry, baby. Papa will protect us, all of us. I won't let those evil men lay a finger on my little flowers."

Sakura wrapped her hands tight around his neck. The bad men were back again? Papa had told her all about them. They would take Papa and Mama away and leave Sakura all alone. Tears welled up in her eyes.

"I don't want you to leave. Don't let them take you, Papa!"

"Daiki!" Her mother hurried out of the kitchen and pulled Sakura away from her father. Sakura buried her tear-soaked face in her mother's soft neck. "Look, you've frightened her."

Her mother bounced her a few times, while Sakura tried to stop crying, knowing she was too big to be held by her mom like this. With a sniff, she struggled until her mother put her in a seat. "There, it's all right, sweetie. No one is going to hurt anyone, okay? Now be my good girl and start your homework."

Another loud sniff accompanied Sakura's nod. Picking up her pencil, she watched warily as her mother grabbed her father by the arm and dragged him into the hall. She recognized that look on her mom's face.

Her mom didn't believe in the bad men. Whenever her dad talked about them, as soon as they were alone, her mom always told her not to worry, to forget about it, that it was just a little joke her dad sometimes took too far.

The hushed voices of her parents filtered into the hall, making it hard to focus on the math sheet in front of her. It wasn't often that they fought, and whenever they did, they tried to keep quiet like they were now, but she still knew what they were doing. She hoped it was quick, so they could have dinner together and it would be like normal.

Her father's voice grew louder. "Hanako, those medicines are bad! They use them to confuse me, to hide the truth so I won't see them coming until it's too late. They want to take you from me, don't you understand?"

"No one is after you, Daiki!" It was the first time she could remember hearing her parents yell. Her mom's raised voice was intermingled with sobs. "Please, just take your medicine and call your doctor."

The hand holding her pencil was shaking so hard it left a scribble on her worksheet. Her mom would be angry at her for messing it up. She grabbed her eraser to try to fix it, but it fell to the floor. As quietly as she could, she climbed out of the chair and reached out for the pink nub.

Her father's voice, too muffled to understand. Then a gargled high-pitched sound cut short. A scream?

Sakura froze, her eyes open wide as she watched the door. The clock ticking on the wall was suddenly as loud as a church bell.

"Mama? Papa?" Sakura called out uncertainly, as she stood there still bent over to pick up the forgotten eraser.

Tick...Tock... The clock was the only thing she could hear.

She straightened, her hands close to her chest as she took one step toward the hall. Then a second, before glancing back at the dining table. She was supposed to study, but she couldn't make herself go back to the table. Even if they were mad, she couldn't take it, standing there alone after hearing that strange cry.

Suddenly she really needed to pee...If they asked, that's why she'd come out. She had to go. To get to the bathroom, she had to walk down the hall after all. Yeah, that would be okay. With the false confidence of her excuse, she moved more quickly toward the entryway.

Her mother was on the floor, sort of sitting as she leaned against the wall near the telephone table. Her legs were bent a little funny, as if she hadn't sat on purpose but had fallen.

"Mama?"

A dark-red stain streaked down the wall behind her mother. The soft, loving hand Sakura reached for so many times was now lying on her stomach, a red stain blooming out from under it, ruining her favorite pale-yellow blouse. Her father stood over her mom, tears wetting his cheeks though he looked calm.

She may be young, but she knew blood when she saw it.

"Mama!" Sakura ran toward her. A steady beeping tone echoed like chapel bells from the phone receiver dangling from the desk beside them.

"Sa...ku...ru..." Her mom coughed. Her head slumped to the side.

"Mama?" Her father walked over to them and knelt down in front of Sakura. With his big, gentle hands, he wiped her cheeks for her. "Papa, what happened to Mama?"

"Nothing, sweetheart, she's fine."

"But, she..."

"I know, it looks strange, but it's okay, I promise. It's a trick, you see. The bad men are coming. They are on their way right now."

"They are?" Sakura asked as she gripped her father's arms. "But why?"

"I wish I knew, baby." He kissed her forehead. "They are just evil and like to do evil things. But we're going to get away, for good this time."

"But how? And Mama, she's hurt?"

"No, no, she's fine. Remember how we read about possums the other week?"

Sakura nodded.

"Well, we're going to do like they do when they are threatened. We're going to play dead. That's what your mom is doing. She's really good at it too. Your mom always had great acting skills." He smiled at her, the loving, reassuring smile he'd given her so many times when a nightmare had disturbed her sleep or she'd found herself on the ground after tripping over her own feet. "Once we've tricked them, we'll leave here and go to a wonderful, safe place I found where no one will ever hurt us. You'll make lots of friends and go to the best school. They even have horses, so you could learn to ride like you always dreamed of."

Sakura nodded and glanced over at her unmoving mother, thinking that if her mother was just acting, she should win an award or something.

"Now we have to get ready too. There isn't much time." Her father held open his arms for a hug. With a smile, Sakura embraced him tightly, happy to know they would soon be free.

"Don't worry, Papa. I did really good in the school play this year, and I'll be the best possum ever."

"That's my little flower," he said with a smile before kissing her cheek. "I love you so much."

A searing pain pierced her back. She couldn't stop the scream that escaped her throat.

"Papa..."

Her father's arm was still around her as she floated backward, away from him. His tear-streaked face blurred in front of her.

"It hurts...Papa. What...?"

He smiled as he lowered her to the ground. "I love you, baby. You're the most precious gift I could ever ask for. It's going to hurt just a little longer, then you'll go to sleep. When you wake up, we'll be in our new home."

With choking sobs, Sakura tried to bear the pain. If this was part of the act, she had to be tough.

Her father's arm loomed above her. With her hazy vision, it took a moment for her to recognize the thing in his hand. A knife...a large, blood-covered knife? She tried to say his name, but then it plunged toward her, sending fresh pain exploding through her chest.

"Altogether, he stabbed me seven times with that knife before lying down beside me and using it to kill himself." Sakura spoke calmly, as she had throughout the whole story, but so many tears streamed down her face that the collar of her shirt was visibly dampened. Unable to stay still any longer, Kazuki moved around the table to sit beside her so he could hug her. Her tears now wet his shirt, but he didn't care. He held her like that, his hands buried in her hair, his cheek against her forehead, until she wiped away her tears.

"The police arrived almost immediately. My father had

killed his boss before leaving work. In a way, it probably saved my life. But it was too late for my parents."

"I am so sorry. I never imagined you had gone through such an ordeal." He wanted to beg her to stop, to say no more. What he'd learned was already horrifying enough to imagine, but he knew she needed to say it, to get it all out.

"The knife pierced my heart and lungs several times. Tenma-sensei, the doctor I visited today, was the one who worked on me when I arrived and has taken care of me since." She pulled back to look him in the eye, again taking a deep breath before continuing on. "Kazuki, the damage to my organs was permanent. As I've gotten older, it has been harder and harder for my body to continue to support me because they are too weak. The medicines I take help some, but they can only treat the symptoms. I…the doctors believe I will die this spring. I could maybe make it to the summer, if I'm lucky."

He caught his breath. Die? But she wasn't even fully a woman yet. How could she die, and so soon? "Is there nothing they can do?"

"A heart–lung transplant might let me live another ten, maybe even twenty years, but it's only been done here once[24] and there are so few donors,[25] especially for someone my age."

"A transplant? What is this?"

"Doctors can take organs that are in good condition from someone who recently died and use them to replace those of

---

[24] The first successful heart–lung transplant in Japan was performed in February of 2013. The recipient, a 35-year-old man, had been on the transplant list 66 months before suitable organs were found.

[25] Due to beliefs about life, death, and medical ethics, organ transplants were banned in Japan in 1968, until the Organ Transplant Law was passed in 1997. In the twelve years following, however, only 81 transplants were carried out, as few people were willing to be donors. Further, transplants for and donations by children under fifteen remained illegal until July 2009.

people who have damaged or failing ones. If their body accepts the new organ, then they can live longer. The best matches come from people with a compatible blood type and body size. It is a very rare thing to find a good match."

"I see." Human medicine had advanced more than he imagined. Never had he dreamed one could replace bad organs with good ones. But they could not do this for Sakura. She was dying. Dying. He didn't want to believe it. Of course humans lived short lives compared to yokai, but this was too short. She wouldn't even reach Hiro's age. He pulled her closer, burying his face in her hair again to hide the pain ripping through him.

Her arms tightened around him. He felt her lips brush against his cheek. She was comforting him, when it should be the other way around. His mind was already racing, though. If human science failed, maybe yokai magic would have the answer. It was a slim chance, at best. King Toramaru held powers that astounded even his sons, powers gained during his millennia rule. Yet his father hadn't been able to save their mother from dying. Still, he had to do something, anything. *I will not let you die!*

He kept his rash declaration to himself, not wanting to give her any false hopes. Now he understood why she had no pictures of her family in the shrine—having her own father attack her and her mother like that no doubt made it hard to look at them.

"I..." What words of comfort could he really offer that wouldn't just be empty platitudes? Instead, he asked one of the questions her story had left unanswered. "How did you come to live with Hiro?"

"My father had no family and my mother's parents wanted nothing to do with me. They were afraid I was like my father. A week or so after the attack, while I was still in the hospital,

Ito-san began visiting me. He'd been best friends with my father since high school and they'd gone to work for the same company after they graduated. He'd always been kind of like an uncle to me growing up. He told me that something inside him had screamed at him to stop my father from leaving work that day. He could tell something was off, but he allowed my father to brush his concerns aside. I think, in a way, Ito-san blamed himself a bit, though it wasn't his fault.

"After I was released from the hospital, he adopted me and brought me here. My parents' estate left me with a little money, as well as the house, which he sold. He invested the money so there would be plenty to cover my medical expenses as I got older. He never took any for himself—though I tried to offer it. After he died, I learned he'd added his own money into my accounts too, and he left me this house, which he'd lived in since he was a child. He was a good man. He was patient and kind, encouraging me not to just laze away what was left of my life. I loved him very much."

"Knowing Hiro, I can say with confidence that he loved you too."

Kazuki held her for a long time, as much for his sake as for hers. Never before had he felt the fragility of her humanity as he did now. He could feel the crumpled letter from Reito stiffening his pants pocket. Since they'd arranged to exchange messages through the tree, new letters had arrived from Reito daily, giving Kazuki updates of the week's news and asking for input on any issues that needed a more authoritative response.

The one thing that never changed was the lack of word on Yuji. Not so much as a sighting of him since he'd attacked Kazuki, or even a notion of where he might be living.

Reito's letters made it clear that things were growing tense, the people restless. Never had they gone so long without someone from the ruling family being visible or active among the populace. How much longer before they grew suspicious, began wondering if they'd been abandoned altogether?

Since the letter had arrived that morning, Kazuki had pondered the situation. He knew he should return home. As Karasu had rightly noted, he could pop back to visit Sakura regularly. As long as he was careful about the timeline, he could probably figure out how to see her every day, even if transporting back and forth would be taxing.

But not now. If he left, she'd be all alone again, alone and trying to take care of herself. He'd already been doing the shopping for her while she was in school and quietly cleaning during the day, just small things, so she didn't have to do them when she got home.

Surely Reito would understand when Kazuki explained it...he had to. Kazuki needed his help. If anyone could find a cure for Sakura, it would be the sharp-brained kitsune who'd served his father for so long.

Visitation Day

IT SEEMED HARD TO BELIEVE only a week had passed since she'd first found Kazuki lying in her garden. His wounds were all healed, so he could have left any time he wanted. Yet he seemed to enjoy staying with her. After learning about her past and her condition, Kazuki had continued to treat her just as he had before. Her cheeks warmed as she thought of the fact that he was still sleeping in her bed. She'd offered again to buy him a bed for the guest room, but he'd just smiled and said he was fine with leaving things the way they were. In truth, she was too, though it certainly was unusual.

And now Karasu was living with her too. He slept in her cherry tree at night in his crow form. He'd usually come down for dinner then would sit in the living room with Kazuki watching TV, but he rarely spoke to her. When he did, it was clear he didn't like her, though he remained marginally polite since Kazuki was always around.

Even when they'd gone out to get him some clothes, he'd been mostly non-responsive to her. If Kazuki hadn't been effusive in his praise of the new outfits, she suspected he wouldn't have worn them. Except the coat and gloves. On the walk there, she'd noticed him shivering a little. Though he hadn't complained, he seemed more sensitive to the cold than Kazuki. When he'd shoved his arms into the coat, he'd actually let a smile slip out.

She still wasn't sure if he hated humans altogether or if it was her specifically. Or maybe he was just uncomfortable with strangers, which to him, she really was. Besides, shopping for clothes probably wasn't very fun for a boy his age, so it was understandable if he'd been bored. Maybe if they went somewhere more interesting it would help him get more comfortable around her. Saturday would be a clear day, perfect for where she had in mind. Kazuki would love it too.

She checked the time again. Five minutes until the start of homeroom and the arrival of parents and guardians for Visitation Day. For most high schools, parents just came at the appointed time, but Saigonohi liked to make a day of it. The administrators believed it helped ensure the parents were fully engaged in their children's academic careers.

As such, after homeroom, students would give their parents tours of the school and introduce their teachers. Eventually, each family would go to an appointment with the student's guidance counselor about the student's career choices. Except for Sakura. She and the counselor had agreed it would just be a waste of his time when she wouldn't have a career anyway.

Was Kazuki already here, waiting in the hall? Had he found the way okay? Last night she'd walked him to the school so he'd know the way. Coming back, he led the way home with no problem, though he said it was also due to following her scent. Since she came this way so often, it was an easy trail for him.

The real question was whether he would find her school as interesting as he seemed to think or would just be bored and want to leave early. Most people wouldn't find touring a school very exciting. It wasn't that she looked forward to his reactions or anything. It was just a harmless way to reward him for being a good house guest. *Yeah, keep telling yourself that.*

Sakura stood with the other students when Mimomo-sensei entered the front door. The parents and guardians began filing in through the other door, huddling together at the back of the room. Fathers straightened ties while mothers smoothed the lines of their skirts, trying not to look out of place. If her parents had lived, would her mother have come today? Would her father have taken off work for the visit?

The brief spurt of sadness fled as Kazuki walked in, wearing the gray suit like a second skin. Female students and parents alike were dithering over him. She had the strangest urge to stand and say, "Yep, that's My Kazuki!" For his part, Kazuki seemed oblivious to all the attention being poured his way. He glanced around the room until he spotted her and smiled. A returning smile curved her lips before she could stop herself.

Mimomo-sensei tapped the top of her podium. "Be seated." Then she took the daily roll and made announcements, followed by a blessedly brief lecture on career choices and the upcoming college entrance exams. Before homeroom ended, the class representative reminded everyone about the upcoming cultural festival. Sakura had forgotten all about it, having done nothing to help with the preparations since she was excused from such things. She hadn't planned on attending anyway, though it might be the sort of thing Kazuki would enjoy.

After they were released, a few of her classmates lingered nearby, staring at Kazuki. Giving in to her earlier peevishness, she threaded her arm through his and led him out of the room. She could almost feel their jealous gazes burning through her back.

"Good morning again, Sakura."

"Good morning. Shall I show you around? Let's start outside."

Saigonohi was a five-story, pale-peach-colored rectangular building with just under six hundred pupils. She walked Kazuki into the open courtyard, which featured in its center a lush garden attended to by the students. It was a pleasant lunchtime and study space. The top floor held the school's nine-lane swimming pool and outside was a baseball diamond along with soccer and rugby fields and four tennis courts. In the gymnasium of a separate building, the students practiced kendo and other martial arts.

Most of the students had grown up in Sumiyoshi-chō, though the school had a few from other parts of the area like Sakura. When she first started attending the school, she'd vaguely recognized a few students from the middle school she'd attended before her parents' death, but they didn't seem to remember her. Not that she'd minded.

The teachers were stationed throughout the school for meeting with the students and their families. Sakura's teachers looked at Kazuki with undisguised curiosity as they politely shook his hand and made pithy remarks about Sakura being such a good student. No doubt they had expected someone around her parents' age, not someone who could almost pass for a student himself. If he noticed their stares, he didn't comment on them as he politely greeted each one.

The first female teacher they reached, her home economics teacher, turned bright pink when he kissed her hand. It was hard to keep a straight face as the older woman acted thoroughly entranced with Kazuki's over-the-top manners. Once they left, Sakura let the laugh out.

"Did I do something wrong?" He looked at her quizzically while she laughed.

"No, no. I just…the look on her face." She smiled at him as she straightened herself. "I know you're being polite, but here it's better to just shake hands."

"Even with ladies?"

"Yes, not too many people kiss hands anymore." She shook her head. "I admit, though, I think you made her day."

They laughed together as they continued on down the hall. They finished the go-around on the top floor, standing in an empty classroom to enjoy the view of Mount Hakodate.

"Human schools truly are fascinating. You have so many extra activities that our schools leave to people to do at home or on their own time, like cooking and all of the different sports. I don't suppose I could sit in on a regular class? I'm curious to see the differences in how the subjects are taught and the way lectures are given."

"They really aren't very exciting…though my history teacher is pretty good at telling stories. You'd probably like his class, but they don't generally let non-students sit in on those. It would be too distracting. Anyway, we should head back to my homeroom to meet with Mimomo-sensei. Then we can head home."

"Ah, the first class, yes? The lecture was quite interesting, but I'm not sure how it related to homes or rooms?"

Sakura slapped her hand over her mouth but it did little to hide her laughing. She hadn't laughed so often in ages.

"Homeroom isn't a subject. It's what we call our classroom. We usually stay in that room all day and the teachers come there to teach us, unless we need to use one of the special classrooms we saw earlier. Our homeroom teacher oversees us for the year, so she tracks our attendance, gives us reminders on things like upcoming exams, stuff like that. We usually only have home-room for the first ten minutes of the day, but once a week we have a long homeroom, like today, where we'll have lectures and plan class activities."

"Ah, I see. That reminds me, the boy who talked at the end of the class mentioned a festival?"

"Yes, the annual cultural festival." She turned her back to the window. "During the day they are doing the usual stuff: booths, cafés, a play, things like that, followed by a fancy dress ball at night."

As she talked, she could practically see the excitement building in him.

"It's going to be held the Saturday after next." She shuffled her feet a bit. It seemed like a dumb question, but still she felt a bit nervous asking. "Um, if you're still here, would you like to go?"

Kazuki pulled her hands close to his chest.

"Sakura, I shall remain here for as long as you are here. And, yes, I would love to go. I cannot wait to see what a human festival is like much less a ball! Honestly, I've never liked the palace balls, as they are all filled with stuffy old men talking politics. But going to one with you will most certainly be pleasurable."

She blushed as she nodded in response. He could be such a flirt, though she knew he meant nothing by it. What girl could pass up the chance to dress up and dance with a prince at a ball? As they left the room, neither noticed their hands still clasped together.

"Sakura-chan, good afternoon. And you are…?"

"Ito Kazuki. Please, call me Kazuki." Kazuki reached out to shake Mimomo-sensei's hand. How would this meeting go? The others had been brief, with each teacher offering some bland praise for Sakura's performance. None of them really looked at her or seemed particularly interested in her at all. He'd heard them talking spiritedly with other families about their kids' studies and their futures, but not for Sakura.

It bothered him that they all seemed to have given up on her. How could she keep fighting until the end if no one was supporting her? Seeing the school was exciting, for sure, but it confirmed for him that he had not misspoken when he told Karasu that she had no friends. Well, she did now. She had him, as well as Karasu.

"A pleasure, Kazuki-san. Are you perchance related to Sakura-chan's late guardian, Ito-san?"

"Yes, we're cousins, though really he was like a brother to me. I was out of the country and only recently returned. When I learned of his passing, I immediately assumed guardianship of his beloved Sakura." He'd embellished the story Sakura had told him to tell if anyone probed, but the teacher seemed satisfied.

"Ah, good good. I'd been told that Sakura-chan had no guardian, so I'm relieved to know someone is watching out for her now."

Sakura glanced at him with a concerned expression before looking at her watch. "I'm sorry. I need to go to the bathroom."

It must be time for one of the medicines. After she told him the truth about her health, she'd explained them all, including the schedules. It had been a daunting list and he couldn't pronounce half the names, but he was glad she was no longer hiding it from him. She'd also told him about the inhaler and the spray, which he'd made sure to learn how to use in case she had any more attacks.

"Of course. We'll be fine here." Kazuki smiled. With another nervous glance, Sakura bowed before leaving them.

"Kazuki-san, shall we sit down?" Mimomo-sensei led him to a set of chairs arranged near the window in a half-circle with no desk or other barriers between them. This teacher seemed a bit more interested in talking to him. None of others had even offered him a seat.

"Now then, Kazuki-san, in terms of grades, Sakura-chan will be fine as long as she continues her current efforts. She is a bright girl and does well in all of her subjects. However, I am concerned about her mental well-being. She is always alone and doesn't seem to have any connections with any of her classmates at all."

"Oh?" Kazuki wasn't sure how to respond, but her concerned expression seemed genuine.

"I realize with her health she can't participate in many activities, certainly not sports, but that shouldn't stop her from making friends. I do not understand why she seems to deliberately push her peers away. I can understand why she keeps her health a secret, especially considering we adults seem incapable of treating her like a normal girl ourselves. Still, even if she feels she must continue to hide her condition from her classmates, wouldn't having people who care about her help her endure it?"

"In truth, I've noticed this myself since my arrival and wondered the same. She carries a large burden on her small shoulders. I hope I am able to ease that load some. I suspected her isolation might be self-imposed, so I will talk to her about that."

"Thank you. I can't imagine how scary it must be for her, or how lonesome. It made me very happy to know she has you now, at least." She clasped her hands together as she leaned toward him, her brow wrinkled with concern. "Please tell me, how is she doing, really? Is there anything I can do to help?"

"As well as can be expected." Kazuki picked up Sakura's footstep approaching. "For now, I would say keep caring. She notices, even if she doesn't seem to, for you are the only teacher she talks about regularly."

He had to leave it at that when Sakura reached the door. At her questioning look as she joined them, he just smiled.

Mimomo-sensei turned to Sakura, her affection easy to see. "Sakura-chan, before you go, I wanted to know if you'd given any more thought to playing at the festival."

"I'm sorry. I don't think I will be able to. I wouldn't be able to devote a proper amount of time to rehearsing, so it wouldn't be fair to the others."

"I see. Well, there is still time if you change your mind."

After exchanging bows and goodbyes with the teacher, they headed to the locker area so Sakura could retrieve her things.

"What did she mean by 'playing in the festival'? Playing what?"

"Our class is holding two concert performances during the festival, one in the morning and one in the afternoon. Mimomo-sensei asked if I wanted to play the piano."

"Oh, I didn't know you played."

"I haven't played in a long time. Not since Ito-san died. He loved to listen to me play."

"Oh…" He took her hand in his and squeezed it gently. She turned and smiled at him, but it was a sad sort of smile.

"Besides, I was never very good at it, certainly not worth playing in public. It was just a childish hobby. Anyway, we should get going."

They headed outside and through the school gates. As they started down the sidewalk, Sakura broke the silence. "Did you go to school?"

"Yes, actually. Our father felt it was important that we have a good foundation in the lives of our citizens, so he sent us to school."

"Did you like it?"

"Oh yes, it was much more fun than being stuck in a room with a tutor would have been. That's where we met so many of our friends, like Aya."

"Aya?"

"Yes, she's the daughter of a neighboring kingdom. Yuji has been in love with her since we were kids, though she doesn't seem to have noticed." He wasn't sure why he felt the need to tell her that, or to leave out Aya's own declarations of love.

"It must be hard on him."

"Sometimes. I told him many times he should just tell her how he feels. She's a nice girl. She can just be a bit blind to what others are feeling, so it would be best to be direct and to the point."

Sakura nodded in agreement. "Hopefully, once he comes home, he will get up the nerve."

"Yes…yes, I hope he will too." He had to hold that hope in his heart—that Yuji would return and they could still make amends. Somehow.

Fledgling Family

ONCE THEY SAT DOWN FOR dinner, Kazuki talked nearly non-stop, telling Karasu all about the visit. She was glad he had enjoyed himself and that thinking about his brother hadn't brought down his mood. It was rather impressive how much detail he remembered. Poor Karasu tried to look interested, but she could tell the boy was getting bored.

As soon as Kazuki paused, she broke in. "Kazuki, you said earlier you went to school in your world, right? What was it like?"

Kazuki turned his attention to her, letting a relieved-looking Karasu focus on his dinner. "We start in primary school, where we learn basic topics, such as history, geography, mathematics, science, language, and the like. Each topic is divided into a set number of ranks. Once you complete one rank in a topic, you advance to the next. Some, like language, have only a few ranks, while others, like history, have nearly a dozen. Advancement is purely based on mastery of a rank. Though Yuji is younger than I, he reached all the mathematics ranks before I did."

"What about universities?"

"There are schools for learning specialized topics, things

like construction, medicine, law, spell casting, and the like; others enter apprenticeships."

"A spell-casting school? So anyone can learn magic?" Sakura leaned forward, excited at the prospect that maybe someone like her could learn magic. Though she'd grown used to the paleness and thinness, it would be nice to use something like Kazuki's glam spell to make herself look healthy again. Then she could wear that dress he convinced her to buy and not feel so out of place.

"Well, to a degree. It is primarily about memorizing spells and how to combine the elements to make them work." He paused as he finished the last of his rice. "It does require some innate ability, though, and more powerful spells require greater ability. The highest level of spells tend to have larger limits, such as with my transportation stone. Then there are powers, which are a separate thing altogether."

She tried not to be too disappointed. *You couldn't do it before, so nothing loss.* Not wanting to kill the mood, she focused on the last thing he said. "What do you mean by 'powers'?"

"For example, Karasu's ability to change into a crow. That's one of his innate powers—something tengu can do pretty much from birth. It requires no spell; he can just do it at will."

"It must feel wonderful to be able to fly like that, Karasu-kun." Sakura smiled at him, hoping to draw him into the conversation.

"I suppose," he mumbled, without really looking at her.

"I do wish you could have come with us. It was so much fun." Kazuki ruffled the boy's hair, which drew a good-natured scowl from him.

"Master Kazuki, I'm already stuck in school for hours a day. Why would I want to go to another one?"

Kazuki put his hand to his chest as if he were wounded.

"Ah, he has no appreciation for culture this one. What am I to do?"

She laughed at his dramatic declaration, as did Karasu though he stopped when he noticed her looking at him. "You know, the weather should be nice tomorrow. Shall we do something, all three of us?"

"Like what?" Though it was Kazuki who asked, Karasu was looking at her with a confused expression.

"We could go to the top of Mount Hakodate. You can see the whole city from there."

"Oh, I'd love to go to the top." He frowned at her. "But, would it be safe for you? To climb a mountain, I mean?"

"Don't worry. We'll take the ropeway up. It doesn't take long at all. As long as I bundle up, it will be fine, promise."

"Great! This will be awesome!"

"I…" Karasu looked at her then back at Kazuki, who looked nearly ready to set out right then as he waited for Karasu to join his excitement. "Yeah. Sounds fun."

Since it was only a short walk to the ropeway, they didn't leave until late in the afternoon. It wasn't quite cold enough to warrant wearing their coats on top of their sweaters, so Sakura tucked all three in a duffel bag along with their gloves and scarves. At his insistence, Kazuki carried the bag, humming to himself with a grin on his face. Sakura and Karasu walked on either side of him, though Karasu didn't seem any happier about this trip than he had last night. He kept his hands tucked into his pockets as he looked at the ground.

Sakura took them on a slightly longer route so they could go through Hakodate Park and see the fountain.

"Um, Karasu-kun, do you like chocolate?"

The boy looked over at her, his usual frown knitting his brows together. "Chocolate? Never had any."

"Oh! Um, well, do you like sweet things?"

"I guess."

"Good! You two wait here a second." She walked over to the vending machine and purchased them all canned drinks. "Here, one for you, and one for you."

Kazuki looked at her in surprise when he took the can from her. "Coffee, in a can?"

"Yep." She showed them both how to open them.

Kazuki immediately took a sip then winced. "Hot!"

"Careful. Like this." She blew on the opening several times before drinking.

Karasu looked at her suspiciously, but followed her example. After the first swallow, he held the can away from himself with a curious expression then sipped again.

"Yours is hot chocolate. I hope you like it."

"I guess it's not too bad. Thanks." He gave her a funny look before tipping back the can to drink some more.

Since the girl's house was near the base of the mountain anyway, it didn't take long to walk to the place they would get a ride to the top. As they stood in line for the ropeway, Karasu looked up toward the summit. The castle at home was the tallest building in their country, but it would be dwarfed by the mountain. Still, he wasn't impressed.

"Kind of small for a mountain," he said matter-of-factly.

He figured the girl would look annoyed at his pointing it out, but she smiled and nodded. "Yep, it really is. Some people even consider it a hill instead of a mountain. Some of the tallest buildings in the world are much taller than this. But, the view makes it a really nice mountain."

Karasu shrugged and looked back toward the summit.

What Kazuki saw in her, Karasu couldn't figure out. She was okay looking enough for a human, but every other woman Kazuki had taken for a lover had been ten times as beautiful, and with much healthier curves. This girl was skinny and sickly looking. And none of his master's other lovers would have ever dared ask him to clean her house or dig around in the ground! Maybe the novelty of her being human appealed to him or something.

Whatever it was, she still annoyed him. Since he'd arrived, she'd been all smiles and nicey-nice with him, but it was only because Kazuki was around. He glanced back at her, now facing toward the front of the line again, watching the gondola pull in. When she said she wanted all three of them to come to this mountain, he'd started wondering what her angle was. Did she plan to get him alone so she could tell him to get out of the picture? Or would she start verbally abusing him or even hit him? Whatever her plan, she'd show her true colors soon enough, he was certain of it.

A few minutes later, they boarded the gondola that would carry them to the top. It had big glass windows all around, making it easy to see from any side, unless you got stuck in the middle. They were among the first to get on, so they were able to get near the front of the car right by the windows. The throng of people loading in made him nervous.

He hated crowds. All the pushing and shoving made him twitchy. It was only after the car began its ascent that he realized he hadn't been nudged even once. Kazuki stood behind him on one side, the girl on the other, their bodies acting as a shield. When he looked up, Kazuki looked down and smiled in that kind way of his. Of course, he knew how much Karasu hated strangers touching him. The girl's positioning had likely been an accident. If anything, she'd tried to get him stuck in the middle or something.

He snuck a look at her as she watched the rainbow of trees flowing below them. *She looks kind of sad.* The moment the errant thought popped into his head, the girl looked down at him and smiled. It'd probably just been his imagination. He turned back to the window and leaned against the glass. It was kind of like flying, though without all the work.

A few minutes later, the gondola pulled up to the station on the summit. Before they left the building, the girl had them put on their coats and other stuff then led them to the observation deck. A bitter wind made him huddle closer to Kazuki as they made their way to the rail.

Immediately below them was the mountain, covered in a quilt of trees colored red, orange, yellow, and every shade in between. Beyond that, the city was littered with buildings and streets. The land narrowed and curved as the seas pushed into it, then it widened again as it stretched on into the horizon, ending in a long line of mountains.

"Sakura, I can see your house!" Kazuki pointed toward it. It was indeed the girl's house—he recognized the roof and the cherry tree. "And I think that's your school?"

She was smiling, again. "Yep. The water on the left side is the bay. See all the ports? On the right side is the Tsugaru Strait."

"Cool! What's that weird shaped bit of land there, the one that looks like a star?"

"Goryokaku, it's a Western-style fort built during the Edo period. It has hundreds of cherry trees in it, so it's really pretty in springtime."

They walked around the platform a bit. The land on the other side of the water continued at first as it curved in a wide arc around the bay, but then it went off into the distance. At one point, there was nothing ahead but a vast landscape of blue-green water. In the far distance, the shadows of more land were barely visible. From the mish-mash of stuff Kazuki was always trying to drill into his head during his "Lessons in All Things Japan," Karasu guessed it was the main island, which lay south of the one they were on.

When they reached the spot they started at, the girl led them back toward the buildings. "Let's go to the souvenir shop for a bit."

The first part bored him, as it was just food, similar to what they had at that convenience store place she'd taken them to the other day. A tinkling sound caught his ear, so he followed it to a display of what appeared to be hollow glass balls hanging from strings. A long string ran through each, ending with a strip of paper and with a glass bead positioned near the edge of the ball. When someone brushed past the display, they swung. As the beads hit the sides of the glass, it reproduced the light, tinkling sound he'd heard.

"Do you like those?" The girl came up beside him to admire the chimes.

"I just wondered what the sound was." Karasu turned and walked down the aisle to where Kazuki stood near some paper lanterns with silly designs on them. As they continued around, he'd sometimes hear the tinkling of the chimes again.

"Ready for the best part?" She stopped them before they got near the door, and he could see it was now dark out. After they were bundled back up in their coats and gloves, she told them to close their eyes. He and Kazuki exchanged glances before Kazuki shrugged and did as she asked. She smiled at him. What was she up to now? Though hesitant, he could see Kazuki was getting excited, so he shut his eyes. A moment later he felt her hand grab his and she began pulling them somewhere.

"Keep them closed." She paused. "Going through the door now."

She continued leading them on, up a slightly inclined path. It had gotten colder outside and the wind had picked up. Even with the thick coat and gloves, he started to shiver.

"Almost there." A few more meters, then she stopped. "Okay, open your eyes."

With the sun gone for the night, the plainness of the buildings had given way to a brilliant display of lights. Beside him, Kazuki murmured in awe. It was as if all the stars in the sky had come down and decorated the land, forming a multi-colored fish on a darkened canvas. Near the port area, a ship floated on the waves like a shooting star that decided to slow down enough to be admired by all who might be watching.

The girl put an arm around him and eased him against her, wrapping her coat around him. It warmed him enough to stop his shivering.

"I'm sorry, Karasu-kun. Is that better?"

Why would she make herself colder like this? Anyone else would have just let him freeze. He knew the score: to Kazuki's lovers he was just an annoying kid they wanted out of the way, a pest to be shoved to the side. That first night in her house, he'd been cold in the thin clothes he'd worn to the human realm, especially after moving away from the kotatsu. The girl had quietly turned up the heater in the room, making it more comfortable for him.

The next day when they'd gone shopping to get clothes, the first things she bought had been the coat, his bright red scarf, and the soft gloves on his hands. Thinking back on it, she'd seemed to take particular care to find warmer clothes for him than for Kazuki. Maybe it was just a trick, a way to get bonus points with Kazuki since they were living in her house, but for now, he'd take the warmth she offered.

"Yeah…thanks."

Unexpected Overtures

HINA TRIED TO IGNORE THE whispers and snide remarks swirling around her as she entered the cafeteria. Since Parents' Day, the lunch-time rumor-spreading had exploded, especially with regards to a certain classmate and her gorgeous companion. Considering that long-haired man had only looked a few years older than them, they all knew there was no way he was Sakura's father.

After looking around for Akari, she went ahead through the line to get her lunch. Their high school was unusual in that it still offered lunch for students rather than presuming everyone would bring their own. It was pretty decent food too. She grabbed her current favorite, the chicken curry and rice, with a lemon cake for dessert.

Back amongst the crowd, she wandered around, looking for a pair of free seats. The gossip continued to swirl around like butterflies. She didn't think it was a big deal, though—probably just her older brother. At least half a dozen other students in their grade had an older sibling who'd attended in place of busy parents. But this was Sakura, so some of the more vicious girls were trying to spin salacious tales.

"I bet he is the son of somebody who owes her family

money, and he's forced to wait on her."

"She probably hired him to be her sex slave."

"Nah, I bet it's the other way around, and he's paying her for her services."

"Like a man that good looking would need to pay for it!"

Though Hina was annoyed at her classmates for their remarks, she had to admit, they were probably right in one regard. It was doubtful he was Sakura's brother, not when he had that long white hair. Not that it mattered. Maybe he was an uncle, or maybe he really was her boyfriend. Why should any of them care? The teachers hadn't seemed bothered anyway.

Moving past the gibbering girls with a slight shake of her head, she dodged a boy who stepped back into the aisle without looking. As she rebalanced her tray, she spotted the star topic in a far corner of the cafeteria. Sakura sat at a table by herself, reading a book as she ate her lunch. Even though seating was at a premium during lunch, she always had a table to herself. Hina had even seen people choose to stand rather than share a table with her.

Though they had been in the same homeroom for all of their high-school careers, Hina had never really exchanged more than a few words with her. The last time had been when she'd asked about donating to Kagura-sensei's maternity-leave fund. Akari had told her not to even bother, that the "Ice Princess" would just bite her head off for approaching her. But she hadn't. Sakura had been polite, even with those horrible remarks from the other students.

She'd heard a few people whispering that Sakura had transferred to their middle school because her father was crazy and that Sakura was too. Still others said she was just a rich, snobbish bitch who thought herself above everyone. If anything, Hina thought she looked sad, and maybe lonely. The only time she'd ever seen Sakura smile had been during the Parent Visitation Day, when she'd seen her walking hand in hand with that man down the hall. She'd looked very happy then.

"Excuse me, is this seat taken?" Sakura looked as surprised as Hina felt. She hadn't planned to go over and join her, but now here she was. The lunchroom grew quieter as Hina's question floated between them. Of course people would notice.

"No, it isn't."

"Mind if I join you then?"

"Suit yourself."

Relieved, Hina smiled as she sat across from her, but Sakura turned her attention back to her book.

"Um, what are you reading?"

"It's a historical narrative on the 1900 hurricane that hit Galveston Island in the United States."

"Oh, that sounds kind of interesting. Do you like history?"

"Yes."

"Is it a good one?"

Sakura finally looked up again, a questioning expression on her face. "It is fairly well-written and the stories about the people in the town are quite compelling. But, it has several pretty basic inaccuracies, which makes it hard to believe the rest."

Hina cheered to herself. Finally, whole sentences! She tried to think of a response to keep the conversation going, but she didn't know much about history or the hurricane, and she didn't want to say something completely stupid.

"Hina, there you are." Akari walked over to the table. "It's so crowded. I was looking all over for you."

"Yes, I was lucky that Sakura-chan let me sit with her. Is it okay if my friend joins us too?" She knew Akari had expected her to get up and go sit elsewhere, but if Hina left now, she might lose her only chance. Though she looked a little wary, Sakura nodded. Score two!

Akari eased into the seat beside her, cutting her a look.

Hina turned back to Sakura and bowed slightly. "I'm sorry. I called you by your first name without even thinking about it."

"It's okay. You can call me Sakura, if you want to." A tinge of pink stained Sakura's cheeks.

"You can call me Hina. This is Takamura Akari."

"Thanks for letting us join you." Akari had that same distant tone she used when she was annoyed with someone. Hina knew she was too polite to make a fuss about where they were sitting, at least for now. When they were alone she'd no doubt get an earful. But, for now, it was worth it.

As the lunchroom decided nothing exciting was going to happen and the noise returned to its previous levels, Hina tried to think of something historical she'd read lately. "Um, do you like the Rurouni Kenshin series?"

"Yeah, it was pretty good. I thought it had a nice blend of historical detail and fantasy, and Kenshin was a great character. I read some interviews with Watsuki that said he based a lot of the characters on historical figures. It made me want to read more about the Shinsengumi." As she talked, Sakura's initial wariness faded and she looked almost excited.

"How about shojo stuff?" Hina asked.

"Love it. I probably read more than I should."

"My mom says that all the time! Though my grades do kind of suck, so she may have a point, but it's so easy to lose track of time when I'm reading a good story."

The discussion naturally led to their talking about favorite anime series and movies. Only Akari remained silent as she focused on eating her lunch, a bland expression plastered to her face.

They were discussing their interpretations of the ending of a movie they both liked when a voice came over the loudspeaker. "Takeshi Sakura-san, please report to the guidance office."

"Awww." *Why did they have to call Sakura to the office today of all days?*

"I'm sorry. I have to go." Sakura gathered her things and stood up.

"It's okay. We can sit together tomorrow, okay?"

"Sure." After taking a few steps, Sakura stopped and turned back. "Thank you." She bowed deeply as she said it. Hina smiled in return, watching until Sakura walked out of the cafeteria before turning to face Akari.

"Hina, what was this all about?" Akari said in a clipped tone.

"What?"

"Don't act dumb. You know what. Why did you sit with Takeshi-san?"

"There were no other seats available. Besides, I've always wanted to talk to her, so it seemed like a good opportunity."

Akari shook her head. "Hina, she is not someone you should be associating with."

"And why not? I'm sick of how everyone, including us, acts like she doesn't exist when we don't even know her. Can you imagine how lonely it must be to be treated like that when she hasn't done anything wrong? It's just not fair."

"She brought it on herself by being so anti-social and cold to people. If she'd quit acting so stuck up, people might be friendlier to her."

"When has she been given a chance? On our first day, people were already ignoring her and saying all sorts of bad things about her. Aren't you the one who's always reminding us about the code of conduct and showing fairness and consideration toward others? Is it really fair to judge her based on rumors without giving her a chance yourself?"

Akari tapped her finger on the edge of the table as she mulled over Hina's remark. Finally, she nodded. "Fine. I'll reserve judgment for now."

"Good. Thank you." She could understand Akari's surprise, but it wasn't an entirely new idea. When they'd first started high school, Hina had wanted to talk to the elegant, solemn-looking girl, curious to know more about her. But then she saw her classmates' attitude toward Sakura and all the gossip that had swirled around her. In the end, she'd been too afraid of being ostracized for breaking from the pack.

But today, finally, she'd found her nerve and she was so glad she had. As the tangy sweetness of the lemon cake melted on her tongue, she found herself eager for tomorrow to come so they could have a full lunch period to talk.

"Tadaima." Kazuki heard Sakura pause to leave her shoes at the door before heading upstairs.

"*Okaeri!*[26] How was your day?" He waited for her by the foot of the stairs. It never took long for her to change out of her uniform.

"It was…strange. Where's Karasu?"

"He went to take a nap."

"Will he be okay out there? It's getting colder."

"So far he hasn't complained. He told me once that it's much warmer in a tree than you might expect, so he is probably fine for now, especially with that thick blanket you gave him for his nest."

"Okay, but it will get really cold once winter comes. Maybe we could fix up the attic for him? It's the biggest room in the

---

[26] The traditional response to the entry greeting, often translated to "welcome home."

house and he could go in and out through the window, if he wanted."

"Hmm, that might work out okay. Even back home, when winter arrives Karasu has to sleep in the castle, usually in my room. But I don't think your bed could hold three."

Sakura laughed. "No, probably not. Besides, I think a boy his age would like a room of his own."

"Yes, you're probably right."

"Since it is kind of chilly, how about hot pot[27] for dinner?"

"Sure! I saw them making that on television the other day. It sounded delicious."

"Let's go to the store then."

Along the way, Sakura told him about Hina's approaching her at lunch. "I'm still not sure why she did it, but talking to her was kind of fun. I don't think her friend liked it very much, though; the whole time she didn't say anything. Still, I liked talking about manga and stuff. Oh, and Hina-chan loves watching Iron Chef too."

"Ah, a girl with good tastes indeed." Since discovering the over-the-top cooking competition, Kazuki hadn't missed an episode.

Sakura laughed. "I thought you'd like that."

"So you will talk with her again, yes?"

"I don't know. I suppose if she approached me again I would, but by now, she's probably been told not to associate with me. That other girl rushed her out of the room at the end of the day." She paused, a smile teasing her lips. "You know,

---

[27] "Hot pot" refers to a variety of dishes, particularly popular in winter, in which a simmering pot of stock is placed in the center of the table. Then diners place ingredients into the pot themselves and watch them cook at the table. The ingredients vary based on the particular dish being served. Sukiyaki is the most popular form of Japanese hot pot; it features thin sliced beef, vegetables, and tofu in a sweet soy sauce base. Before consuming the individual items, they are often dipped in raw, beaten eggs.

since Parents' Day everyone has been gossiping about us, saying all sorts of things."

Kazuki frowned. He hadn't wanted to make Sakura's school life even lonelier, and it bothered him that anyone was saying bad things about her.

"What kinds of things?" To his surprise, she giggled and darted ahead of him before turning back to face him while walking backwards.

"All sorts of things…like that we're lovers."

She spoke in a soft, sing-song voice as her skirt swished around her knees and her hair danced with the breeze.

"Kazuki?" She paused, her smile replaced by a worried expression.

He kept walking until he was directly in front of her, with only a breath's whisper between them. As she called his name again, he lifted his hand and cupped her face before brushing his lips across hers.

He pulled away. "Sorry, you just looked too adorable to resist. Are you angry?"

"No." She stood up on her toes, gifting him a soft kiss in return.

Without another word, they turned and continued to the store. His face felt warm as Kazuki slipped his hand in hers. When he glanced at Sakura, he saw her own face was pink.

After picking up their groceries, conversation returned. Neither mentioned the kiss. Still, he knew the nature of their relationship had shifted in those brief moments.

"Master Kazuki?" Karasu was leaning against the garden fence looking as if he'd eaten rotten eggs.

"What? Is something wrong?"

"What's with that?" he yelled, pointing at their intertwined hands.

"This? It's enjoyable." The bird fumed in place a moment before running through the garden, transforming, and flying off in a huff. Kazuki scratched his head. "Did I miss something?"

"I think he may be feeling a bit jealous."

"Jealous? Karasu? Of what, I mean…" He stopped as Sakura pointedly held up their still joined hands.

"Oh…" He scratched his head again. Why would his holding Sakura's hand bother Karasu? For now he'd let Karasu sulk out his tantrum before trying to talk to him about what was bothering him. As Sakura began preparing dinner, he turned his thoughts to the kiss he'd given her. Any previous thoughts of pursuing her had been fueled more by his own flirtatious nature than any real heat. She was a human, after all. Even if he could find a way to save her from her pending death, she would at most live only another sixty to eighty years. He would live for many hundreds, if not thousands, of years yet.

It was madness to be more than a companion and caretaker, but his heart ached at the thought of her dying, be it in a few months or in eighty years. But how far should it go? A single kiss written off as his being caught up in the moment, or pursuing her fully? Would she even accept him, or would she try to cut him off, as she had everyone around her, in a misguided effort to avoid him future pain?

Stepping Forward

"Good morning, Sakura-chan!" Hina's enthusiastic greeting as Sakura walked into the classroom did not go unnoticed by the other students.

Ignore her. Cut this off.

Sakura forced herself to continue to her desk. Seemingly oblivious to Sakura's attempted snub or the attention she was drawing, Hina skipped over, her blond pigtails bouncing in time with her step.

"Are you ready for the English test?" Hina asked, pulling up a chair so she could sit in front of Sakura's desk.

Now what? Sakura couldn't make herself ignore her again, not with her sitting right there, elbows propped on her desk, with that overly cheerful grin on her face.

"Um, yes, I think so." She kept her tone neutral, unencouraging.

Hina sighed. "I'm so nervous. I suck at English, and especially tests. If I bring home another low grade, Mom's going to withhold my allowance for two whole months! Two months with no taiyaki!?"[28]

"Taiyaki?" Sakura couldn't help asking, curious as to why that was what she lamented. Most girls in the class would have complained about not being able to buy clothes or the like.

"Yeah, there is this little stand a few blocks away. The guy who runs it is seriously ancient, but he makes the best taiyaki ever!" Hina clasped her hands together and raised them by her head as she sung the treat's praises. "Oh, and then there is the ramen from the place by the tram stop. Best broth and perfect noodles every time. Toshi-san's lovely tonkatsu…"[29]

It took everything she had not to laugh. It sounded like Hina's entire allowance went to snacking, despite her trim appearance. Sakura hoped she'd be able to get a good enough grade to keep her allowance up, but bit back the words, while Hina just kept going on about other favorite foods.

Half-desperate, Sakura glanced over at Hina's friend, who watched them with a sour expression that remained unchanged despite Sakura's pleading look.

"Hina, your friend seems lonely." Maybe that would get her to go away.

"Hmm? Really?" She glanced toward the other girl, then smiled and gave her a small wave. "It's okay. Akari likes to spend the morning prepping for her student council stuff. I just get in her way."

At that moment, Sakura was saved by the bell. The ding made Hina jump to her feet. "Oops, time for class. Hey, we're having lunch together, right?"

---

[28] A popular snack food that's shaped like a fish. Made with pancake or waffle batter, it usually has a sweet filling, such as sweetened red bean paste, custard, chocolate, or sweet potato, but it can also be filled with a more savory, meat-based mixture.

[29] A pork cutlet breaded with panko and then deep-fried, usually served with a thick Worcestershire sauce called tonkatsu sauce. Also popularly used as a sandwich filling or with curry.

"Um, okay?" The answer slipped out before she could stop herself.

"Yay!" Hina darted back to her desk, sliding into her seat just as Mimomo-sensei entered and the student with class duty called for the class to stand. As the roll was called, Sakura was able to pick up the full name of Hina's friend, Akari Takamura. She was a bit embarrassed to have forgotten it at all, considering Takamura was their class president. Just when Sakura glanced over at the girl, she found Takamura watching her as well, her gaze dark and assessing. She had a no-nonsense, business-like appearance with her dark hair cut in a straight-lined, chin-length style. Unlike those of many of the girls in class, Takamura's uniform was crisp and strictly to code, no slouching socks, unbuttoned jacket, or skirt rolled up to be higher.

After homeroom was math, but Sakura half-listened to the lesson. Koga had been the one to call her to the guidance office the day before. He'd heard about her having to leave early for the check-up with Tenma-sensei, and once again hinted that she consider dropping out of school. The suggestions were always couched in terms of "focusing on her health," of course. As usual, she said she would consider his advice, but they both knew she was lying. She had no intention of quitting, not as long as she could still attend. The normalcy helped her deal with things. If she had nothing to do but sit at home all day, every day, she'd have let death claim her long ago.

Though she needed to be there, it didn't mean having to hurt anyone. Sakura knew she should be pushing Hina away, just as she should have pushed Kazuki away. It would be better for both of them. *I should just cut this off now, before it goes any further.* The last thing she wanted was to make someone so happy and full of life cry over her. Before lunch, her step faltered. If she left now—rudely didn't show up—Hina would give up on her. They'd just talked a little. It wasn't like they were friends, not yet.

She continued on to her usual seat. Skipping lunch wasn't an option. The medicines she took right after required her to have eaten first, and since the school didn't allow them to eat their meals outside the cafeteria, she'd have to stay there. That's the excuse she gave herself, even though she knew full well that if she asked, she'd be allowed to eat anywhere she wanted.

A few minutes later, she saw Hina making her way through the crowd with her tray. Takamura trailed behind her, grimacing the whole way.

"Hey, Sakura!" Hina grinned as they took the same seats they'd sat in yesterday. "That line was crazy. Hope you weren't waiting long?"

"No, not at all," Sakura said, failing to keep a small smile from lifting the corners of her lips. Part of her had believed that Hina hadn't meant any of it, that it was just some elaborate hoax. Still, she didn't think Hina would do that. She seemed like an honest and forthright girl.

Not sure what else to do, Sakura asked her, "So, how did you do on the test?"

Hina looked down at her tray. "I may have passed, but it was probably really close. Mom will yell, but hopefully, I'll get to keep my allowance. I'm so awful at English. I just don't understand it very well."

Sakura picked up her fork and moved a bite of food around her plate. English was her best subject. But offering to help would mean making an even closer connection. A connection she needed to break.

"Hina-chan..." Sakura started, trying not to look at the sweet girl across from her. If she looked, she wouldn't be able to say it. "You really shouldn't keep doing this. It's best if you just stay away from me."

Hina froze, her eyes wide open in confusion. "What do you mean?"

"I…" Sakura glanced at Takamura, wishing the girl would join in. Oddly, her stare seemed curious rather than hostile. *Oh, make up your mind! You're not helping!* "That is…look, if you keep hanging around me, people are going to gossip about you. They'll stop talking to you. You'll lose your friends and be shunned."

Yeah, that was a good reason. Everyone knew Sakura was an outcast. Instead of putting the girl off, though, the comment just made Hina smile.

"It's so sweet of you to worry about me, but I'll be fine, I promise. Anyone who stops talking to me just because we're friends isn't someone I'd want around me anyway."

Sakura's heart ached. Shaking her head, Sakura gave her lunch tray extra close attention. *Friends…she's already using the F word…*How could she argue with that, or the way Hina beamed at her?

"Sakura-chan?"

"You know…I usually do pretty well in English," Sakura said hesitantly. "Probably because my mom spoke it around me at lot when I was little."

"Was she American?"

"No, my maternal grandmother was. She taught my mom. Mom decided to teach me so I'd do better in school."

"That's so cool!"

This is a mistake…a big mistake. "So, um, if you want, maybe I could help you with it." *What am I saying!?*

"Really? That would be awesome. You want help too, right, Akari? I mean, you get crazy high grades anyway, but you said it was a tough test. Extra studying is good, right?"

Takamura's eyebrows went up so high they disappeared beneath her bangs. She'd stayed quiet the whole conversation, watching but not contributing. Sakura expected her to reject Hina's bulldozing, but instead she turned her gaze to Sakura.

"When?" Her question sounded almost like a challenge.

"Hmm." Sakura frowned. It wasn't like she had a lot of things to do on any given day, but thinking of when meant thinking of where. She didn't want to worry Kazuki by being out too late. Even if he knew where she was, with the colder weather, it was better to stay in at night. Which left only one choice, really. "I'm free this afternoon if you guys are, and um, if you don't mind doing it at my house."

"Where do you live?"

"Not too far, about a mile from the school. I usually walk, but it's on the tram line too."

Hina responded before Takamura could throw out anymore questions. "Perfect! Studying is way more fun at someone's house than at the library. But will your parents mind us just showing up out of the blue?"

"No...they died a long time ago." What was wrong with her? First offering to help, and now telling them her parents were dead? None of her classmates knew about it, as far as she was aware. It wasn't like the teachers gossiped about her to the students, and she certainly hadn't told any of them, until now.

"Oh," Hina said, her shoulders slumping. "I'm sorry."

"It's okay." Sakura tried to give her a reassuring smile.

"You live alone?" Takamura asked, her tone softening some.

"I used to, but now Kazuki and his little brother Karasu-kun live with me."

"Kazuki-san? The man that came on Parents' Day?" Takamura crossed her arms in front of her chest.

"Yes."

She looked unhappy but said nothing more while Hina smiled. "Oh, he's so dreamy looking! I can't wait to meet him. This will be so much fun!"

Sakura tried to calm her nerves as she told Kazuki and Karasu of the expected guests.

"Shall Karasu and I go out while they are here?" Kazuki asked as he and Karasu followed her into the kitchen.

"Of course not. I've already told them you live here. Unless you don't want to be here?"

"Great, I can't wait to meet them."

"Well, I certainly don't want to be around a bunch of chattering humans. I'll stay outside." Karasu stomped out of the kitchen. A few moments later, she heard the screen door slam open. He'd probably change into his bird form and hide in the tree until dinner.

"I guess it's probably best. I suspect Hina-chan would be inclined to pounce on a cute kid and smother him with cuddles. Somehow, I don't think Karasu-kun would like that."

Kazuki laughed. "Not at all. Shall I help you get ready?"

"Sure. I'll go change right quick. Can you start some tea? When I come back down, we can prepare some snacks."

"Okay!"

Though most of the workings of the kitchen still seemed to baffle him, Kazuki had learned how to make both tea and coffee. He told her that spending his days desperate for some had been a great motivator. After she changed, she joined him in the kitchen, humming to herself. She began slicing some steamed sweet potatoes she'd made earlier and arranged them on a plate while Kazuki prepared the tea tray.

Despite herself, she was excited and looking forward to this afternoon. She directed Kazuki to slice up some apples while she poured a bag of chips into a bowl. The teapot whistled from the stove. Kazuki picked it up with the pot handle and set it to the side.

"Thanks for taking care of the tea." Sakura looked over the food. "I hope it's enough."

Kazuki placed his hand over her shaking one. "Nervous?"

"A little. It's been a very long time since I had visitors like this."

"You'll be fine." He kissed her forehead and pulled her in for a hug as the doorbell rang.

"Show time! Thank you." She gave him a quick kiss on the cheek before going to answer the door.

"I hope you had no trouble finding it?" She bowed to the girls.

"No, you write very good directions!"

Sakura stepped back to let them enter and change their shoes. Fortunately, the delay in starting time due to Akari's student council meeting had given her time to dart to the store for some extra pairs of house shoes.

"*Gomen kudasai.*"[30] They called out the familiar expression in near unison. It had been so long since she'd heard it that Sakura almost forgot to reply in kind.

"*Irasshai, dōzo oagari kudasai.*"[31]

"Good afternoon." Kazuki greeted them from the entry to the living room.

"Please excuse our intrusion." Hina blushed and lowered her eyes. Her hands tightened on the strap of the gift box she

---

[30] "Gomen kudasai" is the formal greeting one calls out when visiting a home; it can be literally translated to "please forgive me for bothering you."

[31] Likewise, Sakura's response is part of the formal ritual of visiting; she is basically welcoming them and inviting them inside.

held in her hands.

"Not at all. I'm happy to get to meet Sakura's new friends. Make yourselves comfortable. I'll bring the snacks from the kitchen."

Sakura led them into the living room. The screen door was still open from Karasu's leaving. Hina walked over to it and looked outside. "Wow, I love your garden! It's so pretty."

"Ah, thank you."

"*Kore douzo.*[32] My mom made them so they should be pretty good." Hina handed her the gift box. Inside was a plate of cookies.

"Thank you." Sakura set them in the middle of the table for them to share while Kazuki brought in the other snacks and the tea.

Though Takamura-san had come and made all the appropriate greetings, once they were seated and Kazuki began chatting up Hina, Takamura-san remained quiet, watching. In particular, she seemed to be watching Kazuki, a closed expression on her face.

As if noticing her attention, he glanced over at her and smiled. "Akari-san…is it okay if I call you Akari-san?"

Takamura blinked. "Sure, that's fine."

"Thank you. Akari-san, Sakura tells me you are the class president?"

"Yes."

"Akari has been elected our class president every year of high school. She is a really good one too!" Hina proclaimed.

To Sakura's surprise, Takamura blushed. "I wouldn't say that. I just try my best, that's all."

---

[32] One phrase used when offering the customary gift one brings when visiting someone's home. As Hina already considers Sakura a friend, she uses this more casual form, meaning "this is for you," rather than the more formal "tsumaranai mono seu ga" ("This is a trifling thing, but please accept it").

"It must be hard to balance schoolwork with your duties," Kazuki said. "The president is also in charge of the student council, yes?"

"Yes, it can be hectic at times, but the other student council members give me a lot of support. They are a great team to work with." As she began talking about her duties, Takamura lost her stiff expression and grew more animated.

Sakura was impressed. She knew Takamura was in the top five of their class. Juggling her duties while having to maintain those kinds of grades had to require a great deal of dedication, time-management skills, and patience. In another lifetime, they likely would have been good friends.

Once they finished their snack, Kazuki lay nearby to read while the girls pulled out their books and began to work. At first, Takamura retreated into her shell, studying on her own while Sakura helped Hina with any trouble spots. For ten minutes, Sakura pretended she didn't see Takamura struggling to work a tricky verb-tense problem, not wanting to force Takamura to deal with her. Instead she focused on helping Hina break down a sentence.

"Takeshi-san, would you mind helping me with this problem?" Takamura's voice was quiet, almost demure.

Sakura smiled. "Sure."

After that, Takamura participated more actively as they continued working for the next few hours. When they got to math, Takamura even helped them with difficult problems. Just before dinner, the group began packing up to leave.

As she finished putting her books in her bag, Takamura looked up at Sakura. "Takeshi-san."

"Yes?"

"If you want, you can call me Akari. I never did like my last name." Her tone was almost dismissive, but Sakura had a feeling she added the last bit as an excuse.

"Sure, and please, call me Sakura. I don't really like mine much either."

Once they were gone, Kazuki helped her clean up. "Did you enjoy your study session?"

"Yes. I'd forgotten how much fun it could be to study with friends."

They headed to the kitchen to make dinner. Sakura couldn't stop a heavy sigh from escaping her.

"What is bothering you, little one?" As he'd done before, Kazuki cupped her face with his hand, his thumb stroking her cheek. It was a comforting gesture, one it would be easy to get used to.

"I just…I can't help wondering if this is okay. I shouldn't be making friends like this."

"Since I've been here, I've noticed this: that you hide away from others. You are a kind girl, so I understand your desire to spare them the pain of losing someone they are close to. And, yet, in so many other ways, you are fighting so hard to live a full, normal life. You have not let this illness take away your home, your freedom, your love of books, your garden, so why then are you willing to let it steal away the wonderful feeling of spending time with those you care about and keep you from surrounding yourself with good people?"

"But what if…what if they hate me for it? What if they wish they had never known me when they find out what the future holds?"

"The future is an uncertain thing. We never truly know when we will leave this world, and it is not always when we expect. So I promise you, I could never hate you for letting me into your life, nor could I ever come to regret meeting you. Being here with you now, the days we share together, they are memories I will hold and cherish the rest of my life. And I think, if you give them a chance, you will find that Hina-san and Akari-san will feel the same."

Tears ran down her cheeks as she threw her arms around him. "You…the things you say."

He chuckled before his lips brushed across hers. So light was the touch that if her eyes had been closed, she would have wondered if she'd imagined it.

"You know, Hina-chan may have a little crush on you. If I remember right, she called you 'dreamy.'"

"Ah, she has good taste indeed, but I'm afraid I'll have to break her heart," he said with a hammy-pained stance that looked straight from the romantic melodrama he'd gotten hooked on lately, "for there is only one girl whose affection I seek."

Sakura laughed and danced away from him, wiping her face dry as she turned her attention to making dinner. "You really are too much sometimes."

Chuckling, he came up behind her and wrapped his arms around her waist. With his chin resting on her shoulder, she leaned against him. He wasn't any more serious with his flirting with her than he'd been with Hina and Akari, but it was fun to pretend. Besides, she enjoyed the warmth of his body pressed against hers and the taste of his kisses.

Sometimes at night, she found herself wishing she could turn to him, encourage him to go further. Since meeting him, she found herself hating the idea that she would die without having experienced a taste of adulthood, of making love with a man. Granted, she and Kazuki were not in love, but she felt they had become close since his arrival. That, combined with his generous nature, made her certain it would be the sort of special experience any girl would dream of.

No doubt if she asked, he would agree to it, but that would just be an act of pity, not of mutual desire. Not that it mattered. Her body could never handle the strain. She knew that even without asking Tenma-sensei. Having her die underneath him while he fulfilled some foolish fantasy was not the sort of final memory she wanted to leave him with.

Girls' Day

"SAKURA-CHAN!" HINA BOUNCED over to her desk after class let out. "Guess what? Genji-san asked me to be his date to the ball!"

"The boy who sits behind you?" From the way he watched Hina, with moon eyes, Sakura had started to suspect he was crushing on her. From the way Hina was smiling, Sakura guessed it wasn't as one-sided as it might have seemed.

"Yep, that's him. I was starting to think he'd never make a move!"

"Well, I'm happy for both of you."

"Thanks. So, Akari and I are going shopping this afternoon. I have to get a new dress to wear for something so important as a first date! Want to come with us?"

Sakura glanced at Akari. Since the study session, the two girls had continued meeting with Sakura at lunch every day. Akari had opened up a little more, but still seemed reserved. This morning she had greeted Sakura when they arrived at the room, though. Still, a shopping trip might be too personal. She was surprised when the other girl nodded.

"Well, if you don't mind. I was thinking I should get a new

one too. I just need to call home right quick."

Once Sakura called Kazuki to let him know she'd be late, they headed to the tram[33] stop. It was a quick ride down the line to the stop for the Boni-Moriya department store. Standing seven stories tall, the complex would have everything they needed.

"Where shall we start? Formal wear is on the third floor while shoes and accessories are down here." Akari pointed to various spots on the map as she spoke.

"How about the second floor?" Hina smiled as she pointed toward the escalators.

"Second?" Akari studied the map. "But I don't see anything there we'd need."

"Café Nishimura is there. I've heard they have some amazing Catalana![34] I've always wanted to try it." She glanced back and forth between Akari and Sakura. "Aren't you guys hungry?"

"Hina, really! You're hungry again?" Though Akari's tone sounded exasperated she was smiling as if used to this.

"Lunch was hours ago! And shopping always makes me hungry. Think of it as a pre-shopping fuel-up!"

"Everything makes you hungry."

Sakura couldn't help laughing at the two bickering friends. They both stopped to stare at her.

"Sakura-chan?" Hina looked at her wide-eyed. "You can laugh?" Her remark made Sakura laugh even harder along with

---

[33] Though trams are not as common in Japan as a whole, Hakodate has an extensive network of these streetcars throughout the city. They go to most major locations or close enough to connect to a bus to get the rest of the way.

[34] Crema Catalana, or as it is commonly called in the West, crème brûlée, is a rich custard-based dessert made from milk, eggs, and vanilla with a caramel crust on top. In Japan, the custard is a little thicker than what you might expect, and it is often served cut into squares rather than in a ramekin.

Akari. After a moment, they managed to compose themselves. "I didn't mean to sound so shocked. I just never heard you laugh before." Hina smiled at her. "You should do it more often."

"You're right, I should." She looked at the map then grinned. "Now what was that about Catalana?"

Moments later, they were seated at the café, enjoying the treat with matcha lattes.[35]

"Wow, these are so good." Hina closed her eyes and let her head fall back after taking the first bite.

"Hina!" Akari whispered as she nudged her with her elbow.

Chuckling, Sakura took a bite as well. The rich custard melted on her tongue with the bittersweet caramel. It really was good. She decided to pick up some for Kazuki and Karasu on the way out. Though Karasu tried to act indifferent, she'd figured out that he was as fond of sweets as Kazuki was.

While they ate, Sakura learned that Hina had a little brother in elementary school and a younger sister who was a first year in middle school. As Hina shared another story about her family, she didn't seem to notice that neither Sakura nor Akari were contributing much. Both focused more on their snacks, though they each smiled if Hina looked their way. Thinking back, Sakura remembered that she hadn't seen Akari with anyone on Parents' Day. Instead, she'd been helping various teachers with chores.

Their snack done, once Hina finished her story, Akari stood before she could start another. "Since we're all fueled up, let's get to shopping."

"Yay!" Hina nearly tipped the chair over as she bounced up.

---

[35] Lattes made with matcha, aka green tea, instead of coffee.

As they made their way to the third floor, Hina tapped her shoulder against Akari's. "You know, you still haven't told me who you're bringing to the dance. I know a bunch of guys have asked you."

"It wasn't a bunch, just two, and I declined both offers."

"Awww, so you're going alone?"

"No." Akari paused, looking almost shy. "Aki is bringing me."

"Awesome!" Hina cheered.

"Who's Aki?" Sakura asked.

Hina leaned around Akari to stage-whisper to Sakura. "He's Akari's really smart and super hot older brother!"

"It's nice of him to act as your date." So she did have someone in her family, at least.

"Yes. He spoils me. My mom married his dad just before I started junior high. They are often busy with work and travel a lot, so Aki kind of took over taking care of me. He graduated college last year and managed to get a job at a law firm he likes. I'm really proud of him." Though Akari was smiling, Sakura thought she sounded more melancholy than proud.

"It was more fun when he was still a student. He'd take us to all kinds of places and never complained about hanging out with us girls at all," Hina added with a wistful tone. "He'd go with us to all the festivals in the summer and take us to the beach in his car."

"Hina's had a crush on him for years," Akari said in a teasing tone.

"Do not!" The blush creeping across Hina's face said otherwise. "He's just cool, that's all."

Still laughing, they headed into the formal-wear section. A few hours later, they left the store with new dresses, matching shoes, and even some new accessories. Akari and Hina got off the tram two stops before Sakura. They stood side by side, waving as the car pulled away.

Sakura returned their waves with a happy smile. Once they were out of sight, she slumped down on one of the open benches, glad it was mostly empty. She could almost feel her energy fading away like that of an old battery, but it had been fun, so much fun. How long had it been since she'd spent time with friends?

Friends...yes...friends. There was no turning back now. Kazuki, Karasu, Hina, Akari. They'd made their way into her life, and though it was selfish of her, she couldn't make herself push them away now. Which meant the only responsible thing to do was tell the girls the truth. But not just yet. The festival was only a few days away. She didn't want to spoil the fun by having such a heavy cloud over things, and she wanted to enjoy being a normal girl with them for just a little longer. *Ito-san, please let Kazuki be right.*

"Ah, the fair princess has returned. The sunshine has returned to my humble life once more." Kazuki made a sweeping gesture as he waited for her just past the entry.

"You really will say the wildest things sometimes." Sakura shook her head at him in amusement before switching out her shoes and stepping up into the house.

"Yes, yes. I do." He laughed before stealing a kiss. It was a harder, longer kiss than he'd given her before. "You truly are a light in my life. This you can believe."

He kissed her again and a strange sensation welled up inside her. When he started to pull away, she pulled his head back down. His grip tightened around her as he complied with the unspoken request, brushing his lips over hers again and again, until her lips felt as if they were on fire. She heard a moan through the foggy haze before realizing it had come from her. If this was what a real kiss was like, Sakura could understand why it would drive people so crazy.

SLAM.

They jumped apart at the loud sound. In the kitchen, one of the dining chairs lay on the ground. Karasu stood beside it, his hands balled into fists so tight his knuckles were white.

"You liar!" he yelled at Sakura before running out of the house, transforming, and flying off.

"Karasu, come back and apologize at once!" She was certain Kazuki had yelled, but it sounded more like a distant whisper made through layers of static. Her breaths came in short, shallow pants as the familiar pain began in her chest. Another attack.

She tried to pick up her bag, but she fell forward. Rather than face-planting on the floor, she landed in a pair of warm arms, which eased her down. Then her inhaler was in her mouth.

"Breathe." Following the command, she inhaled as the medicine sprayed out. As it worked, the world became clearer. She could see a fuzzy Kazuki holding up the nitro spray and feel his fingers pushing on her chin. Obediently, she opened her mouth and lifted her tongue so he could deliver the spray dosage. Then the second dose of breathing medicine.

He kissed her forehead before picking her up and carrying her upstairs to her room. Her eyelids grew heavier as the need to sleep kicked in.

Kazuki's beautiful face was marred by worry wrinkles on his

forehead. She reached up to stroke the top of his hair. "I'm okay."

"I am so sorry, Sakura. I do not know what is wrong with Karasu, but this will not happen again, I swear." He ran the back of his finger over her cheek.

Sakura tried to push through the clouds cluttering her mind. Why had he called her a liar? Because they'd been kissing? *Of course…* The day they went to Mount Hakodate. Before they went back down, Kazuki had gone to the bathroom, leaving her with Karasu. Their brief exchange came back to her.

"Hey, are you in love with Master Kazuki?"

"Of course not. We're just friends. Why?"

"I guess it's okay then, so long as you aren't in love with him or anything."

She tried to sit up.

"Sakura, you should rest."

"But I need to apologize to Karasu-kun. I didn't mean to lie to him."

Kazuki pushed her back down and tucked the covers around her. "I will send him up in a bit then, but for now, please rest."

"Okay."

"I'll be back soon." Before he left, he gave her one more light kiss.

Once she was certain he was gone, she eased out of bed and peeked out the window. A few moments later, he walked out of the house and into the garden. Arms crossed, Kazuki looked up at the top of her cherry tree where Karasu was hiding in his bird form, then turned and sat on the bench on the path nearby.

She could hear the ticking of the watch on her nightstand as time stretched on. Finally, the bird dropped down to the ground, changing back to his boyish form as he landed in front of Kazuki. Sakura eased away from the window, not wanting to intrude any further. Sending up a quick prayer that it would go well, she climbed back into bed to rest as she'd promised.

After fleeing the house, Karasu changed to his bird form and flew the short distance to the mountain, letting the wind carry him up along the slope. Below, the colorful trees flowed, broken up in spots by a few that had lost their leaves for the season. He should have realized she hadn't really meant it when she said that she didn't want to be Kazuki's lover.

Maybe it was something more, maybe she wanted more. He didn't think it was money since she seemed to have plenty despite living in that little house. Did she want to be Kazuki's mate, and then maybe queen? It had to be that. Why else would she keep cozying up to Karasu, acting all nice and stuff? Like giving him ice cream and buying him clothes. He hated how she always smiled at him and acted so helpless. She hadn't looked helpless seducing Kazuki in the doorway.

And why was Kazuki so hung up on that stupid human? He swore he wouldn't get involved with her, but there he was kissing her like that. Karasu had never seen him kiss any of the concubines like that. It wasn't as if Kazuki was mean to them, but it was clear he viewed them with the same sort of polite distance he kept with anyone he didn't trust. He didn't laugh with them like he did this girl or spend time with them beyond having sex. And he certainly didn't worry over them all the time.

The palace concubines had made it clear that Karasu spoiled their time with Kazuki. It had always been annoying to be shoved aside, but since Kazuki only spent a few hours with them, he dealt with it. None of them stood a chance of being Kazuki's mate, something Kazuki made sure any woman understood from the beginning. A few had still tried, though. They were the worst, smacking Karasu if Kazuki wasn't around. One had even promised that when she was queen, he'd be their wedding dinner! She'd been particularly scary.

Fortunately, those types clung so hard, Kazuki lost interest quickly and dismissed them from the castle altogether, never knowing about their abusive natures. But this twit hung all over him and Kazuki didn't seem to mind at all.

After flying over the mountain and looping back around, Karasu returned to the girl's home, perching in the tree. A short while later, Kazuki came outside. After giving him the briefest of glances, Kazuki sat down on the bench, his arms resting on his knees as he leaned forward with his head held low. No order came demanding he come down. His master simply sat and waited.

Kazuki could be very patient when he wanted to be. There was no point in putting off the tongue-lashing. Karasu dropped down to the ground. When Kazuki lifted his head and looked at him, the anger he expected wasn't there, only sorrow and disappointment. Karasu scuffed at the dirt beneath his feet.

"You're not going to yell at me?"

"No. I just don't understand. I raised you, so I know you are not a bad person. Why? Why did you do that again? You know she has attacks when she is scared, that they cause her pain. Why did you deliberately try to hurt Sakura?"

"She's annoying. I hate her." Karasu looked away, his pain gnawing at him like a thorn even as guilt began to creep into his heart. "You...she's all you talk about anymore. You spend every minute you can with her, and when she isn't here, you always talk about her. It's like I'm not even here, like you think I'm in the way or something. And you lied, both of you. You said you were just friends, but then you're all over each other. What about the kingdom? What about Master Yuji? You don't even act like you want to go home anymore!"

He knew he was flinging out his feelings like a spoiled child, but he couldn't stop himself. Kazuki pulled him closer and wiped away his tears, stroking his hair the way he used to when he'd been plagued with night terrors.

Once his tears stopped, Kazuki spoke in a quiet voice while still holding him close. "Karasu, you should know I love you very much. You are my brother in all but blood. You could never be a burden on me. I am sorry if I made you feel otherwise. Nor did I mean to lie to you. At the time, I meant what I said. But things changed. In truth, I do not fully understand how it happened myself, but Sakura has become precious to me, so very precious."

Kazuki's voice cracked and he paused with a heavy sigh. "I...I have not forgotten about home, I promise. For now, I have put my faith in Reito, that he will notify us if anything changes. If things were normal, I would likely have gone back home by now, at least for a while. But she does not have long in this world, so I do not wish to lose even a minute of my time with her."

To his horror, he realized Kazuki was crying. "Master Kazuki?"

"Please, my friend, can you endure my selfishness just a little longer that I might stay with her until the end?"

"I...you...you mean she's dying? Not like normal dying but soon dying?"

"Yes." Kazuki swiped at his eyes. "The human medicines

have kept her alive all this time, but they cannot heal her. That is why she has those attacks. Now, she has only a few months left, maybe a year at most."

Karasu dropped to the ground in shame. That girl who smiled at him so kindly was dying? How could she smile like that with such a fate? With his stupid, childish antics, he may very well have sped her death along. He'd just wanted to annoy her, not kill her! So many times he'd told Kazuki and Yuji that he was an adult now, but it was no wonder they hadn't taken him seriously.

"I'm sorry, Master Kazuki. I'm so sorry. I'll never do it again, I promise." Karasu bowed low to the ground, even though he knew the person he really needed to apologize to was inside.

"The fault is mine as well. I should have told you the truth sooner." Kazuki leaned back on the bench to look up at the sunset-stained sky. A light came on in Sakura's bedroom. "It looks like she's awake. She said she wished to talk with you. Will you listen to her?"

Karasu nodded and stood up. "Yes."

"Good. Tell her not to worry about dinner. I shall go pick up something from the store while she rests some more."

"Okay."

Once Kazuki was gone, Karasu made his way up the stairs. The door to her room was cracked open. He pushed it open enough to slip inside. Sakura lay on the bed with her eyes closed. With his eyes no longer clouded by his own jealousy, he could see all the small signs he'd missed before. The unnatural thinness, the grayish undertone in her pale skin. Even her hair seemed a little duller now than he remembered from the first day he arrived.

"Karasu-kun." She started to sit up, even though her voice sounded shaky.

He walked over to the bed so she wouldn't have to raise her voice. "Master Kazuki said you should rest some more. He's getting dinner."

"Oh, okay." She lay back down. "Karasu-kun, I…I'm sorry. I didn't mean to lie to you. I really didn't. I never thought I'd come to love Kazuki like this. I know it's horrible and cruel of me. I don't blame you for hating me. I just…it just happened before I realized it. I…"

"It's okay. Just don't cry anymore, okay?" He grabbed a tissue from her nightstand and shoved it in her hand. "I swear between you and Master Kazuki, I've had all the crying I can take for one day."

"I'm sorry." She gave him a weak smile as she wiped her tears away.

He took a deep breath and bowed deeply. "No…look, I'm sorry, okay? I didn't know about, well, you know, but that isn't any excuse. I've been a selfish brat and I'm sorry."

"Thank you."

"Anyway, I guess I can let you have him for a while. Just make sure you keep making him happy." He nodded, more to himself. "And stay in bed until Master Kazuki gets back, okay? I'm gonna head home."

"Home?"

"Yeah. I'm sure you don't want me hanging around and messing things up anymore."

She reached out and grabbed his hand. Despite her weakness, her grip was firm.

"No, please." He could tell she was fighting to stay awake even as fresh tears streamed down her face. "I…I was so alone before. Then you and Kazuki came. The house stopped feeling empty. I'm not afraid like before because you're both here with me. Please…Karasu-kun…I won't cry anymore, so please don't leave me."

"You're already crying, you know." When he moved closer to wipe the tears away, she hugged him with her free arm. He shook his head as he chuckled. "You really are a greedy little human, aren't you?"

He returned the embrace, careful not to squeeze her thin shoulders too hard. "I guess it isn't so bad here. If you're sure, then fine, I'll stay."

She smiled at him and her grip relaxed as she fell asleep again. After straightening the covers around her, he walked over to the desk and sat in the chair to watch over her until Kazuki returned.

THE FESTIVAL

"**KARASU-KUN! BREAKFAST!**" Sakura called out the side door, but he didn't fly down like usual. She didn't see his little black body in the tree at all. "Karasu-kun?"

"He's not there," Kazuki said from the living room doorway. "I'm sorry. I forgot to tell you, he won't be joining us for breakfast today. I sent him back to our world."

"No! Why? He apologized and we're okay now."

Kazuki smiled and hugged her. "I didn't send him back as punishment. He's running an errand for me, that's all. He should be back by evening, tomorrow at the latest. I promise."

"Oh, thank goodness." She slid the screen door closed and followed him to the kitchen. "We're finally able to really be friends, so I want to talk to him more."

When she'd woken up, Kazuki had helped her downstairs for dinner. While they ate, Karasu had joined their conversation rather than just eating and leaving like he usually did. He no longer looked tense and grumpy, and he'd even agreed to move into the attic once it was too cold to sleep outside.

Once they finished breakfast, Kazuki cleared the breakfast dishes while insisting she stay seated. After he was done, he came back to the table and put his hands on her shoulders, a small frown overtaking his features.

"Sakura, you didn't sleep well last night. Do not try to deny this. I sleep beside you, remember?"

"I'm sorry. I kept you awake?"

"'Tis fine, I do not mind. But will you be okay today? As much as I wish to see the festival, it is not worth risking your health."

She touched his cheek as she smiled at him. "I'm fine, I promise. I'll let you know if I get too tired, and I'll take a nap before the ball."

"Good. Since we have a few hours yet before we leave, will you indulge my worrying nature and rest until then? I know you usually clean the house Saturday mornings, but I shall do your part and mine. So please?"

"All right."

"Thank you." He kissed her forehead then her lips before sending her on her way. She spent the morning lying in the living room, reading the next volume of her favorite novel series. An ad in the front noted that the final volume would be released in December, just before Christmas. *At least I'll get to find out how it ends.* She shoved the morose thought away. It wasn't the day for indulging in such darkness.

At some point, she must have dozed off, as Kazuki woke her just before noon to get ready. They rode the tram down the one stop between her house and the school to reduce the amount of walking they had to do. Hina was waiting for them by the gate.

"Sakura-chan! Kazuki-san!" She bounced over to them, kicking up the long skirt of her winter uniform in the process. "The second concert starts pretty soon, so do you want to go over there first?"

"Sure, we can't miss his performance. What about Akari-san?"

Hina grimaced. "She's stuck running all over the place because of her student council duties, so she'll meet up with us later."

"It's too bad she couldn't get a break for today at least. I guess there is lots to deal with behind the scenes."

In the school auditorium, they managed to find seats close enough to see everyone on stage. Moments later, the lights dimmed and the curtain opened. A spotlight appeared, aimed at a single grand piano in the middle of the stage. A girl came out, bowed, then began playing the first movement of Beethoven's "Moonlight Sonata." Sakura closed her eyes as the haunting notes washed over her. It had always been one of her favorite pieces to play. Kazuki's hand covered hers with a light squeeze, and she turned her palm up so she could hold his hand, pushing aside the tinge of sorrow to enjoy the song.

When the movement concluded, the rest of the performers slid out in a smoothly choreographed sequence, and the spotlight grew bigger, revealing the large drum set on stage. These students played a more upbeat song, with jazz undertones. Hina's Genji Yamaguchi walked onto the stage, taking his place at the drum set. In class, he seemed so quiet and shy that Sakura had expected him to play something with a softer sound, like a flute or a violin, but the tempo surged in a thrilling crescendo before its abrupt end. The audience erupted with cheers as the students bowed before rearranging the stage for their next piece.

After the concert, they went back outside.

"You guys hungry?" Hina asked with a hopeful expression.

Sakura chuckled. Akari had warned her that Hina's priority

would be food. "I suppose I could eat."

"Yes, I have seen much on the television about the foods served at festivals, and I would like to try some. What do you recommend we have?" Kazuki asked. Sakura had already told her friends that he was a foreigner who'd only been in Japan a short while.

"Leave it to me! I scoped out all the food options earlier." Hina pulled one of the festival maps out of her pocket and held it against the nearby wall. "The closest to us is the cooking club's yakisoba[36] booth. It smelled so good when I walked by! Then on to 3-C's crepe café! They have chocolate, strawberry, and banana. Inside, one of the first-year classes has onigiri. Oh, and we have to make sure to get some choco bananas[37] from 2-A's booth."

"Amazing! This looks like an excellent plan, Hina-chan!" Kazuki nodded in approval as he studied the map.

"Oh, Hina." Sakura laughed as she shook her head at them. "It is a pretty good plan, though maybe we could look at some of the exhibits in there somewhere?"

Hina smiled sheepishly. "Sure!"

Once they were done with lunch, they walked around, exploring the various booths and exhibitions. The art clubs had displays of their members' best works: drawings, paintings, floral arrangements, and sculptures. Costumed characters from the drama club mingled in the crowd. Romeo and Juliet

---

[36] Fried ramen-style noodles, made from wheat flour, with a thick, sweetened sauce, vegetables, and a protein.

[37] A popular festival food made by taking a frozen banana, jabbing a stick in it, and then dipping it in a thin coat of chocolate. It is often topped with sprinkles before the chocolate sets. Many vendors offer variations featuring white chocolate coatings flavored with green tea, strawberry, mint, or the like.

stopped in front of them and did an impressive impromptu version of the balcony scene.

The literary club had turned the building by the library into a haunted house.

As they neared the entrance, Sakura stopped. "I'll wait here for you guys. I can't handle scary stuff."

"I hate to leave you here alone, though. We could go look at something else," Hina said.

"No, please go on through. Kazuki has never been in one, so I don't want him to miss his chance."

"Are you sure you don't mind, Sakura?" Kazuki asked.

She smiled and nodded. "Please, go. I'll wait right here."

"Okay." Though Hina still seemed reluctant, the pair headed inside. Sakura waited until they were out of sight before making her way to the nearby bathroom. She'd been trying to think of an excuse to sneak off for the last fifteen minutes, so the haunted house had been a welcome sight. Despite the crowd, the bathroom was empty. Still, to be safe, she filled a paper cup with water then ducked into one of the stalls to swallow the pills.

Just as she arrived back at the entrance, she heard Akari call her name from behind her.

She turned. "Hi, Akari-san. Are you finished for the day?"

"Until the festival part is over anyway. Then I'll have a little work to do before the ball."

"It must be tough."

"It's hard work, but seeing how much fun everyone is having is worth it. Where's Hina?"

"She's in there with Kazuki."

"Not a fan of haunted houses?" Akari smiled when Sakura shook her head. "Me either, to tell you the truth."

Sakura looked around as she realized Akari was alone. "Did Aki-san come to the festival?"

"No, he couldn't make it to this part. With my duties, I wouldn't have been able to show him around much anyway. I'll introduce you to him at the ball, though."

"Okay. I look forward to it."

"Hey, Akari!" Hina called out as she ran out of the haunted house's exit, looking anything but scared. An amused Kazuki followed her. "You're just in time for the crepes!"

"Hina, are you really following that crazy map of yours?"

"Of course!"

Akari rolled her eyes then laughed. "It certainly made it easier to find you, anyway."

"How was your first haunted house?" Sakura asked Kazuki.

"It was interesting, though I must admit, not terribly scary. Even Hina-san seemed unaffected, despite the stereotype that girls scream in these sorts of things."

"Not much scares Hina," Akari said. "Knowing Hina, she was laughing the whole time."

Hina tried to pout as if offended but she started laughing herself. "Only a little. I didn't want to hurt their feelings. Anyway, let's get some crepes!"

By the time they'd hit all of the food places on Hina's map, they were stuffed. Most of them anyway. As they went back to the school gate, Hina wondered if they should get sno-cones.

"No more, Hina, please. My stomach can't take another bite," Sakura pleaded.

"I guess you're right. Should save some room for dinner at the ball tonight! Oh, before we go, we should go to the fortune-telling booth."

Hina led them across the street to the shrine, where members of the Japanese club had been allowed to set up their fortune-telling stand. The three girls running the booth were dressed in the flowing red hakama[38] and crisp white haori[39] that formed the traditional miko[40] attire.

The group took turns shaking the old-fashioned octagonal box before turning it to let a numbered stick fall out. After handing it to the girl behind the counter, she retrieved their fortunes from like-numbered drawers behind her. Each was loosely curled and tied with a paper band.

Kazuki looked so excited as he took his fortune and opened it.

"'Great luck! Your fondest wish will be realized with patience, the one you wish to see will soon appear, and the love you share will be returned tenfold.' This is a very good fortune indeed!"

Sakura unrolled her own fortune. Her smile faded as she looked at the page before her.

"Sakura-chan?" Hina glanced over her shoulder. "What is it? Eh, blank?"

"It's the best kind of fortune," Akari declared.

"How so?" Hina asked.

"It means Sakura can write her own wish, one that is sure to come true."

"Really?"

"Yes." Akari turned back to Sakura. "But you must decide your wish quickly."

---

[38] Long divided trousers or a long, slightly pleated skirt tied with a bow.

[39] A kimono jacket.

[40] Shrine maiden—the closest equivalent in the West might be a shaman. Whether they are working in a shrine or outside, miko traditionally perform various spiritual rites, such as divining, driving out evil spirits, and performing sacred ceremonial dances.

"Oh, okay. Thank you." Sakura smiled at her, then carefully wrote out her wish on the paper and folded it. Together, the group went to the sacred tree nearby to tie their fortune slips to the branches. Though she knew it was futile, she stood with the others in front of the shrine, each with their hands clasped in front of them and heads bowed, and she prayed with all her might.

Please, give me just a little more time.

It was late at night when Karasu stepped through the portal between the human world and Throklana. That Kazuki trusted him with this mission was all the proof he needed that he'd been forgiven for his behavior toward Sakura. He just hoped he could complete his task quickly.

Reito waved at him from between the two columns that flanked the terrace in front of the portal. "Welcome back."

"Thanks." He spotted the guards that usually stood in front of the columns lying in the grass.

"A mild sleeping spell. After getting Prince Kazuki's message, it seemed prudent to avoid having too many people see you. Stay quiet and follow me. We'll take the longer way back to avoid being spotted."

Reito shifted into his full fox form before turning and trotting back toward the castle. Even with his steady, distance-eating gait and Karasu flying overhead, it took them a while to traverse Reito's rambling path to the castle. As they neared the building, Karasu dipped lower, gliding from tree to tree as Reito crept between the trunks. They hugged the sides of the castle for a brief moment before entering through the open window into Reito's chambers.

Once they were inside, they both shifted back. Reito pulled the windows closed and drew the curtains before sitting at the desk nestled in the corner of the room.

"Now then. What exactly is going on in the human world?" He picked up the letter Kazuki sent out just before Karasu left Sakura's house. "The young master says he needs a spell to cure a human of broken organs?"

"Yeah. Well, you already know about Sakura, right?"

"Ah, so this is for the daughter of his late human friend with whom you're residing?"

Karasu nodded. "Her organs don't work right anymore because she was stabbed and now she's dying. The human doctors said she'll be gone by summer, most likely. Since they can't fix her, Master Kazuki thought that maybe a spell could."

"I see. To repay her kindness and honor his old friend is a worthy notion. It is the sort of idea I would expect of him, but surely the prince realizes there are limits to even the greatest of magic? Even our king could not save Her Majesty from death."

"Well, he thought there might be something that wouldn't work for us that might work for her since she's just a human." Karasu debated telling Reito about Kazuki's personal feelings for Sakura, but for now he kept it to himself. It wouldn't help the situation, and could make Reito decide that Kazuki had been in the human world long enough.

Reito rested his chin on his hand, his curled-up fingers covering his mouth. His other hand rested on the edge of his desk, one finger tapping the surface in slow, steady beats. After a long pause, he sighed heavily. "Very well. Let's check the archives. It might be best if you change your form again. I'll carry you under my robe, just in case anyone is wandering around."

Tucked under the heavy garments, Karasu could hear little

but the clicking of Reito's boots on the hall as he made his way to the archive room. Despite the shortness of time, he moved in an unhurried fashion, probably to avoid suspicion. Still, Karasu was glad when he heard the metallic sounds of a key turning in a lock. A door squeaked open. A few more clicks, then the door closed with a solid thunk, and the lock slid back into place. Reito lifted him out from under his robe so he could change back.

"First, just to be safe." Reito turned and chanted something while touching the door. Karasu thought he saw a flash. "That barrier won't stop anyone, only slow them down a bit. It'll seem as if the lock is rusty. That will give us warning while avoiding unnecessary questions. Now then, spells are contained in sections seven through eleven, but most of the ones that might pertain to this situation are in the eighth section, back this way."

The massive room was filled with long rows of shelves that in turn were crammed full with books, so many it made the castle library look like a piddling traveling seller's cart in comparison. In the center of the room were a few tables with chairs lined around them where one could sit and read. At the end of each shelf stood deep cabinets lined with drawers that Karasu guessed contained maps or scrolls. Little signs above the cabinets seemed to indicate the section and shelf numbers. As they walked down the aisles, the lights overhead brightened to light the path.

At the eighth section, Reito walked up to the first shelf and removed a tall stack of books. He carried them to the nearest table.

"Here." He handed three of the books to Karasu. "The shelves are indexed in these books. It will be faster to search them first, rather than the individual books. Look for anything that mentions humans, heavy wounds, or the like."

"Okay." Karasu pulled out a chair and sat down across from Reito. "How many indexes are there?"

"One thousand two hundred and forty-one." Reito seemed undaunted as he began running his finger along the lines of the book he'd opened, his finger just high enough above the page to avoid touching the paper. Karasu took a deep breath and opened the first book. He owed them this much, at least.

Princess Night

THOUGH THE SCHOOL WAS A short distance from Sakura's home, they rode the tram back. Kazuki was certain she'd pushed herself to appear normal while keeping up with her friends. It was on the tip of his tongue to suggest they skip the rest, but he hated to try to pull her back when she'd finally started living again. If she still seemed too tired after she rested, he could deal with getting her to stay home then.

"Akari-san is a kind girl, isn't she?" Sakura murmured as she leaned her head against his shoulder.

"Yes, yes she is." He closed his eyes as his chest grew tight. He hoped Sakura hadn't known, that she'd bought Akari's sweet lie. A blank fortune was an anomaly, one taken as a strong sign that the receiver had no future at all. He squeezed her hand.

As they stood in the foyer of her house and changed their shoes, Kazuki noticed how heavily she leaned against the wall. "Your hands are shaking."

"Oh." She looked down at the betraying body part as if she'd been unaware of it until then. "I...I promised I'd rest, didn't I?"

"Yes, you did." He bent down to tuck his arm under her legs and lift her up. "Allow me."

As he walked up the stairs, she wrapped her arms around his neck. "I didn't get to enjoy this before…It is rather nice. No wonder they are always doing it in movies."

He chuckled as he shouldered open the bedroom door. Once she was settled in the bed, he leaned forward to kiss her forehead, glad to see she was half-asleep already. "I'll wake you when it is time to get ready."

"Lie with me, just for a little while, please." Sleep slurred her words. "It's hard to sleep without you now. It's cold and lonely."

"If you wish." He crawled to the other side and lay beside her, wrapping her in his arms as she turned to face him. He could feel her lips turn up in a smile as she snuggled against his chest.

My sudtama, the day you leave this world, this one shall sleep no more. He brushed his lips against her forehead.

Hiro…if I told you I'm falling in love with your daughter, would you forgive me? I know I am not worthy of her, but I cannot seem to help myself. That blank page in her hand, it only drove it home all the more. If I try to picture a life without her, my heart feels as if it will shatter. I won't let her die.

By the gods, I am one of the most powerful yokai in Throklana. Somehow, surely, I can save her from this fate that she might have a long life yet to come. Please, guide Karasu and Reito. Help them find the spell that will save her. It must be there, buried in the archives, something, anything.

He woke as dusk began to touch the horizon. After checking the watch on her table, he shook her shoulder while calling her name. With a moan, Sakura's eyes blinked open and she gave him a sleepy smile. He was kissing her before he realized it, a deep kiss that left them both panting.

"It's time." He had to force himself to move away and let

her get up. She blushed as she sat on the edge of the bed. For a moment, they were a normal couple waking up with plans for a romantic evening. Then her hand reached for the pills to take her next dose. Her sigh sounded as filled with regret as his own.

He retreated to Hiro's old room to put on the black formal suit she'd bought him. He tied his long hair back into a neat ponytail, held at the base of his neck with a simple black ribbon. Once he'd clipped the bow tie in place, he came back out to find Sakura waiting in the hall.

"It looks really good on you." She gave him an approving look.

"But of course, I am me after all." He struck a pose as he grinned at her.

Once she stopped laughing, she pointed to the stairs with her own imperial pose. "Downstairs with thee and no peeking!"

"Yes, ma'am." He walked down the stairs to wait, pacing back and forth as he tried to imagine how she would look. The little minx had refused to let him see her dress at all. She'd carried it into the house fully covered and when he asked about it, she refused to even say what color it was. Of course, he could have looked anyway since he was home alone all day, but he wasn't about to ruin her fun.

"All done," Sakura called from the landing as her soft steps approached the stairs. "Are you looking? My dress demands nothing less than a proper entrance."

For all the languages he knew, not a single coherent word came to mind when Sakura stopped on the top step. The iridescent royal-blue gown accented her every curve while softening the edges of her thin frame. Silver embroidery adorned its gathered skirt, as well as the long, detached sleeves. A flash of skin separated the sleeves from the similarly adorned strapless bodice.

Simple, but elegant silver drop earrings dangled from her ears. A silver necklace with a jeweled blue pendant dipped down to a point just above the gentle swell of her breasts. She'd teased her hair into a riot of waves that made him want to dive his fingers between them. It was pulled back to one side with the flowered hair clip he'd seen on her dressing table, the white-and-pink ribbons riding the waves as she moved.

Holding the front of her skirt up slightly to avoid stepping on it, she descended the stairs. The way the rest of the skirt swished from side to side had his eyes following it like a cat watching a string. Then she was standing in front of him, a wholly feminine smile on her face as she watched him watching her. He cleared his throat and tried to find some words to properly compliment her, but they still refused to come. Unable to resist, he leaned in to kiss her neck, letting himself revel in the combination of her own sweet scent and the light cherry blossom fragrance she was wearing. Never had he wanted to smear a woman's lip coloring so much as he did right then.

"There are no words for how enthralled you have left me."

"Thank you." Her cheeks turned pink as she floated toward the entry to exchange her house slippers for a pair of royal-blue heels that made her tall enough to brush her head under his chin. He nearly cried out when she put on her coat, blocking his view of her.

"My lady, our chariot awaits." He bowed with a flourish as he opened the door and led her to the taxi waiting outside.

Sakura kept her arm linked with Kazuki's as they entered the transformed cafeteria. Gold velvet bunting decorated the outside walls, while gold silk streamers looped down across the ceiling, softening the otherwise stark lighting. In the center of the room was space set up to allow couples to dance later. Tables of hors d'oeuvres and other finger foods ran the length of the interior wall for guests to pick from.

The usual rectangular tables were gone, replaced with smaller round ones for six set up along the edge of the room. Crisp white linens edged in gold accents covered each table with centerpieces of red, white, and yellow roses tucked around silver candles in glass bases. The school's music club played in another corner, displaying the talent that had enabled them to bring home the trophy from the regional competitions nearly every year.

Mingling among the crowd, underclassman cleared plates, refilled glasses, and kept the buffet stocked. Unlike the festival, the ball was only for the third-year students, a gift from the other classes for the graduating seniors.

Hina waved to them from where she stood with Yamaguchi-san by one of the tables nearest the buffet. She looked adorable in her white silk charmeuse gown. A large red flower motif started in a bottom corner of the A-line skirt and traveled halfway up and around, giving it a splash of color. Her usual pigtails had been set free, her blond hair decorated instead with a large white headband.

Beside her, a beaming Yamaguchi-san seemed happy to look at nothing but Hina all night. With a start, Sakura realized he was missing something. "Yamaguchi-san, your glasses?"

As if remembering the wire-rim glasses he seemed to shove back into position every few minutes, he reached toward his face. With a sheepish grin, he scratched his head instead. "I decided to try wearing contacts tonight."

"It just makes him even cuter," Hina said as she squeezed his arm. The poor boy turned red as Sakura tried not to laugh. "Ah, there's Akari."

Sakura had been shocked at the dress Akari chose. Looking at her now, though, she had to admit, it worked. The bold dark-red chiffon dress managed to be both modest and sexy with its sheer skirt over a matching solid one and its shirred strapless bodice. Walking beside her was the second best-looking man there, after Kazuki of course. Tall with neatly trimmed hair, he wore his black suit well, giving him a dashing appearance as he escorted Akari over to them. Sakura didn't blame Hina for crushing on this man at all.

"Sakura-chan, Kazuki-san, this is my brother, Aki."

"Pleased to meet you." Sakura bowed lightly.

"Good evening, nice to meet you." Kazuki shook his hand with a friendly smile.

"Likewise. I've heard much about you." He spoke with a smooth, deep voice.

After they enjoyed their meal, the couples moved to the dance floor. Sakura placed one hand on Kazuki's shoulder and the other in his raised hand for the waltz that began to play, following his lead as he danced them around the floor. As they swayed in time to the slow rhythm, she found herself wanting to move closer. Every accidental brush of their bodies made her own tingle. Seeing the way his eyes darkened as he looked at her gave her a heady feeling.

"Behave yourself," he whispered, his voice ragged sounding.

She smiled, feigning innocence. She'd realized that deliberately brushing him just so made him draw in his breath, and it was because of her. *So this is the power of a woman.* She wanted him crazy for her. She wanted him to kiss her the way he had before. The barely restrained passion had left her desperate for his touch.

Last night, as they lay together, she'd been aware of his

every breath, of the warmth where their bodies touched, of his earthy, masculine scent. The temptation to turn around and explore the hard muscles that held her so securely every night was strong, but she forced herself to stay still. She was excited yet scared of the things she'd begun to picture, of what it would be like to be with him.

As the first song shifted into another slow number, she berated herself for teasing him and herself. No matter how wonderful it felt or how much she might want more, she knew it was impossible. She'd even visited Tenma-sensei, blushing as she asked if it was safe for her to make love. That led to her telling him about Kazuki, though not how they met.

After she'd addressed his concerns that she was being used and promised to introduce him later, he'd finally answered her. In a regret-filled tone, he'd told her no. The strain would be too great, especially at this stage and with the number of attacks she'd had in the last month.

"No sad thoughts tonight, little one." Kazuki's warm breath teased her skin as he whispered near her ear.

"I'm sorry." She forced herself to smile up at him, letting herself enjoy the song rather than giving in to the sorrow.

At the song's end, Kazuki led her off the floor and through the outer doors to the balcony, grabbing them fresh drinks from a passing server. With the cool air, they had most of the balcony to themselves. Only one other couple was there, but they stood on the far side, the shadows masking their identity.

Sakura sipped at the tangy punch as she leaned on the bunting-wrapped railing and looked out over the school garden. The colorful flowers formed silhouettes of merged shapes that danced in the shadows cast by the courtyard spotlight. A breeze sent a slight shiver up her half-bared arms.

Kazuki wrapped his jacket around her shoulders, then

leaned back on the balcony beside her so he could see her face. "What's wrong? Are you feeling ill?"

It would be easy to write it off as tiredness, letting the evening end early so she could keep her thoughts to herself. What good would it do to tell him? Yet standing there, looking into his eyes, she couldn't bring herself to lie.

"When you look at me like you did earlier when you saw my dress. When we hold hands. When we kiss. Even when you laugh while we watch TV. All these feelings well up inside me. I want more. I want to touch you. I want you to touch me. I want to…" She paused to fight back the desire to cry.

Kazuki didn't look much happier. He lifted his hand toward her face before dropping it back to his side. "I…It is the same for me. Never have I wanted a woman as much as I want you. If I could, I'd take you home this very moment and make love to you until we collapsed in exhaustion. I would kiss every inch of your skin and say to you with our bodies the words my mind cannot form. But I know this is something I cannot do, something we cannot allow ourselves, for I could never risk it causing you harm."

She gripped the railing as his words washed over her. There was no denying the facts. No matter how slowly they took it, love-making would be an exertion and could potentially trigger an attack too great even for the nitro and her inhaler to handle. At best, she'd end up in the hospital for days; at worst, she'd turn Kazuki into a killer. For the first time in a long time, Sakura cursed the fate that left her with this condition.

"You told me before that you'd never regret meeting me. Do you still feel that way now?"

Kazuki straightened beside her and stroked her cheek. "I do not regret the day I fell into your life, and I never will. I want you so much it hurts, yes, but that is only a small pain that I can endure so long as I can stay by your side. Let us not darken this night with regrets for what we cannot have. Instead, let us celebrate these moments that no one can take from us."

"Yes, you're right." She smiled up at him. "I want to make beautiful memories tonight, the night I got to pretend I'm your princess."

After scanning the area for any teacher chaperons, he gave her a quick peck on her lips. "You will always be my princess."

With a sweet smile, he held out his hand to her. Shaking off the lingering sadness, she tucked her hand in his.

As they headed back inside, they ran into Hina. "Ah, there you are. Come on, they just put out the desserts!" With Hina holding onto her other arm, Sakura laughed as she was led back to the buffet table to sample the sumptuous cakes now on display.

THE DOHAME

IT WAS STILL EARLY WHEN Kazuki slipped out of bed and went downstairs. The evening had left Sakura exhausted. He hoped she would sleep in as long as she could. Too restless to sit still, he went downstairs to make some tea and talk to Ito for a while.

He'd just set the pot on the tea tray when he heard the screen door slide open.

"I'm back."

He set another cup on the tea tray before leaving the kitchen, forcing himself to walk at a normal pace to avoid spilling anything. Karasu stood waiting for him, his shoulders drooping.

"Welcome back." Kazuki set down the tray on the kotatsu and sat down. "How did it go?"

"It was exhausting." Karasu plopped down across from him and poured himself a cup. "We really should get one of those computer things or something for the archives. It would be so much easier than spending ten days going through seven hundred and twenty freaking books line by line! Where's Sakura?"

"Still sleeping, recovering from yesterday."

Karasu nodded, and with a tired sigh, he pulled out two

folded-up pages and passed them across the table. "It isn't a cure, but it's the best we found so far."

The top page was a note from Reito.

Prince Kazukiarama,

The recipe Karasu is delivering to you is for a potion called the dohame. I must stress now, before your hopes are raised too high, that it cannot save the girl's life. It can only give her some relief from her symptoms and ease her suffering. It is a spell created to allow a dying person a few hours of peace that they may say goodbye to their loved ones.

It will not erase her injury or illness. Rather, you might say, it will freeze and seal it, temporarily. In essence, while the dohame is in effect, it will be as if she were a completely healthy person.

For most yokai of our stature, its effects would last only an hour or two. In smaller and younger yokai, the potion has been shown to last longer. As such, with her human body, it may last several hours or even a day or two. She will know when the potion is wearing off, as she will grow sleepy and her body will feel a bit numb. This side-effect will wear off after a few hours of rest.

She can drink subsequent doses of the dohame; however, it will lose its effectiveness more rapidly each time. Excessive repeated use or using multiple doses in close succession can create a false sensation of health, causing her to think it is in effect when it is not. Combined with the requirements to create it, I would urge that its use be sparse and with deliberate consideration.

My Prince…though young Karasu has not said as much, I can deduce this girl is someone you hold in high affection. I will not chide you for being close to a human nor will I chide you for remaining there at her side during these times. You are very much your father's son. Yet even he could not prevent a human's life from coming to its unnatural end nor could he heal the late queen's illness, despite his strong desire to save them both.

I will continue searching the remaining indexes for any-thing else that may help your Sakura. However, for your sake and hers, let the dohame help her to fulfill any final wishes she may have that she may pass with no lingering regrets.

Reito

Kazuki crumpled the letter and tossed it aside. He knew it had been a long shot, but still, he hated seeing it written so plainly.

"He said you'd do that." Karasu watched him with worried eyes. "Still, he felt it was his duty to say it. It took him a long time to write."

"I know. I know. I just…" Kazuki forced himself to push aside the pain Reito's words had caused. He had no doubt Reito had measured every word and phrase before committing them to paper.

Karasu set a canvas bag beside the table. "I brought the in-gredients, enough for five doses. Reito said we could make one batch and store it for up to three human months in a cool spot like the fridge. But I don't know if she'll go along with drinking it when she knows how it is made."

Kazuki scanned the second page. "Yokai blood?"

"Yeah. Reito said it would be best if it's yours, since you're the most connected to her and because of the amount of power inherently found in royal blood."

"That makes sense. As you said, though, convincing Sakura is another matter. I hate the thought that this will be what Reito says, nothing more than a way to let her live out her dreams. But I know we must also be realistic and face the current facts. So this will be a gift to her, to use as she chooses." Kazuki read the recipe again. "We can make it while she is in school tomorrow, so she does not have to see the bloodletting part."

"Maybe we shouldn't tell her what's in it? If she doesn't know about the blood, she'd probably drink it without question."

Kazuki leaned back on his hands and stared at the ceiling. It was a tempting thought. Even yokai shared humans' distaste for the idea of drinking blood from one of their own kind, and to Sakura, drinking his blood would be no different than drinking someone like Hina's. But to lie and hide it? If she found out later what they had done…he shuddered to think about how she would react.

It was mid-morning when Sakura was able to shake off the heavy dregs of sleep and get out of bed. From the cool feeling beside her, she guessed Kazuki had been up a while. Still yawning, she threw on a comfortable sweat suit and gave her hair the minimum brushing needed to put it in a ponytail. Her body felt achy and stiff. She was glad Kazuki had made her promise to rest all day. Curling up in a blanket and reading a book or snuggling in front of the TV sounded good to her.

On the way down the stairs, she heard voices coming from the living room. With a smile, she hurried as best she could and threw open the door. Kazuki and Karasu were already looking her way. They both smiled, but they seemed strained. Pushing her concern aside, she continued across the room, happy to see the young boy was back.

"Karasu-kun! Welcome home!" She dropped down beside him to throw her arms around his neck and hug him.

"Oy, oy!" He laughed as he tried to steady himself. "I wasn't gone that long."

"I missed you, though." She sat back on her heels with a smile and clapped her hands together. "Did you have breakfast already?"

His stomach growled in response, making him blush. "Not yet."

"How about pancakes then?"

"With blueberries?" He grinned.

"Of course. So did your errand go well?"

Karasu's smile dropped along with his gaze. "Um, yeah, I guess."

Across the table, Kazuki, who'd been watching her from the moment she walked in, was now absurdly interested in the screen door. Sakura looked from one fidgeting guy to the other. "What? What's wrong? Did something happen with Yuji?"

Kazuki gave her a quick look but refused to hold her gaze. "No, nothing like that. According to Reito, thus far he's stayed quiet since his attempt on my life and only vague reports of sightings have been heard."

"Then what is it? Why are you both acting so strange all of a sudden?"

"It's...I..." Kazuki covered his face with his hand, his brows knitted together. It was the first time since she'd met him that she'd have said he looked unsure of himself. After taking a deep breath, his hand came down and his eyes opened. His gaze was steadier, though the expression in his eyes made her reach out and cover his free hand with her own. He turned his hand up to twine their fingers together before continuing. "Sakura, since learning the truth of your condition, I've thought about how I might help you. I know the human doctors have said there is nothing they can do, but they do not possess the magic we do. When I realized your condition seemed to be worsening, I knew it was time to act, so I had Karasu return home to search our archives with Reito to see if something there could heal you."

"Oh, I never thought about that. I knew you had some magical abilities, but fixing me?" How would Tenma-sensei react if she just walked in healed? But she suspected that wouldn't be happening, no matter how amazing it sounded. Not from the serious expressions on Kazuki and Karasu's faces.

"Yes, that was the idea, at least. The archives are quite large, so it can take time to search. After ten days of searching…"

"Ten days? But Karasu-kun was only gone one day or so."

"Sorry, yes, time passes more quickly there. In the time it takes a year to pass in this world, about ten pass in my own."

"That's right. I remember. Then you really were gone a while?" she said to Karasu, who answered with a nod. That meant, presuming their years were the same length, that to his fellow yokai, Kazuki had been away from home for almost half a year! Did that mean he had to go home soon?

Kazuki coughed. "Anyway, the best thing found thus far is a potion called the dohame. Unfortunately, it is not a cure, but…well, it would temporarily make your body whole again. It is used to…to allow those…those who are dying a chance to say goodbye or do anything they have always wanted to do so they have no regrets on going."

"I could do anything?"

"Yes. While it is in effect, it would be as if you had a perfectly healthy, functioning body. You could run down the street or dance for hours. Anything you would be able to physically do in a healthy body, you could do once you take the dohame. There would be no attacks, no need to fear harming your health."

Her breath caught in her throat. She could do anything? Even make love with Kazuki? A blush crept across her cheeks and she swallowed the question. Karasu was sitting right beside her after all. If it were summer, she could go to the beach and play in the waves? She could climb Hakodate rather than take the ropeway? They could go on a long trip to see more sights in Japan? So why did they not look happier?

"How long would it last?"

"In most yokai, it would only be a few hours, but being human, you will be affected by it for longer, possibly a day or two. In that regard, we won't know for sure until the first time you take it, and that would only be the first time. Each time you take it, the effects are weakened, and thus it would not last as long."

"That doesn't sound too bad. Do you not trust this potion?"

He fiddled with a piece of parchment-like paper on the table. Sharp-lined characters flowed down the page. They were not that dissimilar in nature to katakana, yet they felt foreign. She was fascinated to see what she guessed was written yokai, but it seemed whatever was written there did not make Kazuki happy.

"No, I do," he finally answered. "I know enough of the basics of magic recipes to recognize its nature is sound. It's just…the potion is made using…it…One of the ingredients is blood, my blood, specifically."

"Blood?" Sakura felt the color drain from her face as she pulled her hand free to cover her mouth. She'd have to drink

Kazuki's blood for the potion to work? And Kazuki would have to let some unknown amount of blood be taken from his body? Granted, he'd healed from the stab wounds within a few days, but still, drink blood? She shook her head over and over. "No. I could never."

"Sakura, it wouldn't hurt me, I promise. I have plenty to spare. I know it is a somewhat disgusting ingredient, but wouldn't it be worth it?"

She looked down and shook her head one more time.

"But, Sakura…" Karasu leaned toward her.

"Absolutely not. I appreciate both of you finding such a thing, but I will not drink Kazuki's blood. That's final." She stood, trying to ignore the disappointed feeling growing inside her. If it didn't require someone's blood, she'd already be agreeing. If it were just fish blood or something, she could consider it. But taking blood from Kazuki to have such brief reprieve? Out of the question. "Now, I'm going to go make breakfast."

Later that night, while Kazuki was showering for bed, Sakura pulled out a well-worn piece of paper from her bedside-table drawer. She perched on the edge of the bed and unfolded it, her hands trembling. She'd written it one night after watching a movie from America about two friends who were both terminally ill, like her. Though they were old men rather than a young girl, she'd enjoyed the bittersweet story of their trip to fulfill life-long wishes before they died.

The words on the page blurred from the tears forming in her eyes.

Sakura's Bucket List

1. *Graduate high school*
2. *Stand at the base of Mount Fuji*
3. *Go to the top of Tokyo Tower*
4. *Tour Himeji Castle*

5. *Go swimming with dolphins*
6. *Ride in a hot air balloon*
7. *Visit the Asahiyama Zoo*
8. *Drink a glass of wine*
9. *Fly a kite*
10. *Release a sky lantern*
11. *Go to an amusement park*
12. *Try doing cosplay*
13. *Drive a car*
14. *See a waterfall*
15. *Go to another country*

The dohame would let her do some of the things on the list, but not at the expense of consuming Kazuki's blood. She knew they thought she was being unreasonable, but her stomach turned at even the thought of it. With a cry, she crushed the paper in her hand and threw it in the trash can.

As they lay in bed, Kazuki held her as close as he could. Her fingers dug into his shoulders as she returned the embrace. Could she hear her time ticking away as well, the specter of death looking ever closer?

They hadn't spoken any more about the dohame. The rest of the day had been quiet, normal. With Sakura sitting in a chair, she'd directed them in cleaning up the attic for Karasu after seeing a report that the first snow was expected soon. It hadn't taken long. The few boxes were pushed into a corner, and the futon from the living room moved in along with a small table and a dresser that had been in Hiro's old room. He'd been surprised Karasu hadn't argued that it wasn't cold enough yet, but he'd been cheerful, even solicitous with Sakura. Perhaps he too could feel their time growing shorter.

Kazuki wondered if the pain in his chest was anything close to what she felt during an attack. He'd had sex with several women in the castle. He wasn't a kid after all. But Sakura, the one he could not even physically claim, she would be the one who would haunt his dreams. She he would mourn for a long time to come. Hundreds, even thousands of years from now, she would still live in his heart.

For a moment, he wished he could go with her when she did, but suicide would only dishonor her memory and make her angry with him should they be reunited in the afterlife. It may only be a few months, but he knew the one thing that he wanted, needed, that they could do, even without the dohame.

He shifted so he could look into her eyes. "Mate with me."

Sakura's eyes opened wide, a flurry of emotions dancing across them so fast he couldn't catch any. They settled on a mix of pain and sorrow. "But, we can't. My body, no matter how careful we are."

He smiled and shook his head. "I do not mean make love, though believe me if I could I would be inside you now. I mean be my life mate, my…what's the word…spouse?"

"I…you want to marry me?" A wet drop rolled down her cheek to hit his hand. Then another.

"Yes, that. You, you are my *sudtama*. Even if our time remaining is short, let me be with you as your mate and shower you with all the love I hold in my heart."

"Kazuki…" She wrapped her arms around his neck and pulled him against her body, her face buried in his shoulder. He was afraid to breathe, afraid to think, certain she was about to refuse. A moment later, her mouth moved against his shoulders, her voice muffled. "I want a Western-style wedding, with a white dress and everything."

Thrilled, he kissed her lips, keeping a tight leash on his passion while making sure she knew how happy he was.

When he let her up for air, she blushed. "And everyone has to be there. Karasu, Hina, Akari, Tenma-sensei."

"It will be as you wish."

"What about your family?"

"Ah, yes. While Father has not returned, I will inform Reito. If he can send Father word, I'm sure he will join. As for Yuji, it has been quite a while now. Perhaps his silence is a good sign his temper has cooled and we can try to talk. If we can return to normal, I would very much want him there. I think you both would get on famously."

"Yes, from the way you've talked about him, I think I would like him."

"Do you have a date in mind?"

"Hmmm." Her smile was wistful. "Christmas. I once had a dream about being a Christmas bride. With poinsettias around the church and lots of ribbon and flowers."

"Then I shall make that dream come true for you."

Confusing Encounter

KARASU FLEW THROUGH THE orange haze of the setting sun, coasting on the high winds while flapping as needed to ride from one to the next. Near the edge of the borders of Throklana's main province, he landed on the large, leafless branch of a half-dead tree sitting at the edge of the forest. He looked around, focusing on any movement to locate its source. When he was certain all was clear, he glided down, morphing to his human form before his feet touched the ground.

The darkening sky cast long shadows around him. The Forest of Kuragari was not a place frequented by respectable people. With rumors that ghosts and the undead walked its soft, marshy grounds, it was not a welcoming place. Criminals sought refuge among the trunks, for few would dare to follow them. It was whispered that many who hid there never returned.

With a shiver, Karasu hoped the rumors of Yuji being here were wrong. This was not a place for the prince, no matter how bad he felt toward his brother. He knew Kazuki would yell at him if he learned that he'd come here by himself, rather than sending a messenger or bringing a company of guards, especially since the last messenger still hadn't come back. But he thought it might be easier to get Yuji to come out and talk if he saw a familiar face without a contingent of armed troops.

The wind was chilled and empty. The whole place gave him the creeps. Swallowing his trepidation, he began calling out Yuji's name, keeping a careful eye on his surroundings. Five minutes passed, then ten. His hope began to fade. *Were the rumors false after all?* He couldn't stay too long, as he planned to be back in the human world before Sakura got home from school.

A rush of feet coming toward him made him jump high in the air, turning as he went. He barely managed to get his wooden sword up before a black shadow of a dog sunk its teeth into the blade, its weight pushing him to the ground.

"Get off." Karasu kicked it in the stomach, giving himself time to regain his footing. He kept his blade up between them as the shadow dog began circling. With a snarl, it rushed forward again. A piercing whistle sounded through the clearing and the dog stopped in midair, dropping to the ground before vanishing into the trees.

Karasu wiped the sweat from his brow as he breathed out in relief. He couldn't figure out where the whistle had come from, the sound seeming to have been all around them.

"Karasu?" A familiar voice came from behind him. He turned to see Yuji walking out of the woods.

"Master Yuji!" Caution forgotten, he ran and threw his arms around Yuji, hugging him tight. Yuji's arms wrapped around him as he knelt down to return the embrace.

"Little one, what are you doing in such a place? It is not safe for you here." Yuji pulled back and smiled at him. "But I am glad to see you. I have missed you so much."

"I've missed you too." Karasu stepped back to look at him better. The prince appeared tired and had lost more weight than was good for him. "Are you well?"

"As well as I can be. Do not worry over me. I shall be fine. I heard you have been made Kazuki's attendant?"

"Yeah. The advisers didn't like it and are making me take all these lessons and stuff, but it's kind of fun."

"That's good. I'm sure you will make a good one." Yuji's smile looked almost sad.

Since deciding to come search this spot, Karasu had spent hours rehearsing what he would say. But now, those well-planned words wouldn't come. The questions most on his mind came out in a rush. "Master Yuji, why are you fighting with Master Kazuki? Do you really hate him? Do you really want to kill him?"

"Kill him? Kazuki? Why would you think such a thing? Even though he has hurt me terribly, he is still my brother."

"Then why did you attack him when you met to talk?" The wounds hadn't been accidental or defensive. From Reito's remarks and seeing the healing cuts himself, he knew they had been aimed at vital organs.

"What are you talking about? Kazuki never even showed up when I asked him to come talk. Then I hear he left the castle for an extended trip. How could I have attacked him if I haven't seen him since I left? Besides, you know I've never been able to so much as score a single point on him when we sparred."

"But, I saw the wounds myself. I...I don't understand this at all."

Yuji sighed and stood. "I can only tell you it was not me and hope you will believe me. Is that why you came to find me here?"

"Kind of, yes. I wanted to ask you myself what happened and find out why you are so angry at Master Kazuki. He misses you so much and wants to make up with you, but he doesn't even know what he did wrong."

"Doesn't know? How could he not know? Did he think I

wouldn't find out what he did?" Yuji shook his head with a disgusted grimace. Karasu's heart sank as Yuji turned his back to him. "Go home, little one. For now, it's best if things stay like this. Once Father returns—I'm sure we can sort it out then."

With that, Yuji began to walk back toward the woods. Karasu stood conflicted, watching him leave. He didn't seem angry at Kazuki at all, more annoyed, and he'd denied trying to kill him. None of it made any sense at all. But it did sound like he wanted to resolve things, so maybe…

"Master Yuji, wait! Please, try to talk to Master Kazuki one more time. I'm certain you can still work things out. He's taking a mate soon and wants you to be there!"

Yuji stopped then turned around slowly. "The same Kazuki who has spurned every potential mate since he came of age? He is taking a mate? Then he has accepted Aya?"

"No, of course not. It's a human woman, the adopted daughter of that friend of his he met when they were kids. That's where we've been, living with her."

"A human? A human? Kazuki is mating with a human?" Yuji's eyes bulged as he stammered out the question. "Surely you jest?"

"No, her name is Sakura. She's kind of nice, I guess, though a little sappy." He scratched his nose, still embarrassed to admit that he liked her at all. "They'll be mated next month, in human time."

"That soon? She's with child then?" Yuji shook his head.

Karasu hesitated. He'd already told Yuji more than Kazuki would probably like, but it had kept him there, listening. Maybe it would be enough. "She's sick. Really sick. The human doctors don't think she'll even live to see her next birthday."

"This is insane. Kazuki, of all people, choosing to mate with a human. Their lives are already so pitifully short, yet he picks one who will die even sooner. My brother can be so foolish.

Yokai–human relationships are discouraged just for this reason." Still shaking his head, Yuji turned around again. "The last time I asked to talk to him, he did not show up, but still, I will consider your request. It was good to see you, even under these circumstances."

Karasu watched him leave, unable to think of any other words that might make him stay longer. At least now they knew where he was staying, and Karasu felt he was sincere in his consideration of meeting with Kazuki again. It was a start, at least. Hopefully, enough of one to finally bring their family back together again.

From behind a tree, Yuji watched the young boy transform and fly off. His mind churned over the things Karasu had said, trying to reconcile the difference in his experience and what Karasu seemed to believe. Kazuki was claiming he'd tried to kill him when they were supposed to meet. But Kazuki hadn't even shown up, though he'd waited nearly a day before giving up.

"Did you hear that?"

"Yes, My Prince." His companion, Mumarch, stepped out of the shadows. "Do you believe the boy?"

"Karasu would never lie to me. He's not like Kazuki." Yuji couldn't keep the bitterness out of his voice. It still sickened him to think of Kazuki's betrayals.

"My Prince, I urge you to be cautious. He is still young, and while he clearly cares for you, he also blindly trusts his master. Tricking him into delivering lies to you would be an easy thing for one such as your brother. He stole your love from you, after all, and now it sounds as if he sullied her then threw her aside for a lowly human."

Anger burned in his chest. If Kazuki was taking a mate,

then Aya, who'd chosen his brother over him, would be left behind even though Kazuki had certainly already bedded her. "Curse him. Aya must be a wreck."

"Yes. Though this could work in your favor, My Prince. Perhaps now her eyes have been opened to the true nature of Prince Kazuki, and she will realize that it is you to whom she should turn, you who would never do such a despicable thing."

"Maybe. Even if she doesn't accept me, I hate to think of her hurting alone. I should go see her, comfort her." He began walking back toward the forest hut he'd made his temporary home. "As for Kazuki, perhaps you are right. Karasu could never turn on Kazuki, not when my brother was the one who raised him and not even if Kazuki has turned against me. He would believe anything Kazuki says. I only hope Kazuki isn't using that human girl in his plot as well. Karasu seemed to have met her, so if she is sick as he says, it would be doubly cruel of Kazuki to play with her heart like this."

Feeling low, Yuji continued on, and Mumarch followed, respectfully walking a few steps behind him.

Truthful Friendship

THROUGHOUT THE WEEK, Sakura kept making excuses to herself for not inviting the girls over so she could tell them the truth. She knew Akari had a student council meeting on Tuesdays and Hina had band after school Mondays, so "of course" it would be rude to ask them to come those days. Wednesday afternoon, she was packing her bag at the end of class when Hina and Akari came over to see if she wanted to go to the arcade.

"I'm sorry. Karasu-kun seemed like he might be coming down with a cold this morning, so I really want to check on him." A cold spell had come through, dumping a freezing rain over the area for days, a prelude to the still elusive first snow, at least according to the forecasters. Karasu had gotten caught in it the day before and had been feeling poor since.

"Awww, hope he feels better. We didn't get to meet him last time, though if he's Kazuki's baby brother, he must be adorable!" Hina clapped her hands together as she grinned.

"He's an adopted brother, but he is pretty cute. I'll introduce you next time. Um, actually…" Sakura hesitated. "Would you guys be able to come over Saturday after school? I'd like to talk to you about something."

"Why can't you tell us now?" Akari asked, that strict look

on her face again.

"I wouldn't want you to catch Karasu's cold. Please, I'll tell you Saturday, promise."

"Sure, we can come," Hina answered with an understanding smile. "Hope he feels better."

"Thanks!" Sakura grabbed her bag and fled the room before Akari could question her further. She just wanted to be able to give them time to mull it over after she told them, rather than them having to come to school the next day. It wasn't that she wanted to delay it any longer or anything like that.

Since the ball, Kazuki and sometimes Karasu would wait for her after school to walk her home. Today, though, she'd told Kazuki to look after Karasu, because colds could be serious. Now she was glad she had. She'd have hated for him to stand outside in this weather.

A sharp wind ripped her umbrella from her hand, flipping it inside out and ripping the thin fabric. She squealed as the cold rain trickled down her neck and soaked her shirt. Mentally kicking herself for not taking the tram, she picked up her pace, discarding the useless umbrella and clasping her coat tighter around her. Her chest was starting to burn as her heart sped up.

She stopped to rest under the awning of a store. With her breathing getting more strained, she decided to use her inhaler as a precaution. But the familiar plastic was not in the front pocket of her bag. Frantically, she squatted down to search it. It wasn't her bag. She must have grabbed someone else's in her rush to get going.

Ordering herself to stay calm, she stood. It was just two blocks to go. Then she could use the one she kept at home. Pushing herself out of the doorway, she continued on. She made it one more block before falling to her knees in agony. A sharp pain shot through her body with every breath. It felt as if her lungs were seizing up and would never release the breath she'd just taken. The harder it got to breathe, the harder her heart beat, and the more it twisted and pulled in her chest.

Even as she thought of Kazuki, somehow he was there, kneeling in front of her. She felt him pull her bag off her shoulder.

"Quickly, where is your medicine?"

"Ho…me." The word stretched to two syllables as she struggled to pull in the air needed to say it. "Got…wro…ng…ba…g."

"By the gods no!" Fear racked his words. "Sakura, this morning you said we needed to go by the pharmacy tonight to replace them because they were empty."

"Dammit!" Kazuki covered Sakura with his coat as best he could. Without the inhaler and spray, he knew there would be no stopping the attack. He had to get her inside and call for an emergency vehicle like she'd shown him. He started to pick her up when he heard someone yelling.

"Sakura-chan! Sakura-chan!" Hina and Akari ran up to them, out of breath and panting. "What's wrong? What happened to her?"

"Hina-chan, is that Sakura's bag?"

"Huh, yeah, she took mine by accident. We were just coming to bring it to her when we saw her collapse."

"Thank the gods!" Kazuki grabbed it and pulled out the inhaler and nitro spray. He'd been afraid she was too far gone to respond, but she breathed in when he instructed and lifted her tongue for the spray.

"Is she going to be okay?" Hina asked.

"Can I do anything?" Akari kneeled beside Sakura and helped shield her with her umbrella.

"She'll be okay now, but we should get her home. Please, can you bring her bag?"

Akari kept them covered while Hina carried both bags. At the house, Karasu was waiting with the door open.

"Sakura! Did she have an attack?"

"Yes, but we got her medicine to her in time. Bring some towels up to the bathroom. We need to get her dry. Oh, and get some for her friends too, please."

"Right away." Karasu sprinted down the hall while Kazuki carried Sakura upstairs. The pair followed, silent though he could smell the fear on them. He took her into the bathroom and set her on the edge of the tub. She was still quiet, but held herself upright as she watched them.

"We'll dry her off. You wait outside," Akari said as she grabbed the towels from Karasu and stepped forward.

"Yeah, go get her some clothes to wear." Hina practically pushed Kazuki out the door.

He kept an ear tuned for the room as he went to get Sakura's pajamas. Both girls were talking softly to Sakura, telling them what they were doing and making casual conversation while they worked. Neither asked her any questions, though he was sure they would once Sakura came around.

He mentally kicked himself for not having met her at the school. She'd just been so worried about Karasu, despite both of them telling her he'd be fine soon, that Kazuki had relented and agreed to stay home.

After the girls were done and had Sakura dressed, he carried her to her room and tucked her into bed. She fell asleep before he was done.

"She'll need to sleep a little while before she is able to talk. You two are soaked, and we would not want you to fall ill. Come, I'll make some tea while you change into something dry."

He lent the girls some of Sakura's clothes, certain she wouldn't mind, before changing into drier clothes himself. With all three dry and more comfortable, they sat in the living room around the kotatsu.

"So what happened?" Akari demanded, her gaze unblinking as she watched him.

"It is not my place to tell you; that is Sakura's story to share. I will only say thank you for bringing her bag, thank you so very much."

He could tell his answer didn't please Sakura's friends, but they didn't push it, for now.

"Sakura, are you okay now?" Hina asked in a shaky voice.

Her friends stood beside her bed, watching her with concerned faces. It seemed like an odd twist of fate that she would be telling them now, the anniversary of the day her death had become more imminent. The day her parents had died.

"Yes, I'm really sorry if I worried you."

"You scared us half to death! What happened to you? It was as if you couldn't even breathe!" Akari's voice was sharp as she glared at her.

"I'm sorry." She glanced up at Kazuki, who sat beside her head on the bed, his back leaned against the wall. Karasu had slipped out after checking on her to go make more tea. Kazuki gave her a slight nod as he put one hand on her shoulder, lending her his strength.

"Please, sit down. There is something I need to tell you." Hina sat at the foot of Sakura's bed, while Akari pulled the chair from Sakura's desk up to sit in front of Hina.

"This has something to do with what you wanted to talk to us about Saturday, doesn't it?" Akari's voice was softer now.

"Yes." She paused, and took a steadying breath. "I guess I should start by telling you how my parents died…" They listened intently as Sakura told them of her father's disorder and the day he'd killed her mother and himself, leaving her a half-dead orphan. Hina had begun crying then, but Sakura pushed on, telling them of how she'd come to live with Ito. Then she explained the results her father's actions. In simple terms, she told them about her failing organs and her coming death. The ticking of the Chococat[41] clock on the wall seemed loud in the quiet as she finished talking.

"The scars on your back are from then?" Akari's voice had a strange lilt to it.

"Yes."

"You are…dying?"

"Yes."

Hina broke down and began sobbing onto Akari's shoulder. "I don't want you to die!"

Akari put her arms around Hina, while her own expression seemed to be a mix of confusion and shame. Sakura wished she could offer them some words of comfort, but what could she say? Nothing would change the inevitable.

"Why didn't you tell us before?" Akari's question held no condemnation in it. If anything, her gaze looked apologetic.

"I…I didn't want to be treated any differently at school. The teachers all treat me like I'm going to break at the drop of a hat. I've always been scared to make friends because I didn't want to make anyone hurt like this. Then before I knew it, somehow we'd become friends despite myself. I…I just wanted to be able to be normal with you, for as long as I could. And I

---

[41] A popular Sanrio character, Chococat is a large-eyed black cat, similar in general structure to fellow Sanrio character Hello Kitty.

was scared…scared you wouldn't want to be around me anymore if you knew."

Hina cried anew as she turned and hugged Sakura. "We will always be here for you! You are our friend."

Sakura hugged her back, and finally let her own tears fall. Kazuki slipped out of the room, returning a few minutes later with hot drinks once the crying had stopped.

"I wanted to tell you something else, something good this time." Sakura smiled at them. "Kazuki and I are getting married."

Hina nearly screamed as she hugged Sakura again. "Really!? When?!"

"Christmas Day. It will be a Western-style wedding."

"What, that soon? That isn't much time!" Akari said, her brows furrowed as she ticked things off on her fingers. "You must arrange a location, get a dress, make a guest list. Also, food. Have you started making plans? This will require some serious organization and planning!"

Laughing, Sakura had a feeling Akari had just appointed herself as the wedding coordinator, not that she minded at all.

"I'm on flower duty!" As the daughter of florists, Hina was the natural choice. "I can help make decorations too! I'll talk to Genji about the dress. His big sister works at a wedding dress store."

Sakura had to fight back fresh tears as she smiled, watching her friends throw themselves into helping plan the wedding. With a knowing smile, Kazuki put his arm around her shoulder.

When it was time for Hina and Akari to go home, Kazuki showed them to the door, insisting Sakura stay in bed a while longer. Akari paused and glanced back up the stairs toward Sakura's room, then at Kazuki. She nodded before following Hina out.

"What was that about?" Karasu asked from the door to the kitchen.

"I think Akari-san was giving me her approval, and asking me to take care of her."

"Huh? All that from a nod?"

"Yep. She is a good person. She just doesn't know how to be honest with herself." Kazuki finished locking up, and headed to the kitchen. "All right, now to make dinner."

"Make dinner? Us?"

"Why not? Sakura is always making us meals. Surely we can make something simple for her."

"But the most either of us has done is make drinks and stick stuff in the microwave," Karasu said in a worried tone. "Why don't we just pick something up?"

"Bah, it can't be that hard. Certainly no different than making a potion. The question is, what do humans eat when they don't feel well?"

While Kazuki poked around the fridge to see what they had available, Karasu grabbed a recipe book from the shelf and flipped through the pages. He really didn't think this was a good idea, but maybe having a recipe would help. "According to this, something called okayu."[42]

"Perfect, what's in it?"

"Rice, water, miso paste,[43] tofu, umeboshi,[44] and mirin."[45]

---

[42] A rice porridge commonly given to someone who is sick because it is easy to digest.

[43] A traditional Japanese seasoning made from fermented soybeans.

[44] Pickled ume fruits, which are often called "plums" but are closer to apricots in taste and appearance; unlike either fruit they resemble, ume have a salty, somewhat sour taste.

[45] A rice wine, a core ingredient of Japanese cooking.

As he called out the ingredients, Kazuki found them and piled them on the dining table. "It says you can add other stuff if you want, like boiled chicken, vegetables, and eggs."

"Okay, we have all the basic stuff. We also have chicken and…how about leeks and honey? They are good for when you don't feel well too, right?"

"I think so…but in a rice porridge? Together?"

"Yes, it will be perfect! The leeks for robustness and just a bit of honey for sweetness to keep things from being too sharp. Now then, you're in charge of the instructions."

"Okay. First, boil four cups of water."

"Got it." Kazuki set a pan on the stove and grabbed a nearby coffee mug, carefully filling it four times and emptying it into the pot. He turned one of the knobs to high and moved the pot to the burner that came on in the front of the stove. "Next?"

Karasu felt his nervousness grow. He'd never seen Sakura use a cup like that to cook with, but he knew there was no point in trying to stop Kazuki now. "While we wait, we need to cut the tofu, the chicken, and the leeks into bite-sized pieces."

"That should be easy." Kazuki pulled a large knife from the rack and dumped the tofu on the counter, cutting it into wide strips then cross-cutting it into smaller chunks. The chicken was already shredded, so he ran the knife over it once to break it up some more. He chopped the leeks in equal lengths from the top of the leaves through to the roots.

"Now take the seeds out of the umeboshi and cut it up."

"What seeds?" Kazuki stared at the dried fruits, turning them in his hand. Then he set one down and cut it in half. "Oh, there they are, hiding inside." He finished cutting the fruits into chunks, removing any seeds he spotted. "There, done! And the water is boiling now."

Glancing at the pot, Karasu could see bubbles breaking the surface. "Okay, throw in two to three tablespoons of miso and let it dissolve."

Kazuki grabbed the large spoon from the dining room table and scooped out the miso paste. "Hmm, we had just enough left it seems."

Tossing the empty container aside, he stirred the water around until the yellow paste disappeared.

Karasu was certain Sakura never used that big spoon to measure stuff; mostly she used it for serving up rice. "Now add one cup of rice, one eighth a spoon of the mirin, and then everything else."

Using the same cup he'd measured the water in, Kazuki added the rice. "One eighth of a spoon?"

"Yep, that's what it says."

"How odd." With a shrug, Kazuki poured a small amount of the mirin into the large spoon before adding it to the pot. After that, he dumped in the tofu, the four chopped umeboshi, the chicken, and the leeks. He finished it off with a long squeeze from the honey bottle. Karasu's stomach did a little flip.

"Once it starts boiling again, put a lid on it, and it will be ready in thirty minutes."

As soon as the first bubble broke the surface of the water, Kazuki covered the pot with a square of hard plastic he found nearby. "Ah, see, that was not that hard at all!"

He looked so proud of himself, Karasu forced himself to smile. Somehow he didn't think this was going to make Sakura feel any better. To avoid having to pretend he thought they'd been successful, Karasu began telling Kazuki about his visit with Yuji. As he'd expected, Kazuki was angry with him for going alone, but forgave him quickly.

"So, he denies having attacked me?"

"Yes. He really sounded confused, as if he didn't believe me."

"I do not understand why he would deny it. He has always

been an honest person, one who takes responsibility for his misdeeds. Yet he won't admit to giving in to his anger and striking me? Surely he would know I've already forgiven him."

"I asked him why he was mad, but he said you should know. It sounded like he thinks you tried to hide something from him."

"Then it really must be over Aya. I am glad I sent the formal refusal, even if I couldn't do it in person. Now if only he and I could talk this through."

"He said he'd think about coming to talk to you. I…I told him about Sakura," Karasu confessed.

"That's fine. I should like them to meet, if he is back to himself. Did he seem okay?"

"Yeah, just like always except he's lost some weight."

"I hate to think of him sleeping in such a hideous place…Once he is home, I'm sure our cooks will go overboard fattening him back up."

The timer dinged before Karasu could tell him about the strange shadow dog. As they stood at the stove, Kazuki stirred the thick concoction then spooned some into a bowl.

Karasu looked at the picture in the book and compared it to the strange-colored, lumpy blob in the bowl. "Master Kazuki…"

"It's fine. It's the taste that matters, not the appearance." Though he sounded less sure than before, he put it on a tray along with some fresh tea.

They carried it upstairs where he presented it with a flourish to Sakura. Her smile was a little shaky as she eyed it, but she picked up her spoon and took a large bite. *She may be the bravest person I've ever met.* A moment later, her eyes began to water as she struggled to swallow.

"Sakura?" Kazuki asked in a worried voice.

"—it's just a little salty."

Kazuki took a bite himself then gagged. "I'm sorry. We followed the book's instructions to the letter, mostly, but maybe it was a bad recipe."

More like a bad cook, if Karasu had a guess, but he knew better than to say it out loud.

"It's okay. It's the thought that counts, and it was very sweet of you to try. I'm feeling better now. Why don't we sit downstairs awhile and we can order in?"

When they walked into the kitchen to dump the bowl, Sakura froze. It was a complete mess, with bits of veggies and porridge all over the counter. They'd forgotten to turn off the burner on the pot, so the rest of their mess was burnt and foul smelling.

"Oh…oh."

"*Honto ni sumimasen.*"[46] Kazuki and Karasu bowed in unison as they apologized.

Sakura stood in front of them, her arms crossed over her chest as she glared at them. "This is just too much. Apologies are not enough. You're both going to have to accept your punishments."

They winched as, with a laugh, she threw her arms around them both.

"I love you." She kissed Kazuki's cheek, before turning to Karasu to kiss his too. "And you. You two are the sweetest guys a girl could ever ask for."

Though he swiped at his cheek as if disgusted, Karasu couldn't help laughing. She really was such a simple girl to please.

---

[46] An extra apologetic apology, usually translated to "Truly, I am very sorry."

SHIFTING VIEWS

MONDAY AFTERNOON, KAZUKI went with Sakura to her doctor's appointment. When she mentioned going in for a check-up, he asked to join her, wanting to know more about her illness and to share this part of her life, if he could.

The long hospital building was wide and low, only four floors tall. Inside, everything was white, the walls, the ceiling, the nurses' crisp uniforms, even the doctors' jackets. The stench of disinfectant burned his nose and made his eyes water, forcing him to tune his sense of smell down as low as he could. He hated to think of how many times Sakura must have sat in this sterile, cold room, alone, contemplating her life while waiting to see how much longer she had.

When her name was called, they headed to the specified examination room where her doctor waited.

"Good afternoon, Sakura-chan. And this is?" The slight, bowed man gave him a curious glance over the top of his glasses.

"This is Ito Kazuki, the man I told you about. He is Ito-san's cousin who returned to Japan not too long ago." As Sakura repeated the half-truth they'd used at her school, the doctor shook his hand. "Kazuki, this is Tenma-sensei. He's been my doctor all of this time."

"Pleased to meet you and thank you. Sakura tells me you have been a great support to her."

"I'm just doing what I can. It's Sakura who is her own best champion because she doesn't give up."

"Tenma-sensei, Kazuki and I...that is...um...we are engaged."

"Engaged?" The doctor looked as concerned as a father would have, as if tempted to hide Sakura behind him and demand to know what was going on.

"Yes, I know it's sudden, but he makes me happy, I promise." Sakura smiled at Tenma with one hand on his arm. That smile Kazuki himself could rarely refuse.

"I...I see. Well, congratulations." Though he still looked concerned, the doctor motioned for her to sit at a chair with a fold-down tabletop. Tenma snapped on a pair of white gloves while Kazuki took a seat nearby. "Now then, has anything changed that I should know about?"

"I had another attack, late last week. And I think I'm getting tired more often. I'm having to go to bed earlier and it's hard to wake up on time."

Tenma tied a strange band around her upper arm then began feeling along the inside of her elbow, all the while staring down Kazuki. "How long has this been going on?"

"Hmmm, I guess a little over a week."

The doctor nodded in response, then pierced her skin with a needle. Kazuki did his best to respectfully avoid Tenma's gaze as he watched the glass at the end of the syringe fill with blood. It was fascinating to think they could learn a lot about her current health just from two vials of blood. It was making him wish he'd read more on human medicine. It was one aspect of human culture he'd mostly skipped, figuring it would be boring and close enough to the yokai world's methods, like math was.

Once he had the blood vials capped and labeled, Tenma applied a bandage to the wound and removed the band. "Are you making sure to eat well? Not doing anything too strenuous?"

"Yes, I am and no, Kazuki and Karasu-kun wouldn't let me even if I tried to."

"Karasu-kun?"

"He's my younger brother." It was close enough to the truth that it was an easy lie for Kazuki.

"Ah." The doctor popped up from his seat and stood. "Well, that is good then. Both of you, keep it up. Sakura-chan can sometimes be a bit stubborn."

"Am not!" She smiled as she said it. From the doctor's chuckle, Kazuki suspected this was a familiar routine for them.

"Now then, please change into this gown and we can begin the rest of the tests." Tenma led Kazuki out into the hall then walked down a little bit so he could lean against the window that overlooked the bay. Kazuki followed.

"Who are you, really?" Tenma asked without glancing at him.

"What do you mean?"

"I know for a fact that Ito-san did not have any cousins." Tenma looked up at him, his suspicion plain to see.

Kazuki leaned on the glass beside him, keeping his own gaze steady as he spoke. "I'm sorry. It was not a lie intended to harm anyone. Hiro was a very good friend of mine. I had to return home to my own country not long after we met. As we said, I only recently returned to Japan. Of course, I immediately came to visit Hiro, only to learn I'd returned too late. That was when

I met Sakura."

"What do you want with her? Money?"

"No, believe me, I have more than enough of my own. At first, I simply wished to help her to honor my friend. I felt as if he led me to return at this time so that she would not be alone anymore. Then before I knew it, she'd stolen my heart."

Tenma stared at him a full minute before answering, his probing eyes assessing him. Finally he relaxed his stance some. "How much do you know about her condition?"

"She has told me everything, including that she does not have long left. I admit, I do not fully understand the medical terms and the like. That was one reason I wanted to come to-day, so I could better understand this and what she is going through."

"Okay. Just make sure you're with her because you do love her, and not out of some sense of pity or obligation. You will need a strong heart to endure being with her to the end." Tenma pushed off the wall and said, "She looks happy, so for now, I'll leave it at that. Come, she should be done changing. I'll explain the tests for you as we go along."

"Thank you."

Back in the examination room, Tenma had Sakura sit on the table while he listened to her heart and lungs. Then he used a wide cuff wrapped tightly around her arm to measure the pressure of her blood. It seemed like a strange thing to want to know, but as promised, Tenma told him about each procedure as they went through them.

"Good, now we'll do the echocardiogram." He put a small device against Sakura's chest under the gown and began easing it from side to side while watching a nearby screen. "This device sends out sound waves into the body that bounce off her heart.

It will let us get a picture of her heart's muscle."

Kazuki thought that sounded painful, having things bouncing off her heart. As if seeing his concern, she smiled up at him. "It's okay. It doesn't hurt at all. The jelly is a little cold at first, but that's normal."

"Okay." He held her hand anyway, as much to comfort himself as her. Half an hour later, that test was done and the transponder put away.

"Now then, we'll get an electrocardiogram, or ECG for short." He stuck a dozen patches all over Sakura's arms, legs, and chest. Wires led from them to a machine that began beeping after he flipped a switch. "With this test, we can check the rate and rhythm of Sakura's heartbeat and get an indication of the thickness of the heart muscle."

It took less than a minute. Then the patches were removed.

"The last thing we'll do today is use a catheter to get measurements and blood samples directly from different parts of Sakura's heart." He held up a small hollow tube, explaining that they would insert it into a blood vessel in her neck, and send the tiny collecting needle down into the heart.

"We will apply local anesthesia to the spot so Sakura won't feel a thing. I'll be right back."

After Tenma left, Kazuki moved closer to hold Sakura's hand, unable to stop his own from shaking. The idea of sticking anything down her body like that terrified him.

"It isn't my favorite part, but I promise I barely feel it." She covered his hand with her other hand. "I'm sorry…Maybe it would have been better if I hadn't let you come."

"No, I want to know all of it, even the scary parts. I just wish I could do more for you."

"You love me. That is more than enough."

It was late by the time they were done. Though it would be awhile before some of the test results came back, from what the doctor had seen Sakura's suspicions were correct. Her condition had worsened, but Tenma had assured them that she was still about where they thought she would be at this point. He increased the doses of some of her medicines and confirmed that Kazuki knew how to administer both her inhaler and her nitro spray.

The doctor walked them to the entrance, standing just outside with them as the sun dipped low in the sky. "Be careful as winter really sets in. Take extra precautions to avoid catching a cold. A cough would be bad for your lungs. Bundle up and avoid being outside too much. Kazuki-san, I will be trusting you to take care of her."

Kazuki bowed deeply. "Thank you, I will. You have my word."

Back home, Sakura rested in the living room. Leaving Karasu to watch over her, Kazuki went to a restaurant to pick up dinner. They ate in silence, each seemingly lost in his or her own thoughts, until Sakura set down her chopsticks.

"Um, Kazuki?"

"Yes?"

"I..." He could see her trembling. "If you promise it really won't hurt you, I...the potion...I want to try it."

Sakura forced herself to watch as Kazuki sliced the palm of his hand with a knife. As his blood began to flow, he curled his hand into a fist and held it over the small pot of ingredients boiling over the stove. One...two...three...she counted as drop after drop of the dark red liquid went into the potion. She took a sip of ginger tea to try to calm the tumbling act her stomach was performing.

Kazuki had offered to make the dohame while she waited in the living room, or to even wait and do it tomorrow while she was at school, but she'd refused. If he could give up his blood for this potion, the least she could do was watch. Once Kazuki started, Karasu stayed beside her, holding her hand the whole time.

Twenty drops later, Kazuki moved his hand away, wrapping it in a towel. She was doubly glad she'd insisted he only make one dose—shuddering to think how much more the full five he wanted to make would have needed.

With a wooden spoon, Kazuki stirred the simmering potion. Five times clockwise then five the other way. Then four clockwise, four the other way, and so on until he stirred once each way and set the spoon aside. An almost fruity scent filled the kitchen, not the sort of fragrance she expected from a pot filled with the herbs and vegetable-looking things that had gone in there before the blood.

Karasu gave her hand a squeeze before letting it go and taking the other chair.

"It needs to continue to cook for ten minutes." Kazuki set the timer before joining them at the dining table. Resting his chin on his fingers, Kazuki watched her. The pose felt so familiar to her now, his "contemplation pose" as she called it. When he was done, he lifted his head. "Sakura, may I ask, what caused you to change your mind?"

"It was a couple of things, I guess. The attack the other day...it scared me." She looked down, determined not to cry again as she confessed to the two watching yokai. "I thought that was it, that I was going to die there just like that. It's strange, you know? The whole event only lasted a few minutes, but so many things went through my mind that it felt like hours. So many things I hadn't said yet, so many things I wanted to do that I hadn't done. Then today, Tenma-sensei confirmed my fears, that I'm getting worse. I thought about those regrets, what it would be like lying in that hospital bed at the end for hours at a time with nothing but those thoughts going through my mind."

She paused and closed her eyes, taking a calming breath. "Have you ever heard of a bucket list?"

Kazuki and Karasu shook their heads.

"Well, it's basically a list of things someone wants to do before they die. It's a popular thing for people to do, maybe as a way of reminding themselves to live their lives to the fullest or something." She pulled the heavily wrinkled paper from her pocket, unfolded it and laid it on the table. "This was the list I wrote a few years ago."

Kazuki turned the list toward himself, tilting it just enough that Karasu could read along with him. When they were both looking up at her again, she continued.

"I realize some of those are almost impossible now. We couldn't go to another country, and it's too cold to fly a kite or ride in a hot air balloon. And one day isn't enough time to do it all, but I'd like to do some of them, if we could. Together, the three of us."

"Me too?" Karasu asked with a curious expression.

"Of course. You're my family, the two of you."

His face turned bright pink. "Okay."

"Well then, my lady, have you decided which we shall do?" Kazuki asked.

"Almost. We don't have school this Saturday, so I was

thinking I could drink it first thing in the morning, then we'd make a long day of it."

Kazuki looked at the list again. "Do you have a camera?"

"Just Ito-san's old one. It doesn't work anymore, though."

"Could we perhaps acquire one before the weekend?"

"Sure, if you want. The weather should be good tomorrow, so I'll pick one up on my way home from school."

"Good. I want to have pictures. They are good things to have I think." He smiled at her as the timer by the stove began beeping.

The sun was shining when Sakura left the camera store, her new camera tucked in the swaying bag at her side. She hadn't realized how many options there were now, but the clerk helped her find a model that would work well in the sorts of places they would be going, while still being easy enough to use that she could teach Kazuki and Karasu in a short amount of time.

Part of her was excited about Saturday, a whole day of having fun free of pain or fear. She kept going over her list, trying to decide which things were the most important for her to experience and also the most doable with the constraints of travel and time. There was also one other thing she planned to ask for, but that wasn't something to write on a list anyone could read.

Her anticipation was tempered only by the morbidity of it all. The dohame was giving her a chance to make some final memories before it was too late. While she had always known she'd die from her condition, it was only now that she found herself looking over her shoulder, waiting for a shinigami[47] to come for her.

She hadn't mentioned it to Tenma-sensei or Kazuki, but since the attack, she'd been having nightmares. Dreams of her collapsed on the side of the street with curious strangers milling around, watching her die. Dreams of dying alone at home, her body lying where she fell, phone just out of reach, to remain there for weeks until someone finally found her. Dreams of a funeral with only two or three people attending; Tenma-sensei looking defeated and worn as he stood over her casket.

She gave herself a mental shake, turning into the nearby playground to clear her dark thoughts before she went home. Though it was warmer than usual, there were only two kids there, playing in the sandbox. As she walked toward the swing set, she spotted a familiar face sitting on one of them.

"Akari-san?" Akari's eyes were red and puffy, as if she'd been crying.

"Oh, hey." She looked back down and gave her swing the barest of pushes, sending it into short, slow arcs back and forth.

Sakura set down her bags and sat in the swing beside her, giving her own a slight push as well. For a few minutes they swung side by side without saying a word.

"Sakura-chan, I'm sorry," Akari said in a quiet voice.

"For what?"

"First year, a few days into the semester, I saw you in the bathroom, taking some pills. Of course now I know it was your medicine, but at the time, I didn't know what to think. People were already talking about how you were a pampered rich girl and how the teachers let you do anything you wanted. I guess

____

[47] Death god, believed to collect the soul of one who has died, though some also see it as one who leads a person to death.

people from your middle school started most of that. When I saw you taking those pills, I…I decided you were a drug addict on top of everything else. It was wrong of me. I made so many false presumptions about you without even bothering to get to know you first. Hina was right to fuss at me for being so close-minded. I'm disappointed in myself for how I mistreated you. So, I wanted to apologize."

"I see." The swing creaked as she set it moving again. "Well, I can't say I blame you. I did everything I could to make all of you hate me. I thought it was best to be alone, but I never thought about how much it would hurt, the idea that people would remember me in such a negative way. But then Hina-chan came along and pushed past my walls, dragging you with her. I'm glad she did, though. I just wish I could have gotten to know you sooner. You're smart, determined, organized, and I know from Hina that you make a pretty awesome friend. I'm glad I got to know you, finally, and I'm sorry too, for not giving you a chance sooner."

Akari chuckled. "Here we are, two sorry girls crying in a park on such a pretty day."

"Yeah." Sakura laughed with her as she set the swing going again. "Is that why you were crying earlier?"

"Ah, no. That was something else."

"Want to talk about it? I've gotten rather good at listening, I think." Sakura looked at her with a warm smile.

"Did you know my mom is an actress?"

"No, I had no idea."

"She does television dramas mostly, but her career really took off after she was in a movie a few years ago, so she's in high demand. Dad manages a band that has been really successful here and abroad. So they are always working. It's funny, I could never even figure out how they met, much less why they bothered marrying. They failed the first time. What's one more?" Bitterness stained her voice. "Anyway, that's no way to stay in love, right? So it wasn't much of a surprise when they announced last night that they have decided to divorce."

Akari pushed off her swing again, leaning back to look up at the sky. "I didn't even feel sad when they said it. Just wondered why they took so long. They were so calm about it, almost like they were reading a weather report."

"If it doesn't bother you, why are you crying?" Sakura asked as fresh tears started rolling down Akari's cheeks.

"That's just it, I'm not really sure. I mean, it's not like we were much of a family to begin with, so what does it matter if we split apart? They asked me who I wanted to live with." She stopped her swing, scuffing the ground with her shoe. "I yelled at them that it didn't matter, that it wasn't like they would be around anyway or that they wanted me. They were just being selfish, making me change schools just so they could have a different place to store their stuff. It wasn't like I ever saw either of them, so what did it matter which place they didn't bother coming home to? I'd be alone either way."

Akari's voice hitched as she began crying in earnest. Sakura stopped her swing to stand beside her, wrapping her arms around her shoulders and leaning her head on hers.

"How could I say something so mean? I could tell it hurt them. Mom looked like she was going to cry. Even Aki seemed disappointed in me. Then like a coward, I ran out of the room. I didn't even apologize! They chose their careers over their kids, but they don't leave us wanting for anything either. To say something that horrible to them—I'm the worst."

Sakura held her tight as she cried. When her sobs quieted,

Sakura gave her another squeeze before leaning back to look at her. "You aren't horrible, not at all. You were hurting and all the hurt from over the years just kind of came out at once. It's a normal thing. We've all done it at one time or another. I bet they understand better than you might think, so you should talk to them."

"You're right, I should." Akari pulled out her handkerchief and wiped her face dry. "And I guess I need to tell Hina that I'll be moving away soon."

Sakura sat back in her swing as she realized that the divorce meant Akari would be leaving. "It does kind of suck that you have to go halfway through the year."

"Yeah. They both already have new places to live, Mom in Tokyo and Dad in Osaka. It's too far to commute every day." Akari stood and grabbed Sakura's hands. "But I promise, no matter what, I'll be here for your wedding, okay? So don't start without me!"

"We won't, promise. Can't start without all of my friends there, right?"

"Akari!" Aki called out from the driver's window of his car, parked on the nearby road. After retrieving their bags, they walked over. Aki set his emergency blinkers and got out of the car. "I was looking for you. I got worried when you didn't come back after school."

"I'm sorry. I just needed some time to think."

"It's okay. Hey, Sakura-chan."

"Good afternoon, Aki-san."

Aki wiped a stray tear from Akari's face. "Feeling better?"

"Yeah, Sakura-chan listened to me whine for a while. Sorry I was so bratty last night," Akari said with a shaky smile. "Are Mom and Dad still home?"

"Yeah, they didn't want to leave without talking to you again."

She squared her shoulders. "I guess I better go apologize to them then. Even if I was being honest, I could have been kinder about it."

"That's my girl." He ruffled her hair affectionately as he grinned at her. "I probably should too. After you left, I kind of gave them a piece of my mind as well. I also told them that if you were okay with it, you could come live with me so you don't have to change schools so close to graduation."

"Really?" Akari grabbed his arm. "Would that really be okay?"

"Yep. I know you wouldn't want to leave now. How on earth would Sakura-chan plan her wedding without a certain little tyrant bossing her around?" He winked at Sakura.

"*Nii-san!*[48] I'm not a tyrant. I'm just helping keep things organized!"

---

[48] A polite, but more casual way of referring to one's older brother. While it's often translated as "big brother," the original is more nuanced, as there are many words for "big brother," with differing levels of respect and formality.

Bucket Day

IT TOOK SAKURA ALL WEEK to finalize the plans for Saturday. At first, she struggled with balancing what she thought Kazuki and Karasu would find interesting versus the things she most wanted to do. Then both reminded her it was a day all for her and that they would have fun either way. With their earnest demands that she be selfish, she focused just on her list, but even then it was a struggle.

Some of the things were impossible, at least the way she'd originally written them. Going to Fuji would take half a day, even with the bullet train or flying. She didn't want to waste half the day traveling. Even going to the northern end of Hokkaido was a five- or six-hour train ride, and the flights all went to Tokyo first, an oddity she couldn't figure out. She could hire a private jet, but it would be a lot of money to spend when there were other options.

Going to Tokyo itself would be an easy trip, a quick one-hour flight. The pictures and videos she'd seen of the two Disney parks there looked fun, but after researching them using one of the school's computers, she decided against it. The lines this time of year would be too long.

During her trip to the library, she ran into Akari. The list was beside Sakura's hand, in plain sight, so there was no point in trying to hide it. Her searches for some of the places were still on the screen. Akari looked from one to the other with a frown. Sakura braced herself for the certain chastisement over planning any sort of trip. It wasn't like she could explain the dohame to Akari after all.

"Are you planning a week-long trip?"

Surprised, it took Sakura a moment to answer. "Uh, no, just a day."

"There is no way you can go to all those places in just a day."

"So I discovered." Sakura glanced back at the computer, though the time lines hadn't changed.

"Hmmm." Akari picked up the list, studying it a minute before setting it back down. "Do they all have to be exactly as you wrote them?"

"What do you mean?"

"Well, like going to another country. Is it that you really want to go somewhere else, or is there something about it specifically you want to do?"

"Oh, well, it would be fun to try some food in another country, but mostly I just want to see some of the historical buildings and architectural styles. I love buildings." While, like Kazuki, she loved history in general, architecture was one of her favorite subjects. She had a whole shelf of books on architecture and design elements.

"Couldn't you do some of that in Motomachi?"

Sakura gasped. "You're right, I could. You know I've never been there, even though it's not that far from here."

"Here, move over. If nothing else, I'm good at making plans." Akari winked at her.

An hour later, Sakura had her list. It still would have been insane without the dohame, but with it, it would be doable. As they parted ways at the school gate, Sakura paused.

"Thank you for helping me today. I really appreciated it, though I admit, I thought you might yell at me for planning so much."

"It was no problem. I trust you to know your limits, and I'm sure Kazuki-san will keep you from doing more than you can handle. If you overdo it and make yourself sicker, then I'll yell at you good and proper." Akari smiled.

"Deal."

Saturday, the "Day of Buckets" as Kazuki had termed it, started with Sakura trying her hand at making an American-style breakfast: French toast, bacon, sausage, fried potatoes, oatmeal, and scrambled eggs. During her shopping trip for the ingredients the night before, she'd even found a bottle of maple syrup imported from Canada for the French toast, and she'd splurged on a small bit of cheese to go in the eggs, which seemed to be a popular preparation method. It was a day for experiences, after all.

While she cooked, her two yokai were in the living room, writing their response to a letter from the mysterious Reito. Kazuki said he was his father's attendant and a "noble, if boring" man. If Kazuki trusted him with the kingdom while he stayed with her, he must like him even if he did suspect Reito was hiding knowledge of the king's whereabouts. She wondered if he would come to their wedding with the king, presuming Kazuki's father could be "found" in time.

She finished setting the dining table before calling them in. They both stared for a moment.

"It's Sakura's Breakfast à la American." She giggled at her horrible attempt at a French accent. "I've never made any of this before, so I'm sorry if it isn't very good."

Kazuki scooped up a bite of eggs while Karasu went straight

for a huge piece of the syrup-topped French toast, chomping down simultaneously. To her relief, they both grinned. "Delicious!"

"I'm so glad." She took her own bite of the bacon. It tasted good, but even the fatty bits seemed crispy, making her suspect she'd cooked it too long. The oatmeal was a bit mushy, though she wasn't sure if it was her cooking or its natural state. Still, the meal had seemed to turn out well, and it wasn't long before their plates were cleaned.

"That was a good start to the day. We'll need all the energy we can get!" Kazuki patted his stomach in appreciation.

"I hope my list isn't too long."

"Not at all. It will be great to see even more of the area. And I am looking forward to this amusement park thing. I have seen some on the television and those…what did they call them…roller train things?"

"Roller coasters?"

"Yes, those, they look thrilling!"

"Akari said this park had some good ones. They look a little scary, but people seem to have so much fun on them I want to try it."

Once the dishes were done, Kazuki retrieved the small, antique-looking bottle that held the dohame, setting it in the middle of the table. It was hard to categorize the ball of feelings that hit her as she looked at it. Fear, nervousness, excitement, happiness. The words seemed too simple for it all.

Her hand trembling, she picked it up. The purple-pink liquid inside shifted, coating the sides of the bottle. It was a thick liquid, with a cream-soup consistency. Could what amounted to maybe eighty milliliters, at best, of this strange liquid really make her healthy for a whole day?

"Try to swallow it all down in one go while you hold your

nose. It's easier that way," Karasu said.

Sakura nodded and took a deep breath. The top of the bottle was a stopper, like she'd seen in old decanter bottles. It lifted out with only a little tug. Pinching her nose, she lifted it to her mouth and chugged. The first thing to register was a fruity sweetness, followed by a level of sourness that nearly made her gag, then a metallic bitterness as if she'd drunk melted coins. It wasn't the worst thing she'd ever tasted, but it was close.

Panting, she set the empty bottle down and wiped her mouth with her napkin.

"Sorry, I know it's pretty vile." Kazuki reached out to hold her hand. "You'd think after thousands of years they'd find a way to make potions more palatable."

"I've said the same thing about our medicines. I decided they make them nasty on purpose so we don't bug them if we aren't really, really, really sick." When they stopped laughing, she nudged the bottle with her finger. "How will I know when it's started?"

"You'll just kind of feel better. It is hard to describe, since it's rather individual. But you'll be able to tell, promise. It shouldn't take too long." He continued to hold her hand while they waited.

It was hard not to count down the seconds. In the silence, she was hyper-aware of the sounds around her. The hum of the fridge. The tick-tick of the clock on the wall. The low rumble of a truck passing by. The muffled chattering of two women walking down the sidewalk. The slow, steady breathing of her companions. Her own heart pounding.

Then a warmth spread through her body. Her shoulders felt lighter, her breathing easier. Her chest no longer had the constant feeling of someone constraining it that she had grown so accustomed to. The residual tiredness fled in the wake of a wave of energy that made her want to dance around the room. It was as if she'd been wearing one of those heavy, lead, X-ray vests all this time and someone had finally noticed and taken it off. Or as if she'd been trapped in a corset and the strings had been cut, freeing her to breathe again.

Unable to sit still, she jumped up and ran into the hall to look in the mirror. She touched her cheeks to confirm it really was her staring back. The pale ghost she was used to seeing had a healthy skin tone, with just a touch of pink. Even her increasingly dull hair looked shinier and bouncier. "I…this is…"

Kazuki walked up behind her, put his hands on her shoulders, and kissed her cheeks. She turned and wrapped her arms around him, kissing him as passionately as she could. At some point, he even lifted her up against him.

Behind them, Karasu cleared his throat to remind them he was there. "Not that I mind waiting, but we should probably get going."

Kazuki set her down with a smile. She was panting and her heart was pounding, but neither were in distress, except perhaps at stopping.

Almost giddy, Sakura laughed as she darted around him to grab Karasu's hand. "You're right. Let's hurry!"

It was a quick fifteen-minute walk to their first stop, the Motomachi area, where various buildings from Hakodate's earliest encounters with the Western world could be found. Sakura wondered again why she had never come sooner. It was so close to home, she could have done this years ago, though the hill would have been a mild challenge. Then again, years ago she'd have been alone, which she doubted would have been as exciting.

As they neared the Russian Orthodox Church, the sloped brick road that cut over the hill came to a four-way intersection paved with large cobblestones. The part they continued on, which would take them to the northeastern entrance, became a blend of styles: smaller bricks ran along the outside, with large bricks similar to those on the road they were leaving nestled in the center of each lane, and the large cobblestone design separating the two. Along the center of the road, the large cobblestone design continued in a thin line that flared to larger squares every few feet.

"Isn't this road so cool?" Sakura exclaimed as she walked around the intersection. "It's like touring a history of road laying!"

"Yes, it is very well done," Kazuki said, his tone sounding amused. Sakura shot him a glance, but he and Karasu just stood there watching. Shaking her head at their lack of appreciation for such an amazing creation, she studied the intricate patterns a bit longer before continuing on.

A tall wall comprised of large grey stones marked the edge of the church property. Heavy tinges of rusty color bled down, as if the old, thin wooden fencing that kept people from walking off the top of the wall was crying.

It was as if the wall itself was more of a bricked-in cliff than a traditional structure. Occasionally, sprinkles of green from plants that had somehow found little homes within the tightly woven pattern emerged. At the base of the wall, a thin strip of fading grass separated it from the street, while a few hardy, cold-weather wildflowers gave it some color.

Soon they stood in front of the main gates, which opened inward, pointing visitors toward the long, low dull-red steps that led up to the actual property. Sakura hesitated at the bottom for a moment.

"Sakura?" Kazuki asked as he stopped beside her.

"I can really go up these, can't I?"

He reached out to take her hand. "Yes, you can. Let's go see what's up there!"

With a smile, she nodded and took Karasu's hand, so they could walk up together. At the top, the church and a few small buildings stood surrounded by a mix of pathways, grassy patches, bushes, and trees. If it had been spring, she was certain there would have been flowers in bloom everywhere, but it was still a pretty sight.

The church itself was a magnificent white building with green-tiled roofs that sloped down in gentle curves. An octagonal bell tower rose up over the entryway. Each door and window was framed by a large half-arch that rose to a little point. Over the wooden doors, a second smaller arch was enveloped by the first. The windows were also designed as tall, narrow arches with frames laid inside, forming a grid of panes.

"Now this is quite lovely," Kazuki said as they stood at the entrance, looking up at the bell tower.

"Yes it is," Sakura replied, glad to see they were more interested in the building. "I love the way the arch theme is carried through so much of it. Look, even on the walls, more arches are cut into the plaster as decoration. And those bulb spires are so cute. You can really see the Byzantine influence in the design."

Karasu leaned forward and sniffed. "It smells like it's been here awhile."

"It has. The original church was built in 1859, but it later burned down. It was reconstructed in 1916, making this one almost one hundred years old."

"Old by human standards, quite young by yokai terms."

Kazuki laughed.

"How old are the buildings considered historic for your world?"

"Hmm. Well, as far anyone knows, our kind first appeared in the world about 400,000 years ago. Most of the structures from then have been lost, though. The oldest I know of is about 200,000 years old, an observation tower for studying both the sky and the ground. Our castle was built with the founding of Throklana, making it 105,000 or so, I believe."

"Wow, that is incredible. Even our oldest buildings are maybe 10,000 years old. It would be interesting to see how the building styles in your world have changed over time." Sakura wondered if the yokai, with their longer lifespans, changed their styles more slowly than humans did. She wished she could see it, Kazuki's castle and the rest of his world.

The inside of the church was closed to visitors due to an event, so they took the northwestern path and returned to the street. Their next stop was a few blocks down the road. As they walked along, the properties along the southwestern side continued to feature stone retaining walls, most with tight-set stonework similar to the church's. Sometimes a wall was well over three meters tall then dropped down to just a bare fifteen centimeters or so, with the accompanying house at street level.

At the crest of the hill, they stopped to admire the Old Public Town Hall, which spanned most of the block. The two-story structure had pale-blue wooden walls with columns, railings, windows, and trim all painted in a contrasting yellow. A covered balcony extended out over the porch at the entry, with two smaller balcony-covered porches doing the same on either side of what appeared to be the main building.

Sakura darted through the blue metal gates, doing a twirl in the courtyard before leading them up the four stairs inside.

"This one was built in 1910, during the late Meiji, using nothing but citizen donations after the original town hall burned down," Sakura told them as they headed into the decorated reception room. "Most of the architectural elements and set pieces are indicative of American Colonial styles, but not entirely. You can see some Japanese elements in each of the rooms and the overall design as well, and influences from other Western countries, like this art nouveau. In a way, it is a perfect blend of many styles."

Kazuki chuckled as he examined the wallpaper she pointed to. "Sakura, my dear, would I be right in suspecting you have a fondness for building elements?"

"I...I guess, maybe a bit." She smiled as she tried not to blush. It was hard to contain her enthusiasm as they went around the rest of the building. Before she realized there would be no miracle to save her, she'd dreamed of becoming an architect, in particular an expert in restoring and reconstructing old buildings.

Once they finished the tour, they rented period Western-style costumes, clothes which women and high officials had been temporarily mandated to wear during the Meiji era. The dress Sakura chose was a deep-purple silk with a hoop skirt, and accents in black-velvet and gold thread. The staff helped her dress and put her hair up to the side with a matching gold, laced head piece. When she emerged, Kazuki and Karasu were waiting, dressed in matching black breeches, white waistcoats, and black overcoats. She tried not to giggle as Karasu tugged at the blue silk cravat around his neck.

"Let's get some pictures!" They followed the attendant to the concert hall. The highly polished floor was as reflective as a mirror as they walked across it. They passed the camera around, taking pictures of each other together and separately.

Then one of the staff came and helped them take a few of the three of them together, standing by the hall's large windows, casually admiring the view from the huge balcony, and posed in chairs in front of a painting of the building.

From there, they walked around the corner to visit the old British Consulate. It was a two-story, boxy white building with more simply styled doors and windows, blue trim, and a terra-cotta-tiled roof. In the back, a garden boasted a variety of rose bushes, hostas, English box bushes, and various other flowers, though most were not in bloom. In its paved area stood a hexagon-shaped fountain, several white wooden benches, and a small, white, lace-walled gazebo.

Inside, they toured the rooms decorated with more period pieces, this time primarily from England. Many parts of the building featured information cards, paintings, and other illustrations detailing the history of Hakodate and its importance as one of the few places foreigners could enter Japan through during the Meiji Restoration. It was one reason there were so many foreign buildings in the area, as it became home for many of the consulates there, including the one they toured.

"You said this one was built in 1913?" Kazuki asked as they enjoyed a traditional English-style high tea in the tea shop. When Sakura nodded, he frowned. "The other two had to be rebuilt around the same time because they were destroyed in a fire, so was this one?"

"Yes, the original consulate also burned down. Fire was a big problem in the late 1800s and early 1900s. Then there was a crazy fire in 1907. Nearly two-thirds of the city burned to the ground before it stopped. A lot of historical buildings were lost then. That's why so many of the ones we're seeing now are rebuilds."

"Ah, now I understand."

"Remember the Kanemori warehouses that we saw the first time we went out?"

"Ah, yes, you mentioned then that they too were rebuilds. So they also were lost in the fire?"

"Yep." She smiled at him. "Now that we've finished visiting some other countries, we'll head to Goryokaku Park. It was one of the few places to survive the fire, so it should be interesting to see the differences in style there."

It took them twenty minutes to reach the fort by bus. As they rode along, Sakura found herself still marveling at the miracle the dohame had created. Even with all that walking, she wasn't tired at all. She could enjoy the cold, crisp air, the feel of the breeze playing with her hair, even running down one of the steep hills in the area. No coughing, no pain. *Is this what it would be like to be normal again? To feel alive?*

As soon as the bus stopped at the fort, she darted out to go look at the large moat that ran all the way around the star-shaped area. A small shop near the only bridge across offered boat rides around the moat, but the occasional burst of wind made them decide it was too cold for that. Besides, feeling so active, she wanted to enjoy it more.

"Karasu, I'll race you to the middle!" she said with a grin before taking off.

Moments later, the laughing boy ran past her with Kazuki close behind. Giving it her all, she couldn't catch up, but how thrilling it felt to run at full speed! For a brief second, she felt a tinge of fear when they stopped and she stood panting beside them. But it was just the normal result of exertion, no pain, no tightening in her chest.

"You're so fast!" she said as she ruffled his hair.

"Of course, I've never lost a race yet!" Karasu boasted.

"I'd imagine not. You even beat Kazuki!"

"He had a head start," Kazuki said in an afflicted tone, but his smile ruined the effect.

At the end of the bridge, they walked under a beautiful canopy of twisted branches. Sakura smiled as she walked along the tree-lined paths, imagining what the park would look like in the spring with the hundreds of cherry trees around them in bloom. Not that it wasn't pretty spectacular now, with many of the trees wearing their full fall colors.

"This is the former magistrate's office," Sakura said as they reached the center of the park. "It isn't the original one, though. While the fort survived the fire, before that, the original building was demolished after the fall of the shogunate. The city decided to rebuild it, and it just opened a few years ago. It is an amazing reconstruction. So much attention to detail, even the roof is authentic looking."

Sakura ambled about, looking at the building, getting halfway around before realizing Kazuki was taking pictures of her. When she looked back at him, he shrugged with a grin. "You looked so happy and curious. It was too cute not to capture."

"You really are too much. Come on, let's go up the observation tower back over the bridge. Then we can look at the whole park from above and have some gelato before we head to the amusement park."

ONE NIGHT

AFTER AN HOUR-LONG RIDE alternating between buses and the tram, they reached the newly opened Hakodate Adventure Land. Situated near the northeastern edge of the city, the amusement park was nestled between the city proper and the start of the farmlands that surrounded the area. Several of the roller coasters were visible from down the road as they approached the area, including a massive one that seemed to span the entire length of the place. It had to be over a kilometer long, maybe even two.

They purchased day passes at the entry gate so they could skip having to buy individual ride tickets, then headed straight for that long coaster. While they were waiting in line, the coaster screamed by, heading into what appeared to be the final drops and curves of the ride.

"Wow!" Kazuki stood up on his tiptoes, trying to follow the coaster as it went down into a low point. "That is way faster than a car!"

"The brochure says it has a top speed of over 125 kph! Might as well start with the biggest and the best, right?" Sakura said.

"Exactly!"

"How do they keep the people in there from falling out?" Karasu asked warily.

"A strong harness goes over your shoulder, and a belt across your lap. It's safe, I promise."

"Cool. It'll be fun to go that fast without being in a dive." Karasu grinned at her.

Soon it was their turn to ride. They managed to get near the front of the car. Sakura sat in the middle with Kazuki on her left and Karasu on her right. As the coaster began moving, Kazuki cheered, eager to experience this new sensation. The slow start as the metal train began climbing a long hill was disappointing. Where was the speed from before?

"When we get to the top, I heard it's best to scream and hold your hands in the air," Sakura said as they clicked closer and closer to the sky.

"Okay," Kazuki said, though he wasn't sure what there would be to scream about. Then the train crested the hill and flew down the other side. Kazuki threw up his hands and screamed along with Sakura and Karasu while trying not to panic. Before he could catch his breath, the train whipped around a curve then started up another hill, a shorter one this time, but the descent was still crazy fast, and it was followed immediately by yet another hill!

Three and a half minutes later, they were back on the ground and Kazuki wasn't sure he could walk. His stomach was doing strange flip-flops and threatening to return his lunch. Sakura and Karasu looked happy as they chatted about trying a different one next. He paused to lean against a pole, trying not to let them see how much the ride had affected him, but Sakura gave him a worried look. "Are you okay?"

"Yes…yes, that was just surprising. I let myself be fooled by the slowness at the start. Now I am prepared!"

She and Karasu exchanged looks then shrugged and led the way to the next ride. It wasn't as large, which Kazuki thought was a good sign, but it also looked quite complicated. The white track twisted and twirled all over the place. His stomach gave another lurch, but he gamely got on when it was their turn.

Like the first, it started slow, climbing a long hill. Sakura explained it was one way coasters got up to their higher speeds. Kazuki prepared himself for the coming crest, determined he would be able to enjoy it the same as the two beside him. Then the coaster dropped into a spiral descent that left him dizzy, then up again and down through a second set.

When they got off, he had to dart to the nearest bathroom where he did indeed lose the contents of his stomach. Sakura and Karasu waited for him outside, their concern clear.

"I'm sorry. It would appear my body does not like these coaster things as much as my mind thought I would."

"It's okay. We can go on other rides." Sakura used her handkerchief to wipe his brow.

"I'm sure I would enjoy them better, but I do not want you or Karasu to miss the coasters. You both are enjoying them so much! I shall just wait here on the nice firm ground."

"Are you sure?"

"Yes, this is your day. I want you to ride all the coasters you want!" He smiled as he held her hand.

"Okay."

Once he recovered, they headed to the next ride, which appeared to be a shorter coaster. Though it had a much steeper climb at the start, as well as a steeper drop, it went into a more gradual hill than the last and then into a long straightaway. He observed that after another short climb and a tight turn, it gently sloped back to the start.

"This one only has one turn. It might not be so bad," he

said, still wanting to be brave.

"You probably shouldn't risk it. See that long stretch? In that part, the coaster spins around like this." Sakura motioned with her finger. "You go upside down several times."

Kazuki plopped down on the nearby bench. "Upside down? And this is fun?"

"Should be." Sakura laughed. "We'll be back!"

Holding Karasu's hand, she ran over to the line. The park wasn't super busy, so they didn't have to wait long. Kazuki tried to watch as they rode, but when the car started doing the rolling action, he had to look away before his stomach joined in.

The next coaster had a huge loop that the train rode along the inside of, turning the occupants upside down for the whole rotation. Another had angled turns that had them riding sideways and in long slow twists around. One looked like a giant ship that swung from side to side, but on each swing it got higher and higher until finally the whole thing went around in a circle! There was even one where they stood for the whole ride, held in place by a shoulder harness that didn't look nearly secure enough for his tastes.

He almost tried the tower where people sat in normal-enough-looking chairs and were lifted high in the air. It looked like a nifty way to see the whole park. Then the thing holding the chairs up dropped, sending the people flying down to the ground at a rapid speed, stopping just before what he was sure was going to be a hideous accident. Karasu loved that one so much they went on twice in a row!

Kazuki loved seeing Sakura enjoying the park. Today was the first time he'd ever seen her smiling and laughing so freely. He still did not understand how these crazy rides were fun, but she was enjoying it and that was all that really mattered, though he was relieved when the adventurous pair finished their tour of the coasters and were ready to try some of the park's saner offerings.

The haunted house was much better than the one at the festival; it even made him jump a few times. He loved the mirror house, where the glass walls turned him into a short, dumpling-looking man, then a super tall and unnaturally thin one. Some made his top wide and his bottom small, then vice versa. The mirror maze was a fun challenge to go through without using his sense of smell.

With his stomach calmer, they snacked on strawberry popcorn, octopus karaage,[49] ika donburi,[50] and soft-serve ice cream in between the various rides and attractions. Dusk was approaching when they'd finished going around the park, including Sakura and Karasu taking another turn on their favorite coasters.

Kazuki left the pair under the pretext of going to the bathroom. Once he was out of their sight, he went to one of the pay phones, following Akari's instructions. The call was brief.

"Akari-san? This is Kazuki. We will be departing soon and riding the tram back."

"Good. Everything will be ready."

"Thank you. I know Sakura will love this." He disconnected then went to use the bathroom so as not to make himself a liar. He found the others where he'd left them, standing near one of the rides.

"The sun is going down. Shall we head home?"

Sakura fidgeted, twisting her hands in that cute way she did when she wanted something but was shy about asking. "Um,

---

[49] A frying technique similar to tempura.

[50] A dish consisting of a protein (fish or meat), vegetables, and/or other ingredients simmered together and served over rice. Ika, i.e., squid, is a signature topping for donburi in Hakodate. The fresh squid is known to "dance" when soy sauce is poured over the tentacles.

before we go, do you think you could handle riding the Ferris wheel?"

He looked at the nearby ride she pointed to. It was a large spoked wheel with enclosed cars around the outside. Unlike the other rides, this one turned slowly, never speeding up or doing any crazy maneuvers. "Yes, it looks quite tame."

With a smile, Sakura tugged them both to the line so they could ride it. Kazuki sat on one side while Sakura and Karasu sat on the other to keep the car balanced. This time his stomach had no complaints at the crawling pace nor at the height. As they got higher, they could see most of the city bathed in the red-oranges of the setting sun and dotted with lights as they started to come on. It was a pretty sight.

"Um, thank you, both of you, for today. I can't remember having this much fun before. Being able to run around and spend a whole day seeing and doing things I never imag-ined...I...thank you." Sakura bowed while blinking rapidly, her eyes glistening. Karasu hugged her side while Kazuki reached forward to stroke her hair, unable to embrace her without risk-ing tilting the car.

"No, thank you for letting us share this day with you."

"There is one place I'd like to stop at before we go home, if it is okay with you?"

"Sure." Sakura gave him a curious look but he just smiled and signaled the driver for the next stop. She glanced at Karasu, who shrugged, confused as well. Once they disembarked, Kazuki led them several blocks, occasionally turning down one street or another. He seemed to know where they were going, though Sakura wasn't sure how.

At one point, he paused and asked her to close her eyes while he and Karasu led her the rest of the way. Though nervous, she did as he asked. The sound of the waves hitting the shore grew louder as they neared the coast. Soon she could feel the misty spray on her skin.

"Be careful here; there are some stairs."

Feeling her way with her feet and following their lead, she went down. At the bottom, was a sandy surface. They were at the beach, but why? He took her forward a few stumbling steps.

"Okay, open your eyes."

A blanket lay on the sand, with a covered basket and a paper bag. A small electric lantern glowed from the middle of the blanket, making a cozy scene.

With a flourished bow, Kazuki indicated she should sit down. "Come, let us have dinner."

Once they were comfortable, he began unpacking the basket, pulling out three bento boxes.

"Kazuki, how did you…?"

"I'd like to say it is magic, but that would take credit from those who helped me. Hina-chan and Akari-san got everything set up just before we arrived." He smiled as he pulled three glasses out of the basket along with a bottle. "The wine, however, comes from Aki-san, who says it is quite a good one to try."

"Oh, you remembered that from my list?"

"Yes, it did not make today's plans because you could not buy it yourself."[51]

"Thank you." She clapped her hands as he poured them each a glass of the white wine, even Karasu. Well, he was over one hundred years old, even if he did look and act more like a

---

[51] In Japan, the legal drinking age was 16 until 2014, when it went up to 18. However, you must be 20 to actually purchase alcohol.

twelve-year-old kid.

"*Kanpai!*"[52] They clinked their glasses together then drank. First, a slightly tart taste hit her tongue along with the cool wine, then the delicate sweetness of grapes.

"Aki-san was right. It is good. I like it." She continued to sip at the wine while they ate their dinners, delicious yakotori[53] bentos from the Hasegawa store. When they were done, Kazuki handed her the bag. Inside was a sky lantern, complete with a lighter. Determined not to cry again, she kissed Kazuki on the cheek, then carried the lantern to the edge of the water. Lighting the small paper in the center that acted as the candle, she let it go. The breeze carried it out over the subtle waves, its soft yellow light reminiscent of a glow bug, only larger.

As it floated away, Kazuki wrapped his arms around her from behind, holding her against him, and Karasu came to stand beside them. Sakura sighed with contentment. It was as if the fears that had been growing inside her the last few weeks were being carried away by the lantern, leaving her fully free to enjoy the rest of her time with those she loved.

They stayed there together until the wind had swept the sky lantern out of sight; then they cleaned up their picnic and headed home.

As soon as they were inside, Karasu yawned loudly. "I'm beat. I'm gonna head to sleep." He climbed the stairs to his attic room with a wave. "Good night."

"Good night, Karasu-kun." Despite having done so much, Sakura didn't feel the least bit tired. She guessed it was because the dohame was still in effect. Which was good, as she still had

---

[52] "Empty cup" or "Bottoms up"—a traditional cheer used when drinking. If drinking sake, one would give the cheer then down the whole cup (which is like a shot), but for beer and wine, it's normal to sip as the characters do.

[53] Grilled meat on a stick, usually chicken, though some places, such as Hasegawa— which is particularly famous for its pork—offer several meats.

one last request. She waited until after the house was locked up and they'd both taken their baths and were lying in bed.

Having never seduced anyone before, she wasn't sure how to be cute and coy without looking silly. Besides, it didn't really suit her anyway. Instead, she rolled onto her side and gave him a soft kiss on the lips.

"Kazuki, I…"

He returned her kiss and stroked her cheek. "It would be a shame to waste this opportunity, yes?"

She knew he was giving her the final choice, but there really was only one choice for her. "Please. Even if it's just once…please."

Kazuki needed no further encouragement. His mouth captured her, his kiss more passionate than any before as he rolled over, partially covering her with his body. His hands cupped her face as he kissed her over and over, leaving her lips almost bruised but in the most wonderful way.

One hand slid down her face, his fingers tracing along her throat, her shoulder, her side. The claws of his hands, which looked so scary, didn't leave so much as a tickle behind; it was almost like being touched by a peach. How he could so exactly control it she didn't know, and right now, she didn't care. She was just glad he hadn't shifted back to his false form. Tonight, she wanted him, as he was.

His knuckles brushed the underside of her breast through her nightgown, before his hand turned to cup it, kneading it while his mouth continued its sweet assault down her chin. Her nipples contracted into tight buds as he took her other breast in his mouth, teasing it through the fabric.

She moaned, burying her hands into his hair. A tingling sensation welled up between her legs, making her squeeze her thighs together while pressing against him. It was as if her body had a mind of its own as it reacted to his attentions.

With a groan of his own, Kazuki pushed the nightgown up and over her head, removing the barrier between their bodies so his mouth could fully claim her breasts. He alternated between suckling one while working the other with his hand. The circling of her nipple with his thumb and the light squeezes his thumb circled only intensified the sensations flowing through her.

With her breath coming in short, ragged spurts, she could feel her heart beating faster, but it didn't hurt. No, all she felt now was pure pleasure as his lips reclaimed hers. His hand abandoned her breast to go down further, cupping her mound before one finger slipped between the soft, moist folds.

The touch sent her arching against him with a gasp. Following the signals of her body, she let her hips thrust against his stroking finger even as she felt a strange, tightening sensation.

She reached for him, running her hands over his chest and abdomen. The smooth skin stretched taut over the firm muscles beneath. Her hands slid lower, tickling the ridges of his abs and playing with the band of his boxers. Then he moved away, making her cry out.

He smiled and kissed her again, before shifting so he could remove the boxers. Fascinated, she sat up and reached for him, lightly touching the shaft with her fingers. She'd seen a picture before in health class, but the organ in front of her now seemed so much more alive. And bigger, definitely bigger. It wasn't out of place or anything, and fit with his body, but still. She glanced down at her own body.

"It will fit, I promise," Kazuki said softly, kissing her as he eased her back down. "I just need to make sure you're ready."

He moved down her stomach, easing her legs apart before kissing her there, between her legs. At least it seemed liked a kiss, then his tongue began doing a flicking motion and she lost all sense of thought. All she knew was that her body was hot and aching and needing something. Like when riding that big roller coaster as it neared the crest of the hill, she felt the anticipation building and building.

"Please. Please." She didn't even know what she was begging for, but he responded, coming back up to her mouth, laying his body fully on hers.

"Now you are ready, love." He reached between their torsos, guiding himself to her opening. As he pressed against it, she could feel her body stretching, making room for him. It didn't hurt, not like she'd always heard it would. She did feel tight, even a bit uncomfortable at first, but as he continued his slow entrance, she wrapped her arms around him, digging her fingers into his butt. Taking the hint, he thrust the rest of the way in, making her shudder.

He stroked her face then kissed her tenderly. "I love you. You are the most precious person in my life, my beautiful, sweet sudtama."

"I love you too. You are my prince."

One more feather-light kiss then he began to move, his hips pulling back and forth, thrusting him inside her. As before, her hips moved on their own, bringing her closer against him with each thrust, deepening the motion. As the pace quickened, that tight anticipation from earlier returned, filling her mind with incoherent thoughts. Kazuki feverishly murmured encouraging sounds that formed no words she could translate.

She was crying out, sounds she'd never heard anyone make. Leaning on one arm, Kazuki reached between them again, his finger stroking the nub that he'd licked earlier, while his thrusts slowed and grew more powerful. She went over the crest, screaming as her body convulsed against him. His hands now on her hips, he started going faster. Forcing her eyes open, she could see his face contorted in pleasure. Then his head dropped back and he gasped. With one last powerful thrust, he collapsed on top of her.

Sakura wrapped her arms around him, still trying to sort through the amazing sensations she'd felt. As his panting calmed, Kazuki shifted so they could lie on their sides, front to front, their legs intertwined. They shared shy smiles, random touches, random kisses. No words were needed now, only unwinding from the passion that had consumed them.

Sakura remembered what he'd called her. Sudtama? He'd used that word before as well. "What is a sud…"

Before she could finish asking the question, her breath caught. Not from pleasure, but a mild pain. The heavy vest was enveloping her again, her body instantly growing weary and tired. She could even see her hand, lying on Kazuki's chest, turning pale. She wanted to cry, hating to see this time end, but she didn't. No matter what happened now, this time was a precious gift, one she would treasure.

"Sakura? It has worn off?"

"I think so." Her eyes grew heavy and her head fell to the pillow. There was no fighting off the sleepy feeling, but she tried, even as her eyes closed. "I'm so…happy. Thank you, Kazuki. Thank you."

Her cheeks felt damp, though she wasn't sure why. Unable to hold out anymore, she let go, the dohame's final side-effect pulling her into a deep sleep.

Duty Bound

REITO'S LETTER SAID SAKURA would be "sleepy" after the dohame wore off, but the reality was far beyond that. She'd slept through the night and well into the next day, to the point that Kazuki had been afraid she wasn't going to wake up. When she'd finally started to stir mid-afternoon, he'd nearly suffocated her from holding her so tight. Though the events of the day before shouldn't have left any toll on her body, she remained so tired that Kazuki had to carry her down the stairs.

Settling her in the living room, he went into the kitchen to make coffee, followed by Karasu.

"Is she okay?" Karasu asked.

"I think so. I do not understand, though. The dohame should not have had this much of an effect." Kazuki set the coffee things on the tray, then began making a sandwich since Sakura had missed breakfast. "Since the effects of the dohame lasted longer because she is human, perhaps the aftermath will as well."

"I guess that makes sense."

Kazuki nodded. "We'll just make sure she rests. We already cleaned the house, and I can go pick up dinner shortly. Still, if she is not better tomorrow, I will insist she visit her doctor just to be safe."

The rest of the day she was almost docile as she lay tucked in some blankets on the floor of the living room, her head on Kazuki's lap. At times, he'd look down to find she'd fallen asleep. When evening came, he picked up some take-out, which she ate at the same semi-lethargic pace with which she'd eaten the sandwich earlier.

They'd barely gotten the table cleared off when she nodded off again. Kazuki carried her upstairs. He was too afraid she'd hurt herself in the shower alone, so he took her in the shower with him. With her sitting on the stool, he washed her as quickly as he could while staying ready to catch her if she tilted over. She fell asleep while he was carrying her to bed. Even when he lay her down and covered her, she didn't stir.

When morning came and the alarm went off, she woke up the way she always did. Other than a mild bit of strain around her eyes, she looked normal again as she said good morning and kissed him. He only relented to her going to school when she promised to call him to come get her if she started feeling unwell again and that she would alert Akari and Hina as well so they could help her.

It was early afternoon when someone knocked on the front door. Sakura wasn't due from school for another couple of hours, not that she would need to knock on her own door any-way. Kazuki muted the game show on the television and acti-vated his glam spell before going to answer it, Karasu following close behind. An uneasy feeling settled in his stomach, making him walk faster.

His mouth gaped as he stared at the tall, lithe man with flaming red hair at the other side of the door. "Reito!? What are you doing here?"

"Lord Reito!" Karasu peered out from behind him.

"If I may enter, My Prince?"

"Of course, come in." Kazuki led him to the living room. "Um, would you like some tea?"

"Yes, please, that would be nice." Reito paused to bow in front of the shrine before sitting at the kotatsu. Kazuki darted to the kitchen, his mind racing. Why would Reito come here and why now? He set the tray as fast as he could and returned to the living room.

Reito took two sips before speaking. "Thank you. It has been a long time since I've made this trip, and it left me a bit parched. My age is catching up to me it seems."

"Has something happened to my father? Is Yuji okay?"

Reito set his teacup down.

"I wish I could say I came simply to check on you, but that would be a lie." He paused, his gaze softening. "Princess Aya came to visit you a few mornings ago, to try to persuade you to reconsider your refusal of mating. She stayed, despite being told you were out of the country, planning to wait for your return. I'm sorry, My Prince, but this morning she was found in her chambers, dead."

Kazuki's throat caught. "Dead? Aya? She can't be. No. I...how?"

"She was strangled."

His heart aching, Kazuki's head fell forward as he cried. Vaguely, he felt Karasu's arms come around him. He could barely fathom it. Aya, so bright and beautiful and full of life. Before all the mess with the mating, when they'd simply been friends, her musical laughter, her impishness, had always made him smile. Even when she was being selfish and spoiled, she'd been adorable, with keen awareness of what she was up to and that sweet smile ready to butter up even the most hardened soul.

Kazuki finally looked up to find Reito holding out a handkerchief, a compassionate expression on his face. Kazuki dried his face and patted Karasu's arm in silent thanks.

"Do we know who did it?"

"Nothing's been confirmed yet. Aya's attendants claim to have seen and heard nothing, despite being in the next room. The guards have detained them for now to be safe. However," Reito hesitated, turning his teacup on the table before continuing, "there are rumors that Prince Yujinasanarama returned to the castle sometime during the night and that he was last seen near her room."

"That's ridiculous." Kazuki banged his hand on the table. "Yuji would sooner die himself than harm her. You know how much he loved her."

"Yes, I am aware of this. At this point, I do know that fresh traces of his scent can be found in and around the room." He held up a hand to forestall Kazuki's interruption. "That said, no one in the castle has come forward who actually saw him. They've just repeated what they've 'heard.' I have people trying to find the source of the rumors. However, despite our efforts, they continue to spread."

Unless he heard it from Yuji's mouth himself, Kazuki wouldn't believe it, wouldn't believe that Yuji was so far gone that he would harm Aya over his mistaken belief that Kazuki was going to mate with her. Besides, Karasu had told him about Sakura. "Has word been sent to Yuji yet?"

"I sent a messenger to the Forest of Kuragari where Karasu saw him last. He had not returned yet when I left to come here."

"What about Father?" Kazuki knew it was a pointless question. If his father had returned, he would have sent word. But he had to ask, hoping to somehow avoid what he knew was coming.

"There has been no word from him as yet either. It is enough to make a fox go silver." Reito's heavy sigh filled the space between them. "My Prince, I know you wish to remain with Lady Sakura, and thus far I've been able to allow you that indulgence, but things have changed. Princess Aya's parents will be in an uproar as it is. Imagine if they find out this situation is being handled by a lowly attendant? And the people may well go into a panic if you do not return to keep the calm. This is not the time for our kingdom to be without a ruler."

Karasu jumped up. "But what about Sakura? She's getting worse, and she doesn't have that much longer. We can't just abandon her now!"

Reito ignored him, instead watching Kazuki with that relentless steady gaze. It went without saying. Kazuki knew what had to be done, but the pain ripping through him made him want to cry anew. He covered his eyes with his hand, unable to take that pitying stare anymore.

"Karasu." Kazuki reached out and tugged at the boy's hand until he sat down again. "He…he is right. No matter how much I love Sakura, Aya's death could be seen as an act of war, especially if it is not handled to Osgavenda's satisfaction. How could I continue to live here knowing our kingdom was being torn apart? If she knew I was even thinking about it, she would yell at me to go, to take care of my responsibilities. You know this as well as I."

"I know, but…!"

"We've been here for over a month in human time now. That means our people have gone without a visible ruler for a full year and that I have let this thing between Yuji and I fester for just as long. I hoped he would at least resume his duties if I was not there, believing this was purely an issue between us. But he has not returned. If I am to truly give myself to Sakura for the rest of her time, I must resolve this thing with him and ensure our kingdom will be at peace."

Kazuki glanced at the clock. Two o'clock. Part of him wanted to stay long enough to see her, to kiss her again, hold her. But he knew there was no more time to spare. Reito was calm, but his being there alone was a sign of how critical this was.

But, still, he couldn't stop himself from asking. "Can we take her back with us? It will just be a few hours until she comes home."

Reito was shaking his head before Kazuki even finished the question. "From what you have told me of Lady Sakura's condition, it isn't possible. You do not have enough magical power to transport two via a gem, and while your power might be sufficient to enable her pass through the portal, it would be too taxing on her. It could very well kill her to even try it. In truth, I cannot remember the last time a human without some latent magical abilities did so and lived to tell about it. If by some miracle she did make it over, she'd be under intense scrutiny. Would you want to subject her to that sort of welcome?"

"I know. You're right." Taking someone else between the worlds on one gem required significantly more magic, particularly if the other person had no innate magical powers to contribute to the spell. Nor would he ever gamble her life on his abilities to enable her to pass through a portal. His father could do it, if he were home…but then, if his father were home, he wouldn't have to leave at all. And bringing a human mate to court now? That would be an insult to Osgavenda.

With a shaky breath, he forced himself to retrieve a pen and paper. He knew if he waited until she came home to say goodbye, his resolve would crumble. Reito and Karasu remained silent, watching as he wrote a letter to her to explain his absence.

He filled the first page and part of the second before scrawling his signature on the bottom. After he folded it, he held it out to Karasu.

"Master Kazuki?" Karasu looked at him, confused as he reached for the letter.

"I trust you as I do few others, Karasu. That is why I am asking you…no, pleading with you, please watch over her, my precious Sakura."

He knew it was a lot to ask, that Karasu would most likely want to go home with him. But Kazuki would at least keep that part of the promise, to never leave her alone again. Though Karasu's bottom lip trembled, he nodded, holding the letter against his chest. "I promise."

"Thank you." Kazuki stood and hugged him tight. "Send word through the tree if anything happens. We'll keep you updated, and I'll be back as soon as possible."

Hatching Connections

"I'M OFF." AKARI WAVED goodbye before heading to her student council meeting. Sakura returned the wave before finishing packing up her things. Nearby, Hina leaned against her desk while waiting for Yamaguchi-san to finish packing his bag so they could head off on a date.

"See you later." Sakura smiled at the pair as she left, answering a few other farewell calls along the way. She passed Mimomo-sensei in the hall.

"Ah, Sakura-chan, good afternoon." As usual, Mimomo-sensei looked bright and chipper. Rather than scowling as she might have in the past, Sakura replied in kind.

It seemed so long ago that she would have made this walk in absolute silence, her nose in the air if she passed anyone. Since meeting Hina and Akari, she'd started to forget to wear her cold mask of disdain, and now it was just too much trouble. Maybe her classmates were responding to that. Or maybe they just liked Hina and Akari too much to go against their becoming her friend. Either way, it made the school feel warmer, and the days didn't drag on like they used to.

Near the lockers she spotted Koga-sensei, his hands behind his back as he watched to make sure no one loitered in the halls.

Because of a cold, he hadn't been at school Friday or Saturday. She smiled brightly and waved to him. "Glad you're feeling better. See you tomorrow!"

His hands fell to his sides as his mouth gaped open. "Uh, um, yes, thank you. Good afternoon."

She could barely keep from laughing as she continued on to her locker. After exchanging her school slippers for her street shoes, Sakura headed outside. The sky was overcast, but no rain was in the forecast for the week, only more cautious talk of potential snow, the same first snowfall that had been "coming" for three weeks now.

"Yo!" Karasu leaned against the wall near the school gate, his hands clasped behind his head.

"Karasu-kun, you came to get me today?" She wondered where Kazuki was. They had sometimes come together to get her from school, but Karasu had never come alone before.

"Yep, thought it'd be a nice change of pace. Disappointed?"

"Of course not!" She smiled. "It is a nice surprise, thank you."

Though he seemed nonchalant, something was happening, she was sure of it. If anything bad had happened to Kazuki, there was no way Karasu would be so calm, so it must be something else. She wanted it to be something good, like Kazuki's father or his brother coming home, but surely Karasu would be acting all excited if that were the case. Her unease made her babble about whatever random things came to mind about her day. He walked beside her, his hands in his pockets, listening intently as if she were telling him global secrets.

They were in the park, the same park in which she'd run into Akari, when he stopped. She'd gone a few steps before noticing.

"Karasu-kun?"

His hands were out of his pockets now, and he stared hard at the ground. "He's not there."

"What?"

"Master Kazuki. He isn't there, waiting I mean. He's gone. He went home."

"Home…back to your world? He's…" She looked back over her shoulder toward the direction of her house. Her foot lifted as if her body was ready to give in to the urge to run there, to prove it was a lie. He wouldn't have just left, without even saying goodbye?

"Something happened. He had to go back. He didn't want to, but he said you'd understand." She turned back to Karasu. He was bowing deeply, a letter held in his outstretched hands. "He left this for you."

She took the folded pages, her vision blurring for a moment. With mechanical steps, she walked over to the swings and sat down. The movement set the swing into a shallow sway as she unfolded the letter and read it. She could understand his leaving because of Aya's death; she would expect no less of him. Not that it made the words any easier to take. He was gone. Her Kazuki was gone.

Wet drops discolored the trembling paper as she read his final words again.

> *Never have I felt so great a terror as I do now, at the thought that something will happen while I'm gone and that I will return to find you have left me. Please, my love, mind your health and let Karasu aid you in my place. Until I can return to you, I pray you will wait for me.*
>
> *Eternally yours,*
>
> *Kazuki*

The letter fell to the ground as she looked up at the sky, wishing it was a terrible joke. But it wasn't…He was gone, just like that. With nothing more than a letter to say goodbye.

With a sob, she buried her hands in her face and cried. Karasu's arms wrapped around her shoulders as he leaned his head against hers, whispering an apology even as his own tears dampened her hair.

After her tears ran dry, she hugged Karasu tight. "Are you okay, staying behind, I mean?"

"Well, yeah." Karasu sniffed as he swiped at his nose with his sleeve. "Master Kazuki loves you. If he's worried about you being alone, it will just make him get things done that much quicker and come back sooner, right?"

He turned his head away from her, but looked back at her from the corner of his eye. "Besides, if I left too, you'd just cry even more. Crying isn't good for your health, you know."

A small laugh sneaked out despite her pain. "I suppose you're right, it isn't."

Karasu relaxed a bit and pushed a tissue into her hand. After drying her face, she reached down and picked up Kazuki's letter, running her hand over the surface.

"Can I write him back?"

"Yeah, just give it to me when it's done, and I can send it to him just like how we sent letters to Reito." He swiped at his face again. "Don't worry, okay? It shouldn't take too long. With the time difference, he'll probably be back by the weekend."

"That's true…" She folded the letter carefully and tucked it into her pocket. It wouldn't do to sit around moping. Even if he had stayed to say goodbye, she knew he was right, she'd have told him to go. While she loved him being with her, she wasn't so selfish that she'd keep him here when his people truly needed him.

Kazuki doesn't love some weak girl who throws a tantrum at him taking care of his duties, some girl who can't stand on her own. I have to be strong. It isn't like he's gone forever, and I still have a few months left.

Karasu watched Sakura warily. She'd cried a long time. He hadn't meant to cry himself, but then she'd started going, and next thing he knew, he'd been bawling too. Now she was looking at the ground after putting Kazuki's letter away, her toe occasionally giving the swing a push.

"You going to be okay?" he asked quietly.

She nodded and looked up at him, her expression resolved. "Yeah." Her face softened in an affectionate look. "Besides, you're still here with me, so I'm not alone."

He tried not to blush at her sappy remark. "Yeah, yeah, I'm not going anywhere. Wanna head home? I'm getting hungry."

"Karasu-kun, I understand why he left, but it still rather bugs me a bit. It doesn't seem fair, you know?" With a slight smile, Sakura stood from the swing, but she didn't start walking. "What about you?"

"Yeah, a little." In truth, he hated being left behind, hated not knowing what was going on, but he knew why Kazuki hadn't wanted to leave her alone. He just hoped her health would hold out. She'd been noticeably weaker since the Day of Buckets.

"So let's splurge on dinner tonight and go to Shabu Shabu[54] Kirari."

It took him a moment to recall the name. "Wait, that place from the TV Master Kazuki was going nuts about wanting to try?"

"Oh, is that where I heard of it?" Her smile grew bigger as she gave him a wink.

Karasu grinned back as he caught on to her scheme. It sounded like a fitting way to pay Kazuki back for leaving them both behind. Of course, they both understood why, but as she said, it still sucked. "Yeah, that sounds good! Let's do it!"

Located in a hotel, the restaurant was a more expensive place than they usually went to, so they returned home first to change. Sakura put on a long blue dress with a dressy-looking pair of boots, and Karasu took a picture to give Kazuki later.

He was able to get away with wearing one of the nicer pairs of pants she'd bought him and a long-sleeve shirt. The bow tie at his neck, borrowed from Kazuki's clothes, was itchy, though it was still better than wearing a full necktie. He hated having nooses around his neck.

They rode the tram there and soon had a small pot of boiling dashi[55] broth sitting between them, along with plates of locally grown beef, Chinese cabbage, onions, carrots, and shitake mushrooms. Bowls of tart citrus ponzu[56] sauce for dipping and

---

[54] Shabu-shabu is another form of hot pot, featuring a kelp-based broth in which ingredients are "swished" back and forth. They are then dipped in ponzu sauce before being eaten. The remaining broth is combined with any remaining rice and eaten as a soup to finish the meal. As the beef is only cooked to a rare state, high-grade meat is used, resulting in Shabu Shabu predominately being "fine dining," unlike more common forms of hot pot.

[55] A basic stock used in many Japanese dishes, made by boiling edible kelp (kombu) with shaves of preserved fermented tuna (kezurikatsuo) and straining; considered one of the five basic tastes of Japan.

[56] A thin, dark-brown, citrus-based sauce known for its tart flavor.

individual servings of steamed rice took the last of the space. She showed him how to cook the meat and vegetables to go on the rice.

It was a relaxing meal, the silence as they enjoyed their food a companionable one. Learning the truth about Sakura's health and getting over his childish jealousy of Kazuki's feelings for her had turned out to be a freeing experience. Without the stress and self-generated angst, he could enjoy his time in the human world and better understand Kazuki's fascination with it. He'd even gotten used to sleeping in the attic, though he did miss being out in the open—having walls around him was just too confining. Given a choice, he would still rather be home, but being alone with Sakura now wasn't the burden he would have considered it a few weeks ago.

"You know, we've never really had a chance to talk before, have we? Just the two of us, I mean." Sakura tilted her head as she gazed at him from across the table. "It's like I know lots about you, and yet it's also like I know nothing at all."

It was true. He hadn't deliberately avoided being alone with her or anything. It just tended to work out that way because Kazuki had wanted to spend as much time with her as he could. "So what would you like to know?"

"Well, I know Kazuki said you were like a brother to him and you've been together a long time, but how did you meet? And what about your actual family?"

"The answer to both questions is kind of the same." He set down his chopsticks. "I don't have a family, not anymore. I mean, I had parents who made me, but they aren't a part of my life now. Master Kazuki and Master Yuji are my family in the ways that matter."

"Oh." She didn't ask him to explain, no doubt wanting to respect his privacy. But thinking of her history, of how she came to be in her current state, he decided he wanted to tell her.

"Tengu parents have multiple children at once, just like regular birds do. I was born as part of a clutch of four, but none of my siblings lived even five years. I don't know why. Maybe they were born sick or they got sick later. Either way, they just drifted off one by one. Because I was the only one to survive, my parents blamed me. Said I stole their food or that I tried to kill them on purpose, all sorts of lies."

"How could they blame a baby for something like that?"

He shrugged. "Maybe losing so many kids so close together warped their minds or something. Or maybe I was just a convenient target for their pain. Whatever the reason, they would sometimes ignore me for days, leaving me hungry or cold. If they did pay attention to me, it was usually to insult me and smack me around. Then, one day, my mother picked me up, flew far from our home, and dropped me."

She gasped, tears forming in her eyes. It didn't surprise him, not anymore. When it came to those she cared for, she was almost too empathetic.

"I was only ten at the time, so I couldn't fly yet. We can't assume our other form until we're fifty. Somehow, I only ended up with a broken arm and some bruises. I knew if I went home, they would probably just kill me, so I went to a town not far from where she left me."

At the time, he hadn't known it was the main city of Throklana, the one where the royal castle was housed. He just knew it was large and that people there would likely care nothing about a small child on his own. "At first I begged for food, but I would get so little that I stayed hungry. It got worse and worse, so I started stealing. Usually I went for stuff that no one would buy anyway, like meats that were getting too old, stale bread, stuff like that. Since they were just going to be tossed, it wasn't watched as closely. Sometimes it made me sick, but it helped keep the edge off. Then a shop keeper caught me stealing some molded fruit from his stand. Even though it was trash, he was furious and chased me. Some other people joined him. I've never been a fast runner, so they caught me and beat the gizzards out of me. They left me lying in some alley. I thought I was going to die then. I kept waiting, almost hoping for death to come."

She gave a slight nod, a sad, understanding look in her eyes.

"A few hours later, Master Kazuki found me. He took me back to the castle and treated my wounds. He stayed with me the whole time I was healing, with Master Yuji helping. They were the first people to show me any sort of kindness. Once I was healed, I was allowed to stay at the castle with them, and we've been together since."

"It must be pretty hard on you, seeing them fighting like this."

"Yeah, I wish I knew what was going on. Master Yuji has always had a more even temper than Master Kazuki…You actually remind me of him a bit. He almost never gets angry or yells. So him being so furious that he would leave home? It just makes no sense."

They paused the conversation while she paid for their dinner. Outside, they arrived at the tram stop just in time to catch the next one. Once they were in their seats, he quietly told her about the meeting he'd had with Yuji.

"That really does sound odd. They both seem to want to end this dispute, but they think the other is angry and refusing to listen."

"Yeah. And unless he's really changed since he left home, Master Yuji is a horrible liar. So I believe he was telling the truth when he denied having anything to do with the attack."

"We must be missing something." She crossed her arms, tapping one finger against her upper arm. "Could either be under some kind of spell?"

"I don't think so. That kind of magic is hard to work, even on a low-level animal. To do so against royalty of levels like Master Kazuki and Master Yuji and have it last this long would require someone with crazy abilities. As far as I know, even the king can't do that kind of spell."

They got off the tram at the usual stop and began walking the two blocks home. Sakura put her arm around his shoulders as the wind picked up. "I read once that a single misunderstanding can cause people to forget the many things we love about someone, that it's like a poison that clouds our minds."

Her words made sense. In a way, the two had cast a spell on themselves, making them view everything the other said and did in a negative way, continuing to fuel the very misunderstanding that started it.

"If we could get Master Yuji back to the castle, we could just take both of them and lock them in a jail cell or something until they got it all out and started listening to each other again." Karasu chuckled as he pictured the scene he described. "As stubborn as they both are, even they couldn't hold out more than a year or two."

Shifting Pawns

THURSDAY NIGHT, A LETTER arrived through the tree while Sakura was making their dinner.

Karasu,

Please return to me as soon as possible. The situation has grown dire, and I urgently need your assistance.

Kazuki

No matter how many times Karasu re-read it, the brief lines didn't change. Had Osgavenda declared war? It had to be horrible for Kazuki to write such a short note, one that made no mention of Sakura at all.

"Karasu-kun, dinner's ready," Sakura called from the doorway. "Oh, is it from Kazuki?"

He gave her a brief nod, glad the letter was written in their native language. "He said to tell you he loves you and misses you lots. Things are still kind of tense, but getting better."

"That's good. Maybe he'll be able to come back soon." Her smile made the pang of guilt at lying to her worth it.

"Probably. Though I'm going to have to leave for a bit."

Her smile fell away sharply. "You too?"

"Yeah, he asked me to run an errand for him. It's just a quick one, though." He stood and walked over to her, holding her hand. "Really quick, okay? I bet I'll even be back before you get home from school tomorrow. So don't cry, please? You'll start coughing again." She'd been coughing for two days now. At first it had just been a little thing, one or two at random times. But it was getting more frequent, to the point she'd had to use her inhaler.

She sniffled but managed a shaky smile. "Okay, then I'll make that udon dish for dinner tomorrow."

"The one with the squid? Yay!" He forced himself to grin. "Speaking of dinner, I don't exactly have to rush off right this minute and that curry sure smells good."

They laughed and went back inside to eat. But the uneasiness clawing at him only got louder. He could tell she was trying to keep on a happy face, but she didn't want him to leave any more than he wanted to go. Her eyes were as pitiful looking as those of a lonely morcet asking for someone to pet it. What could Kazuki need of him that Reito couldn't do?

While they were clearing the plates, the coughing started again. Karasu stayed near with her inhaler ready as she leaned on the counter. Her thin body shook each time she coughed, seven times in all. That was more than last night.

"I'm sorry."

"It's okay. Why don't you go shower for a bit? The steam helped yesterday, right?"

"Yes, it seemed to."

"I'll be right here if you need me, okay?" He handed her the inhaler to keep with her, just in case. He went upstairs with her, continuing on to the attic to retrieve the wooden sword he'd brought with him there. The day he first met her came to mind, when he'd attacked her and threatened her with the dull weapon. Then, she'd just been a stupid human to him, an annoyance hindering his return home with Kazuki. Now, he was trying to find a reason to ignore Kazuki's command so he didn't have to do just that.

Karasu went back downstairs. Sakura was still in the shower, so he ducked into her room to search Kazuki's things for the dohame recipe before darting back downstairs. The ingredients he'd brought for it were a few weeks old, but none looked spoiled yet. They'd kept them in the fridge, as per Reito's instructions when they'd told him they hadn't made it all.

Working as fast as he dared, he followed the steps outlined. His was paler than the last batch. In terms of pure power, he knew his blood was nowhere near as potent as Kazuki's, so this dose wouldn't work as well. He just hoped it would be enough. He'd just finished pouring the lavender liquid into the bottle when she walked into the kitchen.

"What are you doing?" She stared at the bottle as he capped it off.

"Here." He pressed it into her hand. "That cough of yours doesn't sound good, and it's supposed to snow again tomorrow. Knowing you, you'll go to school anyway, so take it with you. If you get sick, you can drink it."

"You made this for me?"

"Yeah. I know you don't like how it's made, and you said you wouldn't take it again, but with that coughing, I wanted you to have something in case anything happens while I'm gone."

She wrapped her arms around him, hugging him tight. "Thank you."

He hugged her back. The same feeling that drove him to make the dohame was practically screaming now that he shouldn't leave. But Kazuki needed him, and that was where he belonged. Forcing himself to let go, he strapped his sword on, put on his coat and gloves, and then walked with her to the side door.

"Stay warm and don't stay up too late studying. If you start to feel worse, go see that doctor of yours, okay? And keep that bottle close. The stopper won't fall out unless you pull it, so you can carry it with you anywhere. If you feel an attack coming on, drink it. It's a weak dose since it's made with my blood, but it should still last a few hours since it will only be your second dose."

"I'll be careful, I promise, and I'll keep it on me all the time. Travel safe and tell Kazuki I love him." She paused, her expression shifting to a shy smile. "You know, I always wanted a little brother. If I could choose one, he'd be one just like you. Though, I guess, technically you're older than me, so you'd really be the big brother I never had. I mean…so…if it's okay, I think of you as family now, and I love you too, so hurry back, okay?"

"I will, I promise." He walked off the porch before stopping to look back at Sakura, who stood in the doorway. "I guess you'd be a pretty good little sister, even if you are taller than me."

Her laugh mixed with a sob and followed him as he transformed and flew toward the small island just off the Hakodate shore where the portal home was located.

Friday morning, Sakura had to force herself out of bed. The deafening stillness of the empty house had kept her up all night. She debated staying home from school, but so far, the cough hadn't made an appearance that morning. Besides, being alone all day would only make her miss them more.

After she dressed, she picked up the dohame bottle, taking comfort in the slight warmth it exuded as she held the precious gift against her chest. With a smile, she tucked it into her jacket pocket. Throughout the day, her thoughts kept drifting back to her missing yokai. It was the loneliest she'd felt since Ito-san had died. It really wasn't much different from a normal day, since Karasu would be home before her. But, somehow, it still felt different, knowing they weren't at home. A voice inside her kept whispering that there would be no one waiting, that she was alone again.

No, I'm not alone, not anymore. She glanced across the room toward Hina, who sat watching her with a worried expression. In the next row over, Akari was also looking her way regularly. Between the next class, they both came over to her desk.

"Sakura-chan, are you feeling okay?" Hina asked as she leaned over and put one hand on her forehead, the other on her own head.

"I have a little cough, but I'll be okay."

"What else is going on? You've been sighing a lot and looking like you're going to cry. Did you get some bad news?" Akari asked, putting her hand on Sakura's shoulder.

"Kazuki had to go home for a bit to deal with a family problem. Karasu stayed behind, but then he had to leave yesterday too. It just feels weird without them around now."

Hina took her hand away, seemingly satisfied that Sakura didn't have a fever. "That sucks. Will they be back soon?"

"I hope so. Maybe even tonight." She tried to make her smile hopeful, but she suspected she'd failed.

"It's supposed to snow pretty heavily tonight. The trains might stop." Akari looked toward the window where the snow was already picking up again. "Sakura-chan, you want me to come spend the night? That way you won't be by yourself if anything happens."

"That's kind of you, but I wouldn't want to burden you. You already have to travel so much further now to get from Aki's house to here. I'm sure I'll be okay. Thank you."

In reality, her chest was feeling increasingly strange, like flies were trapped in her lungs, tickling the sides with their wings in an effort to escape. Then, mid-morning, the coughing started up again. Just before lunch, it got so bad the whole class was staring. With a blush, she apologized and asked to be excused to go home. But, first, she stopped by the hospital where Tenma-sensei gave her a cough suppressant to try to keep it from weakening her lungs further, making her promise to call immediately if it got any worse.

On the tram home, she watched the snow-covered landscape sliding past. If they were here now, Kazuki would be pulling Karasu into a snowball fight while she sat bundled up on the porch laughing. Then she'd make them hot chocolate and cookies to enjoy while they warmed back up. She gave the bottle in her pocket a light squeeze to push away the renewed sadness.

When she arrived home, she was surprised to find a young man with long white hair standing on her front porch. He turned as she walked up the walkway, looking at her with a familiar pair of deep, purple-tinted eyes. "Yuji-san?"

"You must be the girl, Sakura?"

She nodded and moved past him to open the door. "Please, come in."

"Thank you." He followed her inside, looking around with a curious expression. "How did you know my name?"

"You look a lot like your brother." Perhaps it was foolish to invite him in when he supposedly wanted to kill Kazuki, but he didn't make her afraid. His voice was as soft and gentle as his demeanor as he stood with her in the kitchen, watching her prepare tea. As Karasu had said, it was hard to picture him being violent. He looked more delicate than Kazuki, thinner of build and with a more feminine face.

Once she had the tea loaded in the tray along with some leftover cookies, she started to pick it up, but he moved first and took it. It was just as well, she started coughing at the living room door.

"I'm sorry. You can set it down over there. I just need a moment to take my medicine." She went back to the kitchen and forced down a dose of the syrup from Tenma-sensei, trying not to gag on the bitter taste. When she returned to the living room, he had the tea set up and a cup waiting for her. "Thank you."

"It is no problem." His gaze stayed on her as she sat down and sipped her tea. "I'm sure you are wondering why I am here."

"A bit, yes. Kazuki isn't here, you know."

"I know. He is in Osgavenda, talking with Aya's parents." Pain distorted his beautiful face.

"I'm sorry. Kazuki said you loved her very much."

"Yes, if she would have had me, we would already be mated. But she only had eyes for him."

"Is that why you attacked him?" *Talk about jumping in with both feet!*

"I did not attack him! While I'm angry at him, yes, and all the more so for all of these lies he keeps telling about me, attacking him would be foolish. He has always been a better fighter than I and could kill me with little effort."

"Whether he's told any lies about you or not, I can't say. I do know that I treated his wounds myself. I also know that every time he's spoken of you, he has told me how wonderful you are, how worried he is about you being away from home, how much he wants to reconcile with you, how much he loves you."

Yuji shook his head with a frown. "Loves me? No, he doesn't love me, not anymore. I don't know what I did to make him hate me like this, but there is no love left."

"It would seem stubbornness is another trait you two share." Sakura sighed as she refilled his teacup. "Look, I love Kazuki, so you may not consider me a neutral party in all this, but I'm willing to listen. I know what Kazuki has told me and the things Karasu-kun has seen and heard. Perhaps if you told me your side, I could help you figure out why you are all saying different things. There must be some missing link that connects your stories."

She almost laughed when he rested his chin on his fingers to think before nodding. They really were similar.

"Growing up, I worshiped him. I wanted to be just like him. To me, he was strong, brave, kind. We were always together. As we got older, though, things started to change. We started to have different interests and disagreed more. Then there was Aya. Though he swore he had no interest in her, that she kept making it clear she intended to be *his* mate, it made me jealous. This I admit." He paused. "Has he told you of being the future ruler of our kingdom?"

"He told me he had promised to stand down as potential king, as he doesn't want to rule. And that you would then succeed your father, which you both preferred."

"Yes, this is what he once told me too. While I disagreed with his assessment of himself as a ruler, that he had no desire to do it was enough to make me accept the arrangement. But then, I learned he had changed his mind and was heard talking of what he will do when he is king. When I questioned him about it, he denied it, but I continued hearing it more and more."

"And you started to believe the rumors?"

"I didn't want to, but then I was attacked while visiting my mother's grave by an assassin. I easily fought him off and demanded to know why he would try to harm me. He told me Kazuki had hired him to kill me, to ensure I didn't claim the crown and to leave him free to mate with Aya. It was then that I knew my brother hated me."

Sakura moved around the table so she could sit closer to him and hold both of his soft, smooth hands. "Kazuki had no way of knowing we would ever meet, so there would be no reason to lie to me about not wanting the throne, right?"

"I suppose not. If anything, he would brag about being future king."

"And you said yourself that Kazuki could best you in a fight, yes? You've been together all of your lives, so surely he knows your skills well. If he wanted you dead, would he not do it himself or at least hire someone he knew to be a better fighter?"

He frowned. "That is true. At the time, I took it as an insult that he sent someone so weak. And I was so hurt and angry over the thought of betrayal, I just accepted what I was told and decided to leave home until Father returned."

"Does it not all seem odd to you? Someone attacked you, a weak fighter easily captured and ready to tell you things to make you believe the rumors you'd already heard. Then he was attacked. You both agree that he is the stronger fighter, yet no one has questioned how you, as his supposed assailant, were able to wound him multiple times? And that he only survived more serious injury by escaping?" As she finished speaking, she tried not to fret about the true trouble Kazuki and his family were potentially in.

Yuji's frown deepened along with hers. "You're right. It is as if we are being manipulated, but who would stand to gain from making us turn on one another?"

"That I don't know. Together, perhaps, you can figure that part out." She squeezed his hands. "Yuji-san, you love your brother, yes?"

"Yes…of course, even now."

"Then shouldn't you have more faith in him and he in you? How can you love someone you don't trust? There may be someone else behind the scenes, pulling you both along, but they never would have been able to do so had you both been honest with each other and trusted in the love you've had all this time." She kept her tone soft as she admonished him. "The good thing is it's not too late. You haven't lost him yet. He's waiting for you to come home, waiting for his brother to return."

Yuji nodded. "Yes, it is time, time to return home and deal with this. I feel like such a fool, to have let this go on so long without noticing the strangeness of it all. It should have been so obvious!"

"The thing about love is when we think it's been betrayed, the hurt can make us blind. There is a story I like that talks about the need to view situations with eyes unclouded by our negative emotions. Now the clouds have been lifted from your eyes, so you can see each other as you really are again."

"Eyes unclouded…yes, that does sound fitting." He stood up from the table. "Thank you for lending me your ear, Lady Sakura, and for helping to uncloud my eyes. I shall take my leave, for now."

They were almost to the front door when Yuji stopped and turned back toward her. "I almost forgot."

Awakening Awareness

KARASU FLAPPED HIS WINGS to thrust himself up from the fading wind current to a higher one. Since returning to Throklana, he'd yet to talk to Kazuki, who was still in Osgavenda. From what he gathered, Kazuki hadn't even been in the castle when he sent the note, yet the note hadn't mentioned going to Osgavenda to meet him. At the castle, Reito had seemed puzzled to see Karasu.

"He did not mention any task he had for you before leaving or even that he'd sent for you. Strange." Reito shook his head. "It would be best if you not follow, as the people of Osgavenda are already on edge. That said, from his last reports, things are turning in a more positive direction, so he should return here in a few days. Until then, I received word a short while ago that the king was seen near the village of Uragiri. It's probably a false report, but it still needs to be checked."

That was how Karasu found himself out searching for the missing king. Karasu guessed it meant that Reito really didn't know where the king had gone either. With his stature and importance, it was amazing King Toramaru could be so difficult to locate, unless he was deliberately ensuring he wasn't found. Thinking back to his conversation with Sakura, about how someone was likely trying to split Kazuki and Yuji, Karasu wondered if the same person could be behind the king's absence.

With a scoff, he dismissed the idea. The king had left of his own accord and announced his departure. He hadn't vanished; he was just taking some time for himself and wanted some privacy, for whatever reason. Though it did seem dangerous and even a bit irresponsible for him to do so without even telling his attendant. What if something had happened to him? Or, heck, look what was happening with him gone! But King Toramaru would have a good reason for all this, even if they didn't know what it was yet.

The sun hung low in the sky as the remnants of what was once the village of Uragiri came into view. Now a desolate ghost town, it was once a regular, homey place peopled by a few hundred citizens, mostly farmers, who grew an abundance of crops in the rich soil. A few of the old irrigation ditches were still visible in the land, leading from the river to where the fields once stood.

According to the stories he'd heard, long before he'd been born, a series of pounding storms sent the once life-giving river raging over its banks, flooding the village. The same storms had unleashed mudslides from the hills above, burying a quarter of the town. The survivors were decimated with disease, and only a handful had managed to escape. Declaring it a cursed town, they'd left and never looked back.

A shiver ran through him as he flew over the village. As if to throw a final insult at the town, a fire had burned through at some point, leaving the wood-framed houses a mix of charred shells and stone foundations. Near the back of the village, a couple of houses had avoided the flames, but they still looked shaky, apt to cave in at any minute.

Nothing stirred, not even a breeze. Even as Karasu landed on the remnants of a fountain near the village square, he knew there was no way the king was here. "Bah, Reito was right, just another false lead."

Though anyone would be hard-pressed to stay hidden in such a place, he flew over the area twice more. It had taken most of the day to fly there—a long flight for nothing. Grumbling about having to fly back at night, he turned back toward the castle. He'd just cleared the river when he realized he was no longer alone.

A large shadow swooped down from above with a screech. He barely managed to avoid the dracnor's sharp talons.

"What the…you stupid bird, leave me alone!" It was rare for another bird to bother him, due to his yokai aura, but this dracnor seemed not to care. It was already coming around again for another attack. Karasu flew toward it, twisting past it at the last second to disorient it, then dove toward the forest below.

"I'll just lose you in the trees, you nut."

Halfway down, Karasu was forced to pull out of his dive to avoid another dracnor that had burst out of the trees below. Its claws whisked past Karasu's tail feathers, knocking some loose. Before he could fully recover, the first bird came at him from the side, and he had to roll back down to avoid it. Maybe they were mates, desperate for food for their young. Then a third slammed into him, slashing his back and sending more feathers flying.

Despite the pain in his back, he went into a sharp dive toward the forest again. The dracnors continued attacking, forcing him to veer one way and the next to avoid them. He was only meters from the treetops when a fourth, arriving, ripped into his wings and rendered one useless. His dive became an ugly spiral toward the forest. Using his one relatively working wing and his tail, he managed to dodge another attack before hitting the trees.

Branches battered him as he broke through the canopy and fell through the lush branches. Meters from the ground, he morphed back to his humanoid form, landing with a painful crash.

"Ouch. What was with those crazy birds?" Shaking his head, he looked around the shadowed place. He could hear the dracnors screeching above, but they didn't seem to be willing or able to fly through the thick foliage. Relieved, Karasu leaned against a tree to assess his injuries. With the damage to his arm, he was grounded. It would take days to walk back to the palace, unless he was lucky enough to find a village that would let him borrow a cart.

He ripped some strips of cloth from his shirt to use as bandages, wrapping one around his arm and pressing another to his side. The forest around him grew darker; it would be pitch black before long. He could feel his hair standing on edge among the silent trees; even the dracnors had stopped their screeching.

A twig snapped behind him, causing him to spin around. Through the leaves, several sets of glowing eyes approached.

"You've got to be kidding me!" He bolted as the pack of shadow dogs charged him. Grabbing a low-hanging branch, he swung himself up into a trees, barely avoiding the sharp snap of one dog's teeth. Jumping from branch to branch, he kept going toward the edge of the forest, the pack following along, jumping and foaming at the mouth.

When Karasu neared the forest's end, the dogs just stopped, standing and watching him as he continued on. His arm burned with pain as he stopped to rest. Balanced on the thick branch of a tree, he watched the pack sliver back between the trees. Was it over, or was something else coming?

Several long minutes later, the sounds of the forest returned. With a sigh, he walked along the branch toward the trunk. Finally, his first stroke of luck! He'd stopped on a reiki tree. Its sap had healing properties that could have him ready to fly by morning. After securing the tree's permission, he pulled the small knife from his belt and gouged the trunk enough to get to some of the sticky sap, pasting it on the worst of his wounds. The pain began to ebb before he was done.

"Thank you." He waved his hand over the gouge in the trunk, healing the damaged spot. The helpful tree showed him an abandoned nest further along its branches. With a yawn, he morphed back to his bird form to settle in for the night.

In the morning, there was no sign of the shadow dogs or the dracnors. The reiki sap had worked well, healing his wing enough to fly, though it was still a bit sore. He stayed low to the ground, keeping a vigilant eye and ear on his surroundings until he reached the palace.

"What happened to you?" Reito asked as soon as Karasu landed in front of him in the castle courtyard.

"I was attacked." He gave him a brief summary of the events in Uragiri.

"I see. Do you still have the note Prince Kazukiarama sent you?"

"Yeah, right here." He handed the page to Reito. "Lord Reito, is something wrong?"

"This handwriting is not the same as Prince Kazukiarama's. I should have realized it before when you showed it to me. Nor could that long-winded boy ever pen such a brief note." He shook his head. "We've received confirmation that the person who reported the sighting of the king was the same one who claimed to have seen Prince Yuji near Aya's room."

Karasu could feel his stomach knotting. The note was a fake? Kazuki hadn't recalled him? "But why would anyone call me back here? They couldn't have known you'd send me to Uragiri, right?"

"True, though they may have suspected I would, as you are the only one currently in the castle capable of flight." Reito turned and walked out of the courtyard. He didn't run, but he walked fast enough that Karasu was trotting to keep up. "Earlier when we talked, you told me of Lady Sakura's thoughts regarding the argument between the princes. I was not certain before, but this is enough to make me think she may be right. Which means the real question is why someone would trick you into returning here."

"Sakura...I left her alone. You don't think he's after her, do you? I mean, the only people who know about her are you and Yuji, right?"

Reito stopped and put his hand on Karasu's shoulder. "As far as we know. As you said, other than me, Prince Yuji is the only person who knows of Sakura's existence or that you two were living in the human world. If I could, I would go myself, but the prince should be here within the hour. Hurry and go to his Lady Sakura. I'll send him there as soon as he arrives."

Kazuki dropped into Sakura's garden, near the base of her cherry tree.

His heart raced as he looked around, the scent of his own fear filling his nose. Not a sound came through the open side door of the house, though he knew Karasu had already returned. As he stepped on the porch, he spotted the overturned kotatsu lying in the living room. He sprinted into the home.

"Sakura? Karasu?" He ran through the living room and into the hall. Sakura lay on the floor near the stairs. With a cry, he dropped to his knees beside her, unable to even speak her name. His trembling fingers stroked her still-warm face. He pulled her into his arms, clutching her tightly as he cried, begging her to wake up, though he knew it was futile. He couldn't feel her heart beating anymore. Lifting his head, he kissed her lukewarm lips, apologizing over and over.

"What...?" Blue-purple bruises circled her neck, bruises shaped like fingers. Wiping his eyes, he laid her back down. Her shirt was torn in spots, and scratches littered her arms. If she'd had an attack, she would not have these wounds. He looked toward the stairs. The telephone table that usually stood near where Sakura lay was now in pieces at the end of the hall. Blood was smeared along the walls.

Kazuki stood, his fear mounting. "Karasu? Where are you?"

He strode toward the kitchen before glancing back at the front door. A large pool of blood stained the entryway. Sakura's injuries were not enough to warrant so much blood. As he moved closer, he spotted a familiar wooden sword lying nearby, the blood staining it a dark color. Karasu's scent was heavy in the air. "You tried to protect her, didn't you, old friend? But from what, from who? And where are you now?"

He kept his hand on the sword at his side as he made his way upstairs. Sakura's bedroom door was broken, the surface marred with claw marks. More marks dug into the windowsill along with bloody handprints. Only one other scent overlapped Sakura's and Karasu's: Yuji's. It was strongest in the living room and kitchen, but he could smell it everywhere Sakura had run as well. Some parts smelled odd, particularly around Sakura's body, but he couldn't put his finger on why.

Something twinkled near Sakura. With a snarl, he snatched up the broken chain, staring at the rectangular pendant that dangled from it, identical to the one around his own neck, as it had been on the day he and Yuji had been given the set by their mother. He hadn't wanted to believe Yuji was involved in this, especially not in harming Karasu, yet the proof was irrefutable. Closing his fist so tightly around the pendant that it cut into his hands, he howled in rage. "Damn you."

Puppet Master

KAZUKI MATERIALIZED NEAR the castle, intending to go straight to the stables to get a steed to take him to the Forest of Kuragari to find Yuji. Instead, he heard a familiar voice call to him from behind.

"Kazuki! I've been waiting for you." He turned to see Yuji walking toward him, smiling at him even.

His rage and thirst for vengeance lent him speed as he ran forward, drawing his sword. Yuji managed to block the blow with his own sword at the last second.

"Brother?"

"You are no brother of mine, not anymore. This I will never forgive." Their swords crossed between them. Kazuki kicked Yuji back and swung, just missing his cheek. With renewed rage, he began a series of rapid strikes. Though Yuji managed to block them, Kazuki pushed him further and further across the grassy expanse.

He feigned to the right. When Yuji tried to block it, Kazuki struck him from the left side with his scabbard, sending Yuji's sword flying while Kazuki kicked his legs out from under him. Yuji lay panting on the ground.

"I thought you wanted to talk, to work this out. Yet now

you will kill me?"

The tears pooling in Yuji's eyes made Kazuki hesitate to deliver the final blow. Then the image of Sakura's lifeless body returned.

"That was before you took her from me. Brother or no, I will avenge her death."

"Whose death? I've killed no one!"

Kazuki flung the pendant at him. "Quit playing the innocent. You killed Sakura, your pendant was by her body and your scent fills her home."

"I swear, Kazuki, I did not harm, Lady Sakura. We only talked! And I lost this a few days ago. It was she who told me to come look for you."

"Enough of your lies." Ignoring the aching in his chest, Kazuki thrust his sword forward, intending to run it through Yuji's heart. But the blow never landed. A ghostly image appeared between them, her arms out to the side, shoulder-height, shielding Yuji.

"Sakura?" Kazuki's sword lowered as he reached for her with his other arm, but his arm went through her. Of course she couldn't be there, she was dead. He'd held her body himself. Yet the sight of the spirit was not wholly surprising, given the magic of his world. What confused him was why she was stopping him from avenging her death, from giving her the peace of justice served that would let her soul rest.

She looked over her semi-translucent shoulder at Yuji then back at him, shaking her head. "But he killed you! And Karasu!"

Again she shook her head, then held her hand out toward him. Warily he reached for her. This time he was able to touch her, but her ethereal form was cold, wispy. It lacked the warmth he remembered so well.

Turning, Sakura reached out to Yuji, who pushed himself to his feet. Though he'd gone pale at her appearance, he took the offered hand.

A blinding light flowed over them, forcing Kazuki to shut his eyes. When he opened them again, they were floating above Sakura's home, watching as she came home to find Yuji waiting for her.

"I knew it!" Kazuki shouted.

"I told you, we only talked!"

Sakura put a finger over each of their mouths, giving them a stern look, then pointed down as Yuji started to leave but paused to find out when the wedding was. After he left, the scene changed to the next day, with Sakura sitting in the living room at the kotatsu, reading.

Sakura stayed up late into the night, hoping Kazuki or Karasu would return, but finally, she'd been forced to give up and go to sleep. In the morning, her coughing had grown worse, even with the medicine, so she had decided to stay home and sleep in. Close to lunchtime, she woke up and ate a light meal before going to the living room.

She carried a book with her, but set it down and went to the shrine to pray, whispering the fears in her heart to Ito, of the dark sense of dread that had been her companion since waking. *What's wrong with me. I just have a cough. It's nothing to be so afraid about.*

She started back toward her book. Instead, she found herself at the shelf, looking at the picture of her with Karasu and Kazuki. Taken on the Day of Buckets, the picture had made her so happy when she saw it, she'd made copies for each of them. Hers was framed on the shelf, the first such picture she had ever put up.

"If what I'm feeling is true…" Sakura picked it up and held it against her chest. It was a poor substitute for hugging them, but it was all she had. Giving in to her worries, she returned to the kotatsu, stationary in hand, and began writing.

Some time later, a sound almost like a ping made her look up, but she couldn't see anything unusual. With a shrug, she presumed it was just the metal of the heater popping, as it sometimes did, and she turned her attention back to the letter in front of her.

Just as she was signing it, she heard something hit the side of the house. *Was there supposed to be high wind today?* She opened the door and went into the garden, but it was calm and nothing looked out of place.

"How odd…I must be hearing things." She headed back inside. Absentmindedly, she reached behind her to slide the door closed, but her hand hit fabric instead. With a squeak, she whirled around. "Kazuki!"

The man who stood in the doorway was not Kazuki or anyone else she knew. He was so close to her, she instinctively took several steps backwards. He followed, sliding the door closed behind him. The click echoed through the house.

Even before glancing at his clawed hands, something told her he too was a yokai. But he was nothing like Kazuki or Yuji. Everything about him was dark. His short hair was jet black, his eyes a dark charcoal that seemed to absorb all light. A dark-blue cloak covered his black tunic and pants. The only part of him that was light was the grape-green tone of his skin and the single golden hoop earring decorating one ear.

His still manner and the predatory way he watched her frightened her.

"Who are you?"

He chuckled as he took two steps forward to grab her arm, pulling her against him. With one hand, he grabbed her chin, turning her face from side to side. "So you are the prince's little human mate, eh? For someone with his tastes, I expected something more impressive."

"Let me go." To her surprise, he did, laughing while she rubbed her jaw. "Who are you?"

"Ah, forgive my poor manners. I am called Mumarch. You will not have heard of me."

It was true, she didn't know his name, but her fear grew as she realized who this man had to be. "I thought everything seemed strange. You're the one behind this, aren't you? The one who's been manipulating Yuji-san!"

He grinned then moved toward her again. She continued stepping backwards until her back hit the wall. Mumarch planted his hands on either side of the wall, pinning her arms as he pressed closer, leaving barely enough room for a breath between them.

His position kept her from even being able to knee him like they told you to do to an attacker. His proximity disturbed her, much to his seeming amusement. She willed herself to stay calm. Having an attack around him would not be a good thing.

"Ah, you are a clever girl, aren't you? Yes, it is true. Those two fools were so easy to turn against one another. A few rumors and one well-paid assassin were enough to send Yuji fleeing the castle. Afterward, the stupid boy believed every sweet little lie his loving new friend whispered in his ear."

"You..." Her mind raced as the final piece fell into place. "It wasn't Yuji who attacked Kazuki that night either. That was you, somehow, wasn't it?"

"Sad, isn't it? He was so upset at the thought of his brother betraying him that he couldn't see past my mimicry spell to tell the difference between me and his brother. As I said, fools both of them."

He bent his head down and began nuzzling her neck. Her attempts to push him away only made him laugh more. "I thought you liked yokai? Is one not as good for mating as another?"

"What are you going to do to me?" She tried not to flinch as he pressed his knee between her legs and rubbed it against her.

"Alas, even after planting the idea that it was Kazuki who murdered Aya, that soft-hearted fool Yuji got it in his head to come and meet his brother's future mate. The nosy twit convinced him to talk to Kazuki again. Said twit being you, of course." He ran a hand over her abdomen, making her stomach roll. Sakura forced herself not to react outwardly, realizing he was enjoying toying with her.

His hand played with the edge of her shirt. "Despite the doubts he has, that idiot still loves his brother. Thanks to you, if they talk, they will realize that a third party has been leading them by the nose. Therefore, I'll make sure Kazuki never lets his brother get so much as a word out. Instead, he will slaughter him in a rage."

"Why? I thought you wanted to support Yuji?"

"I don't care either way. As long as one kills the other, I'll have removed one obstacle to getting the crown. If Yuji dies, I'll ally myself with the grief-stricken Kazuki until I can get rid of him as well. It won't be too hard; he is as much a fool as his brother." He tried to kiss her on the mouth, but she managed to turn her head to the side. His tongue left a wet trail along her cheek. "Aren't you wondering how I intend to send Kazuki into such a mindless rage?"

Sakura couldn't stop herself from shaking. He was already

making his intentions clear enough.

"Just think how he will feel, coming here to find his precious human's lifeless body, blatantly violated, and his brother's scent all over her."

"Do you think Kazuki can't tell the difference between your scent and Yuji's?"

"He didn't before, did he?" Mumarch's laugh was as cold as an arctic wind. "My mimicry spell is two-fold. Not only does it allow me the option of disguising my appearance, but also of masking my smell. I cast it before I came. This cloak is a favorite of Yuji's, so it is heavily imbued with his scent to take the place of my missing one. And, of course, there is this, which will be lying on your body, between your naked breasts."

He held up a golden chain with a pendant dangling from it. She recognized the crest emblazoned on the rectangular piece; Kazuki wore a similar pendant around his neck all the time.

In her pocket, she could feel the dohame Karasu had left for her. Praying for strength, she waited until he tried to kiss her again. He had loosened his stance as he talked, perhaps thinking she'd given up fighting.

As soon as he leaned in again, she punched him in the groin, forcing him back enough that she was able to just get away from him and run toward the front door. She didn't even make it halfway before he tackled her from behind. A sharp pain flew through her chest as Mumarch flipped her onto her back, straddling her as he grabbed her arms and held them over her head.

"Behave yourself. I was intending to make this nice for you, give you a last thrill before you die." He pulled a bottle out of his pocket with his free hand and set it beside her. "But for that blow, I think a little punishment is in order first."

His mouth covered hers as he grabbed her face with his hand, forcing her to open her mouth to his probing tongue. She squeezed her eyes closed. He held her jaw so tight she couldn't even bite him. Tears ran down her face into her hair as she continued to struggle, not just to be free but to breathe, his weight a terrible burden on her already overtaxed lungs.

When he broke the forced kiss, she gasped, desperately trying to snatch in air. He released her jaw, his hand sliding down to push up her shirt. A moment later, he released his grip. She opened her eyes to see Karasu on Mumarch's back, raining blows around his head.

"Run!"

Sakura coughed as Mumarch climbed off her, trying to reach Karasu. Half-crawling, she reached the front door, but when she looked back, Mumarch flung the boy down the hall. Karasu hit the wall with a sickening thud.

"Karasu!"

"Get…going…" Shaking her head, she could only watch in horror as Mumarch stalked toward the boy. He was larger and no doubt stronger. There was no way a boy Karasu's size could defeat him, even as he staggered to his feet, drawing his wooden sword.

"Leave…my…sister…alone."

Mumarch seemed to hesitate at the determined expression on Karasu's face. Taking advantage of his distraction, she forced herself forward, grabbing up the telephone table and smashing it into the back of Mumarch's head. He slammed into the wall as she called out for Karasu.

Karasu darted forward and grabbed her hand as they staggered toward the door. Just as they reached the entryway, something grabbed her collar. She flew through the air, landing in a painful heap near the stairs, the last of her breath knocking out of her.

"Stay there, girl. I'll deal with you in a moment." It was

Mumarch's voice, but she could not turn herself over to see what was happening. She heard a strangled sound, followed by an eerie silence and a thud that made her cry. "Ka…ra…su…"

"He was a stupid child."

Mumarch's footsteps approached her. Somehow, her body responded to her desperate plea, her lungs snatching another breath. She scrambled up the stairs, reaching her room and securing herself inside before he caught her.

Though she locked the door, she knew it didn't matter. The bigger enemy was inside now. Only the door at her back kept her standing. Blindly, she reached into her pocket for her medicine, but all she found was the small crystal bottle, somehow still intact despite her fall. Praying it would work fast enough, she guzzled the bitter liquid.

The light in the room dimmed. Mumarch was crouched in her window, laughing at her. Blood covered his hands. "If you prefer the bed, I suppose I can still be convinced to make it easy on you."

She turned the lock and escaped the room. Dimly, she knew he was only letting her get away on purpose, no doubt enjoying the chase.

Halfway down the stairs, her feet gave out. Her scream was brief, her strained lungs cutting off the waste of air. Over and over she tumbled, pain radiating through her body. By the time she came to a stop, lying on her back with her legs still on the stairs, she knew she was done.

Near the front door, Karasu's bloodied and limp body lay in the entryway. She pulled herself up and tried to crawl toward him, but her body refused to obey anymore. In a mixed blessing, the pain burning through her chest drowned out the rest. Her vision blurred as she stretched one hand toward Karasu's body. It fell lifeless to the ground.

Mumarch eased her over onto her back, his sardonic smile replaced by that pitying look she hated so much. His dark eyes showed the first flicker of real emotion she'd seen. Even chasing her, while he'd laughed, his eyes had remained cold, dead. Now she thought she saw sorrow in them as he watched her gasping for air. His hands were oddly gentle as he cradled her in his arms.

"Shhh. It's all right, Safina. You'll be free in a minute." He kissed her forehead, an almost loving touch even as his hands wrapped around her throat. "Sleep now, little one."

Violent Confrontation

THEY WATCHED AS MUMARCH laid Sakura's body down on the floor, closed her eyes, and arranged the necklace beside her. After picking up Karasu's body, he vanished in the blue-white flash indicative of using a transportation gem. Moments later, the brothers stood in the grass near the castle, where they'd started, Sakura's spirit nowhere to be seen.

With a sob, Kazuki fell to his knees, his sword forgotten at his side. His hands shook with targetless rage as he forced himself to put aside the images they'd just seen. He needed to stay calm and think rationally.

Now he knew what had bothered him about Yuji's scent in the house. Where Yuji had been, the scent had been fresh, barely a day old, but the false scents Mumarch had laid were a mix of many ages, due to Yuji having worn that clock for decades.

"This Mumarch, you know him?" he asked Yuji as he recalled Mumarch's words to Sakura.

Beside him, Yuji had pulled his knees against his chest, wrapping his arms around them as he buried his face in them. Now he looked up, nodding his damp face. "I met him a little over a year ago. He was always kind to me and we talked often.

Once, I was nearly crushed under a falling rock. He saved me. I thought he was my friend. When he started to tell me rumors he 'heard,' I didn't believe them at first, but he kept feeding them to me, always as if he was reluctant to share, and as if he thought I should dismiss them. Over time, I started questioning everything you said and did. He told me you intended to kill me the day before that assassin of his attacked me. It never occurred to me to wonder how one who hated being near the castle and seemed to have few friends could always learn these things…or how he could've found out about any supposed plots you might have had. I am such a fool."

Yuji picked up Kazuki's sword and handed it to him. "It is my fault Lady Sakura is gone. Please, I deserve no less."

"The fault is shared. I could no sooner kill you for her death than kill myself." Kazuki sheathed the blade as bitterness filled his mouth. "I should have known it wasn't you that night at mother's grave. Everything about it was wrong. The lack of scent, the fighting style. But I accepted what my eyes saw and didn't question it until it was too late. You are my brother, my best friend, yet even as I proclaimed your innocence, I doubted, all too eager to accept the barest of circumstantial evidence instead of hard proof."

Yuji wiped his face and stood. "Mumarch…that he was behind all this means that he is the one who killed Aya."

"And no doubt tried to have it pinned on you while telling you I had done it."

Yuji held out his hand. "He has stolen those most precious from us. We can wallow in our self-loathing later. We have a duty to uphold."

"He must be stopped and justice served." Kazuki took the offered hand and pulled himself up.

"Let's go. I have a good idea where he will be."

Within minutes, they were standing in the town square of the abandoned village of Uragiri. The roads in the town remained, the stones broken up, but no grass grew between them. No vines struggled to reclaim the burnt shells. The empty fountain had no bed of dried leaves filling the bottom. It was as if even nature did not feel the area deserving of life. The only sign that anyone was there was a single plume of smoke coming from a house near the remnants of the mudslide from long ago.

As they walked closer, swords drawn, they realized it was in fact only half a house. What had looked like the other side was a mud-covered pile of rubble behind it, a pile Mumarch was now walking over to approach them.

"The princes of Throklana come to visit me? To what do I owe this pleasure?" His sneer matched the goading tone of his voice.

"Mumarch, you are under arrest for the murder of Princess Aya of Osgavenda, the murder of Lady Sakura of the human realm, and the assault on Karasu, an attendant of the high court of Throklana." Yuji stood straight, his gaze unwavering as he spoke. "Surrender and let the council decide your fate."

"And if I refuse?"

"You can return dead or alive; the choice is yours," Kazuki replied, his fist tightening on the grip of his sword.

"A serious choice, yes. I suppose you don't mind if I think about it a moment. It is a big decision to make. To die here or to die there, that is." His voice had a manic sound to it as he joined his hands behind his back and began pacing back and forth. "My dear Prince Yuji, do you remember when you came here with me before? You wondered why I would have any interest in such a place, the cursed place, the haunted lands?"

"I remember. At the time you said you found it curious how an entire village could be forgotten so easily."

"Indeed. Even now, I wonder, what sort of ruler could so casually erase hundreds of people without so much as a thought." He stopped and gestured to the house behind him. "This was my home, you know, long ago, when our village thrived. My mate, our son, my sweet little girl, and our newborn babe. We lived here together. It was a simple life then, working the fields and sharing our bounty. The people here were good people. Then the rains came, an unending torrent of water that filled the river. As it droned on, we did as any would do, we cried out to our king, our protector."

Mumarch spat on the ground. "The Great King Toramaru. With a wave of his hand, he could have shielded our village from the floods or even cleared the skies and turned the waters away. But he ignored the village's cries. Even as the river overflowed its banks and began to fill the streets, he ignored us. Then the hill there, swollen from the water, lost its grip on itself and came crashing down."

He swept his hands in front of him as if reenacting the mudslide, his voice growing louder.

"In an instant, my mate was gone, buried under the collapsed half of our house. By some miracle, I was able to get my children out, but it was a short-lived one. After the floods came the plague, the plague that stole the life from my baby. Even then, some in the village had faith, faith our king had not abandoned us. Then came the dry storm. Nature was determined to erase us from existence. Lightning arced through the sky, setting what was left of our village to flames. My son died here"—Mumarch stopped at a small pair of mounds near his house—"his sister wrapped in his arms as he tried to shield her from the inferno till the end."

"So you did all this because you blame our father for their deaths and wanted revenge?" Kazuki asked.

"It took me a long time to grow powerful enough to avenge them. I wasn't born with spell-casting skills, you know, nor did I go to any school that taught them. But I learned, years and years I studied, learning all that I needed so that I could do to him what he did to me. You blame me for your women's deaths, but you point your fingers in the wrong direction. Don't you see, had the king done his duty, my mate and my children would still be here now. Your precious Aya, your human girl, they would be with you. If you wish to arrest someone for their deaths, arrest your father, for it is he who could not be bothered to protect those who most needed it."

Kazuki shook his head. Mumarch's losses did not excuse what he had done nor could he shift the blame to their father. He gave Yuji a questioning glance. He nodded once, confirming he too knew why their father hadn't come to save Uragiri.

"Mumarch, I won't pretend to understand your grief." Yuji spoke in a soft, calm voice. "But Father never abandoned this village. He was not told of the floods nor of the fire at the time, because he was at our mother's side as she lay dying. Don't you remember? The council did what they could, sending doctors with medicines to try to combat the plague, but they were ill-prepared. Half of them fell to it themselves, and two others died in the fire trying to save people. By the time Father was told, it was all over, and there was nothing he could do."

In fact, the king had been furious with the council for keeping the village's needs from him and had dismissed them all, replacing them with the current council. Even now, mentioning Uragiri around their father made him grimace in pain.

Mumarch laughed, a harsh ugly sound. "You expect me to believe that? You think I'll just say 'oh, it's okay then since he didn't know'? Just how stupid are you? Their blood is on his hands. My mate, my children, the other people who lived here.

He killed them as surely as if he'd smitten them himself! Their blood is on his hands, his!" Mumarch raised both arms above his head and began chanting in an undecipherable tongue. "He already lost his mate, and now he will lose his children and know my pain."

Dozens of shadow dogs appeared, their heads down as their snarls pulled back their lips to reveal razor-shop fangs. Kazuki turned so he and Yuji stood back to back, braced for the massive attack. Kazuki struck them down as fast he as could, some with sword and some with his claws. Behind him, Yuji grunted as he fended off more.

With a yell, Kazuki ducked down and swung his blade, taking down three of the dogs with one stroke while grabbing a fourth in his claws and flinging it into the nearby river. Out of the corner of his eye, he saw something else move.

"Yuji, watch out!" Kazuki managed to block Mumarch's sword, which had been aimed at Yuji's shoulder. Yuji jumped to the side, then rushed back toward Kazuki to kill the two dogs that had pounced on Kazuki's unprotected back, ripping into his flesh with their teeth.

With a growl, Kazuki swung at Mumarch, but he dodged and charged. They exchanged a vicious set of parries and thrusts as Yuji kept the remaining dogs away. With one swing, Mumarch sliced Kazuki's cheek, leaving an opening that allowed Kazuki to leave a deep wound on his arm. Mumarch jumped back, panting, and held up a hand in a sign of yielding. The shadow dogs vanished.

"Drop your sword," Kazuki demanded.

Mumarch lowered the weapon, but kept a loose hold on the grip. For a moment, his shoulders dropped in defeat and his face looked worn and haggard. Then he began chuckling. The sound made Kazuki's blood run cold as Mumarch looked up at them. "Did you not forget someone in all our talk earlier, My Princes? That foolish child, the one who thought he could protect that slip of a human from me?"

"Where is he? I know you took him from Sakura's. What did you do with him?"

His smile was even more chilling as he stood again, holding his sword in front of him in a weak stance. "You'll find him in my house there. He should be just about done."

"Done?"

"Yes. A bit premature, I guess, but to celebrate my victory, what better than a bit of crow stew?"

"You monster!" Kazuki rushed forward, burying his sword deep in Mumarch's heart. With a gurgling gasp, Mumarch fell backwards, a strange smile flashing across his lips before he expelled his final breath.

LOVE'S SACRIFICE

KAZUKI AND YUJI MADE THEIR way into Mumarch's house, climbing over the pile of rubble as he had done. The remaining part of the house held what was left of the cooking area and the family room. A fire burned in the stove and a pot boiled on top, but inside they found only clear water. The family room was barren of any furniture it might once have held. Now there was only a jumbled blanket and a thread-worn pillow, to indicate where Mumarch had slept.

A framed picture sat on the floor beside the sleeping spot. A pretty tanuki[57] stood with a smaller version of herself snuggling in her arms. Beside them, a fawn-haired man smiled with his hand on the shoulder of a young boy who had his mother's eyes but his father's skin-tone and hair. The man in the picture barely resembled the one outside. Had he stained his hair to disguise himself for some reason, or had it been an effect of the dark magic he'd learned?

Kazuki spotted a book peeking out from under the blankets. It seemed to be a diary kept by Mumarch's late mate, but then

---

[57] A raccoon dog yokai; tanuki are canines with raccoon-like features, hence the name raccoon dog.

the writing changed near the end. Newer entries added by Mumarch included details on his lengthy studies of magic and things he'd learned from forbidden texts. They would need to try to find those books to seize them.

"What is it?" Yuji came to stand beside his brother.

"A diary. Mumarch wrote down pretty much everything he did, including killing Aya."

"Does it say what he did with Karasu?"

Kazuki flipped to the last entries, hoping they'd been written within the last day or two.

Risa Half, Kisa Full, Twelfth Cycle, 219 AU

Tomorrow I will go to the human world and take the girl's life. I will make Kazuki think Yuji defiled and murdered her. If he is any sort of man, it will drive him insane and he will kill his brother before Yuji can act on his newfound desire to "work things out." Indeed, this change in plans is fitting. Just as our youngest went first, so too shall the king's.

After a suitable time has passed, I will arrange to meet with Kazuki. I think it best to approach him as a friend of his late brother who was privy to his thoughts before his death, then use these ramblings to continue to drive him further into grief. Once I have him broken enough, I'll arrange his death to look like suicide. No one will question it when he'll have lost so many he loved.

Do not think ill of me, Safina, I am no ogre. I know that girl is a true innocent in all this. I will only scare her enough to ensure her fear scent fills the area. I have made a potion to kill her as quickly and painlessly as possible, so it will be as if she is asleep. I have no intention of bedding another woman, though I may have to touch her a bit when frightening her. Believe me, it will be no different than my touching the dirt outside.

The prince will be so shaken by her death that simply seeing her with her clothes torn will be enough to convince him. And I've already taken care of the child. The boy should be back in Throklana, running a fool's errand where my pets will keep him safely out of the way long enough for me to get the deed done. By the time anyone realizes he was tricked, it will be over.

Risa Half, Kisa Full, Twelfth Cycle, 220 AU

Things did not go as I planned. The girl's illness, I did not know it was of such a nature that running from me brought her to death's door. I did not get to deliver the potion to her; by the time I realized what was happening it was too late. I was afraid to use it, for I wasn't sure she could swallow it properly.

Believe me, Safina, I did not mean to make her suffer. Did I not set her free, even as she seemed to take on your countenance while lying in my arms, gasping for air? How many more times must I live out that day?

And that boy, oh, that foolish, stupid child. He returned sooner than I expected. Surely he knew I was far stronger, yet he jumped to help her. I reacted without thinking, not realizing it was the child at first, and my fighting instincts took over. How much it hurt to see him standing there, looking so much like our Raiowano, ready to protect that human whom he called sister. It shook me, I admit, but at that point, I had no choice. There was no more time, and he was in the way.

I forced myself to dispatch him, and yet, how could I leave him there? Before I fully realized it, I'd picked him up before leaving the girl's home. Upon returning home, I carried him

"Carried him where?" Yuji asked.

"The entry stops there." Kazuki glared at the page, trying to make meaning of Mumarch's ramblings. What had he done with Karasu and who was the Safina he kept referencing?

"Let's search the rest of the village. I think he lied about eating Karasu," Yuji said.

"But why would he say such a thing?"

"Who knows? Maybe he realized he was wrong to blame Father and wanted to goad one or both of us into killing him, so he wouldn't have to answer for his crimes."

Yuji led the way out of the house. They split up and searched every remaining structure, even ones comprised of little more than a few burnt wooden beams. There was no sign of Karasu. Mumarch must have hidden his body elsewhere.

Heavy-hearted, they decided to return to the human world to retrieve Sakura's body and send a search party back to find Karasu's body. It would eventually cause some twittering among the populace; there'd be no way to keep it secret that a human was buried in the royal cemetery as Kazuki's mate. But, right now, he didn't care. They could fuss all they wanted. He wanted her there with him.

First, they stopped at the castle to fetch a second transportation stone to help move her without having to take her body through the portal, allowing Kazuki some privacy while he buried her. When they arrived, Reito stood near the entrance. Beside him, was their father. For a moment, Kazuki felt a burst of resentment. *Too late, yet again.*

Hating himself for even thinking such a thing, Kazuki dropped to one knee along with Yuji, bowing deeply.

"Father, you've returned." Yuji managed to smile as he went forward to shake his father's hand. Toramaru pulled his younger son in for a hug.

"Yes. Forgive me for being gone so long." He looked at Kazuki over Yuji's shoulder. "Reito has told me of the spat between you and that some other party was involved who wished you separated. From the wounds you bear, am I correct in presuming you identified this person and dealt with him?"

"Yes, Father. It was a man named Mumarch, a survivor of Uragiri," Yuji answered for them both, giving his father a brief summary of what transpired.

When Reito heard of Karasu's death, his pain was visible before he hid his face behind his hands. It was one of the few times Kazuki could remember his emotions emerging in public.

Toramaru put a hand on Reito's shoulder as he let out a heavy sigh. "The curse comes home at last. I only wish I'd known it would touch the two of you like this. We will send a search party to Uragiri at once to look for the child. If he took him home with him, he may have hidden him in the surrounding woods and hill country."

After the order had been given to a nearby guard, Kazuki stepped forward. "Father, I am glad you are home. I know we have much to talk about, but for now, I would like to return to the human world. My Sakura, I would like to place her beside mother."

"Of course. I shall go with you."

Yuji remained behind to coordinate the search for Karasu. Before they solidified in Sakura's garden, Toramaru used his magic to create a shield that ensured no one would see him or Kazuki when they appeared, a fortunate thing, as police officers had overtaken the residence.

Yellow tape stretched across Sakura's side door and around the front of the house.

"What is going on?" They maneuvered around the officers, taking care not to touch them, as the spell only hid them from sight. After they ducked under the tape, Kazuki led his father inside. In the hall, more officers stood. The place where Sakura's body had been now bare. In the door, two officers kneeled in front of Karasu's pool of blood.

"Dammit, where did they take her?"

"Stay calm, Kazuki. First, to ensure we don't have any unnecessary questions—" Toramaru held up his hand. It glowed briefly. The blood near the front door changed, though the humans didn't react. "Now it is only spilled liquid. As for your girl, where did you see her last?"

Kazuki pointed to the spot by the stairs. Toramaru walked over and held his hand above the area, his eyes closed. He stayed that way a few minutes, then stood.

"Two girls about her age came and found her here. It was they who called the emergency services." He walked over and put his hands on Kazuki's shoulder. "My son, when they found her, she was still alive."

"What? Then where…a hospital, they would have taken her there!"

"Yes, and I know which one. Let us get away from this scene, and we shall go there and see what has become of her."

Once they were near the hospital, they used their glam spells to attain human appearances, and Toramaru dropped his shield. In the emergency area, Hina and Akari huddled together on a bench, with Genji and Aki standing nearby. Akari saw them approaching first. She marched up to Kazuki, slapping him in the face.

"Akari!" Aki grabbed her as she leaned forward, her hands balled in fists.

"Where have you been? You couldn't even leave a number or something to reach you at? How could you leave her alone like that?" Tears ran down her face as Aki continued to hold her.

The initial sting had dissipated, but the burning sensation that remained paled compared to the sharp barbs thrown at him. It was his fault; he'd left her. "I'm sorry. I didn't think anything would happen in the few days I was gone. Please, Sakura, where is she?"

"In there." Hina pointed to the window across from the bench on which they'd been sitting. Kazuki looked through the tinted glass. Sakura lay on the bed with so many tubes and wires coming out of her that she looked almost inhuman. Several doctors and nurses stood around her, including Tenma. He briefly looked up at Kazuki, but his expression offered no hope.

Her body was so still. From inside, the same sort of beeping emanated as during her doctor's visit, the one for the heart monitor. Only now, the sounds were spaced much further apart than before. Turning his senses up, he confirmed her heart barely beat. Somehow she was alive, but for how much longer?

Hina walked over and put her hand on the glass. "She stayed out of school today, so we came by to check on her because she hadn't been well yesterday. When no one answered, we got worried. Then we saw that the side door was open. We found her inside, lying on the floor. And there was blood on the wall and by the door, so we called for help. The police said she probably surprised a burglar or something, but they couldn't explain the blood."

"We went to the house first. They told us it was not blood, only spilled juice," Toramaru replied before Kazuki could.

"Who are you?" a calmer Akari asked. Aki released her from his grip, but took one of her hands in his.

"This is my father." Kazuki moved away from the glass. "He returned with me to meet her."

"Pleased to meet you." Akari bowed, a light blush covering her cheeks. "I'm sorry for my outburst."

"Do not fret. In a time like this, it is an understandable reaction." His father bowed in return.

With nothing left to do but wait, Kazuki sat on the bench, his head bowed as he prayed to every deity he could think of to somehow grant her a miracle. As Hina reclaimed her seat, Genji moved closer to hold her hand. Calmer, Akari leaned against her brother's shoulder. In silence, the group waited on.

An hour later, the doctor came out and walked over to them. Kazuki bolted up. "Dr. Tenma, how is she?"

"I wish I could say she is improving, but so far…" The exhausted-looking man shook his head. "I…I'm sorry, but you should prepare yourselves for the worst. We'll keep working, and I know Sakura-chan, she's a fighter, but this time…I'm not sure if she'll even wake up again. For now, we'll have to wait and see."

Toramaru looked at the can the human child Akari pressed into his hand with bemusement. How long had it been since he'd had one of these hot canned coffees? As he drank it, he watched his oldest son. He hated that he and Yuji had ended up paying the price of the mistakes of Uragiri. As well as losing young

Karasu, Yuji had lost his long-beloved Aya, and Kazuki would soon lose his Sakura. Toramaru knew the doctors' efforts were futile. They were only prolonging the inevitable. Her body was failing and had passed the point of human salvation. She would be dead by morning, at the latest.

Though death was inevitable for all mortal beings, he'd hoped his sons would be spared such pain until later in life. He thought of his beloved Kita and having to watch helplessly as she left them. At least he'd had the comfort of his sons, in whom he could see bits of her. His boys would have nothing but memories and regrets. So many regrets. There was nothing Toramaru could do for Yuji other than support him as he healed, but perhaps for Kazuki…

He shifted so that he could ensure the edge of his cloak, which masqueraded as a coat in his human disguise, was touching Hina. Closing his eyes, he muted his regular senses to open his sixth one. Like all rulers of Throklana, he'd been blessed with many powers during his reign. New ones were bestowed upon him each century during the ceremony to renew his right of sovereignty.

No one quite knew where the powers came from or how it happened, only that they came during the ceremony and only once every one hundred years. His shield of invisibility was one such power, and one well known to all. Others, like the ability to read people's memories when touching them, he kept well guarded. Unlike his other powers, this one had come upon him after the loss of Kita. The only one who knew of it now was Reito, who he knew would carry the secret to his grave.

Since he'd gained the power some two centuries ago, the few times he'd used it had been to ensure those he was dealing with were acting with honest intentions, in cases where duplicity would have jeopardized the kingdom. No usage came without a heavy dose of guilt at spying into people's intimate thoughts and memories.

Today was the first time he'd used the power for personal reasons, as a father wanting to help his sons, if possible. If anything, the guilt was worse, but it didn't stop him from using it to read Hina, and through their clasped hands, Akari.

Their emotions came first, a combination of colors and simple tastes. The black, bitter grief and sour yellow fear for the girl who lay in the room across from them, followed by the sweet pink warmth of love and blue shades of respect that lingered like a rich sauce. Then he began shifting through the memories, including the things Sakura likely did not know, such as how Hina had stood up to some others who'd tried to force her to stop hanging out with the girl. And Akari scaring them off with her own defense of the girl, even though she'd still been torn between what she'd seen and the person they'd come to know. The two spending hours together over the last week, folding one thousand origami cranes to bring Sakura good fortune.

As his only interest was in learning more about Sakura, he tried to keep the power focused to just those areas, but it was an inexact science. A few extra memories slipped through, based on tenuous associations to her, such as Hina's wondering where Sakura would want to go to college and Akari's contemplating talking to Sakura about her recent first kiss while being afraid of what she would think.

Satisfied he'd learned all he needed to know, he closed the connection and let himself rest a bit. From what he'd seen and heard from Reito, despite her being human, Sakura was a good sort for Kazuki. He could see how much his son had matured since meeting her, putting aside much of his self-important way of talking and starting to consider how his own actions affected others. There was no doubt in his mind of his son's love for her, that she was his sudtama. Her loss would leave Kazuki deeply affected. But was the alternative worth the price, for Toramaru and for the kingdom?

Later in the evening, Hina's parents called, asking her to come home to rest. After Kazuki swore to call if anything changed, Genji escorted her. It took Aki a bit longer to convince Akari to go home for the night. Both girls promised to return in the early afternoon, as soon as school let out.

The hall they waited in was quiet now, with little foot traffic about.

Not long after Sakura's human friends left, the doctor came out again. The man looked as if he'd aged even during the time they'd been there. Toramaru didn't need his other sense to tell him how much the man cared for his young patient; he'd seen it in how tirelessly he'd worked over her. Even now, he looked ready to fall over as he approached them.

"Dr. Tenma?" Kazuki looked up, his own worries lining his face.

"So far, she's remaining stable." He sighed. "I'm sorry, my boss has ordered me to go rest a little and eat dinner, so I'm going to my office for a bit. I have a futon there I can lie down on. The nurses will let me know if even the smallest thing changes, and if so, I'll be right back here. Another doctor will also be keeping an eye on her until I return."

"No, please, she would not want you to make yourself sick. You must take care of your own body too," Kazuki said in a reassuring tone.

"Thank you." He bowed. "Oh, I almost forgot, this was found in Sakura's pocket. It's addressed to you."

The doctor handed Kazuki a pink envelope decorated with

cherry blossoms. Kazuki returned the bow. "Thank you."

Once the doctor left, Kazuki examined the envelope in his hand, looking both confused and scared. He glanced at Toramaru before turning it to the side and tearing off the end to retrieve the letter inside.

Kazuki,

If you're reading this, then I'm probably already gone. When I woke up, it was with a certain feeling that I would die today. I don't know why I feel this so strongly. Maybe I'm just in a fatalistic mood because of this cough, but something is screaming inside me that this is it, the end, and that I won't even get to see you one last time. It was that thought, more than the rest, that made me want to write you this letter.

There are so many things going through my mind, things I want to say, but where to start? I wonder if you're doing well. Are you making sure to eat properly and get plenty of sleep? I hope that right now you're sitting with Yuji having a good long talk. I met him, you know, as he came to visit yesterday. It was nice getting to talk to him. You have a lot in common, yet you're also so different. You're bright and bold, like a rich coffee, while Yuji seemed warm and sweet, like hot chocolate. That seems like such a silly comparison now that I think about it.

Anyway, I hope you've apologized to each other for letting someone trick you like that. Before he left, Yuji asked when our wedding was because Karasu hadn't told him the date.

I was happy he planned to come. He even asked me my favorite colors so he could bring an appropriate gift. Yes, he is just as you said he was. I can see why you love him so much.

Kazuki, I'm sorry. I'm so very sorry. I told you I had until spring, and now here I am, dying months earlier than I was supposed to. When you left, I swore I'd be here when you got back, that it wouldn't be like with Ito-san. I ended up lying to you. I'm sorry.

Please tell Karasu I'm sorry too, and make sure to give him a big hug for me. It was hard not to cry when he gave me the bottle of dohame he made just for me. I have it in my pocket even now. It's comforting to have it with me. He's such a good boy. I know he'll be a wonderful young man when he grows up.

I also wanted to say thank you. Thank you for coming here, even if it was by accident. Thank you for staying with me and making me laugh again. Thank you for making me want to live, even when I knew I wouldn't. Most of all, thank you for being you because having you in my life has made the last few months the happiest moments I can re-member.

I know it will be many hundreds of years before you're old and hopefully even more before you come to the afterlife. It seems like such a long time for me, time in which part of me hopes you'll find another love and forget about me. That you'll move on and be happy. If, though, you do still remember me when that time comes, I'll be waiting for you under that big cherry tree, kind of like when we first met.

When that day comes, you better tell me what that word means! You know, the one you kept calling me? It's been driving me crazy wondering.

I love you, Kazuki, now and always.

Sakura

Kazuki cried unabashedly as he finished Sakura's letter. He cried over her being alone as she sensed death approaching. He cried over her lying across the hall in that room, halfway there. He cried for Karasu, who'd even made her another dose of dohame before leaving her. Then he realized what she'd written and what it implied.

"The dohame," he said aloud as he wiped his face. "I didn't even realize before, when she showed us what happened. That must be how they were able to save her. She drank the dohame Karasu made her, and it kicked in after the attack."

His father nodded. "That could be. Being a child still, his blood would not have a great deal of power, so it would take longer to work."

Feeling antsy, Kazuki stood and walked over to the window, leaning his head against the glass as he looked at her. The light in the room had been dimmed for the night when the nurses left, a small courtesy in case she could somehow still see the brightness of the harsh overhead lights.

He could make another dose of dohame, to give himself a chance to talk to her one last time, to tell her how much he loved her. That was the original purpose of the potion anyway. But would that really be best for her? It would mask the pain, but she'd still be stuck in that bed with all the wires and machines hooked to her. It seemed kinder to let her sleep until the end.

"Kazuki." His father joined him. "You said this girl is your sudtama. Are you certain of this?"

"Yes."

"My son, there is something I should tell you, though it may make you angry with me. When your mother was ill—I could have saved her."

"What do you mean?" Kazuki asked.

"There was a way I could have restored her health so that she would live out her normal, natural lifespan."

"Then why didn't you?"

"Your mother and I agreed, using the spell was too great a risk. It could have left you and Yuji without a father and the kingdom without a king. Do not think it was an easy choice to make, for it was not, but I know even now that we did the right thing."

Kazuki gave a brief nod. As it hadn't come up in the search of the archives, he knew it was not normal magic. It would make sense for a spell with that power to potentially claim the caster's life.

"Were Sakura a yokai, I wouldn't even tell you about this, as it would not be an option. However, as she is a human…"

"Let's do it!" Kazuki grabbed his father by the shoulders, uncaring how desperate it made him look. "I want to save her! I don't want to lose her. Please, father!" Kazuki wondered why his father would even act as if there were another option.

Toramaru shook his head. "Listen to me well. This spell, it cannot extend her life beyond that of any other human. It will heal all the illnesses and wounds currently on her body and make her more resistant to disease, but she will still age like others of her species. This spell will not act as some sort of immortality serum. She can still die early if she has an accident or is killed on purpose."

"I understand."

"Like all life magic, the spell has a price. The question for you, Kazuki, is, are you willing to pay that price? Are you willing to give up all of your magical abilities, your power, including your own longevity?"

All of his abilities? He'd never be able to go outside in the human world because he couldn't glam himself? He'd lose his ability to use transport gems or activate the portals, in essence making it impossible to go home again unless someone came to fetch him. Without magic, he wouldn't even be able to exchange letters with his family. And what sort of lifespan would he have if he no longer had his natural longevity? As these thoughts flooded his mind, his father asked him one more question.

"Are you willing to give all of these things up for her, even if you will both forget all that has happened, including your feelings for one another? Will you lose all that you are for a woman who will not know your name or what you have done for her?"

The thought rendered most of his other questions moot. Did it matter which world he was in if he would no longer know her, nor she him? Kazuki pictured a life having lost all that his father outlined, a life that would leave him as something neither human nor truly yokai. Then he thought of Sakura, healthy and smiling as she had been on the Day of Buckets. That image, that future, was worth any price to him.

"Yes. Even if it means that she will forget me and find a new love, I'll be happy as long as she gets to live out her life. If there is a way to save her, please tell me what I must do."

"Very well." Toramaru looked to ensure no one was in the hall, then held his hand up to the glass. It glowed for several long seconds before he removed it. "We will need to return home, but that spell I cast is similar to the dohame and will keep her alive while we prepare. If you wish to say anything to her…"

Kazuki nodded then slipped inside the room. The machine monitoring her heart continued its slow steady beeping as he made his way to her side. Another hissed as it breathed for her. Her hand was almost cool as he held it, nothing like the vibrant warmth he was used to. He leaned down and kissed the small corner of her lips that was not blocked by tubes and tape.

"Sakura, the night you told me of how you came to be like this, I swore to myself that I would find a way to heal you. Finally, I can keep that promise, though it means I will not be able to see you again. I hate the thought of living without you beside me, but the thought of a world without you in it at all hurts even more. Once we cast this spell, you'll be healthy again, able to live a full, rich life." He bent over, touching his forehead to hers as he cupped her face with his hand. "The spell will take our memories away, yours of me and mine of you, but know this, you are now and always will be my sudtama, the one who holds half my heart and without whom I could never be whole. Goodbye, my love."

He gave her a final kiss before rejoining his father. They found an empty stairwell of the hospital and transported back to their world. His father gave Reito a list of things he would need, and then led the way to his royal chambers.

There he had a special room where he could cast spells that required larger amounts of power or privacy. In holders around the room, various gems and minerals enhanced the ambient magical power, lending strength to his spells.

Reito slipped into the room carrying a large bag and secured the door behind him.

"A moment ago, I received word that Karasu has been found. It would appear Mumarch left him alive just outside of town where he was discovered and taken to the doctor. He has some broken bones, but should make a full recovery."

Kazuki sighed in relief. "I'm so glad. Has Yuji been told?"

"I sent a messenger to retrieve him. According to the report, Mumarch used a low-level healing spell on him, stopping the bleeding. It likely aided in his surviving. After hearing your story of what happened, I looked through the records of Uragiri. The son he lost was not much younger than Karasu, so it may be that he couldn't bring himself to harm a child of a similar age."

Reito walked over to the long table that spanned one wall of the room. "Oh, the name from his diary, Safina. That was his mate. When the building collapsed in the mudslide, she was trapped under it. However, it did not kill her outright. He dug her upper body free, but it was clear the injuries were fatal. Rather than forcing her to endure a long slow death, he killed her by suffocating her."

Now Kazuki understood the strange things Mumarch had written, and his actions with Sakura. The man's tragic past had led him to his plot against Kazuki and his family, but it also had, in a strange way, kept him from completing it.

"Reito, when you see Karasu, please, tell him thank you for me. That even though I won't remember by the time I see him, I am grateful to him for protecting Sakura, and proud of him. He has grown into a fine young man."

"Yes, My Prince. I will let him know." Reito began pulling some things from the bag. Kazuki recognized some of the items as common spell ingredients, including some minerals and plants known for their magical abilities, a kagorin egg and feathers, a lakmanine stone. The last items Reito put out were a picture, one of the ones of Sakura and Kazuki taken by Karasu during her bucket day, and the locket from Sakura's room.

Toramaru moved over to the large stand in the middle of the room that held a thick book. Though his father had been gone over a year, there was no dust visible on the tome, rather it seemed to have the barest hint of a glow. He opened the book, softly turning the pages until he found what he was looking for.

He directed Kazuki to the middle of the room. "Now then, let us begin."

New Future

SAKURA WOKE UP LYING IN A hospital bed, confused. She didn't remember getting there. Presumably, she'd had an episode, but even that seemed strange because she felt good. Tired, but good. There was no pain at all. No machines clung to her, not even a heart monitor. No IV lines connected with her body. If not for the sterile white walls around her, it would have been like waking up in the morning in her own bed.

"How long have I been here?" she said aloud as she sat up. Glancing down, she held her hands up in front of her. Her healthy, normal-colored hands. "What is going on?"

A shudder ran through her as she realized no heavy weight pressed on her chest, her breathing came free and easy. She took a deep breath, then another, reveling in the feel. But how was this possible?

Am I dead?

The door to her room clicked open. Tenma-sensei entered, a huge smile on his face as he walked over to her. She couldn't be dead if he was here.

"Sakura-chan, good morning! How are you feeling?"

"Sensei, I don't understand it. I feel better than I have in years. But I had an attack, right? That's why I'm here? But why can I breathe so easily?"

"What's the last thing you remember?"

"Um…" She thought back, struggling to recall the previous day. "I had a cough, and I stayed home from school to rest. I…I can't remember anything after that, not even what I had for breakfast."

"From what the police have gathered, you surprised an intruder who probably thought no one was home. It caused you to have an attack. Fortunately, your friends found you in time and you were brought here." He reached out to hold her hand. "To be honest, last night I thought I was going to lose you. You were fighting hard, but it seemed hopeless. Then earlier this morning, one of the nurses ran to get me. I thought that was it, but instead I came back to your room to find you sleeping naturally and healed."

"Healed?"

"Yes, completely. We've run every test I could think of twice, and I'm still not sure what to think. Every bit of damage to your organs is gone, as if you'd never been hurt at all."

Sakura pulled the hospital gown away from her body and peered inside. The thin white lines marking her father's attack were no longer there. "My scars…they're gone." She pinched her arm, but that only resulted in a moment of pain. This must be a dream, right? How can I suddenly be cured?"

"I wish I knew. I'm half afraid to be happy about it without knowing how it happened. At this point, I don't know what else to call it but a miracle. Maybe Ito-san worked a little magic from beyond. All I know for sure is, you will live." He put his hands on her shoulders, beaming even as his eyes grew misty. "You will graduate, you will go to college, get married, have kids."

"I'll live? I'll live!" She hugged him, her happiness at being healthy overshadowing her questions of how it happened. Tenma-sensei quietly filed the paperwork discharging her. It seemed prudent to keep the miracle of her recovery as quiet as possible to avoid press attention. Since so few people in her life knew about her illness anyway, it would be an easy thing to do for her, though she decided she would tell Hina and Akari. She knew they would keep her secret. There were only a few more months of school, so she could slide by with the administration and teachers. If anyone else found out or asked later, then she would just say she'd been able to go to the West and get a transplant in time.

Before leaving the hospital, she called the police investigator who left his card to tell him what little she remembered. He sounded almost bored, asking one or two questions before telling her to let them know if anything was missing and that, otherwise, there wasn't much to do. As far as they could tell, the intruder had panicked at scaring her and ran off, most likely not realizing she'd been sick.

Outside, the sun glinted brightly off the snow-covered ground. Feeling energy brimming inside her, she half ran the whole length home, too excited to wait. She had to tell them the good news.

Them?

Her step faltered. Who was it she needed to tell? With a shrug, she continued on. It had to be Hina and Akari of course. Who else was there? She ran through the side door, throwing open the shrine doors with a huge smile.

"Ito-san, I'm all better! My heart and lungs are perfectly normal now! It's so strange! I don't know how it happened, but I bet you had something to do with it. Thank you! Thank you! I do miss you so much, but I know you'd rather I take a bit longer to come be with you. Oh, I better hurry and call Hina and Akari. School should be out by now, and they'll be heading to the hospital if I don't catch them."

In the hall, she paused. The police officer said there were cranberry juice stains around the house, including a large puddle by the door, but she didn't see anything like that now. He'd also said her hall table was broken, but it looked the same as it always had. *How odd.*

Shaking her head, she called Hina's cell phone.

"Hello."

"Hina-chan, it's Sakura."

"Sakura-chan!" Hina's voice was so loud Sakura had to hold the phone away from her ear. "You're awake! They said you weren't going to wake up again. Akari and I are on our way to the hospital now."

"Actually, I'm home now. Come on over. I have so much to tell you!"

"Home? Already? But…" She sounded scared.

"I'm okay, I promise. I'll explain when you get here."

"Okay, we'll be there in a few minutes."

Sakura went upstairs to change. The last bit of damage the officer had mentioned were scratches by her bedroom window, but that too looked fine to her. Maybe he'd mixed up the report about her house with another one or something. The only thing that held true so far was the police tape outside. It seemed to her like she had just had one of her breathing attacks and been fortunate that her friends had come by when they did.

She'd just finished changing when the doorbell rang. Hina and Akari hugged her tight as soon as she let them in. The house was filled with squeals as she told them of her miraculous recovery, though Akari was skeptical until she showed them that her scars were gone.

"I can't believe it!" Hina said with a sob. "Our wish came

true; it really came true!"

"Wish?"

"Yeah." She held the bag they'd brought with them out to Sakura. Inside were dozens upon dozens of origami cranes. "We made one thousand, Akari and me, to help you get better."

Sakura hugged them both again, knowing how long it must have taken them. "Thank you, both of you. To be honest, I'm still not sure what to think. For so long, I've thought I'd never be an adult, so I hadn't really thought about the future, you know?"

"Yeah, you can go to college now!"

"Oh, I haven't looked at schools or anything. I mean, I studied for the test just to pass the time, but…"

"Don't worry. We can help you get caught up! It isn't too late yet," Akari said as she pulled a book out of her bag with a smile. "To be honest, I'm still trying to decide where I want to go myself, so we can look together."

"Thanks." Sakura went to the kitchen and fixed them cups of hot chocolate. When she returned and passed them out, there were two extra cups. She laughed at her absentmindedness. "That's strange, I didn't even notice putting them there."

"It's chocolate. It won't go to waste," Hina said with a grin, having already downed half of her cup. With a laugh, they flipped through Akari's book. With their help, Sakura was able to come up with a list of schools to consider that could help her achieve her once impossible dream, renovating and restoring historic buildings.

Near dinnertime, the girls left after a final round of hugs. Now that she was by herself again, the house felt strange, as if something was missing. It was too quiet, though it hadn't changed from the day before. When she made dinner, again she found herself preparing more food than she needed.

"Maybe it's my subconscious's way of telling me I'm lonely. Now that I'm healthy, I could get a pet…maybe a cat? Though a dog might be better since cats don't like birds."

She stilled, wondering where the errant thought had come from. *Why would it matter if cats like birds?* Deciding it was just tiredness from the events of the last twenty-four hours, she went upstairs to lie in bed and read awhile.

When she opened the novel she'd been reading, a photograph fell from between the pages to the floor. She picked it up, surprised to see it was a picture of a beautiful young man with long white hair and a gentle smile standing in front of her house beside a grinning, dark-haired boy.

On the back of the picture, written in her handwriting, were the names "Kazuki and Karasu." The date under the names indicated it was taken just a week ago.

Who are they? Why do I have their picture? Something about the picture made her heart ache worse than any attack, as if she'd lost something precious. "Ito-san, what is going on? It's like I'm forgetting something, something really important."

Ripping the covers off, she searched the entire house looking for clues. There was a futon up in her attic along with the dresser from Ito-san's room. She didn't remember moving either up there, nor would she have had the strength. Someone had to have done it for her, but who?

It looked as if someone had been staying there, though there wasn't much else there. Most of the drawers of the dresser were empty, except for a bright red scarf and matching gloves. *I hope he isn't cold without them.* As the thought crossed her mind, she dropped them, startled. Hoped who wasn't cold?

Back in her room, she found a purple tie buried in the closet. Somehow, she was certain it belonged to the man in the picture, selected because it matched his eyes. But why was it here and in so intimate a spot? There were new cups in her kitchen too. Did they belong to the man and the boy?

Going through her notebooks from school, she found the name Kazuki written several times, sometimes surrounded by a heart. A few doodles of a crow, sometimes nesting in a tree, other times flying, accompanied them.

The most mysterious of all was a sheet titled "Day of Buckets" with a schedule written on it. The date near the top was the same as the picture's. But that was impossible. There was no way she could have seen all those places and gone to an amusement park then. It would have killed her.

What did *I do last Saturday?*

Yuji stood over his brother's bed, willing the pale figure to move. After the spell had been cast to heal Sakura, Kazuki had fallen into a coma. His father, exhausted to the point of being unable to stand, told him not to worry. Kazuki would wake up eventually, though it could be many years from now.

They'd put him in his bed so that he'd be in a familiar place when that time came. Attendants came daily to move his body around so his muscles wouldn't atrophy. The healers used magic to keep him from starving, but he'd lost a noticeable amount of weight.

"Master Yuji?" a sleepy Karasu said from the other bed in the room. They'd moved him there so he could recover from his injuries and stay by Kazuki's side to watch over him as best he could.

Yuji crossed over to his bed and sat on the edge. "I didn't mean to wake you. I'm sorry."

"It's fine. Is everything okay?"

"Yes, I just came to check on him since I was stuck in that

meeting earlier and missed having dinner with him." He knew the castle staff thought it was odd and sweet that he now tried to eat all of his meals in Kazuki's room, but he didn't want Kazuki to feel lonely. He talked to him all the time, certain his brother could hear him. "Any change?"

Karasu shook his head sadly.

"I see." Yuji let his head drop into his hand. What he was planning could end up being the cruelest thing he'd ever done, if Kazuki stayed sleeping for decades. But he had to do something, anything to make up for his foolish mistakes. Firming his resolve, he looked up. "Karasu, I'm going to be away for a few days, okay?"

"Oh, sure. Work?"

"No, I'm going to the human world to try to unseal Sakura's memories."

Karasu sat up so fast he winced. "What are you talking about? How would that even be possible?"

"When Reito and I cleaned up the traces of our existence, we were both a bit, um, sloppy about it. Lady Sakura seemed like a bright girl, so she must be teeming with questions by now. I'm going to go answer them for her."

"But what good is it for her to remember now? It will just make her sad. I hate that she's forgotten us, but it's for the best. She can have a happy life now."

"But would it be as happy as what she had with him?" Yuji stood. "It may make me a monster, but I have to try, for both their sakes."

First thing in the morning, Sakura called Tenma-sensei, hoping he could explain what was going on.

"There was no sign of brain damage or anything that should

be causing memory lapses." He paused. "It does sound strange, though. Even stranger, now that you've asked me about it, I feel like I should recognize them, and yet I don't. I'm sorry. I wish I had a better answer."

"No, it's okay."

"Are you doing well otherwise?"

"Oh, yes, I've never felt so alive. Thank you!" she told him cheerfully. Though consumed by this mystery, she'd awoken that morning wanting to sing and dance. "I even ran around the house a few times just for fun."

Tenma-sensei chuckled. "Good, just don't overdo it. Part of me keeps thinking it can't be real, but as much as I care for you, I hope you don't need me again for a long time yet."

"Don't worry. I won't forget you. I still need to introduce you to Mimomo-sensei so you can finally get married!" Sakura said with a laugh before hanging up.

At lunchtime, she met up with Akari and Hina. While they ate, she told them about the strange things she'd found and showed them the picture. Like Tenma-sensei, neither recognized the two people in the picture, but they both gave her strange looks.

"It's funny you asked about it. I found this in my desk and was starting to question my sanity a bit," Akari said as she pulled a small notebook from her bag. On the cover was written "Sakura's Wedding."

"Wedding?!" Sakura exclaimed as she flipped through the book. Several pages of plans, including potential locations and catering options. All for a wedding dated Christmas Day. "But to who?"

"To one of these two, I guess. Going by the names, the taller one is probably the one named Kazuki. His name is written down in there, on the page about tuxedos."

"This is insane. How could I be marrying someone I don't even know…" She looked at the picture again with that same aching. "No…I think I do know them…I must. But why can't I remember?"

"Hey, that schedule you found, maybe you should ask around at those places?" Hina suggested. "It's so weird that none of us can remember them, but it might be worth a shot."

"You're right. I have to keep searching. It makes no sense…none of this. My being all better, but losing my memories. I realized pieces of other memories are missing too. Like the day of the cultural fair, I remember going to the ball and being there with you. I danced with someone, a lot, but I can't remember who. Not his name, his appearance, anything."

Following Hina's idea, Sakura went to all the places from the bucket-day list, showing the picture to the people there. At first, it was the same answer: no one recognized them. Yet each place she went to, despite knowing it was her first time there, felt familiar.

At the Old Public Town Hall, the attendant on duty smiled when she showed her the picture. "Yes, I remember. The three of you came here a week or so ago. He looked so handsome in the period suit, it made even my old heart flutter. I hope you find him, dear. I've been around quite a long time. Men can sometimes get an urge and go off for a while, but the ones that love you, they will come home again. Not that looking for them hurts, so they know they're wanted, you know."

Sakura smiled and thanked the woman. So they were real, and she had been with them. It also seemed to confirm that she and the one she was calling Kazuki were a couple. It didn't seem likely he had just run off, though, and if he had, it still didn't explain her forgetting him.

She remembered going to school, eating meals, everything

else, so why not that one day, and why was she certain the gaps in her memory all revolved around these two men? At the amusement park, the ride operators laughingly told her how Kazuki hadn't been able to handle the big roller coaster and how they'd wondered if he was going to throw up while she and the boy had ridden it several times.

With no more clues to follow, she headed home. A man stood in front of her house, a man with long white hair. She ran up to him, but even before pulling out the picture, she knew it wasn't the same one. "You look similar, but you're not him, are you?"

"No, I'm afraid not." The man's voice was warm and gentle as he pointed at the photograph. "That is Kazuki, my older brother. He is currently in a coma far from here."

The man she was looking for was in a coma? How could that be? "I'm so sorry. I hope he'll be okay. What happened to him?"

"Well, you see, he fell in love. He came to love someone so much that he was willing to give up everything he had to help her."

As he looked at her with those dark-purple eyes, she could hear her heart pounding in her chest. This man, he had the answers to all of her questions, she was certain of it. "Do you know why I have this picture? Why I feel like I should know these two? Please," she begged, "tell me, why can't I remember them?"

"Let's go inside, and I shall tell you a story, a very special story whose ending is still being written."

As the days and weeks passed since Yuji's visit, bits of memories began to return to her. Little snippets of the time he told her about, when Kazuki and Karasu—the two yokai—had lived in her home, sharing their lives with her. One night she'd awoken terrified, having dreamed of the attack by the hideous yokai, Mumarch, and Karasu's courageous defense of her.

In the camera she didn't remember owning before, she found a memory card full of pictures. More proof that Yuji's story was not some fictional tale. Picture after picture of Kazuki, Karasu, and her—some taken around her house, some taken at other places.

Her favorite was a picture of the three of them at the Old Public Hall, wearing period costumes. As the older woman had said, Kazuki was very handsome in the suit, and she beamed as she stood holding his hand while Karasu posed in front of them. She framed it and put it on her bedside table, wondering if she'd ever remember it all, or if she'd ever see them again.

Sakura told Akari and Hina the parts she could about Yuji's visit and his story. They agreed it had to be true, given the things she'd discovered. Though confused by the feelings she was experiencing over a man who was still more stranger than lover, she did not doubt that she had loved him.

Before he'd left, Yuji had told her that, if Kazuki woke up, he too would have forgotten her and that his loss of memories might run deeper. But that they would bring him to see her, though he didn't know how long it could be. It might even take years. Despite knowing that, she craved to meet him again, him and Karasu. No matter how long it took.

Winter drifted into spring with no sign of the yokai. Mimomo-sensei helped her further narrow her college choices down and complete the applications. Sakura passed the National Exam with high marks and did well on the exams for her top two choices. She'd considered going to the local school, Hakodate University, so she could still be where Kazuki could find her, but it didn't have an architecture program. If she was accepted into the other schools, she could keep the house and maybe leave a note or something in case they came back.

On the third day of April, Sakura graduated with her class, cheering as loudly as the rest of them at the end of the ceremony. She celebrated with Hina, Akari, Genji, and Aki with lunch at a restaurant, happy to have made it to this day and to be able to spend that time with such good friends. Before heading home, she rode the tram across town to the cemetery where her parents were buried. She carefully cleaned the gravestone and site, grateful that others had tended the grave during her long period of neglect. Once she was done, she set the fresh bouquet of tulips, her mother's favorite, in the holder and lit incense for both of her parents.

"Mama, Papa, look, I did it." She held up the diploma for them to see. "I'm sorry I haven't visited in so long. It isn't that I forgot you. I guess part of me was angrier than I realized, so I kept making excuses for why I couldn't come. I thought I was coming to join you soon, but I hope it's okay if I stay a while longer. There is someone I'm waiting for now, someone I want to see again and spend more time with here."

On her way home, she got off the tram a stop early so she could walk through the park and see the cherry blossoms. For some reason, her own tree had yet to bloom. It had a full amount of healthy leaves, but the plentiful buds remained tightly closed.

She smiled at the delicate pink-and-white blooms on the park's trees, enjoying the light breeze blowing through her hair.

"Hey, girl!" At the oddly familiar voice, Sakura spun around. Standing behind her, a little taller than she remembered from the photo, was the boy, Karasu. "Remember me?"

"You're...Karasu-kun!" She threw her arms around him, holding him tight. He hugged her back, his grip stronger than before.

"Still a crier, huh?" he said with a smile as he wiped the tears from her cheek.

She hugged him again. "Thank you for protecting me. I'm so glad you're okay."

"I'm glad you are too." He gave her a mischievous look. "But is it really me you were hoping to see the most?"

She gasped and looked around the park. But there was no one else around them. "Kazuki?"

"Karasu, where did you go?" It was that voice, the voice that had haunted her dreams since her memories had begun to return.

With a grin, the boy turned and ran down a nearby path. Sakura followed as fast as she could.

Standing under a cherry tree was Kazuki, looking almost like a lost child. He was thinner and his long white hair had been cut. Now it just barely brushed his shoulders.

From what Yuji had told her, she knew he was not using his glam spell anymore, as he had no more magic; that and his human appearance were just part of the price he'd paid to save her life.

When Karasu ran up to him, he smiled.

"There you are. I was worried." He glanced up as she stopped in front of them, bent over while panting from the pace. "Oh, hello?"

"Good afternoon." She straightened, smiling as best she could.

"Master Kazuki, this is Sakura. Remember, I told you about her?"

"Ah, I see. Yes, you said she's like a sister to you. My name is Kazuki. Pleased to meet you." He bowed politely. "Thank you for treating Karasu kindly. He also said you knew an old friend of mine, Ito Hiro?"

"Um, yes, that's right. He was my adoptive father." She threw Karasu a questioning glance.

Karasu shifted closer to her and motioned for her to bend over so he could whisper in her ear. "He only woke up a little while ago. Master Yuji thought he'd have the best chance of his memories returning if he saw you as soon as possible, so we brought him straight here. He thinks we're just visiting a friend of mine."

She nodded then glanced back at Kazuki. Before she could figure out what to say next, he tilted his head and took a step closer.

"Um, this may seem like a strange question, but do I know you? I feel as though I have met you before, yet when I was last here, you would not have been born."

Sakura smiled, holding back her tears as she reached out and took his hands. "Please, will you come with me for a while? I'd like to tell you a story. A wonderful story about a dying girl whose life was saved by a beautiful prince who transformed her into his sudtama."

Thank You for Reading!

Want to know when my next novel is coming out? Head to my website, SherelleWinters.com and get a free novelette as well!

Also By Sherelle Winters

Deviations

At Week's End

Broken Wing

A Few Final Words

AISURU IS A SPECIAL NOVEL FOR me, as it was my very first "win" for National Novel Writing Month, and only the second complete novel I'd ever written. Of all my stories, it has always been special, one that I loved from the moment it first came to mind.

Even as my revision time grew from "just a few months" to a ridiculous six years, I never stopped loving this story. In the end, with more novels under my belt and a greater maturity in my writing, I was finally able to finish what I began back in 2009 and bring the full story of Sakura and Kazuki to life.

I hope you, dear reader, will forgive any transgressions I've made in the geographical or cultural aspects of this work. I myself have never walked the streets of Hakodate. I've never tasted the famous cheese soufflés at the Kanemori Red Brick Warehouses nor have I gotten to partake in the joy that is the Catalana from Café Nishimura. I have not smelled the sea breezes of Hakodate Bay nor felt the biting cold at the top of Mount Hakodate.

In crafting the finer details of *Aisuru*, I conducted extensive, and sometimes even excessive, research into the various locations my characters visit and the experiences they have. To bring this city to life, my imagination was fueled by my studies of numerous pictures from tourists and local residents shared on the Internet, reading stories and descriptions of people's experiences there, extensive use of Google's wonderful street-level views, and various local Hakodate websites (and the often humorous translations Google made of them; especially restaurant menus!).

Of course, some locations are strictly my own creations, and I occasionally modified settings and the like to better fit the story. Sakura's house does not exist, and I took a bit more artistic license with the neighborhood she lived in versus what that area really looks like. Saigonohi High School is a fictionalized high school, though I based its outer appearance and some of its features on Hakodate Ryoujoku Senior High School, which is many miles from where I placed Saigonohi. The hospital where Dr. Tenma works, Hakodate City Hospital, is entirely of my own creation and bears no resemblance to any hospital in Hakodate. Hakodate Adventure Land is also fictional, but it is based on various real amusement parks. Most of the roller coasters are based on ones found at the renowned Nagashima Spa Land, including the first two the characters ride.

In all these cases, I tried to create these places in such a way that you could easily picture them being there, if they did exist. It is my hope that I have given a respectful representation of Hakodate and that this work pays fitting homage to this beautiful port city.

While writing this final bit to wrap up my novel, I am elated that it is done and will soon be on its way to you, yet I also am a bit sad. After six years together, I must depart Sakura and Kazuki's world to move on to the next story waiting for me. It's almost like saying goodbye to a friend. But, I know, it isn't really goodbye, for they will always live inside me, ready to say hello whenever I stand under the snow-like petals of a cherry tree.

~ Sherelle